# PHANTOM

## KEVIN KING

Published by Open Books

Cover image "Feb Rowing Camp" Copyright © 2017 by Steve Burt

Learn more about the artist at www.flickr.com/photos/sburt/

ISBN-10: 099780629X
ISBN-13: 978-0997806298

*This novel is dedicated to the chief, George Mangan, and to all of my sparring partners at the Harvard Boxing Club and the Boston Sport Boxing Club. I apologize to all the Harvard Boxing Club members whose names I cannot recall. Here follows a list of those whose names I remember:*

*Father Dave*
*Father Paul*
*Doug (c)*
*Doug (Big)*
*Soph*
*Seth*
*Seth*
*Jimmy (crazy)*
*Jimmy (c)*
*Dennis (c)*
*Pete*
*Marcus*
*Jeanine (?)*
*Charlie*
*Gene*
*Red (Paul)*
*Peter*
*Clark (c)*
*Kevin*
*Jake*
*Staney*
*Seeb (?)*
*Janar (c)*

*"I didn't say a good life. I said a life."*
—James Wright

*"Grace can be found ...*
*in the energetic and muscular stroke of the rower."*
—George Mangan

.

# Chapter 1: Fire

*November 9, 1872.*

Halfway between the Civil War and the new century with its electric lights and motor cars—1872, the first year of France's *Belle Époque*, Waddy Googan's, too, though he had no idea what was imminently and literally about to befall him. Trotting his Stanhope Spider buggy across Boston's cobblestoned West End, he was thinking more of the Civil War. Working his tongue around his mouth he found the small hole in his cheek, invisible under the thick red mutton chops, that was a reminder of Gettysburg, where he'd fought for the Union as a teenager. He was a man in perpetual thrall to Lady Luck, who on this day carried a pocket tinderbox full of 'lucifers', careless as ever, loose as an *apache*—in the *Belle Époque* argot sense of the word; her guise this day in 1872—fire.

He was thinking *rainbow*—multifarious colors compressed into a singular hue at the horizon, almost as if the sky, weighted down with vapor, were about to explode. Brick—which seemed to define Beacon Hill, reflecting heat and color. Exterior warmth. The arrogance of the insanely high white church steeple, lightning rod to God's wrath for a city of sin? The tall, lead-latticed stained glass windows were compressed vertically. The gas lamp posts, hitching posts—architecture's commandment—*up*. Up, the commandment, too, of flames.

A fish stenciled into a wooden plaque hanging from chains over a shop informed passersby not of what the shop beneath it sold but rather of the purveyor's name— Sam Fish, one of Waddy's Friday night poker buddies. Outside Fish's smoke shop stood a cigar-store Indian, carved by a logger in winter, time on his hands and with as much skill with an axe as with a chisel. It looked more Egyptian than Wampanoag. The tall cigars clutched in a bundle looked like dynamite. The Indian's complexion, the same muddy brown as his cigars, offended Waddy's sense of historical decorum. One thought *Redskin* when one thought *Indian*. And the statue itself seemed a monument to bad haberdashery.

Fish's smoke shop occupied the corner of Hanover and Court, and Waddy marveled at how rectangular brick could be molded into a perfectly circular tower. The puzzlement was one of those irritations that felt good— simply because it was his, like a small cinder of Boston brick in his shoe, reminding him that the common man too could fit into the tight boot that was Brahmin society. Whose city was it, in 1872? The Brahmins'? The proles'? Episcopalians'? Lutherans'? Fire's? Destruction and ruin seemed Waddy's constant companions. Grace, opined Martin Luther, was not something earned. It simply spilled, like smoke. Fire and grace, then, a city's unearned heresy.

~~~~~~~

There had been a suicide on Appleton Street, a robbery on Commercial Street, fights on Elm and North Streets, and parts of a dismembered body were found in the

Charles River. Not a bad night for a city of around 270,000. The weather was clear and calm. Indian summer. The regularity of the clop, the rhythm of the horse's hooves over the cobblestones through the short-cut alleys of the West End and onto the wider avenues approaching Beacon Hill invest Waddy Googan with a priceless feeling of comfort and security. He contemplates the cobbles. It's their tuckedness he loves; in his Friesian-drawn Spider he feels like a child again in a trundle bed. The proletarian aspect of the cobbles makes him feel at home, the myriads of them that, working together, create a soft but rugged shine under the drooping gas lanterns and the moonlight.

He regards the mansions, the cloistered, barred windows and imagines the demoiselles presumably behind them, the comely Irish maids in the basements, and the heavy bolted doors that keep out the riff-raff, the croppies. What is opulence if not these concentric cobbles reflecting the dim gas light and the light of the full moon rising over the State House, swathing Beacon Hill in cobalt gray?

He settles into a V.S.O.P. memory of being a part of the fancy just hours ago, feeling as in a pilgrimage from Sodom-by-the-Sea—the Chelsea Sporting Club—to the taverns of the North and West Ends of Boston. All the more curious since that white urban elephant—the Chelsea Sporting Club—a decade from now would be his, at least in name—on the mortgage held by Foxhall Codman's Charles Street Bank.

And the simple twist of fate that turns Waddy Googan's dreams of proprietorship into reality is the twist of the reins of his Spider toward Summer Street rather than down Tremont. The horse disagrees with his choice of direction and bucks in its traces, reminding him of Bobby Dobbs' convulsions in the 42nd round just hours ago at the hands of 'The Deckhand'—Mike McCoole, self-proclaimed boxing champion, while future black champion George Godfrey and future white champion John L. Sullivan filled the Sporting Club with their dreams from orthogonal ends of the cheap seats of the cavernous edifice.

Of a sudden Waddy's horse stops with no command, whinnies as if approaching a pack of wolves. Then he notices the stillness, the absence of cricket chirp, dog howl or bark. There is no breeze yet the air feels as if it is moving en masse. There is a sensation of stillness before a hurricane, the air in some kind of quiet panic. It seems bizarre that out of the stillness and quiet there comes such a clear loud clamor of bells, and it becomes clear to him even before he sees the firemen just what has come to pass. The Latin declamation champion of last year's senior class at Harvard is thinking 'tintinnabulation,' but the connotation seems so fey for what he sees now as he turns down Hawley Street.

To say that Waddy was a fuse burning at both ends would be to discredit his love of loafing, but his career would begin as his life ended—in fire. This one destroyed most of Boston's commercial district. He never intended to view the 1872 conflagration up so close that his white linen suit would be singed, but he took umbrage at a foul-mouthed, starched-dickeyed fireman's ordering him off the street, never imagining the treasure that was about to literally befall him and jumpstart his career in fashion.

The firemen were late because Engine 11 was being pulled over the cobblestones of Franklin Street by a single ox and a gang of thirty volunteers. Epizoic distemper had made its way south from Canada and was epidemic by October of 1872; horses were dropping dead all over Boston. Conductors and drivers were pulling hansoms and horse cars in the South End while granite coping exploded, streaming bits of stone on the firemen. It reminded Waddy again of Gettysburg, and he stroked his thick reddish mutton-chops that covered the invisible wound with a peppering of gray. The fire was sucking air. Franklin Street, wide as it was, became a flue. Hats and bonnets flew off, his own silk top hat a victim.

Shopkeepers were throwing boxes of merchandise onto the street—gloves, hosiery, corsets, hoopskirts—hoping to cart it off. It was descended on by the men of the rag and the bone, soon followed by men and women in fashionable dress with axes. Women in hoopskirts were fighting each other for boots. The merchants fighting off scavengers were getting the worst of it.

Rooting for the hoi-polloi, Waddy was surprised and indignant when the driver of the Engine 15 Amoskeag steam-pumper shouted, "Hey, high-hat, get yer fucking oat-burner off the road."

Moving his buggy, Waddy sneered, thinking, 'Asshole, I don't even have a hat.'

"Hey, croppy, wanna race? Five bucks we get to the Beebee block before you do." Engine 15 was a rarity—it was pulled by horses.

Waddy smiled. He figured his Spider could take the 9,000 pound steam-pumper with ease. Albeit prohibited, racing was the major perk of fighting fires, and racing was the reason the inveterate gambler had dumped his Stanhope Phaeton in favor of the faster Spider.

"You're on."

Gambling was his singular addiction. And sometimes even when you lose you win. With no warning, and before Waddy was completely turned, the clumsy $5,000 steam-pumper, drawn by three horses abreast, was off the mark, its four kerosene-lit lamps shaking and clanging off the central boiler. It had one chance—get a lead and force the charging Spider off the road. Waddy gained rapidly. The pumper's driver turned his head and saw Waddy's horse coming hard on his left. He yanked on the reins and angled toward the horse, closing off the street. Waddy had no choice but to rein in his horse and try to pass on the right, where he ran out of real estate. But the victorious firemen of Engine 15 were distracted from collecting on their bet by another looming battle. A hydrant-sitter from Engine 11 had covered the only hydrant with a wooden stave barrel and was reserving the fire plug for *his* company's engine, which was turning off Federal Street onto Franklin. Unlike the multiple-outlet Lowry hydrants used in neighboring communities, the 'Boston' model had just one outlet, which meant only one company would be able to use it.

The sitter was a pugilist, well-chosen for the job. He took on four firemen from Engine 15, while Waddy watched and eventually made his chiseling getaway when the ox-pulled Engine 11 arrived to reinforce their sitter, who was taking a pummeling from the white-dickeyed men of Engine 15. When the sitter managed to get back to his feet, a fragment of exploding granite hit him on the temple, sending grains into his eye. Screaming in pain, he staggered out of the fray while the men from Engine 11 engaged the Engine 15 men trying to connect their hose to the plug.

A man in a suit arrived in a Brougham and screamed, "It's down to Pearl Street."

The men from Engine 11, having lost, scrambled back to their ox-drawn pumper. "No more shoes for the Brahmins," shouted a drunk. It got Waddy to thinking— the whole city would be short on shoes. It was an opportunity, one that would literally fall on him shortly.

Franklin Street, the world's wool capitol, was in flames, and so were the boot and leather warehouses and shops of High Street, Water Street, and Broad Street. Granite facings, thought to be imperishable, crumbled, and the fashionable mansard roofs were fire-fodder. Though most firefighters were moonlighting thugs, they took pride in their work. Waddy was mesmerized by the men on the engine brakes working one hundred and eighty strokes per minute. They took turns, going a half-minute at a time, then were spelled by another firefighter. As fatigue set in, fingers got cut and heads broken by the peculiar descending brakes.

Hours later, Chief Damrell decided to level an entire

block to stop the fire from spreading. Gunpowder proved easier to obtain than adequate water or couplings that could fit out-of-town hoses to Boston's antiquated hydrants. Two tons of powder arrived by ox- or man-pulled wagons at North Market Street. One and a half tons were schlepped to Dock Square, and one ton to State Street. Stewart's was yet untouched by flames when firemen broke the showroom windows and carried in eight twenty-five pound barrels of powder.

A head stuck out a third-story window. "What are you doing? Don't blow it up! Put it out!"

"Better get the fuck out of there, mister, and fast."

Waddy watched as the man appeared in the window of the adjacent building. Minutes later, Waddy was almost hit by a large tarpaulin filled with goods and sealed with rope, which did not burst on impact. He cursed and looked up at the man admiring his salvage job.

To get away from the explosion, Waddy drove farther down the street, in the direction of the fire. Suddenly it broke out in the building in front of him. From a third story window, a woman's form appeared, the window to her right bleeding red and orange flames. The third floor was where seamstresses worked. The woman's features were not visible, but he was fairly sure she was looking at him, trying to communicate something to the last man she would ever see. Then she retreated, and flames were visible in the background. He was hoping she had found a way downstairs, but the second floor was burning more intensely than the third. Then he saw her again at the window, clutching something the size of an infant to her breast. His own heart beat like the brakes of the Amoskeag steam pumper. She raised it over her head, as if an offering, an appeasement, but her eyes were on Waddy, as if the offering were intended for him. He understood it was hopeless, but he moved closer to her. She clutched it again to her breast. Momentarily, hoop skirts ablaze, she was a candle *and* the birthday cake at once. He had the sensation of a flaming lampshade coming down at him. Halfway down she jettisoned her bundle and Waddy's arms involuntarily struck out as if they could catch it as the woman, who never unfixed her gaze from his eyes, engaged in her final earthly act—modesty—pushing down the flaming skirt that had flown up over her waist before her feet, which had lost their shoes, dug into Franklin Street at the same time that a man-hole cover shot upwards from exploding gas. He felt his bowels loosen at the thud of her striking the cobbles. Bouncing towards him was no infant but the sewing machine she must have scrimped for a year to buy. What strikes him is a strange sense of violation—in witnessing her planting herself into Franklin Street. Stranger was the sense that in her descent she recognized him, she who was now faceless. For who he was? What he was? Witness, death's voyeur, accidental looter? Heretic—for sure, fancying that a man of charm, persuasion, good looks, talent, and modest wealth, Harvard man but no Porcellian, could seduce his way into the high ranks of Boston's rarefied, stratified, class system.

The man-hole cover hit the ground and also rolled towards him, scaring his horse. Then he heard a louder explosion. The Stewart building was reduced to rubble. The heat was getting intense and his horse was getting jumpy. He turned his Spider back up the street, away from the fire. The merchant in the building adjacent to Stewart's was back at the window with another canvas bundle, long-fingered flames pushing him out, not *with* his bundle but *on* it. He intended to cushion his impact with the bundle and added to his chances of success by draping a Persian carpet, a gold-threaded, silk Qom prayer rug, over the bundle, as if in the Beantown version of the *Arabian Nights* carpets also could fly.

The rug was precious but not magic. Still, the merchant who mounted it managed to fold his arms as he threw himself, the rug, and the bundle at the cobbles below. The cushioning in fact worked, to an extent, but the merchant flew off of at impact almost as fast as he had fallen, his headfirst momentum stopped by an iron lamp post.

Waddy spread the valuable Persian rug over his seat and hung the two bundles of shoes and garments on either side of him, then trotted quickly northward up Devonshire Street, which had just erupted. He paused on the corner where fifty thousand Cuban cigars were aflame, got a pleasant noseful, and kept on. Some building were burning; others were being blown up. Merchants continued throwing their shoes, boots, leather and cotton goods into the street, hoping to salvage them, while men and women of every class were ravaging the same warehouses and fighting the merchants for their goods. It looked to Waddy like an anthill had been stepped on, with thousands of ants gone berserk. Higher-class women with bustles were getting the worst of it, since it was easy to grab one by the fanny and tip her like a cow. Kids were running about clutching mismatched boots. It looked like King Solomon's cloakroom being sacked. Waddy is alternately appalled and attracted. He imagines a Biblical camel loaded with this treasure heading toward the eye of that needle. Women on their knees to God-as-a-bundle. Curious, he thinks, how fire transforms scarcity into abundance. He had to use his whip to keep his loot from being relooted. He managed to get to Dock Square, then up Commercial Street to the bridge over the Charles River. He would retire now from gambling, impelled not so much by virtue as by intermittent success. He wasn't good at gambling, and he was seldom a lucky man. *Manta* from heaven—it had been a sign, an offering. Now he was Waddy Googan, clothier, soon to be couturier. His would not be an empire, like Brooks Brothers with their quirky but popular button collars. Googan Fashions would be known for innovation. If you had the nerve to wear the cutting edge of fashion in stodgy Boston or the more rural Cambridge, you wore Googans. Strange—how he is already thinking of fashion. What he recalls most from the

McCoole fight is *the Deckhand's* bright scarlet cummerbund rolled and passed through six belt loops, tied and hanging in a red splash down the side of the off-white, loose linen pants.

Trotting his treasure over the Prison Point Bridge back to Cambridge, what he remembers now—the image that sticks with him from that extraordinary kaleidoscope of human folly, greed, and calamity—is a note on white paper, on fire and in darting descent to his feet, and his need to read it before it was consumed.

> *Dear Patti,*
> *Please let the dog ou ...*

And he is as sure now as of any bet he's ever made that what sticks to the hairs in his nostrils is the smell—though he has never actually smelled it—of burning dog hair.

For the upstart crow—or rather, weaver—the main thing lacking, for respectability, was a wife. For the arriviste, the woman of choice would be a fallen aristocrat, but that would have to wait. With a few thousand girls now out of work, there were other opportunities to be exploited. As he approached Cambridge, it occurred to him that he could make a killing in sperm oil, now that Boston's entire inventory of gas was gone. And in candles. It was daybreak, November10, 1872. By nine o'clock he had acquired a church-full of candles, and though he didn't pray *for* fire, his gratitude was some smoky kin to prayer.

# Chapter 2: Gratitude, 1891

*T*hink of gratitude as a trough. Think of Waddy Googan and Rebecca Casey dipping their cups in it, celebrating their marriage nineteen years later. Gratitude for the night they met, for his delivering her father's corpse to the door and for her washing his puked-on shirt. She lifted her glass, silently toasting convenience, necessity, and relief. She had nothing better to do, penniless, twenty, and itchy about love. That clink of glasses, Waddy thought, was a rough facsimile of how she embraced him, not that night but in the nights to come.

Gratitude from George Washington, too. The last dollar the bride's father, Sam Casey, touched before leaving the Hub of this world in 1891 was tucked into the G-string of Fanny LaFlamme in Paddy The Pig's, a Scollay Square saloon. What else to do with a single dollar? Sam winked at the unblinking eye at the apex of the triangular brick shithouse on the greenback's backside, and eased George into the musky sporran. His pulse raced as his fingers brushed her whiskers. She ground him an ellipse of appreciation, and he joked to the dapper man beside him that he heard her cheeks flap together in thanks. That buck broke Sam Casey, and his brain cells moved in an orbit similar to Fanny's hips. Ten minutes later the broad-shouldered 'stroke' for the Riverside Boat Club Eight staggered outside in time to catch a hansom that was about to leave.

"Get me out of here," he told the hack. "I've got money back at the house."

"I've already got a customer," replied the driver, Hugo Bartolini, swiveling his neck toward the dapper man. Leaning forward, Waddy Googan recognized the man from the bar and sensed the desperation in his voice. He nodded. Sam Casey got in.

Hugo could tell that the man was a club member from the 'Riverside Cut' of the man's hair—long on the top and short on the sides. He could also tell from the English cut of his suit—what newly-minted couturier Waddy Googan would call *el corte ingles*—that the man was good for the fare. He could not tell that the fare would go stiff on him on a starry night on Massachusetts Avenue. Sam felt an acute, searing pain in his chest. When it passed, he huffed, "It's a shame to have only one life. We ought, like baseball men, to have three."

Waddy nodded in agreement. Sam looked out the hansom window at the river. "Do you know what a sculling draw is?"

"No."

"It's a stroke. In a large arc, to move a boat sideways," Sam said, looking back out the window. After a very long pause to wonder at the moon's reflection off the water he added the nexus. "Life's like that."

Waddy gazed out the hansom window opposite him, saw the infinite stars sparkling around the man in the moon with his one, eternal, nocturnal life and reflected that life was more banal than Sam had suggested, more like a single toothbrush and a thousand choppers all vying for it.

For Sam Casey it was an ideal way to go. His last cent spent. Passed out with his puke-covered thumb in his mouth when his heart again panicked and skidded to a halt in its forty-ninth year.

—*My life*, thought Waddy, *is circumscribed by vomit.* The first time, he recalled, was at ten, at Shraft's, mixing Moxie and chocolate drops. In between he recalled the time with the debutante in the Northampton cottage, in the loo, taking turns, puking, so hot they shrugged and shoved tongues down each other's throats. Then the drunken dive off the staircase of Grays Hall at Harvard, setting up the double gainer, backwards, off the balcony at the Harvard Club in Boston, watching emulsified stars catch up with him, tumbling against a lit up sky, mixing his own effluent with the Milky Way.

Crossing the bridge from Boston to Cambridge, Waddy brushed off his shirt with a monogrammed handkerchief and noticed that his companion was, literally, stiff. He leaned forward and whispered, "I think he's dead."

Hugo panicked. He galloped the four-in-hand onto the man's street, Putnam Avenue, looking for a convenient place to dump the body. But lights were still on and dogs were still barking. He reined in the horses, got out, and checked the dead man's wallet, then his pockets. The stiff had been telling the truth about paying with money from his house: his pockets contained nothing but lint.

Hugo tried Sam Casey's top hat and tossed it to the floor. Wrong size. Total loss. Exactly what it was that prevented him from demanding the fare from the recipient of the goods he was about to deliver he did not know. But he nixed the thought. Then it dawned on him. "You've got to pay his share."

"You tell his wife," Waddy retorted.

A deal Hugo could live with, as long as his living customer helped carry the stiff. He tried to think of a suitable way to put it, but his lines always came up something like, "Excuse me, I think this is your husband is and he's dead."

Surprise, surprise. A beautiful, twenty-year-old, raven-haired woman with *Moxie bottle* glasses answered the door. Holding the corpse, Waddy and Hugo were speechless. She divined for herself what had happened and insisted on washing the monogrammed shirt of Waddy Googan. He insisted on taking her to dinner. Not that night.

"I don't have money for the burial," Casey sobbed. Waddy had the answer to that problem. If she put a Torah in his pocket and just dropped him, incognito, an hour away, the Hebrew Free Burial Association would pick up the tab. He was about to suggest it, but something held him back. As the idea dissipated, it was replaced by what seemed clearly a better one. He could almost see the glitter of stardust from the good fairy's wand, the idea crystallizing, taking form, the Big Bang transformed into ordinary words of deliverance. "I'll pay for it."

As he spoke, the sporting man had no more money than Casey did. But a gentleman could always hit another up. Burial would be a sure thing. She thanked him, and Hugo wasted no time urging his Friesian to a working trot.

"Wait!" said Waddy. "Did you hear that?"

"Yeah, she screamed."

"But it was a man's voice."

Hugo thought on it and nodded. He whipped the Friesian. A stiff in his hansom was creepy enough. Nothing more was spoken, even when Waddy got out at his rooming house, the same one he had lived in since his Harvard days.

A fortnight later the *jolly noisings* of sparrows woke him from a dream in which he stood before a mirror wearing a top hat and a dressing gown emblazoned like a boxer's robe with his trademark: **WG**. The would-be prince of Boston fashions drew back the gown, exposing a warm pink room that he looked down into. A dressing room. Empty, pink, warm, lonely; not a hanger or even a hook to hang it on.

*Hey, ho, nobody home.*

He looked out the window obsessively, till the clouds finally gave up and the sun came frisking through. On this auspicious note he rose, feeling potent, and in the reality of a spring morning looked at himself naked in the full-length mirror and took mental inventory:

*Sporting man—a lover of prizefighting, horse racing, rowing, and rat baiting. But above all a lover of women, no bones about it; a designer of their clothes from the bonnets that adorn their heads to the shoes that envelop their feet, a man knowledgeable in the warp and the weft and the seam of it all.*

On the bathroom table were shaving soap and whiskey, a mug of each. When he was through with both, he put on a pinstripe Italian cut suit, starched collar, and a black tie with a diamond stick pin he'd just won in a card game— one large stone surrounded by thirteen miniatures. As dapper a man as you would find in Boston.

Spring. There were tremors of violets. Lilacs dabbed against his chops. The sun felt so good it was putting him to sleep in his new Stanhope Phaeton in Boston's Public Garden, among the proper ladies and their parasols, their prams. So many majestic derrieres that seemed designed, by nature or bustle, to catch the eye, while part of him wanted simply to be left alone to enjoy the peace, the warmth, and the good smells of a very good day. He was starting to doze when a woman's foot caught his half-conscious eye and brought the buggy to a standstill and got his old heart going two-forty. The tips of her toes were red, with a slim band of leather covering the metatarsus. A short-heeled shoe hung loose from her foot. Her legs were crossed. And he became obsessed by the arch's bursting distention and tautness, reminding him of the belly of

Fanny LaFlamme arched over backwards.

She cocked her foot upward. A visitation of feet, in Boston's Public Garden, feet worthy of the shoes of Waddy Googan, cobbler of material imagination. These were the fleshy mold to stretch *his* leather. The big toe's bending accentuated the extreme arch, the foot a microcosm of the body itself, and the body a metaphor of creation, hinting of God at the helm, or hem, His spirit throbbing in Yr. Hmbl. Srvt, *WG.*

"They're flat!" He immediately repented his tone, which seemed to him almost an accusation.

"Excuse me?" she said to the man she would ordinarily ignore, just another horny gent in a high hat and a Phaeton, but the tone was so high, serious, as if she were a patient in distress and the resident physician was informing her of it. Her instinct told her that the man in the high hat with the dazzling smile, dancing blue eyes, and rakish moustache had more than arch on his mind. As she lifted the broad-brimmed blue hat with a single red rose in the cloth trim, Waddy recognized her a split-second before she recognized him.

"Rebecca Casey."

"My benefactor."

"Waddy Googan," he reintroduced himself, bowing and doffing his hat.

"What did you mean 'they're flat'?" she said, looking at her feet.

Waddy laughed. "Not your feet. Your feet are divine. The *shoes* are too flat! God knows *Henry Marshall*s are excellent shoes, but they're not *you*! Your legs, your feet, that arch," Waddy gesticulated histrionically yet genuinely. "Everything is screaming, 'High! High! Elevate me!'"

She could not help smiling. "I know—you're one of those ... ministers. You want me to repent and follow the Lord." She did not know why she had joined in the badinage. The man was just somehow irresistible. And the approach was nothing if not original. The jury, of course, was still out on the man himself, the most impeccably tailored gent she'd ever spoken with.

"Follow—no. Repent—yes—the sacrilege of diminishing yourself in short heels. High heels ... will change your entire orientation."

"They will?"

"Like a ship sailing *into* the wind instead of luffing along downwind."

"Is that the impression I make? A schooner?"

Waddy slapped his knee and laughed, squinting in the bright sun. "I'm being metaphorical."

"Metaphorically speaking, then, high heels just put women on an erotic pedestal. Is that what you want?"

Waddy squinted, bit his lower lip, and truthfully answered, "Yes."

"Oh," she said sarcastically.

"But what's wrong with that?"

"I don't need to be crippled."

"During the reign of Louis XIV, all aristocratic men wore high heels."

"They should try walking on Boston cobbles."

"That's just the point. They didn't have to."

"Before the Enlightenment, no doubt."

"Touché." He smiled, then sniffed audibly with his eyes closed. "Jicky."

"How did you guess?"

"I know my Guerlain, and I like *Jicky* a lot more than the *Cuir de Russie* or *Le Jardin de Mon Cure*—too flowery." Waddy's eyes turned skyward. He did speak like a minister, some sort of crusader, but it was all from the heart. "I see a new vestimentary discourse, less prosaic, more egalitarian. I see demimondaine fashion stripped of its coarseness and made palatable to the American woman of the '90s." He looked her intensely in the eye and extended a white gloved hand. "Perhaps I could expand my views, over tea?"

Casey rose. "Sorry, I've got to be on the river in an

17

hour."

"You've inherited a yacht?"

"Hardly. A single scull. I row. My father and I rowed together all the time."

Waddy lowered his gaze and nodded very slowly, recalling how recently her father had died. He repressed a smile at the sudden and not entirely welcome inspiration for a mourning cloak. She stood and extended her hand. He'd forgotten how tall she was. He considered kissing her hand but shook it instead. "Perhaps lunch, sometime."

"Perhaps," she said, turning and heading toward Arlington Street.

The next day she received two letters from Waddy on top-of-the-line Marcus Ward linen paper; one sealed with purple wax and the other with chocolate-colored wax. She was a welter of emotions, opening first the *purple*-sealed letter that signaled condolence, then breaking the seal of the *chocolate-colored* dinner/lunch invitation.

At the Café Marliave the following Saturday afternoon, Waddy studied her face—her lips in profile, ruby colored, with the same bursting sensation as her great toe. His eyes focused on her *décolleté* as she studied the menu. "I'm so glad you accepted my invitation."

"I surprised myself. I hardly know you."

"You did wash my shirt."

"Yes, but you could be a democrat, a reformist, a know-nothing; you could be a socialist as far as I know."

He pushed the last two peas onto his fork. "I lean toward anarchy. Other than that, I have no political views that I can think of."

"Do you think women should vote?"

"I think that if women continue to develop mentally, there should be no impediment to their voting in ten years or so."

"And now?"

"On the whole, the better half still displays too much irrationality."

"How so?"

"Let's start with the bustle. If fashion is the body's architecture, the bustle is its outhouse. It's an insane distortion of feminine anatomy, yet outside of Boston women still wear them."

"Those are women who could never afford a good bustle when they were in fashion, and now that they're out, they can get them for pennies. It would be irrational for them not to."

"Then there's the corset—a *debilitating* distortion."

"Men wear corsets, too."

"And I wouldn't let them vote, either." Waddy was taken aback by Casey's assertiveness, combativeness, not to mention her rationality. He leaned forward, animated, as if she were rational enough to be convinced of women's irrationality. "And rice powder? The lengths to which women will go to make themselves look like cadavers?"

"You seem to know women, but I'm wondering if you *like* them."

He inserted his fork in the last piece of rare steak with béarnaise, marbled with blood. "I wouldn't have become a couturier if I didn't like women, would I?"

"Some artists paint beautiful nudes but treat their models despicably."

He looked out the window at the downtown women in French fashions and reflected, "At the time of Louis XIV, the couturier was a dress fitter, which was a somewhat exalted position. A man at that time, Balzac said, could be an artist of dressing *and* undressing."

"Let me guess—Waddy Googan is leading the revival, of the latter."

She found him blunt, witty, intelligent, outrageous, but charming. If nothing else, he was refreshingly different. She imagined that he would be capable of sweet nothings, but without the unctuousness of so many flattering gentlemen.

She was silent, parsing it all—the man, his views.

"I'm not shocking you, am I?"

"I'm not exactly a tabula rasa."

He proposed a walk through the Public Garden. Where she saw sadness in the women selling corn from cedar-stave pails and in 'mint girls' selling their wares from willow baskets, he saw opportunity. In the Public Garden they were on his turf; and the Harvard-educated naturalist commented on the flora and fauna, using their Latin names. "This is *tilia vulgaris*, the common linden."

He stared at the weeping willows—solipsistic green huddles, and at the linden frosted with gold, but nearly opaque, as if opaque were the result of ingested sunlight. He stopped, inspired again. "I have just the thing for you," he said exuberantly. "A green muslin *décolleté* with Vallencienne lace." He stared at her neck. "An enormous diamond pendant."

"I don't think I can afford that."

He smiled with promise and looked her directly in the eye. "You'll be the talk of the town."

"Your gown will."

The green huddle of himself smiled. With unusual coquettishness, she removed her silk scarf and twirled it above her head, where a strong breeze blew it into an *ulmus*. "It's caught."

Waddy's eyes fell on a robust adolescent bootblack with a strange looking pair of tongs. "You," he said to the lad, "come here. Let me borrow those tongs."

The lad hesitated, but getting an eyeful of the woman, he complied with a smile. Waddy retrieved the scarf with the tongs and handed it to her, then handed the tongs back to Laz Godfrey.

"I don't think I've seen the likes of those, with a rasp at the end."

"They're special. For rattin'. All you need is a piece of the tail, and it's in the bag. One time I bagged three hundred, at the Parker House kitchen." As he spoke, Laz's eyes were diverted to Casey, and hers returned the gaze.

Waddy was oblivious to Laz's attentions, studying the man's physique. He was, in the vernacular of Mooney's tavern regarding pugilists, a *specimen*.

Casey saw Laz in the foreground of the statues on the Boston Common: George Washington—his legs sadly straddling a horse, and another general, sword poised to run through an invisible enemy. Violence—even the statues in the Museum of Fine Arts tended toward it—the Greek gods locked with their serpents, unto Leda with her swan—violent love. The statues in their marble eternities embraced no one; and no one reciprocated. It was just as far—no?—from reality to contemplate the embrace of a strapping, handsome, young black man. The blush of a thought washed through whatever conjured itself as boundary in her mind, where she saw their lips brushing. Then it was banished, just another image in the mental album, piled under thousands of others, just another window closing in one of the Victorian bungalows of Beacon Street. It recalled for her the marvelous kaleidoscope her father had bought her when he was on a winning streak. These images—she wondered as a kid— did they inhere in the instrument itself or did she create them by a twist of the hand? Or the neck?

Waddy discarded the scarf tainted by ratting tongs, for which Casey felt some relief. "I'll make you a new one." He looked again at the muscular young man. "Are you by chance something of a sporting man?"

"I bet on the dogs where I sell my rats—the Band Box, Worcester Street Crib, Mooney's pit ..."

"Why don't you take the scarf?" Casey offered. "Wear it for good luck."

Laz picked it up, grinning, still looking at Casey. "Thanks. I will."

"You know, if you were as fast as you are strong, you'd make another John L. Sullivan."

"How fast is fast?"

Waddy stepped closer to the kid and said *sotto voce*, "I

know a Colored who can squeeze a bull terrier by the balls and not get his hand taken off."

The kid smiled, showing a set of strong teeth with which he manipulated a toothpick. "Can that boy pull a rat out of a full bag and not get bit?" Laz displayed scarless hands and fixed Waddy with a glare that loosened his bowels.

"Come down to the Chelsea Sporting Club some time. Tell them Waddy Googan sent you. We're always looking for new blood. If you can put your hand in a white boy's face and not get hit, you've got a career ahead of you."

"I done that," said the kid, with a serious mien that reverted to a big smile that unsettled Waddy.

"What's your name, son?"

"Lazarus Roger Godfrey."

"I like the ring of it. *Grappling Godfrey.* Any relation to the pugilist George Godfrey?"

"We're cousins."

Waddy nodded and escorted Casey towards the Charles Street gate of the Public Garden. Laz watched the tall svelte brunette recede, then he fastened her scarf around his neck. Casey had been cleaning her glasses to give her poor eyes a better look at the young man. There was something about him, something more than the hickory-knotted arms, something about the energy that reminded her of someone. And it wasn't until the next time she saw him, in boxing trunks, that she realized it was—herself.

"That was Ulysses-like, retrieving my scarf. A clever man doesn't need muscles like that lad's."

"I am not without muscles," Waddy responded, not without some pique. "I studied boxing with Professor Mike Donovan."

"A professor ... of boxing?"

"He wrote the book on it, literally. The world's authority on training. He could take a muscularly endowed lad like that one and make him a champion."

"Well, if he can, why can't you?"

"Me?"

"Why not?"

On the Common, a governess stood watch over a group of boys in basted white linen collars and jackets buttoned up to the neck, playing with a *locust*, a round wooden match box with one end torn off and replaced by a piece of goat skin. A grooved twig was tied to it with horse hair. When swung, it made a sound like a locust.

Casey directed Waddy's attention to the boys just up the street, by Boylston Place. "I went to school right over there. Dixwell's Girls' Latin School. When the boys next door could get away with it, they'd shoot at the felt top hats with putty balls and smokeless powder."

Waddy stopped his Phaeton under a gas light whose glass bubble drooped, twenty feet over Charles Street. Catching the reflections of a setting sun, it looked already lit. Bugs spiraled, dissolved, and re-collected in a shiver of sunlight, a living barber pole. He laughed. "I was expelled once, for something like that."

Just what, he didn't say, and she didn't ask. She reciprocated his dinner invitation—tea, on her porch. She served pancakes, remembering her mother's adages regarding suitors: *If he puts a handkerchief on his knee during tea, he'll be prudent. If he picks up the last griddle cake, he'll be selfish.* Waddy failed on both counts. But charm outweighed a mother's adages. She invited him back four consecutive Sundays, the last of which was fateful. He glanced at her leaning against the door frame of the kitchen, projecting lassitude—but dynamically, a standing contradiction; she appeared a kind of ornate frieze, her breast in silhouette ruffled with taffeta, one hand on hip, the stasis of a one-handled wine jug and the soaring potential of a one-winged butterfly. It took his breath away.

He picked up the book she'd left on the table. "You read Balzac, in French?"

Casey nodded.

Waddy closed *Splendeurs et misères des courtisanes* and smiled. "That seals it for me."

"Seals what?"

He dabbed his lips and put down his napkin. "*Les noces*. Our marriage—if you consent. Balzac was the first novelist to deal in depth with fashion. I'm a fashion designer. I think you are someone who would understand me."

She looked away, thinking. She walked to the window that looked onto the unfinished backyard maze, then returned. She took a deep breath. "There are two things I need to tell you."

He raised his chin one notch, the facetless blue gems as open as they ever got—Waddy always holding something back.

"First, I'm a virgin, and second ..."

"Yes?"

"I'm a vegetarian."

A pencil-line of ivory shone beneath the thick bushy mustache of the Harvard-educated declamation champion. *Therein lies no impediment to love's banquet*, he mused. In partial thrall to his charm, intelligence, and the cuteness of his middle-aged dimples, the utterly destitute, about-to-be foreclosed on damsel found no abiding impediment to matrimony. Waddy took and kissed her hand, already imagining the bridal dress and train that he would confect. The courtship might be summarized as:

> —*Your shirt.*
> —*Your ring.*

Time was just the mortar for the building blocks of shirt and ring, themselves extensions of gratitude. He was ostensibly wealthy and dashing and forty-three. Love was yet one more thing to gamble on. She was jobless, skill-less, in as dire straits financially as he was emotionally. Her father's creditors were banging down the door. Sam had been a broker who gambled professionally and privately.

His wife had run off with a Russian aristocrat and left him with a daughter, Rebecca, who disowned her feminine, given name and wanted to be a boy, which was fine for Sam, who raised her as a boy.

For Waddy, love was as true as desperate. Fidelity was a horse of another color. A vow coerced in a church was no vow at all. He vowed to himself to love Casey. In that he never wavered. He saw fidelity as everyone on 'the continent' did, a mental construct. Men had physical needs that women didn't. Was Casey not smart enough to see that? As for her vow, Waddy would later say she had her legs, in lieu of fingers, crossed. True love would not *come* to her; she would later run it down, literally, on a horse.

In the meantime, did he not provide? And those times when gambling trumped provision, was she not better off than before he made her a Googan? Was there ever a time when, provision notwithstanding, Rebecca Casey Googan was not the best-dressed woman in Cambridge, if not Boston—the hub of the known world?

If one married not for love or not *just* for love—say for money, etcetera, when etcetera loomed large in the female dreamscape, was it not normal for some version of love to grow, especially when the man was as loveable as Waddy Googan was to a large coterie of Cantabridgean ladies, with his wit, charm, intelligence, talent, robin's-egg-blue eyes, rosy and chuckable mutton-chopped chin?

So maybe it was there—love—in the beginning or the thereafter. Maybe it was there all along but poorly expressed or poorly processed. Then again, for a gambler, denial was de rigueur. Waddy denied that he was an addict, denied the fact that his losses exceeded his winnings, that he was a stochastic deadbeat. Did denial extend to the wager his emotional life depended on? Who could forget the day he created a heart of rose petals on their bed and the intricate, artistic petal-designs all about it that took an entire morning to elaborate? Or the love made there where the rose-petal arrow pierced the heart. Or that bed itself—

what she wanted, the largest bed procurable, what he wanted as well—the freedom, the expansiveness. The luxury of enormity, himself that daVinci mandala of a naked man, arms extended to reveal the perfect symmetry of man. His fingers and toes could row and never go over the edge into the void. But it didn't turn out that way. The enormous bed would not fit up the stairway to the hundred-year-old Putnam Avenue house. But two singles would do the trick. With the practiced tucks of a matrimonial sheet Casey turned two into one. Yet he could feel the edge beneath the sheet, the stitched rope enclosure of his and hers. He sank into the formless form that was so familiar, so undeniably himself. There was a dream of sheets with no wrinkles. Was is Waddy's, Casey's, the sheet's, the wrinkles'?

See it from a bird's eye view, make that a swan's eye, of Waddy on those cold Cantabridgean winter nights, Casey at her toilette, he in tippled and tumescent anticipation, and the daVinci mandala comes to life, those outstretched and naked arms and legs making a snow angel in the bed— that's what the swan sees, but on terra/bed-firma what he is doing is warming the bed for his love. Did she know? Did she feel the strangely warm sheet beneath her and reckon that he was the creant? He would never mention it. There just were things a man did. A good man.

Waddy moved into Casey's Putnam Street house. He had stopped foreclosure on it thanks to a tip from Foxhall Codman on a fixed race at the Franklin Trotting Park. Their first morning he is on the patio thinking that the sweetest thing would be Casey in a morning coat holding a cup of coffee in the sunlit doorway with a 'How are you?' And in his mind he gives it back—'How are you?' he says to this vision in the Cambridge mist, and he hears, from above, her cough. He can only wait and see... Minutes later—she must have been barefoot—he's surprised by the softest 'Good morning.' Then a kiss and the 'How are you?' Though she has forgotten the coffee. She stares at him as if she has discovered something. Then she looks away, almost troubled, surprised at not having already noticed something.

"What?"

"You have loving eyes."

Her morning coat is some Nubian vision of sunlight mobbed into a fanciful vision of what the King of Hearts would wear if he could wear himself. That's the stuff she wears from the heart, communing with, decked out in, the emerging Cantabridgean sunlight. The mourning doves whoo-whoo. The home team is ahead for good. Shadows recede from the Gloucester-quarried granite, and the air is so full that his nose feels absolutely animal—that acute. Even the sound of neighbor Charlie Neblung's sharpening wheel is co-opted by the redolence as the sun, god, comes trundling down.

But it was not long before the girl raised as a boy insisted a job. Waddy gave in only when his gambling debts overwhelmed. But *he* would get *her* the job. He conceded, no doubt, out of love. The job he would get her was at The Holly Tree, a Harvard Square restaurant where all the swells had breakfast. Which meant she had to get up even earlier to indulge her passion—rowing.

She had grown up on water, with her father's collection of boats. He'd been a member of the Wharf Rats Club, whose gavel was a whale penis. When he gambled away the money necessary for the annual dues, he joined the Riverside Boat Club. Casey fell in love at an early age with shells, especially singles. Sam taught her to row, and she rowed exceptionally well. Her rowing was pure miscegenation—the marriage of muscle and wood. She dressed like a boy, and as she grew she kept her hair short like a boy's. To the men at the Riverside Boat Club, who had known her since she was seven, the female sculler was an anomaly they were used to. They predictably ignored how fast she rowed, only nodded in acknowledgment of her technique, and never allowed her to race. But race she did, secretly, with the men as they practiced their sprints. And not entirely in secret. When Casey knew she was beating the men on the water she would let up. She was wise enough to know that there would be repercussions if it were known that a woman was besting the men. Still, a spectator with some knowledge of sculling and who watched intently could see what she was doing. Such a swell was Charlie Hot Dog, as he was called for his present occupation—Charlie Neblung, their neighbor—whose last name few people knew, though once upon a time it had been engraved on brass plates affixed to the shells he constructed.

She got up before dawn, too, because daylight was urgent. Her eyes were so bad it was hard to read at night. So the daylight hours after work became precious, especially since she thought her sight was worsening, and the piles of necessary books to read grew. She had finished one semester at Bryn Mawr where, as a freshman she captained the newly-formed women's-eight crew team, but was forced to withdraw when her father was unable to pay the second-year's tuition. As a female sculler, she was somewhat unique, but Mt. Holyoke women's eights were also rowing—on Lake Nonotuck, and Wellesley women rowed their cedar shells on Lake Waban. Brwn Mawr girls rowed on the Schuylkill in matching beanies, collar-less shirts, and ankle-length skirts that answered the question of where ten missing American flags on campus went— stripes without stars billowing from the girls' waists. Rowing in the 1890s was becoming a national pastime.

At Bryn Mawr she developed a taste for French authors, and read them in their own language until she decided that time was running short. As she read *Madame Bovary* in English, even the seat of her pants got urgent— she felt the romantic part of her life was slipping past her too, the way she would slip past a prudent Foxhall Codman on an early morning on the Charles, where fog leveled the watery playing field, when Boston's sculling champ let up on his sculls to avoid crashing into a bridge that she could not see and wouldn't have cared about anyway; the moment was all that mattered.

# Chapter 3: Possessed

*T*his foggy spring morning Rebecca Casey Googan was up before the sun. She loved dawn and dusk, those doppelgangers, for their sameness, two sides of the same coin. The morning star and the evening star—one in the same. Venus, sole schizophrenic mistress of the heavens. Casey, mistress of the water. Dusk—with the Big Dipper slowly blinking in. And dawn, announced by the roosters and the *orchestra d'ucelli*, with the sun just starting to scale Putnam Street's thick fortress of sycamores, when warmth teased, the perfect equipoise of heat and chill. The sun's reflection on the kettle on the stove-top flashed and bounced, accentuating the kettle's bobbing and weaving. Single-nostriled, bull-snorting morning. Not the kind of day to remain at home.

The fog on the tidal Charles seemed to roll down the banks where small ridges of snow still clung to the thawed earth. The twenty feet between the street and the river created a temperature differential of ten degrees. From the river's edge, Casey saw the outline of the dim sun at the horizon. From the cold racing shell on the river she saw nothing but white and gray. The shoe plate was visible as she tucked her feet in, but even the tip of the stern disappeared in wisps of rolling, roiling, marshmallow fog.

~~~~~~~

This early on a cold morning Foxhall Codman expected no one else on the river. No one else could be that obsessed. Swinging his shell out to mid-river, he knew how many strokes it was to the bridge, and he'd turn at five strokes from it, with a comfortable margin of error. He enjoyed the feeling of disaster at his back and closing, knowing that it would never strike this Brahmin, the wet air seeping through his two woolen sweaters and settling in his bones notwithstanding. He took the shell out at moderate speed, glad to be moving, blindflying through the fog, and did a neck-snapping double-take. To his right, a brown woolen cap appeared, then instantly disappeared again, in the fog. His heart jumped at the apparition. He stretched his torso at the end of the power stroke as if the added three inches might put his eyes above the fog. As he settled back in his seat and began to push back the sculls, he caught another glimpse of the brown-capped figure who threw off his rhythm, and he caught a crab. Regaining his balance, he realized that the apparition was rowing through him. Instantly, his muscles tensed. A surge of adrenaline sped down his arms and down his legs. He took two power strokes. On the next stroke, with no visible water-level reference point, he dipped his scull at the catch and nearly capsized, something he hadn't done since his novice days. He put all his skill and strength into the next three strokes and sensed, from the sound of the challenger's boat, that he had pulled even. By his calculation, he was now five strokes from the bridge. The game had become a game of chicken. Four strokes now to the possible crash, and the fog gave for an instant. He was still not ahead. If anything, he had lost a half-meter. With three strokes to go, the fog blanketed the challenger's boat. One last hammer, then panic in mid-stroke, and he backed his sculls to stave off collision. He turned the shell, and the darker fog over his left shoulder signaled the imminence of the bridge. The upstart boat slid ghostlike past him, at full throttle through the semi-circular stone arch of the bridge, leaving him wondering if it has been some kind of mirage or dream. He decided later that the laughter he thought he heard was just the water lapping against the bridge. But the sculler? Was he hallucinating gender from the disconcerting blindness imposed by the fog? Or was he hallucinating the whole thing—the phantom sculler lucky and crazy enough to slip between the stone pillars of the bridge?

He hadn't been bested in years. But this wasn't *really* a race. How could it come to pass that the sculling champion of Boston should feel like a Rube? A bit-player in someone else's game—a woman, perhaps—who couldn't beat him with a ten length lead over a thousand meters in a fair race? She had put one over on him. He'd been a bit player in her drama, the way an occasional runner along the river bank would—unawares—be the victim of a race Casey would enter him in.

Codman was so unnerved he misjudged his docking at the Union Boat Club boathouse. He swung the bow around, but not enough. He struck the dock and was jolted forward, off balance, and into the water. He had redamaged the Neblung shell that was made at his father's boat works in 1881, but was still one of the fastest boats on the river. He vowed to focus even more on his rowing. This night, after a bottle of Chateau d'Yquem, he fell asleep dreaming of the *woman* on the water. And from her dream-laugh he reconstructed a mouth, a face, a head from which a brown woolen cap was rendered as yet another trophy. Then came again the sound of the shell's wood splintering against the dock. His body snapped forward, awake, his heart hammering. And how he wanted to race the phantom sculler again, on the fogless water that was his *Hub*.

~~~~~~~

Casey was soaked. The fog and drizzle had penetrated her wool sweater, her cotton shirt, and undershirt. She shivered, as cold as the naked bronze statue on the river bank of the athlete coiled up to throw his discuss. But between paroxysms of shivering, she laughed, feeling frozen but good. She knew who the man was and what he was. It had been worth every shiver of it. She had no trouble docking her boat at the Riverside Boat Club boathouse.

Codman's Union Boat Club and Casey's Riverside were polar opposites, and one reason they had never met on the water. From the junction of Brimmer and Chestnut streets in Back Bay, the exclusive Union Club looked onto both the Charles River and the Boston Common, while the Riverside was a working man's club, located between River Street and Western Avenue in Cambridge. Déclassé perhaps in comparison to the Union, but its hundred or so members had coughed up $13,000 for a new, shingled, two-story structure. Casey had lived on rice and lentils to afford her share, her membership more important to her than food.

~~~~~~~

Rowing, she was perfectly centered, feet, knees, thighs all perfectly aligned for maximum power. Her hands crossed unerringly, with precision, the same distance between them at every stroke. She seemed born with technique as much as with strength. When she threw her head back, it moved straight back, favoring neither side. Even her grimace was marked by symmetrical retreat of her lips from slightly gat teeth.

After a good practice, the one hundred and forty pound sculler thought that if she were a man no one could beat her. She would bet her life on it. Her competitive spirit came from her father, who took her to the Cottage Farm Bridge to watch the boat races. He would hold the young girl on his shoulder for a better view. The colors impressed the child most: the crimson of Harvard, Yale's bright blue with white letters, and the brightly painted oars, all of which had the flavor of a medieval pageant. She once heard a man with a crimson sweater describe how Edward Hanlan could really "move a boat." And the phrase was magic. It was beautiful. She wanted to *move a boat* like no woman ever had, and not like Hanlan, with his choppy, dogged stroke. She would emulate the smoothness of the nonpareil Charles Courtney. Sam Casey was not normally a man to share his feelings with anyone but himself, yet some years later he sidled up to the girl that he had always wanted to be a boy, admiring her arms and shoulders and voicing his thought, "You know, I can't help thinking that if ever a girl was born to move a boat, it's you." He then slapped her on the back like one of the lads.

For hours she would watch the scullers go by, feeling the strength of the sculls pulling on the water and the boats lurching. The rhythmic quality of the power entranced her. She would tense up her small biceps as the sculls hit the water and pulled. The obsessed girl began with a rowboat whose oars she could barely manage. As soon as she was big enough, Sam Casey taught his daughter to row a wherry. And by age twelve she was sneaking off with her father's single. Little got in the way of her obsession. Not the weather. Not boys. In winter she would skate on the Charles—backwards, the same way she would row, getting a feel for the landmarks and how far she was from a bridge at any given point. She did not understand what possessed her to skate backwards at full speed, not sliding to a stop till she was as close as she could get without crashing into the bridge. The bridges were a problem on the tortuous Charles. In every regatta you would see the eight-man shells get their oars tangled as they headed for the same arch under a bridge. And the Western Avenue bridge pylons were so close together that only one boat could fit between one section.

They called her a tomboy, and she liked it. As she matured into an attractive, 5' 9" adolescent, she tended to ignore boys—who did not ignore her. Her fantasy took another direction. During the long hours of almost hypnotic practice on the Charles, she would sometimes feel that she was living another life from another time. At times the feeling was so strong it was something other than fantasy. In that other time, the colors were softer, the river took on an earthy, orange tint. She began to live her recurring dream. The pain then was in the back of a broad-shouldered slave on a Roman trireme, pulling on his oar for hours at a time. If the ship went down, no one would bother to unshackle him. Casey awoke some nights tasting the brackish, force-fed, warm Mediterranean water in her throat.

Pulling a power twenty on the Charles, her back breaking, her stomach knotted like ironwood, her heart trying to burst its cage, she would be transported, rowing for her life in a trireme where the power twenty became meaningless; there was another power ten to simply save her life as the whip of the burly officer came down on *his* shoulders. Then on the Charles she would row through anyone ahead of her. These scullers didn't know who it was rowing through them between matins and lauds. She looked like any young man at a distance and always wore a woolen cap. Anonymity was important because she knew there would be a backlash if the men knew it was a woman who had rowed through them.

And she felt just as strongly that she was somehow letting down her long-haired doppelganger, that if she could row strongly enough she would burst his shackles, that she would row *himself* to freedom. Then the picture got cloudy and she knew that she had to stop or lose consciousness. She would come off the river shaking. She would shake her head at the power of the fantasy and give a small anxious laugh to reassure herself of who she really was.

She rowed from ice-out to ice-in, and the months in between were miserable. She loved most the fall, the smell of the apples on the Alston side of the Charles river, sliding the bow through the reflection of bright yellows, oranges, crimsons. She loved the smell of leaves turning, browning, letting go, loved how the trees shuddered, how a certain species she could not name unleashed a flotilla of oblong, boat-shaped leaves that would oscillate synchronously in their descent into an afterlife as boats.

Resting, she would feather her oars while the Harvard eights sprinted by, oblivious to her presence, fully interred in their own pain. So intense was their concentration, she felt, that were she to strip off her sweater and row half-naked, they wouldn't notice.

*Stroke* ... the coxswain bellowed, coming through the bridge, and it echoed ... *stroke* ... and the echo dissipated into the next bellow ... *stroke* ... so that there was almost no interregnum. It reminded her of church bells that rang and echoed similarly—matins, lauds, terce—and the call, to Casey, was much the same, the rowing as liturgical. *Stroke* ... *stroke* ... *stroke* ... *stroke* ... The perfection of it ... It was the moments between pain, that absence, that made pain noticeable. A world where pain was all there was was not pain at all. The joy—*why not?*—of it. Where she dwelled.

But she felt too a kind of exhilaration, a feeling of freedom. And most of the time on the river for her was good time. It was by the sound of the boat that she knew that it *swung*, the full sound of the catch and the way the sculls came out of the water, when full power had been garnered. She listened till it clicked. Sometimes she would push and pull till she felt her muscles would pop from their sheaths, but the sound would not be there. Then she would let up slightly and it would be there, a synchronicity. But the synchronicity was a sound, a pitch, that could be duplicated an octave *higher*, no? The harmony of rower, boat, and water was a chord that could be played in a higher key, one with more power, and pain. What was the limit? Sometimes she felt, in ecstasy, afraid to pull any harder, afraid she would dissolve into the dazzle of light in the water—which was all that she would see. And the rhythm, that chord of *swing* was all that she heard. Her arms and legs were numb. The only feeling she had was the blood beating for an exit at her temples. Now, she thought, with the good yet guilty feeling of swiping a finger-full of icing off a cake—just one more surge, one more power level and poof, she would disappear, boat and all, row right into the orange, earthy-tinted, Trastevere dazzle.

She rowed, too, because what was more natural—she thought—for an organism that was seventy-five percent water? She rowed to live, and lived to outrow anyone living. But then, thought Casey, *what if you did? What if the whole world bowed down in adulation and no man or woman, dared to take up oars against you?*

~~~~~~~

*I'm not <u>ob</u>sessed,* Casey decided. —*I'm <u>po</u>ssessed.*

# Chapter 4: Mooney's

*W*addy's favorite watering hole was Mooney's. Proprietor Skeets Mooney attributed the popularity of his Central Square saloon to his changing its name from *Mooney's Temple of Friendship* to *Mooney's Temple of Bacchus* in 1880. More likely, it was the introduction of free lunch—soda crackers, raw onions, cheese, and one of the best chowders in town—with the purchase of a five-cent schooner of beer or mug of ale. Outside Mooney's Temple of Bacchus you could still read the whitewashed-over lettering *Café Majestic*, which it once was. It still had an attractive ambiance. Carved marble pillars in the marble floor, cut glass windows, elaborate woodwork and embossed leather-backed benches in desuetude. A few dead light bulbs like cataracts in their sockets. An immense but cracked three-part mirror on the wall. Dust collected on the ornate, peeling, gilded decorations around the mirror, the thighs of child bacchantes decorously matted with a century of it. The ceiling paint peeled, and a smoke patina covered everything.

Skeets promoted his joint to first-timers as having

"Good ale, raw onions, and no ladies." That didn't mean *no women*. Mooney's was open to every wandering creature, but only after 10:00 p.m. Then the doors were thrown open to *les belles impures*, as Foxhall Codman called them. Before 10:00, the only woman allowed in the bar was Fanny Bronsky, who sold oysters for a penny each. Fanny's husband had been a friend of Skeets and died of a rattlesnake bite at the Battle of Bull Run.

In the main room a sign read:

*Profane, indecent & boisterous conduct prohibited.*

Behind the polished mahogany bar was a long mirror, and at one's feet was a polished brass rail. The mahogany around the mirror was studded with shoes of famous retired horses, including Stonewall Jackson and His Nibs. The walls featured portraits and lithographs of John L. Sullivan, Tom Sayers, Joe Choynski, and other pugilists. Between the wainscoting and the ceiling were photographs of Harvard crews and of local scullers, including Foxhall Codman. A huge fireplace occupied much of the rear wall, with a chimney wide enough, Waddy discovered in 1885, for a man to climb into but not out of, mystifying the bookies who were searching for the deadbeat couturier.

Ale was drawn from a brass-bound pump. Regulars had pewter mugs with their names engraved with an ice pick. On the bar sat a quart of tobacco and a rack of clay and corncob pipes—free with drink. There was no cash register. Coins were kept in soup bowls, bills in a mahogany box. The two clocks on the walls were never in agreement. The floor was covered with sawdust and the ceiling was of patterned, pressed tin, painted white. Gas lamps threw flickering shadows on the cobwebbed tin ceiling whenever someone opened the door. The main room was large enough that chairs and tables could be moved to accommodate prize fights, and rat-baiting pits were located through a door under a sign that read:

*Sanctum Sanctorum (Miscellaneous Entertainment of High Character).*

Mooney's became the closest thing north of Manhattan to Harry Hill's establishment on Houston Street. Lined up for blocks were the stately black Broughams and Landaus of the Boston aristocracy, along with Bachelor Broughams, Coupes, the Barouches of the smart set, and the four-in-hands favored by the avant-garde bored with the St. Botolph's Club. Brahmins could rub shoulders with the hoi-polloi with minimal fear for their well-being and their wallets. It was an opportunity to "study humanity," as Foxhall Codman put it, to see how the other half, or 95%, lived and sported. The gentry called it "hunting the elephant," the metropolitan beast. There was squalor, depravity, spittoons, sawdust, and spilled beer. *Les belles impures* plied their wares, and sailors were immediate targets for men with plucked eyebrows.

Behind the bar, Skeets kept order with a baseball bat that he used for sporting purposes on Sunday afternoons on the Cambridge Common with Mooney's Cantab Nine, and which he referred to as his shillelagh. Known pickpockets had their heads, hands, or any available limb, shattered. The unruly were cold-cocked. But a gentleman could pass out on his bar stool with four-hundred dollars in his pocket and wake up in one of Skeets's back-rooms with four-hundred dollars in his pocket, as Foxhall Codman's pals Deke Merriwell and Cosmo Croninshield well knew.

There was musical entertainment most nights from a partially-burned pulpit Skeets had rescued from the Episcopal church destroyed in the fire of 1885. Skeets had a short range of musical taste that included fiddles and accordions. Mick Lawless played, the accordion for hours, with Waddy offering vocals of his favorites *The Girl I Left Behind* and *Benny Heaven*. When Mick quit, usually around

2:00 a.m., he was replaced in the pulpit by *Father Divine-who-changed-the-first*-e-*of-his-last-name-to*-i. After retiring from active ministry in 1886, Father Divine took up active drinking. He railed against evil of all sorts, but primarily the kinds he saw being pursued around and below him. The demon rum took it on the chin. The more epithets he collected ("Shut up, you fucking moron"), the more he was impelled to take on Satan in his many garbs. His sincerity was as intense as his hypocrisy about alcohol, and Father Divine would rant mellifluously for an hour before he passed out or keeled entirely out of the pulpit.

The next time Waddy Googan saw Lazarus Roger Godfrey was the day Moose took over Mooney's, but he did not recognize the lad who had retrieved Casey's scarf that day on the Boston Common. Moose found his last name unnecessary and unexpressive. The police, who generally found law enforcement urgently needed in Harvard Square when Moose was in Central Square, logged him in simply as *Moose*.

Moose was 6' 5" and went about two-hundred and fifty. He had those oversized teeth that seemed an inbred inheritance amongst mountain men from Maine and Vermont, and he could straighten nails between them. Like the British pugilist John Jackson, he could write his name with an eighty-four pound weight suspended from his little finger. He hadn't lost a bar-fight in the two years it had taken him to work his way south, lumberjacking and brawling, from Jackman to Boston.

"I seen Little Egypt in every joint in Scollay Square," Moose uttered to every man in his vicinity. "What I want to see is Big Egypt. Where the fuck are they keeping Big Egypt? I'm tired of Little Egypt. I wanna see tits you can wrap around your head and bury it in like a groundhog. I wanna get lost in tits."

Meat House Slim was every bit as drunk as Moose and had an edge in truth-telling and stupidity. "You want your mama."

Moose turned toward Meat House. "I want *your* mama."

"You ..." The world never learned Meat House Slim's intended defamation in its entirety as he lurched at Moose, for the lumberjack without turning his head lifted his nearly full mug of ale and stove in Meat House's face. Slim fell instantly, out so cold so fast he had no time to groan. Moose smiled, ostensibly more proud of the fact that he'd hardly spilled a drop. Father Divine came over to check on Meat House. Moose took no chances. He heaved Father Divine over the bar, which drew Skeets Mooney into the fray, reaching for his shillelagh. Skeets gave his standard exculpatory warning, "Make haste and remove yourself from the premises." Moose reached over the bar as Skeets wound up, grabbed him under the armpits, pulled him over the bar, and threw him headfirst onto the floor. Then he squaled the bouncer and threw him out the window. Skeets shook out the cobwebs and scurried around to the back of the bar where he kept a miniature cannon loaded with powder only. When things got really out of hand he'd fire it off and deafen everyone into submission. Now Skeets aimed the canon at Moose. Moose grabbed the barrel with one hand and threw it through another window, followed by the canoneer.

Most of the patrons were scared pink and left en masse. The remaining were stout-hearted, stupid, drunk, or some combination of the three. In any case, they cowered and made no eye contact with the rampaging Moose, who scoffed the cheese from Waddy's plate. "Not every man's a mouse that eats cheese," he jested, drinking Waddy's ale and making a threatening gesture with his arm. Waddy retreated to the street, quickly followed by a cohort of the better-dressed inebriates. Hugo Bartolini moseyed up. "What's going on?"

"Moose."

Moose proceeded to chase the rest of the patrons out and drink their beer, all but one, a young black man sitting quietly and calmly in the corner shelling a small pile of peanuts and sipping a beer. At first, Moose didn't notice him. Then he prowled the area adjacent to where the man was sitting, as bewildered as perturbed by the young man's permanence.

Hugo peeked through the broken window with Father Divine, saw the young black man, and shook his head. "He's had a few too many."

"What? Peanuts?"

"Days."

Waddy heard only part of the conversation. "Days to what? To pay up?"

"I think he means Moose is going to kill the nigger," said Skeets, wiping his forehead with a white bar rag that turned as red as a Tom turkey's wattles. "The elevens are up."

"Yup. I can see 'em," said Waddy.

Skeets had a theory, developed over two decades of bartending, that a man was itching to fight when the two cords on the back of his neck stood out, forming the number eleven. And Skeets was right. Moose picked up the black man's beer and drained it. "Not every man's a monkey that eats peanuts, but some's chicken." Moose chuckled and added, "but you do kind of look like a monkey."

The young black man calmly shelled another peanut.

"Piss ant! I'd piss on you, 'cept that I respect the dead." Moose didn't wait for the man to prove he was neither a chicken nor a piss ant. He thrust the beer mug at the man's face like he had at Meat House's. This time the mug was intercepted by a hand, almost as big as Moose's, that wrenched the mug from the big man's maw. The six-foot black man was now on his feet, giving away almost sixty pounds but with a big edge in hand and foot speed. He stepped back out of range as Moose came forward with a left and a right. Before Moose could set himself to throw again, the black man sprang forward with a stiff jab that startled Moose, snapping back his head. Moose took another jab to the face and looked bemused as he felt blood trickling from his nose. When a right cross crushed his nose, startle turned to daze. Moose's eyes went glassy. He looked upward, like a cherub in the faux fresco still dimly visible in the barrel-vault ceiling of what had been the Café Majestic, before falling in a heap.

The black man emptied a plate of cheese onto Moose's face. "Not every man's a cracker that gets his mug full of cheese." And young Laz Godfrey strode out the door with a mug and a notion. Maybe his fists really could make him a living.

Skeets looked at Waddy. "Was that John fucking L. in black face?"

"Holy fucking cow!" exclaimed Hugo. "He fixed Moose's flint. What do you think, Father?"

Father Divine rubbed the lump on his forehead. "I think Jesus changed water into wine, but I've just seen a lad change the cartilage and bone of his right hand into dynamite, and praise the lord for that."

"I didn't want to tell him," said Waddy, "but there *is* a Big Egypt. At Paddy The Pig's. Little Egypt and Big Egypt—they're sisters. Little Egypt is about five feet even, and she does what she calls a camel dance, bending over backwards, her breasts ersatz humps, and her hair's so long it drags over the sawdust on the floor. Big Egypt has similar facial features, but she's about six feet tall, a stepsister, and she's weird. When she sings or just talks to you, she always stands sideways, in that Egyptian pose. I think she's on the pipe."

"That *is* fucking weird," said Meat House, who spoke kind of weirdly himself, through a busted jaw, as the patrons reentered Mooney's Temple of Bacchus.

"Where's Foxy?" Waddy asked Skeets. "I've got to tell him what he missed."

Skeets drew himself a pewter mugful. "Codman? He had to see a man about a dog, a terrier with a pedigree as

45

long as his own."

~~~~~~~

Codman was in a shop owned by Nemo's cousin Jans Mangin, checking out the terrier, Jugs, who had a sleepy air to him, eyes barely open, chin nearly dragging the ground. But confronted with four rats in the pit, he became a different animal. His hairs seemed to all raise up in unison, his eyes bulged, and he showed a formidable set of gleaming teeth.

"Ain't had a chance to clip his ears yet," said Jans, "but there's just four rats. Shouldn't be a problem, with his breeding. He's the son of Jack, who's on tonight, and Jack was begat by Apollo, who ..."

"... who fled Ireland along with the snakes and the rats," Foxhall Codman groused. "I'm interested in what he can do, not in his ancestors going back to the ark."

"He's a bull terrier, not an Irish."

"I don't give a fig about his nationality or his pedigree, as long as he's mayhem incarnate."

Jans put Jugs in the pit with the four rats for his audition. Jugs was instinctively inclined to dismember them but seemed wary of the gigantic one. Jans put a foot under Jugs' arse and propelled him into the rats, who converged on all four sides. He sank his teeth into one rat and shook it while two others latched onto his ears. The one on the right ear was so heavy Jugs listed his way while disposing of the second rat, who put up a fierce defense. He managed to get a grip on the rat that took off half of his left ear, and tossed it on the other corpses. After a long tussle, he disengaged the gargantuan rat, leaving it with a triangular swatch of his right ear. The two retreated to opposite corners and snarled at each other. Jans put a foot under Jugs's rump again, but the animal was dug into a defensive crouch and barely budged.

"You want him?"

"I'll take him."
Jans picked up a collar and reached for the dog."
"Not him. The rat."

# Chapter 5: Boxer

*T*he Chelsea Sporting Club looked like a matchbox sitting on a brick. The gleam in the architect's eye was an armory, but Councilman Curley rerouted the armory funding to his own wharf project. So John McKane, aka *the King of Coney Island*, picked up the unfinished white-elephant for a song and turned it into a sporting club. Under indictment in Brooklyn, he sold it to Waddy, whose fashion emporium had become the destination of Cambridge's and Boston's wealthiest women. That was a month after The New England Society for the Suppression of Vice had shut down Franklin Trotting Park, leaving Waddy hard-pressed to gamble away his earnings.

The first floor windows of the Chelsea club remained little more than slits, but the second floor of the armory was remodeled into gym space, with seating and more light. Plumbing was an afterthought with low priority because of expense. Water was collected in rain barrels, and kids like Swipes were paid pennies to haul it around in buckets. A cement staircase, twenty feet wide at the bottom, wound and narrowed to ten feet at the top. Under the cement staircase, a cavernous vestibule led down to a locker room.

Stepping into the dark shadows in the vestibule out of the brilliant early June sunshine, Lazarus Roger Godfrey couldn't see the knotted cord that led to a cow bell inside. From Waddy's office window, the trainer Nemo watched Laz approach the building, climb the six cement stairs, then try to decipher the lettering on the plaque next to the oak door that was wide enough to drive a milk wagon through. Nemo paid no attention to Waddy's tirade on Foxhall Codman's luck and his own lack of it. Laz slapped the door, kicked it, but the pummeling did not resonate enough even to make the roaches scurry.

"See what that stupid bastard wants," Nemo shouted down to Swipes, the kid who ran errands for Waddy. With his shoulders against the wall while the rest of his body curved outward, Nemo sculpted an inelegant letter *d*.

Swipes opened the door.

"Mr. Googan told me to come by."

"What for?"

"I'm gonna be a fighter, I guess."

Swipes relayed the message to Nemo, who stubbed out his cigar and went downstairs. Waddy followed. "Set him up, and make it snappy. I've got an appointment with Archbishop Williams in the South End in an hour. Put him on Big Paddy, and get him some skins."

"None left. The kids keep stealing them."

"All right, let *Big Paddy* chew on his hands a while. We'll see how tough he is."

Nemo wore a high-necked, moth-eaten sweater and a narrow-brimmed derby that looked like it had gone twenty rounds with John L. Sullivan and lost. He slept in his clothes and, as a rule, didn't bathe, which didn't distinguish him from a sizeable minority of men of his generation and class. On the hottest days of summer he would assault the Chelsea River, and twice a week he would wash his face and neck, preliminaries to shaving, which was a hit or miss venture, but an egalitarian one. If he made three sweeps of his razor on one side of his face, he had to make three on the other side. The middle of his face was problematic, a Balkanized zone of intense negotiation that his face was seldom up to, the result of which was an occasional stump or hedgework of hair. Nemo kept his egalitarianism to himself, leaving people to mistake his visage as the result of fecklessness rather than ideology.

—Nemo? said Waddy a propos and in dialect—He don't shave. He landscapes.

Nemo looked Laz up and down. "You don't look like you've been in many fights."

"Maybe you should look at the other guys."

"Your daddy beat you up regular, take a strap to you?"

"No. Why?"

"Any fighter who's any good knows what it's like to get beat up regular, so in the ring it ain't nothin' new."

"I never had no daddy. My mama invented child abuse. I got thrown down the stairs more times than I walked."

Nemo's eyes opened a little wider. "Don't bring your mama around here." He smiled and introduced Laz to Big Paddy.

The heavy bag was Nemo's conception and Waddy's confection. It was nearly two hundred and fifty pounds, while most bags were between sixty to eighty. Waddy used twelve burlap bags, tarred an interior layer of Osnaburg to keep the sand in, and cut the sand with peanut shells and sawdust to get the right amount of give. A couple of layers of irregularly cut circles of sail cloth formed the bottom, and a single layer of canvas covered the burlap. Twelve grommets were triple reinforced with canvas at the top, and the end-product was the biggest heavy bag on the East coast, finished with typical Googan panache: **'BIG PADDY**—whitewashed in great, vertical, calligraphic letters. The bag nonetheless would sag with use and get bottom heavy. Like a hole that you dig and there's never enough sand to fill it—no matter how you packed the bag, it would inevitably settle, flare, then sag at the bottom.

Laz looked the bag up and down the way Nemo had looked at him. If Nemo's philosophy of being paternally pummeled was right, the bag—with limbs—would be one hell of a fighter. At the top there was a two-foot slit, trussed tight with rawhide laces, through which more sand could be added. For reasons of his own, reasons that went back to his mother, Pearline Godfrey, and reasons that he thought he'd never tell anyone, those laces were all he needed to see. After a score of punches, the bag was bleeding sand, both high and low, and Nemo was behind Laz, stretching out his left hand to tug lightly at Laz's scarf, the one Casey had given him, but on his toes in case the wild man turned on him. Laz did turn, bleeding at the knuckles, but with a wide grin at the destruction he had wreaked, which scared as much as it pleased Nemo.

"Holy cow, kid! You shoeshined him! Cut him high and low. What do you file your knuckles with?"

"Aw, it's just an old rat bag."

"Looks like the rats chewed their way out ... Hey, Waddy!"

Waddy was already rushing back with a contract and a gold-topped pen.

"You've got a punch, boy, a natural punch. What was your name again?"

"Laz Godfrey. And I ain't a boy."

Waddy noticed the scarf and did a double-take. "The kid with the tongs. The same kid who took out Moose!"

Laz nodded.

"You need a moniker," said Nemo. "Something that'll stick in the public's mind. Like *Kid Chocolate*."

Waddy shook his head. "What do you do when the kid gets old?"

Nemo shrugged. "Old Chocolate?"

Waddy turned his attention back to Laz. "Jesus, your hands are a mess. Something about that *rat bag* you didn't like?"

Laz looked away, with a smirk, unwilling to reveal the traumatic reprise brought on by a laced bag.

"You take the same dislike to your opponents, and you'll go places. And if you've got speed ..."

"Like I told you before, I been rattin' since I was a kid, and I ain't never been bit." Laz held out his hands with skinned knuckles.

"I've seen prettier." Waddy turned to Nemo. "For Chrissake, get him some skins. And patch up *Big Paddy*. I want Laz working out tomorrow morning."

"I can fix it," said Nemo, "but he'll bust it again."

"Then put some cement in it."

Waddy unscrewed the pen top, handed the pen to Laz, who had never touched such an instrument and held it like a cigar. Waddy pressed the contract form against the heavy bag that was still pouring sand from the lowermost hole.

"Sign here. Ten dollars a week, fifty dollars for every fight you win, plus bonuses if the gate is good. You get a fight with a tip-topper, and you'll be pulling in hundreds." Waddy pulled the contract away, signed with an X, cautioning Laz not to get blood on it.

Laz sat in front of the locker on which Nemo had white-washed an **X** instead of a name. Nemo took both of Laz's hands in his, staring at the bruised knuckles, and Laz felt a strange tingling in the middle of his palms which spread through his hands. Nemo poured his own solution of cannabis, alcohol, arnica and more esoteric ingredients over the knuckles. "Nothing broken. They'll be okay."

"I done some bare knuckle fightin'. Never broke nothin'."

"On you, or the other guy?" Nemo smiled.

"On me. I always break something on the other guy."

"I've seen you with the rats, kid. Waddy don't know it, but you've got the speed. You got what it takes. Fast hands. You'll be ready for Sullivan in a couple of years. You're still growing and you're almost as big as he is."

"I'm already taller, and I ain't waitin' that long," Laz

said with an air of presumption and certainty.

"Tomorrow, about ten."

Laz nodded and tapped the X on his locker with a short left. "Was that a joke, or can't you write neither?"

Nemo leaned on a broom. "So long, killer. Don't suck your knuckles."

Laz stared at the locker room door till Nemo was out of sight and he was alone. It was dark. One bare electric light hung high overhead with no reflector. The ceiling was so high and dark he couldn't see it. A bit of light came through a thin, barred window ten feet above his head. The window slits were fifty feet apart. The walls of heavy stone were always damp. Everything seemed to be missing a leg—the chairs, lockers, towel racks. A towel thrown over an open locker cast a shadow on the wall like a sharp-toothed open mouth. If this was a lion's den, it was his den. As Laz leaned back against the wall, his head drifted into that shadow, and in the dim light he was smiling, happier than he could remember being.

~~~~~~~

"Your new fighter," said Casey. "Is he really black?"

"Such a dusky orb as never rose on Chelsea."

# Chapter 6: Godfrey vs. Lyon (December 31, 1891)

'Grappling Godfrey'—was how Waddy had him billed. Over time *the fancy* changed that to '*Old Chocolate*'. The grappler's hands seemed short only because they were disproportionately wide and thick. When Laz put his hand down flat next to a Bible, his knuckles were nearly level with the cover. Only Bobby 'The Beast' Caspar had bigger hands.

In Chelsea, there were a couple of bars where you could get a bare knuckle fight any night of the week. Pass the hat for the winner, and beer for the loser. No Marquess of Queensberry here. London rules, adapted to the circumstances of the locale. There Laz learned to hold and hit. With those strong fingers he could catch a man in the interstices between the ribs, then rip up and spin the man to get a good shot at the kidney. Years later, Jack Dempsey had a move and a punch like that, but Dempsey never fought without gloves.

—This Lyon, any good?

—Relentless as a cataract. And a *soaker* with the right.

The collective mind of Chelsea this dark night was reeling with one question—*Are you ready for the Big One?* Not Godfrey vs. Lyon, but the Nor'easter. Now it was here—in small frozen shrapnel from a marbled grey cauldron. It would be a night to test the mettle of the Fancy—the crowd of boxing aficionados who attended every match, or tried. Laz packed his gear in a bag and walked in the direction of the Chelsea Sporting Club, just six blocks away. He knew he was close when the three functioning electric lights on the marquee became visible, like one arm of a constellation being born. From the lip of the smokestack of the Chelsea power plant behind the Sporting Club hung a great lump of cloud like belly layers of a fat man, a stuck Santa. Laz imagined this smokestack a poor boy's stocking, the cloud an offering with no takers, and the poor boy with nowhere to go.

Walking down the aisle, Waddy Googan's eye was caught by two corpulent black women. One, dressed like a tart, smiled at him. He guessed correctly from Laz's description that the other, the glaring one, was his mother, Pearline.

~~~~~~~

Come in. Go the distance—down the rectangular tube that leads to and from the locker room where Laz Godfrey throws a few jabs in a broken mirror. Across rectangular cement slabs once painted *yellow*—or are there, ground into the floor wall to wall, comestibles that never stayed down before the count started? Yellow. In the smoky light of the Sporting Club, Sonny Lyon looked anemic, and Laz's skin turned the color of an old chocolate fingered daily by a maiden aunt and left in the sun. The fighters heard a round bell, a sick toneless ringing, like sound passing through water, through sweat.

It's time.

The noise at ringside was getting louder. A cloud of smoke gathered under the dim lamp with its one bulb over the ring. The men in black suits taking bets in the aisles were sitting down for the show. No particular attention was paid to the androgynous figure in a brown woolen cap pulled low over the ears, sitting far in the back. Sonny Lyon's manager Hank Broyard was making a stink. "We want the north corner, so when Sonny knocks this punk out they can carry him south with the other birds."

Waddy snarled at the lowbrow humor. "Let 'em have any corner they want."

So they switched. Nemo carried the pail, sponge, towels, ointments, tape, and assorted paraphernalia to the opposite corner. Sonny Lyon had fifteen wins, no losses, one draw. He figured to be a contender. Laz was 7 and 0 with a lot of tomato cans on his record. In his first big fight he was seen as a stepping stone for Lyon. The first blood was drawn on Godfrey: before he entered the ring, he tripped, his shin coming down hard on the third wooden step.

"Hey, ref! Stop the fight! He's cut already! Too bad it's your knee, kid. Now you can't even pray."

Laz gave Hank Broyard a look that made the many hairs on the back of Nemo's neck stand up.

Sonny shouted across the ring, "It's your funeral kid. Don't care if you walk, run or crawl."

Sonny looked at Hank and spoke loudly enough for the men in the opposite corner to hear. "Why do niggers always look like they're sleeping?"

"I don't know," said Hank. "If I did, I'd tell ya."

"Remember," Nemo told Laz, "he's a bleeder. When you throw the jab, twist it, like a corkscrew. It'll open him up."

Laz barely heard him. He didn't even notice Sonny stomping around in his corner like a horse with the blind staggers. Laz was going into a different world. One where he heard no taunts, felt only the severest of pain. But he saw. Saw the hundreds of washed out circle-stains of blood on a canvas floor that had almost no trace of the original white color. Suddenly, everything became clearer under the intensity of his gaze. He saw pores in the canvas, strands of hemp in the ropes, each one wound tight, as coiled as he was. His other senses seemed to lose sovereignty to sight, so that he never really heard the opening bell or felt Nemo's push on his backside to get him out of his corner. Laz felt his eyes controlling the world, and the world now was cut down to a twisted rope enclosure accessible to the feet of three men and contested by two. He danced around the ring, and to Waddy it looked like his fighter was tip-toeing to the bed of a dozing child, one who would soon be asleep and silently rolling.

The first two rounds were uneventful, both fighters feeling each other out, Laz winning the rounds with his jab, Lyon already bleeding above both eyes and growing frustrated at his inability to hit the fleet black man. Father Divine nudged Hugo Bartolini. "I tell you, the lad was baptized with fairy water. He can't be hit."

In the third, Lyon followed a jab with a haymaker. Laz saw it coming from its inception. Overhand right—Sonny Lyon's trademark, his elbow lifting out to the side gave it away, and Laz was *stunned*—by the beauty of the parabola being cut in the air by the punch. Beautiful, and in slow motion. There was time for a short, quick breath in the stillness where he heard nothing, the breath like coming up from under water, precious, pure, sudden. Breath that he drew at the same time that his elbow automatically rose, interposing his forearm and the red glove's long kiss.

Before the bell ended the third round, a strong corkscrew jab tore open the skin under Sonny's left eye as his head snapped backward, blood squirting. Dazed, Sonny turned towards his corner, but the referee was in his way. He lurched to his left to go around him, but the ref simultaneously stepped the same way. The referee, with a towel in his hand to wipe the blood on the canvas, felt absurdly like a toreador, and the crowd was laughing. Sonny shuffled to his right and pushed the ref out of his way. The ref watched the trail of blood, made one great swath at it with the towel, and walked to a neutral corner.

Sonny could taste the rivulets of blood pouring over his lips. He sank into his stool. "Bad, ain't it?"

Truth was—Sonny looked like he was having a nosebleed and his whole face was a nose. His cutman, Gil, had never seen worse, but it never helps to see a cutman puke, so he steeled himself to his job, applying his homemade coagulant containing yarrow, salad burnet, Epsom salt, egg whites, and gunpowder. Arcane but remarkably effective.

Gil slapped him gently and beseeched, "You're gonna win this with heart!"

"He ain't gonna win it with face," scoffed Pearline, leaning forward on her shaky ringside chair.

Hank took Sonny's face in his hands, inspecting the damage and shaking his head. "Your eye's swolled something awful. There's not much holding your eyeball in your head."

"The nigger's got a jab like a hogee's fending pole. I can't get inside it," Sonny lamented.

"Touch it off, then hook him," advised Gil.

"I tried. He's like a squirrel with a tick on his tail. I can't reach him."

Hank concurred. "Sonofabitch bobs like a crow in a cornfield. Best way to kill a crow's to use a shotgun. Get in close and hit him everywhere. Put a good one on his balls."

"I've been trying for three rounds. Ain't hit him a good one yet."

"You were a farmer, right?"

"Yeah. So?

"You wise in the ways of livestock?"

"What are you gettin' at?"

"What's a mule do?"

"Kicks."

"All right, then."

"I can't kick him. It's illegal."

"Well, you ain't hit him, and you got to do something or they won't pay you."

"I could butt him, like a ram."

"Now, you're talking."

Sonny motioned toward his eye without touching it. "Patch me up so it won't be annoying me no more."

Gil could do nothing about the eye, but he applied some of his coagulant as a placebo along with a glob of goose-grease.

In Laz's corner, Waddy was ecstatic. "You snake-bit him. The flesh is going to keep swelling under that cut. They couldn't keep it closed with a vice."

"That was a beaut," said Nemo. "He's going to be covering the eye all the time. The body's gotta be open. Keep shoeshining him."

"Look out for the haymaker, Laz. Go for the cut."

Laz gave Waddy a peeved look as the bell rang for round four. Waddy walked down the ladder to his seat. He turned and smiled at Foxhall Codman right behind him.

"Didja see that eye? Banged worse than a two-bit mill-town whore's twat on a Friday night."

"Speaking of which, where did you get that scar?"

Waddy's face bore a few scars from his tangle with Casey's backyard maze, his spatial orientation and sense of direction nil. He refused to be told the path to its center, determined that the Harvard man could bootstrap his way in and out. The bell sounded for round four. Sonny used his head. He butted Laz in a clinch and spent much of the round hissing, like a snake, which disconcerted Laz while not hurting him. The next time they clinched, Sonny snake-bit him on the ear and drew blood. It hurt like the devil, and Laz knew he had to take Sonny Lyon out before the fighter wise in the ways of livestock adopted some animal attribute that could leave him maimed.

At the end of the round, Laz pointed his glove to his

ear in his corner. "Is it bleeding?"

"Ears don't bleed much, 'cept when it's coming from way inside. Then it's bad," said Nemo.

"He got his teeth in you, but he didn't bite it off. You'll be okay. You better take him out soon. No telling what he might do. Kill the bastard," Waddy urged.

"I don't want to kill nobody. Nobody ever kill me."

"You can't ride to heaven hanging on Jesus' coattails. You've got to take charge." Waddy gesticulated with an uppercut.

"Sonofabitch's got a hide like a razorback and a chin like granite," Laz groused.

"You got the sledgehammer," said Nemo. "Remember what you did to Big Paddy. The sonofabitch will crack, you hit him a couple good ones in a row. Straight right, left hook, one-two, okay, baby?"

"Okay."

The round bell rang. Waddy called out, "Laz."

Laz turned quickly.

"If he don't fall, keep hittin' 'im."

Laz nodded at Waddy's supererogation. Ten seconds into the fifth round, Sonny Lyon went down under a barrage of body punches and did not get up for the count. He lay on his side, propped up on one elbow, motionless, looking like he was posing on a chaise longue. The young man wise in the ways of livestock looked like a rabbit on display in a butcher shop window. Waddy looked at one after another of the old-timers trying to compare Laz to anyone in their memories, and Waddy knew that something special had happened in that ring, and he, holding Laz's contract, had himself a piece of it.

There was little cheering for the victory of the black man, but Laz was elated. He held his hands high over his head and grinned. He saw his mother Pearline with her arms folded across her stomach and a rictus on her face. Then he noticed Waddy's ringside companion, Patti the Cantatrice, with an empty chair next to her. Her hair was cocked high in a pony tail that tumbled in an array of long hooking blonde curls to the base of her neck. So frail, so perfectly proportioned, that rare twenty-eight year old body that looked like a sixteen-year-old girl's. He stared at her profile as she turned to meet Waddy with a wide smile and high cheekbones and frail arms with wrists cocked and fingers folded into aggie-sized fists hammering jokingly on Waddy's arm like a pair of woodpeckers.

Laz asked himself how a man could be so calm as Waddy beside a woman whose flesh hit you like an avalanche. He did not notice the effeminate figure in a black suit, a brown woolen cap pulled down over the brow, cigarette hanging from the lips and looking at him through opera glasses from the last row. Nor did Waddy. But Casey saw all, albeit poorly, her imagination long used to fleshing out details her eyes might not physically perceive.

Nemo sat on the middle-one of three ropes and stretched the top rope up as far as he could. Laz ducked through the opening. Waddy, with blonde companion on his arm, started toward Laz, who grabbed Nemo's arm as he sprang up off the rope.

"I can't listen to two people at once. Tell Waddy to get the hell out of my corner. All he knows is hems and skirts."

Nemo wrinkled his mouth. "I'm in kind of a sensitive position appertainin' to that. Why don't you tell him?"

"You're my trainer. You tell him."

Waddy and Patti were waiting at the bottom of the steps to congratulate him. When Laz saw her, he felt a nervous urge to stuff his hands into the pockets of his old robe, but his gloves were still on, and the gesture looked silly. After a few words in private with Waddy, Laz walked to the locker room he shared with Sonny Lyon, whose bruised and welted skin blended in with the dirty cold wall against which his handlers had braced him. They had put a towel around his neck and left him sitting so calmly that he seemed to be waiting for the barber instead of the doctor. His robe was draped over the locker door next to him, a lion embroidered on the back with a ridiculous grin that Sonny was not wearing, his one unswollen, wistful-looking eye closing slightly more now.

Hank Broyard reappeared, and Sonny spoke to him with tears in his good eye. "I never lost before."

"Yeah, well, there's always a first time."

Laz was unlacing his shoes when he noticed Waddy smiling at him. "I didn't mean to offend you," Laz said before Waddy could get a word out. "It's just that you and me got different ways of doing things."

"I admit I was overzealous." Waddy smiled. "I'll let Nemo do the talking from now on. Hey, can't argue with success, right?"

"I just don't want you to misunderstand."

"Don't worry about it. I'm smiling all the way to the bank."

"How much did I make?"

"Fifty plus a percentage of the gate. I'll figure it out in the morning. Here's twenty. I thought you might want to celebrate."

"Thanks."

Waddy walked to the door. Opening it, he was met by bookie Stu Steerman. Stu just smiled. They said nothing. Waddy removed the gold clip and slapped the cash on Stu's outstretched hand. Stu turned away and Waddy heard the slam of a metal locker door and a "Goddamn!" He nervously turned back and saw Laz tracing one half of the X on the locker door with his toe, grinning and fingering the scarf around his neck that once belonged to Casey, the scarf that Waddy told him would bring him luck. Waddy exited as Hank Broyard entered, giving Sonny his last instructions:

"Take a shower. Go home. Go to bed."

~~~~~~~

*Veni. Vidi.* Went to bed.

~~~~~~~

There were no showers at the Chelsea Sporting Club. Swipes waited with a bucket of lukewarm water where the shower ought to be. Laz nodded and Swipes tossed half the bucket. Laz turned his back for the other half, while Sonny Lyon still looked at his feet, through one eye.

"Goddamn," said Laz, who also went home, and went to bed, which was often on the roof. As far from Pearline as he could get. Until it was freezing out, he slept with the cannabis and other herbs growing on the buckled-tar roof that slanted to let the water run off. No one else slept up there, what with the rats and the fear of falling off or of being pushed off, not to mention the cold. Tonight before crashing inside his unheated room, Laz stood out on the roof as the snow shape-shifted with the rising temperature into what Waddy called 'Teddy Owen's feathers,' those broad flakes curved in their descent into miniature curraghs. Laz watched a rat moving across the roof go snowblind—it couldn't seem to find where it was going. The snow fell wet and fast, covering the rat's back and head and even the whiskers that flexed to shake it off. He was fascinated at the white-topped black rat moving across the roof and getting whiter, till the snow was thick enough that the rat slowed down. It was breathing hard, its sides puffing out, when he walked up to take a closer look at the rat that had stopped moving but kept puffing out its flanks till they were covered: white, heaving white, white.

~~~~~~~

Leaving the Chelsea Sporting Club, Casey figured that roughly one man in four looked at her longer than at a spanking new *Steamer* hissing down Massachusetts Avenue.

Luxurious, thick black hair coiled up under the brown woolen cap drawn low over her ears and brow revealed nothing feminine. Breasts, too, a dead end, under the loose, ribbed lisle jacket that drooped over the cheviot trousers. Not the shoes—canvas, the same style as worn by all the scullers on the Charles. Not her height, as tall as most men. Nor her shoulders—beneath the jacket undifferentiated from any thin male's. So it would have to be the porcelain face, the thick black eyebrows, the curve of the jaw, the high cheekbones, the fuller lips, the altogether of the unblemished, uncovered face that caused the eyes of one in four to drag over her like a trawler over a clam bed.

She'd gone in late, when the preliminary was finishing. She had meant to leave immediately Laz's fight was over, but was entranced by the spectacle, the thick cigarette and cigar smoke in the lemon light, the homoerotic spectacle of men cheering wildly for muscular men in short shorts, men with buckets and big floppy sponges, the whole dramatic atmosphere of neo-gladiatorial combat, the strange camaraderie alongside the partisan scuffles, the private world of men that she had experienced only second-hand—in the smell of Waddy's body and hair at 2:00 a.m. She felt now like a blind person suddenly restored to sight. She figured she would still be home before Waddy, and even if she did not have time to defumigate her body and hair, he would be drunk enough not to notice.

She left after the fight, hailed a cab, and got out at the Grand Hotel, just past Central Square at midnight. Crossing Mass. Ave., she was nearly run down by a silent Morrison electric car. The driver sneered and spat tobacco juice out the side of his mouth. Suddenly she was shouting words Waddy had never heard her use, and it felt like a corset had been loosened at her diaphragm. The driver gave her the horns with his free hand and shouted back over his shoulder. A half-block away, the man was still craning his neck back and gesticulating, while Casey felt empowered by her own curses. In the hotel lobby, she took off her hat, shook off the snow, and let her hair down, then entered the ladies room. She emerged in a dress with high-heeled boots, the men's clothing stuffed into her large bag. Still elated, she took a shortcut down a one-carriage wide alley, where she was arrested by a snow-dusted black form sliding between broken, tarred shingles in a garbage heap. A black woolen topcoat, like a puffed sail, moved as slowly as a beetle. An empty bottle of Imperial whiskey flew at her, then rolled to her feet, but did not break. Closer now, crouching, the beetle turned its soft side to her. One of its arms stuffed into the dark slit down the torn leg of his trousers and emerged from the folds holding by the legs a dead seagull that flew in an upward arc from his feet to his shoulders. She ducked out of the bird's trajectory, which ended directly over his head. He whooped and took a step towards her with the bird coming back down in an overhead arc. She turned, caught a heel in the cobblestone, and started to fall. Felt her heart hammering. Heard the man whooping and stumbling after her. She reached out with her hands to break her fall but only her fingertips touched the ground. Regaining her balance, she realized that the drunk could not run. He tried, but stumbled, slipped, and weaved. But neither could she run, in her high-heeled boots on the slick, snow-covered cobblestones. She strode quickly, trying to catch her breath and regain her composure. The intersecting street, with gas lamps, was only fifty feet ahead, out of the shadows. He pursued her. She turned her head in time to see the seagull rising again to its zenith, then coming down. The air beneath the lifeless wings forced them open, though not to their three-foot span. She stumbled again, but with less panic, as the sidewalk was several yards away. The drunk left off his pursuit and hurled the gull, which flew past her shoulder into the street. She walked quickly to her Putnam Avenue house. She opened the icebox and reached past the remains of Waddy's chicken in wine sauce. She took one chocolate from a box, then another, then took the whole box with her, eating as she ascended the stairs to the bedroom.

~~~~~~~

Celebrating at Mooney's, Waddy was ecstatic when he spied Foxhall Codman walking toward him. He relished the slap on the back and the generosity of his high-hat Harvard classmate.

"Shall we tap the juice of the grape?"

"*Waugh*, I'm as thirsty as a goat," said Waddy. "Ready to tip the whole nine. What did you think?"

"Magnificent. Molineaux reincarnated."

Waddy took a slug of top-shelf whiskey and let it burn his throat. Codman was already in his cups. "With Blacks, it's the vigor. The vigor and calm, as if they weren't contending for their lives in a ring but working in a field."

Waddy nodded. An hour later, Codman paid for the whiskey, including the bottle of Teacher & Sons Highland Cream they exited with. He put his arm around Waddy's shoulders, and they stepped outside with a few for the road. Codman signaled for his chauffeur, Sawyer. The Benz *Vis-à-Vis* came down the incline with a terrible racket, grumbling to a halt.

Waddy laughed. "Sounds like the clutch."

Sawyer got a can of collan oil from the trunk.

"Too late for that. We'll get Hugo in the morning." Codman turned and addressed Waddy, "You have that antiquated buggy of yours?"

Waddy cleaned some snow off the buggy and Codman got in. Visibility was poor. Waddy put on his gloves and angled the Phaeton into what he thought was the street under six inches of wet snow. The cold flipped his mood from elated to morose. "The high-hats find a way. I'm lost out here, Foxy. Astor waltzed up the Hudson with nothing and came back with a fortune in beaver pelts. Vanderbilt, Morgan—how do they do it? When they short a stock, it goes down. They buy a swamp for peanuts and the next day it's a metropolis."

"I can only tell you what they *don't* have."

"What?"

"Self-pity. Still whining about not being punched by the Porc," as Codman referred to the Porcellian final club at Harvard. "Googan, you've got everything you need. You've got a beautiful wife, a roof over your head, damsels to stick your pins in. By some standards, you're a wealthy man. Be satisfied."

"Those guys don't just have *wealth*, they have *vintage* wealth."

"There's nothing vintage about money. Not anymore. Cabot's dollar is the same as yours."

"Do you ever think about things, I mean, cogitate, the way we did at Harvard over sherry with William James, Langdell, and Agassiz?"

Codman raised his arms cynically like bird wings and chuckled, quoting Agassiz, "Soar with Plato."

"I can't afford to waste my time making money, he said. Remember?"

"Yes. After he married a Cabot."

Among the impressions Agassiz left on Codman were his disdain for materialism and his drunken romanticism, quoting his good friend Longfellow and dishing out rhapsodic tidbits like—*Inhabit the music of the spheres, boys*. It made him think about Pilâtre de Rozier and his hot air balloon. He had only disdain for Agassiz's disdain for materialism.

"*Inhabit the music of the spheres*—remember that? That's how we did it," Codman japed.

Waddy remembered, even treasured the evenings swilling brandy with Professor Agassiz. He exhaled and watched his hot breath condense, forming miniature balls of ice in the measure of his thick red moustache.

"Inhabit the music ... of the spheres."

The Googan that Codman knew would as lief joke about the twin furry spheres frozen between his thighs, but the shivering Googan who inhabited this moment, a vulnerable, drunken, borderline desperate Googan, found himself fancying that the aristocracy were the aristocracy precisely because they understood Agassiz on a different plane, one where a Back Bay swamp *could* turn into gold, as it did for the Codmans; one where an ordinary Jack like Astor could sail up the Hudson a pauper and came back a sultan. Waddy recalled Casey's father with his last breath saying that life was like a sculling draw, moving a boat sideways.

"Do you remember how Agassiz used to say *You have to ask yourself, 'Have I done enough with my life?'* He got it wrong. The question is 'Have you done anything with your life?'" Waddy hung his head and confessed what was most depressing him. "I've been rejected by every club I've applied to. Well, not *rejected*, exactly. They just haven't replied."

Codman shook his head. "That's just the problem. You don't ask *them*. They ask *you*. Or some friend or business associate puts you up for membership."

"Why don't you put me up?"

Codman turned and raised his hands, fingers splayed, half in anger, half in supplication. He laughed. "All you belong to is the fucking Dante Society. The *Dante* Society!"

"I love Dante. Dante understands hell."

"*You* don't understand."

"No. *You* don't understand *Dante*," Waddy defended his favorite author. He had his own *Inferno*, a rare edition bound in soft red Moroccan leather with silver quatrefoil vines designed by Tiffany.

Waddy rattled the reins before divulging, "There's also Clan na Gael."

"Oh, Christ! Fenians."

"Nationalists."

"Bruit that and you'll have as much a chance of getting shot as getting elected."

Codman threw up his hands and looked away. "What's the use?" Then he turned back to Waddy. "It helps to be a pewholder, at least. You're not a pewholder anywhere."

"I'm not religious.'

"You can't be an atheist in Boston. It's Episcopalian or Unitarian."

"Unitarians are *religios* without the courage to be atheists. And the appalling thing is that if you say that to a Unitarian, chances are he'll agree with you."

Codman chuckled. Waddy continued, "If I held a Unitarian pew, the first thing I'd do would be to smash it to pieces and bring in some good Adirondack chairs. And when it was my turn to announce the day's theme, I'd tell them it was brevity and order them to all go home. And the insane thing is that no one would bat an eye at the whole business. They'd all just go home."

Codman slapped Waddy on the shoulder. "That's why I slum with you, Googan. You're damned entertaining. By all rights you're a vulgar parvenu, but you lack most of the flaws of *arrivisme*. In fact, *your* taste *elevates* you. You know what you are? A goddamn *arriviste manqué*. I shouldn't tell you this, but I've admired you precisely because you're *not* as rapacious as Vanderbilt and Gould and the like. Ask any stitcher in Cambridge who they'd rather work for, and they'll all say 'Googan.' You pay them thirty-five cents an hour and downtown they're only making thirty."

"They have to eat, Foxy."

Codman shook his head. "You're destined for something. It may not be the Somerset—you aren't cut from the right Boston cloth, but you *are* club material. Look, the first thing you do is get a pew at King's Chapel. Then I'll put you up somewhere you haven't applied."

Waddy had a tear in his eye and was not sure if it was from sadness or appreciation. Codman thought out loud, "There's the Union Club ... but you don't boat.

Algonquin—no, that's Jack Gardner's club, and you dress his wife. They'd never take you. What about the Boston Athletic Club?"

"Applied there."

"St. Botolph ... no, they're artists and intellectuals."

"I *am* an artist."

"You're a dress-maker."

Waddy slammed his fist on his knee. "I am *not* a dress-maker. I am a fashion designer, a couturier! Fashion is the architecture of the body. You design it, blueprint it, then you decorate the body. The Acropolis has nothing on a good evening gown."

Codman slowly clawed at the night air, mocking Waddy's anger. "Don't get your Irish up. What I'm trying to say is that it's hard to say to a gentleman in the afternoon, 'What side does Sir dress on?' and at night be accepted as a peer."

Codman gazed at the heavy falling snow backlighted by a gas lamp, then back to earth. "Wharf Rats? I don't suppose you know the fifth verse of *the Star Spangled Banner*?"

"I don't do patriotism, goddamn it! I had enough of that at Gettysburg."

Codman snapped his fingers. "I've got it. The Monday Evening Club. I've been sculling on Monday evenings and I'm usually too tired to go out afterwards. I'll resign, so there'll be a vacancy. I'll put you up. It's a cinch."

Waddy put an arm around his buddy's shoulders. "Foxy, you're a *mensch*. Thank you."

"Don't call me that at King's Chapel."

Waddy looked up at the snow illuminated by a gaslight, so many stars falling, a cascade of opportunity lost, wishes never made. "I'm wondering, Foxy, if after you die you're more than nothing."

"Well, for a while. Until the records are expunged, till the Googan garments are worn out and everyone forgets."

"And when you're alive?"

"What?"

"Are you more than nothing, when you're alive."

"You, Googan? You're the essence of unforgettable. A veritable scourge. Think of how many husbands wish you *were* nothing. How about that girl who tried to stab you twenty years ago? I can't think of anyone more 'more-than-nothing' than Waddy Googan."

Waddy looked at the dark sky. "Time is terror, Foxy."

Codman unscrewed the top of a pocket flask, throwing Waddy a puzzled look.

"Time is a cloak thrown over pure perception."

"Only you would think of time as a garment, but what in blazes are you talking about? Or are you aping Agassiz again?"

"You're an idiot, Foxy." Waddy took the flask from Codman's hands. "You wouldn't understand." He took a long slug and stared into the snow. "What do you want engraved on your tombstone?"

Codman took the flask from Waddy's hand and sipped. "Here lies Foxhall Codman, brought down finally to Googan's level. And you? Wait, I know, 'Farts really were funny.'"

"Here lies Waddy Googan. He loved too much."

"Lied. Here lied." Codman sipped again. Waddy stared again into the snow. How gravely his closest friend misunderstood him.

Waddy's foul mood proved contagious. That and the cold air on his face turned the recently divorced Brahmin just as saturnine. "I was going to sit around the Ritz bar tonight just to hear the carolers and pretend I'm part of a family ... get warmly tippled, last call would be bruited, and the music would stop. The Maitre d' would wish me," Codman paused and chuckled, "a *good* night."

Waddy held his tongue longer than customary for the glib sporting man that he was. When he did speak, it came with a chortle and a pause. "A man without a woman ... is like a bird without a four-in-hand." He slapped

Codman reassuringly on the back.

Feeling patronized, Codman got out at the Ritz, watched Waddy trot away, and reflected on his ambivalent friendship:

> *How maddening the man is! Why we love him is a mystery. Why we despise him is clear—class. He neither was born with it, like the Lowells, nor earned it, like the Rockefellers. Yet he has the chutzpah to want everyone to bow down to him, to admit <u>his</u> superiority. If he weren't such a howling swell, I'd pay him no heed. He knows I envy the ease with which he enters and exits the world of pimps, prostitutes, pugilists, ratters, gypsies, homosexuals and transvestites. The man can step in shit and it will not adhere to his heel. But when you do it does. And Googan is there with the affable smile and the condescending pat on the back. One can't compete at slumming with one who is both of it and not of it. And if one tries, if one dips into the nether world of pimps and rat baiters, Googan goes one step farther. He spars with his black man who never hits him in the nob and only love-taps him to the body, then he insists that Godfrey fight him like a true opponent, and Godfrey draws the claret with a nobber and Googan is ecstatic. He leaves the faucet open and sits at Mooney's with blood all over his starched white monogrammed shirt and expects every man to lift a glass to his bravery. And then all the Pierce Egan ring slang, the* fib *and the* chaffer *and the* fancy, *as if anyone still spoke that way. So Googan has no inner circle of companions. No one will pay the price of admission. He has no intimate friends. No intimate male friends. Female—a horse of another color. He runs the gamut, as if this too were a competition, where he has you beat, hands down. And he lets you know it, with no scruple to the jealousy it creates. He has every class represented in his collection, from trollops to servants to demimondaines to the highest class of ladies whom he pricks with his pins till they are in an ecstasy of pain to which he must apply the stanch of his own. Then as he pricks the Constance Lodges and the Mrs. Jacks of this world, he sidles up to their husbands when they go slumming to Mooney's and he*

*almost expects them to toast his prowess at seduction rather than taking a knife to his throat. The man has no peer as a womanizer and he expects the men who envy him to glorify him. But hubris has its way with Googan as with every man. The* nonpareil *of sporting men, who* has *to possess the most beautiful woman in the hub, has her, who does not love him. A common enough phenomenon. But Googan is not a common man.*

Waddy savored the snowy late night, driving his *rattler* back to Cambridge. He was to be a Monday Evening Club member. It made him feel even more defiant than usual of the automobiles encroaching on the turn of the century, and in particular of the roadster usurping Massachusetts Avenue and bearing down on him. In the seat of his buggy, he felt like a medieval knight in a joust. He gave no ground to these *Jack*s, their fenders like foreshortened rats' ears. The roadster swerved to avoid him. His panicked horse reared, stumbled, and finally seemed mystified at stumbling. On the ground, it seemed to contemplate the harness and traces as if trying to solve some gigantic, hopeless puzzle. Waddy was in less of a quandary, but more abused by the earth he was dragged across. The French Trotter got to its feet shortly before he did. An approaching car slowed, but the snow-dredged man in its lights was anything but a deer. The car stopped and the driver asked if he could be of assistance.

"Yes," Waddy said, putting his foot on the fender and tying his shoe. He put his foot down. "You can go now." He turned his white back to the motorist and righted his Phaeton.

Sunday morning, at breakfast, Casey was sadder than a pan, sitting like a brood hen over a cup of coffee. She rested her chin on her fist, then raised her eyes to meet Waddy's. The bright morning sun illuminating his face below the eyes, he reminded her of a raccoon.

"You look so pensive," he said. "What are you thinking about?"

"Nothing. And you?"

*I have been thinking for the last few minutes of bending Mary over the chopping board and dropping those cotton drawers of hers, of inhaling her earthy smell. I have been thinking about how I resent the way you corset up your beauty.*

"Waddy." Casey extended her hand as far across the breakfast table as it would go, and waved it in front of his eyes. "Anybody home?"

"Yes." He smiled and gulped his coffee. "Did I tell you? Foxy is going to put me up for the Monday Evening Club."

"What do they do?"

"Eat."

"When?"

"On Mondays, obviously."

"No. When is Foxy putting you up?"

Waddy waved dismissively. "These things go at their own pace. You don't ask. They'll be in touch. Soon, I suspect."

"I don't know why you're so hot to join some eating club."

"A man needs to be accepted by his peers, needs to be respected, be a part of something."

"But you're an artist. By definition, you're an outsider. You should be glad those stuffed shirts haven't wanted you."

"It's not that they haven't wanted me," Waddy said defensively. "I just didn't follow the proper procedure."

"Waddy, you just don't get it. You're such an outsider you didn't even know what the procedure was. I wish you'd just forget about it. Those highhats don't want a dressmaker ..."

"I'm not a dressmaker!"

"All right, but you don't find artists like Henry James or John Sargent in those clubs, do you?"

"Can you stop badgering me for just one day?" He reached for the marmalade.

Casey breathed deeply and stretched out her legs. "While we're on joining, I'm thinking of joining the temperance movement."

Waddy huffed, then laughed.

"What's so funny?"

"The irony. You tell me *I* don't belong in a club, but *you*—there's nothing about you that in any way speaks of temperance. And it's more like a parade than a movement. A bunch of big bustles marching in a phalanx with hatchets."

"They're interesting and they're smart."

"And as joyous as the Harvard line. The temperance movement has no chance. Do you know how city officials get paid?"

"I assume the city pays them."

"Out of what revenues?"

Casey shrugged.

"Excise taxes. Taverns provide half of the revenues. Nuf ced?"

Casey was angry at herself for not knowing. She considered herself very pragmatic. She disliked Waddy's lumping her with the irrational if not mindless do-gooder Brahmin ladies. She threw her book on the chair. "I'm getting cabin fever. I've got to get out more, especially when spring comes. You know, with practice, I think I could row faster than most of the men."

Waddy folded his newspaper and swatted at the cat Alice, which was rummaging in the remnants of his breakfast. The black cat's tail breeched, and it made a black arch with its back. "Which is precisely why you won't. I won't have my friends humiliated by an Amazon who happens to be my wife."

"With that kind of mentality I'll be the last woman in Cambridge even to ride a bicycle."

"You're right ... following a few grand dames unable to

mount anything more than an armchair."

She poured herself a cup of coffee and dropped three sugar cubes in it, which appalled Waddy. "I bumped into Jânos Esterhazy last week. He said he would be delighted to give me lessons, at a reduced rate. He's the best jumper on the East coast."

"Jumping into beds is what he does. Isn't he that prince of something or other ... Bohemia ... Sardinia ... the prince of bed-jumping?"

"He's uprooted."

"Ah! He's either Armenian or Jewish."

"He's Hungarian. What does it matter what nationality he is. Every suggestion I make, you snaffle."

Waddy took a deep breath. He was on the brink of giving in when Casey suggested, "Let's arm-wrestle." She put her arm on the table, cocked at the elbow. "I win, I get riding lessons."

"If I win?" he said, putting down the newspaper.

"I wear one of your horrible dresses."

"You love my dresses."

She smiled. "Just kidding. You win—no lessons."

He found the arm-wrestling proposition on the one hand humiliating, but on the other so patently absurd that he could run with it. So without another word, he smiled and put his elbow on the counter. Her arms were unusually long. His hand was only a centimeter higher than hers. Her hands too were large for a woman, but the mass of his was still considerably greater. She gripped his hand with a grin that was both playful and fierce, which bemused him utterly.

"Go," she said.

After thirty seconds or so of stalemate, it was time for him to put an end to the charade. He pushed full force, but her arm went nowhere. He felt like looking around for some contraption she was using, some chinoiserie used in séances when the lights went out. There was nothing but the crinoline of her sleeves and her arm that was moving his past 1:00.

"Your tea, Mr. Googan," Mary interrupted.

Deus ex-Ireland. He released his grip, his concentration gone, and slid his hand and arm from the match. "Good show. We'll continue later."

"And my lessons?"

Waddy sighed in exasperation and turned his eyes to the heavens. "Whatever will make you happier, with one condition—you start eating again. You're as skinny as Harlequin's bat. No chocolates, no salad ... Food. If my wife is to be an Amazon, she'll have enough strength to get into the saddle without a Hungarian giving her a push on the rump."

She took an apple from the bowl of fruit on the table bit with a crunch that sounded like Moose's jaw shattering. Waddy watched her chew. He admired her moxie. He felt proud to be her husband. In the past year she had grown even more beautiful while he had grown more dissolute. At the same time, he was deliriously in love. In that he never wavered. And she? Did she love him when she married him, at least a bit? Was it simply an expression of Jamesian pragmatism: your shirt/your ring? Was it just that? And did she love him now? He could always take refuge in his confidence in winning a woman's love ... or was even that beginning to erode? He told himself she'd come around. For all practical purposes it was a good marriage. It just lacked certain manifestations of love, which made it indistinguishable from virtually all the marriages he was familiar with, a fair number of which he was intimate with. She'd come around, the way the years had a habit of going by, would she not?

# Chapter 7: The Best Day of His Life

*T*he only Cantabridgians who watched the scullers as intently as bookie Stu Steerman were Charlie Hot Dog and Billy 'Swipes' Unger, for very different reasons. The patrons of The Holly Tree virtually set their watches by Charlie Hot Dog. He left his house, next door to the Googans, at 5:30 each morning, walked the same circuitous route, arriving at the restaurant at precisely at 7:00, leaving Foxhall Codman to compare him to Emmanuel Kant. The allusion was not lost on Charlie, who grew up not far from Kant's home town of Konigsberg. Watching the scullers was both a hobby and an obsession for Charlie Neblung. He'd been a boat builder for years, till arthritis slowed him down and Codman Senior fired him. He took to selling wurst and hot dogs at sporting events. But his first love was the regattas on the Charles River. He watched the four-man barges of the Cambridge Police Department and the Boston Fire Department, the Harvard eights, the pair-oared shells. But he focused most intently on the single shells—thirty-five feet long and just fifteen inches wide.

As Charlie pushed his *shtupvegel* past the boathouse, Swipes awoke in panic, in the darkness under the eaves of his hovel under the boathouse. Usually, no one bothered him, because they were afraid of the boathouse ghost. Twelve years an orphan and nursed on the twin teats of the alms house and the saloon, Swipes knew that there was a lot more to fear than ghosts. He knew from the noise this morning that another homeless drunk had stopped to piss in the rat-hole entry. The drunk quickly caught a poke of a stick and howled, doubling over and stumbling down river toward Stu Steerman, who was following Casey who—in Swipes' imagination—had stopped rowing to wave hello.

Swipes helped farmers unload their carts in Haymarket early in the morning, grabbing a free ride, hanging on to the side of the street car. He ate what he could steal or what was discarded, too bruised to sell. By nine o'clock he was free to pursue his less consistent but more lucrative vocation, petty thievery, often in collusion with the Quayside Rats.

The sun sparkled off the Charles. By nine the tide had gone out, leaving pools of dazzle lingering in the stinking mud on a Sunday morning when most of the world was in church. The tide also left booty of all sorts to pre-adolescent pirates like Swipes.

For Casey, much of the past year had been a fog. The time on the water was the only time she did not feel partially in a daze, in a bed she did not entirely know how she got into, with a man for whom her love was intermittent and fuzzy, an attentive lover who did love *her*, she knew, almost desperately. He loved her enough to let her keep working at the restaurant where he used to breakfast with his *asshole buddies*, as he referred to them, a common expression both at Harvard and at Mooney's. Casey had thought that marriage would make her freer.

But Waddy pressured her not only to quit her job but to stop rowing. She compromised, agreeing to row only in the early mornings, when no one would notice Mrs. Googan still acting the Tomboy.

Waddy wanted her to do volunteer work, take piano lessons, join a *Bee* and spend the day sewing and gossiping like the other Cantabridgian ladies did. But Casey felt about these enterprises the way her cross-town neighbor Alice James did. The similarity went no further. Alice disapproved virtually everything physical, while Casey embraced it. Alice felt like "an animated meal bag" on a horse's back, while Casey felt herself an extension of the animal. In Waddy's view, Casey had retreated from life— female life as he perceived it. She had transformed herself into a *dollar dead*—a baseball of the era—with the cover knocked off, rough edges of anger remaining on the surface. A *dollar dead*, especially in bed. Casey did not know that on her way to work at The Holly Tree that morning she was being followed by the bookie Stu Steerman, uncommon harbinger of good news. A week earlier Waddy had bought a bunch of grapes at a fruit stand in Harvard Square. He sniffed at the blue sky, tilted his head back and popped a grape into his mouth, filling his eyes with more blue, thinking

—*God, give me a sign.*

It seemed that God had consented. Waddy saw a dog with a gimp foreleg and knew he had to bet on Crooked Finger in the 3rd at Mystic Park. He saw a man carrying a chicken, so it had to be Blue Goose in the 8th. But those were bum omens Waddy saw, for neither of the horses finished in the money. He pleaded with Stu's runner Paddy Mahon, who worked the luncheonette across from City Hall, to carry him for a week. Now, time was up.

He awoke in the late afternoon and assessed the night before's excesses. No breast had been beaten, or caressed, in the Googan homestead. He showered and shaved meticulously, put on his ironed underwear, his white shirt, his Harvard tie, his blue suit, and stepped lightly onto the sidewalk of Putnam Avenue with no intention of throwing in the towel. He felt an enormous energy. He felt he could take young Laz Godfrey to a cat house and be the last one out the door.

At The Holly Tree, Stu was disappointed but not surprised that Casey's deadbeat spouse had not showed up. He ordered his toast from a counter stool where he could see the door and out the window. He put on his rimless glasses to read the racing news. With them off, he always appeared to be squinting, with small deep-set isinglass eyes, over which his eyebrows were *one*—a long black continuity of hair across his forehead. His moustache totally covered his upper lip. Hair sprouted from his nostrils and ears in such abundance that plucking was out of the question. He had to shave even his Adam's apple— which usually sported one or more nicks, but the hair that shot up from the neck hole could not be shaved. He wore a white shirt and a tie all the time, which covered most of it, but when he raised his chin the outrageous hair followed like an untrimmed hedge.

He had scarecrow shoulders beneath the padded suits that wrinkled on his back. A stogie lodged in a groove on the left side of his mouth, through which came a cold, flat, condescending, and derisive voice, as if the interlocutor was born a sucker and Stu was ordained to inform him of it. When he paid off some lucky sucker, he made him feel like he had stumbled onto a pot of gold from which he would soon be parted. He worked strictly on a bookie's margin, except when he had engineered a fix or was privy to information that no one else was. But success came largely from hard work. He set the odds right because he watched the fighters and the horses, and spent hours on the riverbank with a stopwatch, timing the scullers. It paid off. From time to time there would be a stunning discovery, like the figure in a brown woolen cap rowing secret races on the far side of the river.

Stu was on his third cup of coffee. His new henchman, Moose, was on his third donut, everyone waiting for Waddy Googan. Having given up on finding 'Big Egypt' and on finding work as a lumberjack in Boston, Moose put his skills to work beating up deadbeats and protecting Steerman. It turned out that Moose also had a soft side and he was soft on Casey, even though she was now married. Waddy knew what was on the minds of every man at The Holly Tree. It set his stomach going so that at times he could not eat, and it made him wonder if being married to one of the comeliest women in Cambridge was more of a curse than a blessing.

Moose was still hungry. He stared indecisively at the assortment of pastry and donuts and finally said, "Give me a curler."

Charlie Hot Dog laughed. "Where you been all your life, you don't know a cruller?"

Moose sneered. "Forget the cruller. Give me a jelly donut ... No, make that a glazed."

"You want magic, or you want a donut?" Casey replied with just the right, coruscating combination of sarcasm and affability that had everybody laughing, and Moose uncharacteristically laughing at himself. Even Stu laughed. Then Swipes entered with his boot-blacking stool, on an errand for Skeets Mooney, but he also had a weekly date with Charlie, who always tipped the kid a penny for the shine. Swipes checked out the counter for leftover scraps of pastry. He did not notice Stu, who caught him by the ear and twisted it painfully. Swipes pretended it didn't hurt. If the other urchins saw him cry, they'd steal his brushes.

"Little Swipes the snitch."

"Let go. I'm no snitch."

"You're Googan's errand boy. You tell him I'm looking for him, or I'll get Mud Foley to burn you out of that rat hole under the boathouse."

Casey was frozen to a spot just within earshot. It *seemed* that Waddy had money. He was always buying things. He'd paid off their house and bought a new horse and buggy. Maybe that was why he was out of cash. Swipes approached the counter. "Skeets wants a bag of them soggy quoits."

"You mean donuts?"

"I reckon so."

"Why so many?"

Stu laughed out loud. "He wants to see how many it will take to kill Nemo's pig."

Casey didn't understand why she felt better, freer, why she didn't even holler when Swipes took the bag and then snatched a cruller and ran out the door. Subconsciously she understood that Waddy's circumstances would make it more difficult to put limits on her.

Swipes delivered the quoits, then took refuge in the front seat of the parked, chocked Peugeot in Charlie's front yard, next door to Waddy, lost in the walnut and leather upholstered security, the multiplicity of buttons, knobs and handles, the functionality *cum* mystery of all of its parts. The Peugeot was worth almost as much as the hovel Charlie lived in. Waddy resented the old man's leaving the Peugeot poised facing his yard. He resented even more the noise, the pollution, and the mechanical problems that you did not get with a horse. The Peugeot just sat there because the eccentric hot-dog man enjoyed rubbing materialism in his neighbors' faces. But if Waddy felt hostage to this potential battering ram he did not admit it.

It was quitting time, and Casey was about to commit a domestic violation of her own. She had agreed to row only in the early morning, but this early spring evening was beautiful, and Waddy's financial woes loosened the domestic noose. Everything was politics. And her campaign was just getting started.

She waited impatiently on a customer, then grabbed a donut herself and her satchel of rowing clothes. She stuffed the donut into her mouth to open the door and was met there by Hugo Bartolini, the hack who had delivered her father's corpse to her door. She turned sideways to let him enter. He mimed biting at the donut still in her teeth and said, "Hey, Casey, going out to row, row, row your boat?" with a girlish motion of his arms.

She closed the door with the donut still in her teeth, and hammered a response with her knuckles.

"Hey," said Father Divine, "you know Morse code?"

"No. Why?"

"I'm not sure, but I think the first letter was an *F*."

"Hey—Fuck you, Hugo! Ha! Ha! Ha!"

"I'll be ... She didn't ... Did she? A broad like that?"

Father Divine was trying, inconspicuously and with a modicum of success, to suck the jelly from his donut. The goal was not so much the jelly proper as the act itself, the pink jelly-insertion-hole so deliciously anal.

"Tell us about Godfrey," Hugo addressed Father Divine. "Some are saying he could take Choynski."

"Doubt it," said Nemo. "The old professor has the hardest one-two in the ring. Hits harder than Sullivan. The only man alive hit as hard was Bobby the Beast Caspar, but God knows what happened to him."

Father Divine put down his cup. "Godfrey is not as ring-smart as the old professor, but he's got the fastest and strongest hands I've ever seen, and I've seen 'em all. He's got a short left that will break a man's ribs like toothpicks. Choynski can hit, but Godfrey has ten pounds of muscle on him." The retired priest threw a few punches in the air. "He told me his mother locked him out once, and he punched the door down. Hands were a mess."

"So, who's next?" asked Hugo.

"Knucksey Doherty of Donegal Square, most likely."

"Fastest heavyweight in the ring," said Nemo. "He'll give two ticks to a jaybird and beat him to the peck."

"He drew the claret on Choynski. Took Joe twenty rounds to put him away."

"Maybe Johnny Haystacks."

"You mean Haystacks Johnny?"

"No. 'Haystacks' is his real name. Funny thing is, he's not all that big."

Stu did not see Waddy enter. He was busy scratching his head and watching the dandruff fall onto the polished walnut and mahogany bar. Crystal-sized pieces of dandruff combed from the various parts of his head formed a speckled, irregular ring at the base of his neck. He pushed the flakes together with a long pinkie-nail, then pressed them to the fleshy part of his forefinger till they adhered. He held the forefinger up before his lips, then blew them to Kingdom Come.

"Hey, Stu, buy me a beer," said Father Divine sarcastically.

"I never buy nobody nothing."

"Stu is so tight he wouldn't give a pregnant slut a clothes hanger to relieve herself," Hugo added.

Waddy felt sick to his stomach, looking into the grinning face of Stu Steerman, accompanied by the taciturn Moose. Moose had a head like a potato. His hobby was extorting pennies from school kids. At just twenty-six, his hair was already severely thinning. Only a few rows of dirty brown hair remained over the dirty ears. Waddy didn't have the dough and he knew what was coming. But the imagined physical pain did not bother him so much as the humiliation—being roughed up before his peers.

"Look who's here—Mr. Fancy Pants. You're a hard man to find."

Waddy tried to appear calm. "Let's not beat around the bush, Stu. I don't have it."

Stu shook his head. "Blue Goose—I could have told you that horse has bad knees."

Jogging down Mass. Ave., Laz noticed Waddy's Phaeton. Seeing Steerman through the window, he decided to take a breather and be sure Waddy wasn't in jeopardy. Moose sized up the Negro more attentively than he had in their first encounter, and he was undaunted. He knew Laz was a professional boxer now, but how did 190 pounds deal with 260, with brass knuckles on his right hand? The incident at Mooney's he believed was an aberration. He'd been drunk and got sucker-punched. Now he was sober and looking for revenge.

Waddy did not see Laz. He saw Moose move around to his left, while Stu remained to his right. He thought of himself as a piece of green effete lettuce in the enforcers' sandwich. Why hadn't he been born with more muscles—or brains—instead of good teeth and a killer smile?

He rubbed his tongue over the perfect teeth he might part with in just moments. It was time to put Professor Donovan's First Commandment—that no one remembers *how* you won the fight, just *who* won it—to work, however poor the odds. He slid off the stool and faced Stu fawningly, asking him to, "Listen ..." Without another word, and with the momentum of his shoulders turning one hundred and eighty degrees, his fist flew at Moose's nuts.

Professor Donovan hadn't told him that that a heavy's overcoat might catch a piece of his knuckles and deflect the shot to the thighs, or that it might all be useless when the guy was twice his size. Moose grunted a cough, as if a doctor were checking him for prostate problems. It hurt him more than Waddy thought it had, but it was not an incapacitating pain. Before Waddy could aim a better punch at the nuts, Moose cuffed him a forearm blow on the neck that sent him to the floor, where he expected momentarily to see his perfect teeth scattered and staring back at him from the sawdust. But what he saw was one of Moose's legs flying up, then his body crashing ass-backwards to the floor. Waddy didn't know Laz had these moves in his repertoire, or even that the Black Knight had appeared at The Holly Tree.

Moose had the wind knocked out of him. He got to his feet, too far away for Waddy to throw another shot at his nuts. But this time Moose paid no attention to the fashion designer. His eyes were fixed on Godfrey.

The crowd cleared out to give Laz and Moose some room. Cheers were equally divided for the White and the Black. Moose slid the brass knuckles onto his right hand. A small stream of blood issued from a cut on his temple. His face was so dirty that it looked to Laz like a red mudslide coming down his cheek. Built like a potato, Moose had the same propensity for dirt. The Negro did not look the slightest bit intimidated. Except for the brass knuckles, this was business as usual. And the big man's right hand was easy to duck. Laz grabbed his arm and twisted it behind his back. Moose screamed but nothing broke. Laz threw him into the coat rack, turned, put his shoulder to Moose's back, grabbed his head backwards with both hands and snapped. Moose could not remember being so high off his feet. When he hit the floor and the barstool at Waddy's feet, he felt like his arm and back were broken, along with a couple of ribs. His head hurt so much he could not see straight.

Waddy could not resist kicking the sonofabitch. Stu lifted a root beer bottle and was about to let Waddy have it on the head when Laz stepped in and put him in a full-Nelson. Waddy sucker-punched the bookie, who bled profusely through the nose. This did not sit right with Laz. He never intended to hold the man so Waddy could take unfair advantage. He released Stu, who again picked up the bottle and went at Waddy.

"What are you doing?" Waddy screamed, incredulous.

"Fair is ..."

Stu stung Waddy on the forearm, then on the shoulder, and finally broke the bottle on his skull. Waddy's blue suit was stained with blood. The two were tangled in a stalemate when Laz finally pulled them apart, sending Stu headfirst toward the door, out of which he crawled as fast as he could, leaving Moose still stunned and immobile behind him.

Unlike Stu, Waddy still had all his teeth, though his suit, shirt, and tie were all ruined. But as he looked around, the men were lifting their cups and glasses to him.

"Why did you let that bastard go? He could have killed me?"

Laz smiled and flattered him. "You're tougher than you think. Now you can tell everyone how you kicked his ass."

"Why didn't you just *punch* Moose, knock him out."

"I'm a professional now. I can't get my hands busted if I want to be champion."

Father Divine handed Waddy his pocket flask of brandy and congratulated him.

"Here's how," said Waddy.

"Same here," the others echoed, Waddy thinking—*This is the best day of my life.*

~~~~~~~

Meanwhile, Casey was in as much pain as Stu and Moose, but it was self-inflicted. The pain if anything felt good. It was her choice. Unlike the pain of being kept outside the sculling fraternity. The solitary female artist created a series of two circles, perfectly equidistant in length and width from each other. They widened into each other and disappeared on the flat river surface. Casey absorbed the ephemeral perfection as if to store it away, waiting for the next secret race. She rested for a moment, leaned on her long sculls like outriggers on the sleek shell, and reflected on her own solitude and peace on the water. She finished four miles before the devouts could finish their rosary at St. Paul's. And when the bells peeled the end of the last mass, she pulled one last power twelve, chuckling at her version of *Hail Mary* on this watery ro*w*sary.

How does one come to see one's life as a mistake? At the end of a stroke pulled hard in anger, suddenly? Or does it take a mile up and a mile back? Where in that run is the modicum of domestic luxury jettisoned? The closest she could come to describing the whole phenomenon was that she was allergic to her husband.

She hated to admit it, but emotionally he made her scratch.

# Chapter 8: Sorosis

*If* Waddy was going to avoid being a constant target of Steerman and other bookies, he had to bring customers into Googan's Emporium of Fashion. And to do so he had to vie with fellow couturiers Haliburton, John Brooks, C. E. Quimby, Drew Lashton, and George Lee, the vanguard of Boston fashion. They attended each other's openings and heckled. Googan and Haliburton had an edge in this. Waddy had excelled at declamation at Boston Latin and at Harvard. Haliburton had an acid wit. When Brooks put on his 1891 opening, the two hecklers, competitors but friends, arrived by serendipity at Brooks Brothers on Newbury Street at the same time.

"It's Waddy Googan, the Black Prince of Fashion." Hal removed his tall black tile and bowed with a flourish.

Waddy reciprocated Hal's hat gesture. "Maitre d'Elegance. How is His Foppishness today?"

Hal laughed. "Shall we torment poor John ensemble?"

"I can't think of anyone more deserving. After you."

Boston's two most provocative couturiers linked arms and sauntered into Boston's most conservative fashion outlet. It was packed, primarily with women. Hal and Waddy stood in the back. John Brooks was in a gray swallow-tail coat, with a Bodier cravat beneath a Dundreary beard, holding a Verdier cane for affect. His eyes dilated when he noticed Haliburton smiling and waving effeminately at him. Hal immediately let him have it. "Isn't that the coat Lincoln was shot in?"

John Brooks was still trying to live down the fact that Lincoln was assassinated wearing a black Brooks Brothers frock coat. John ignored the comment, but he looked like he'd just swallowed a wad of Redman. He knew the Hal & Waddy routine, how they and other rival couturiers would band together and razz, kvetch, and bad-mouth the presenter, and he knew that the press would crowd around them for their *bons mots*, their one-liners. Worst— Haliburton and Googan were the wittiest cavilers in the business.

The conservatively dressed Master of Ceremonies Bleekman took the floor to present Brooks' new line, paradoxically billed as 'Boston's Avant Guard Fashion.' Bleekman expostulated, "Mr. Brooks' collection demonstrates that clothing serves two purposes— protection from the elements and adornment."

"There's also the pleasure of taking them off," Waddy gibed, "especially if they're made by John Brooks."

The entire audience laughed except Brooks, who turned livid. To compete with his less conservative rivals, he went with a sporting line for women based on race track attire, with a male edge to it. His model walked across the floor and stood before Mrs. Jack, Isabella Stuart Gardiner, whose favor every couturier curried, as Bleekman read from a card, "The informal outfit begins with a stunning Norfolk jacket with front and back pleats, lined with velvet and moiré, clearly an avatar of adornment. A perfect outfit for a day at the races."

"It's as loose as a shirt on a shad," Waddy scoffed.

"Now I know what happened to my horse blanket,"

Hal taunted.

Waddy imitated the master of ceremonies' countertenor voice, "Brooks' cuffs are larger this year, to hold three aces rather than two."

The men from the press guffawed. Brooks was getting more agitated by the minute. His face had reddened. The master of ceremonies tried to ignore the clowns. The first model retreated and a second one strutted forward.

"For formal attire," began the master of ceremonies, "Brooks' model sports a Prince Albert coat with satin lapels and a white piqué shirt. The feminine cravat is worn in a sailor's knot."

Waddy laughed. "Add spats and stir with a cane."

Hal rubbed his chin pensively. "Why does it assume the body an inopportune presence, with all the jollity of a snuff box?"

"Did she wear that on a dare?" Drew Lashton added.

Skeets Mooney would have said that Brooks *had the elevens up*, as titters progressed through the crowd and emboldened the critics.

"I think Archbishop Williams ordered her to wear it as penance," Hal jibed.

Heads turned toward the two dapper comedians and the laughter grew louder. The model tried to ignore it. She strutted forward and turned on her heels. Brooks started toward his competitors with fists clenched and veins bulging on his neck and forehead. Taciturn couturier Lashton restrained him. Another model appeared, in more traditional female garb. Bleekman read, "Now for evening wear, Brooks offers an organdy muslin gown with elbow sleeves trimmed with deep lace. The gloves are in Sultan red, ornamented with gold studs and finished off with gold-mounted tassels. The hem is encrusted with precious stones—emeralds, rubies, and sapphires, and the bodice is virtually ablaze with diamonds."

"Looks to me like a dumpy lighthouse," Hal commented, followed by a rush of laughter.

"It's beautiful, as long as no one is wearing it. Then it's ostentatious, obscene." Waddy threw his arms out, palms up, with a look of non-comprehension at Brooks, who was striding toward him. "It's supposed to be a dress, John, not a tapestry."

Haliburton jeered. "She looks like a tramp steamer at midnight. The pokeberry lipstick makes her lips look like purse clasps."

The *Town Topics* reporter guffawed and wrote down the comments. Brooks grabbed Haliburton by the collar. Hal reciprocated the grip. Fights between designers were never with fists. They pulled on each other's necktie till one fainted. Hal had the advantage of youth and was able to hang on till Brooks dropped. Hal affected a trauma greater than Brooks's, and Waddy supported him as they left the building, whereupon Hal whooped it up and Waddy whistled for a hansom parked nearby.

"*Waugh*, I'm as thirsty as a goat," said Waddy. "What say, duck, aren't you dry?"

Hal smiled and ordered the driver, "Mooney's Temple of Bacchus, with all possible haste."

"Cheese it!" Waddy added.

Watching the debacle, Mrs. Jack knew there had to be a better way to do fashion shows, one that would keep the men from each other's throats. She resolved to do her own show, inviting Boston's couturiers to compete for prizes at her residence. It would be, of course, outrageous. It would locate the avant-garde squarely in the hub, the hub of which would be 152 Beacon Street, the house that Mrs. Jack built.

Back on Putnam Street in the early evening Waddy was in an apron of his own design, moving with purpose from the counter to the stove, his eyes wet from cutting onions and his own moving rendition of 'Dear Old Pal of Mine,' a cup of too cold tea and a glass of too warm brandy on the counter on the maid's day off. This was how he relaxed. He brushed the inquiring cat off the counter and hopped it in the ass. Casey had a Maltese cat, talking birds, and shitting dogs. Waddy had a Malacca stick with a silver knob to swing at the cat and to clobber the French poodle that shat on the Persian rug. Now he heard feet coming downstairs to the kitchen. Casey put a bag on the counter.

He stared at her. There was clearly something masculine about her which wasn't conveyed by height alone. How easy it would be to impersonate a man. His eyes were fixated, captivated, as if it were the first time he saw her. How long her face looked, almost anticipating Modigliani. She had an understandably sleepy air, given her grueling schedule, rowing and riding between stints waitressing at the Holly Tree and simply being Mrs. Wadsworth Googan. When she was angry or competing, her face could appear almost demonic; traces of it were also there simply in the person of Mrs. Googan, wearing the finest evening gown in the room. But when she smiled, all notions of demonic, all insinuation of masculine, were erased, and his chest was utterly clobbered from the inside; when she smiled, and her lower lip hung almost obscenely delicious.

"What kept you?"

"I went rowing."

He stopped slicing and contemplated the betrayal of their agreement—that she would row only in the morning. "You're making me look ridiculous, you know that? Waddy Googan—his wife truckles at a diner and runs roughshod all over him."

"So, put me in a cockle shell?"

Waddy put down the long chef's knife and threw the chopped onions into the salad bowl. "Have I ever done that?"

"I'm not trying to make you look ridiculous. If Isabella Stuart Gardner can ride a bicycle in men's clothes ..."

"Isabella Stuart Gardner thinks she is George Sand. She makes a social career out of *outré*-ing the bourgeoisie. She is probably fucking the butler."

"Or somebody."

"You are not Mrs. Jack," he said, pointing at her with the knife.

"Clearly."

Casey emptied two ashtrays, letting the irony of rumor seep in. "I don't understand why you let Mary have the day off, just when the rats are coming out and the kitchen has become the depository for dirty ashtrays."

"Sometimes," he paused to wipe the blade twice on his aproned thigh, "I want to design you a head-sized tea cozy."

She started to laugh, and quickly stuffed her mouth with a duxelle mushroom he had just carved. "Do you have any objection to a person and her dog spending the night here? I've invited Rosemary Frothingham."

"What's the dog's name?"

"I don't know. Why on earth do you ask?"

"I want to be able to tell them apart." Waddy slammed the knife and his free hand down on the counter and braced himself for his histrionic laugh, stomping with one foot.

Casey bit on another mushroom and gave an affectless ha-ha.

"Your friend Rosemary is amazing. I've never seen a tongue wag so much. Like a bitch's tail in springtime."

"You don't seem to object to bitches' tails, so I assume you won't have any objection to Rosemary."

"I've never met a suffragette speechifier that wasn't more cock than hen." Waddy untied his apron and threw it down on top of the knife. "I've lost my appetite. You and your harpy friend can have it all. This started out being one of the best days of my life, and now..." He hammered his fist on the solid oak counter and it seemed to him effete. He shook his head and found his body involuntarily shaking with it. He hoped it wasn't noticed. "I even cook for you." his voice faltered slightly. How many other men cook for their wives? Do you think Foxhall Codman cooks for his wife?"

"He has enough money to afford a cook."

"Oh, so that's what this is about."

"Have you asked me what I want? You cook, but you cook what *you* want."

"All you ever want is salad, with the occasional box of chocolates thrown in, a little garnish."

Casey moved toward the window and stared at the sun melting into a burnt-bean horizon. "Pumpkin."

"What?"

"Make me a pumpkin."

Staring into his ratatouille, dour Waddy *Peter*ed it out: *Pumpkin Eater.* That was the allusion, that he kept her in a cockle shell.

"It's always about *you.* You don't cook for me. You cook because you like to. It's narcissism."

"Sheer tosh! It's not narcissism. It has nothing to do with narcissism."

"So, it's your crazy wife again."

"It doesn't fit." Waddy's mouth turned down at the corners. Casey took the histrionic tea cozy off her head and let it fall silently onto her plate.

"I never said you were crazy. I said the idea of rowing against men was crazy." Dour Waddy Googan regarded his cozy creation and found himself oddly speaking from the heart without running his words through his well-worn censor. "The problem is that I love you, and ..." He could not finish, but stunned himself by the admission that felt emptily good. He had no idea where it was coming from. He felt some combination of ridiculous and sentimental but felt more than these the need to confess, "All I ever wanted was love."

"And sex?"

What could he say? That too. And love was what *he* wanted, for *himself*—so the next cudgel to come down would be narcissism, again. He didn't have a Chinaman's chance. And he didn't know why. He felt helpless. He'd painted himself into a corner from which the only exit was the greenhouse. Wordless, he imagined fashioning a daisy chain into a noose, uncertain whether it was meant to hang himself or his beloved.

"I'll be back late. I've got some errands to do."

"Errands ..." she said quizzically, giving no quarter. "I've always been stupefied by your errands. That's not what men say when they mean *assignation*, is it?"

Waddy swirled and drained his glass of brandy.

"Mrs. Jack is coming, too, later."

"Is she spending the night, too?"

"No. I suppose I should have told you ... I've seen so little of you lately ... I've joined Sorosis." Casey was reluctant to mention it, as it might remind Waddy of his failure to be invited to join a social club. The Monday Evening Club had not contacted him and he'd been clearly chafed by it after being put up by Brahmin Foxhall Codman.

"Sorosis—sounds like a disease."

She laughed. "That's what *I* said. It's a society of women. We're dedicated to women's suffrage."

"You smoke," Waddy translated, and Casey gave him a sidelong glance. "Turkish cigarettes. I've seen it. Fifty women in a room, all puffing away for equality and choking each other. They have a canary, like coal miners, and when it keels over they open the windows, and minutes later there's a steam-pumper ringing its bell."

She poured herself some black tea, imported by Madame Demorest's company, which was funding Sorosis. She refrained from telling him of its provenance but couldn't hold back a small smile.

"Why are you smiling?" Waddy asked, tying a scarf around his neck.

She hesitated before speaking. "Sorosis was founded in New York by Madame Demorest. It has chapters in Philadelphia and Washington."

"So, it's not a disease; it's an epidemic."

She smiled wanly. "I've volunteered to host our next meeting. In fact, it's here ... tonight."

"Here?" said Waddy defiantly. "You know I despise that harridan."

"Madame Demorest? She's not coming."

"That's not the point. This is *my* house." It felt hollow. He almost regretted saying it. The bank was threatening to foreclose and Casey knew it.

The timely knock at the door was Rosemary, Waddy's cue to exit. He strolled first through the greenhouse, among *the four-hundred*, as he called his collection of flowers, which usually calmed him. *The four-hundred* was the term Lady Astor used to designate the desirables, the fashionables who rose above the rich arrivistes. Here are daffodils, pansies, violets, sunflowers, magnolias, daisies, black-eyed susans, marigolds that represent the Mellons, Goulds, Fricks, Huntingtons, Crokers, Flaglers, Rockefellers and Hearsts.

This evening it's the unassuming begonias Waddy is in love with, the begonias spilling over an old pot, *no*—better said—vessel—for the transport of their magenta and proletarian green. And what catches his eye in the whole profusion of bloom is one simple white begonia proclaiming itself not a tossed piece of some high-hat's hanky but one of the risen—above the four-hundred. Begonia—outrageous prole. He is in love again with his creations. Florist cum gardener—his male friends know nothing of his avocation, and Casey understands the unspoken need to keep secret this side of her man, what the swells at Mooney's would consider an underside.

The simple begonia has inspired him to attend to the four-hundred, to extirpate the wannabe weeds, pale stringy schlumps, arrivistes in Googan's garden, warm and steamy. It's made for sex, one might say, and the maid Mary could attest to it in something less than four-hundred places, but who is counting? Not the nearly-crushed Vanderbilts. Not the immaculate Morgans. *Twenty-seven rows of* manured

stems *and tell me—who do you love? Who do you love?* Special
care for the Gardners, of course—Mrs. Jack is a poppy. It
is clear there's something about a poppy more human than
flower, thinks Waddy—the way its four petals, for
instance, resemble skirts tossed over a banister, that
absolute languor, the self-effacing beauty, *malgre lui*, just a
*schmatta* thrown on for the occasion of sun, and the thinly
striped pin cushion at the center—little ottoman for bees.
This clump of poppies—the Gardners—red dripped
*voluttá.*

But on closer look some of the poppies are toppled,
racked by love's zealotry—manly enthusiasms and the
plump servant's broad bottom's thumping, a very
memorable sound, so much like priming a pump that
Waddy turns now to the old water pump and pushes down
the long handle just to remember again the near-sack of
Mr. and Mrs. Gardner's ersatz mansion. Not 52 Beacon
Street but the far left corner of Googan's garden of oh-so
earthly delights. Suddenly, struck with an idea the way a
dress design inspires him, he grabs the wooden step-ladder
and rushes out to Casey's backyard maze. Rising above it
all, he imagines he could plot the course to and from the
center. He makes just two turns in the maze, to be sure to
remember the way out, before planting and mounting the
ladder.

Head popped above it all—this is what it is like, he
imagines, to be born. To see everything and comprehend
nothing of the new world—half of the maze paths still
inscrutable. It's all been an ocular coitus interruptus. He
descends his wooden ladder and folds it over his shoulder
the way he stuffs a half-stiffy back into his trousers.
Submits once more to the bush. Makes his way back to his
floral charges. Out there he is an interloper in the bush
that one day will be burning, on the day he departs this
world. But now he is back in the steamy comfort of his
own ersatz world, floral paradise, dazzling storm of color
that represents eighty percent of the country's wealth. His

pockets are empty and that's okay. He inhales deeply this rich air, and somewhere inside the mental chasm he knows where he is—in this. But like scar tissue over a wound, access is denied to the reality this world represents. So many scars has Googan, and the wounds they close are like the blocked passages of the maze. Contemplating that real world, it's as if he's gone color-blind here in this visual feast but retains the sense of smell, and the scent is lovely. The scent is enough.

He looks over at the Gardners—the cluster of poppies that defines them, keeled over. And—he thinks—if these are ruins, is it not love that razed? His love for Casey that, unrequited, drove him to seek its doppelganger in someone else?

He turns now to the nasturtiums and waters them, contemplating the sadness that is his marriage, then heads for a long celebratory night at Mooney's.

After dinner, Rosemary offered Casey a cigarette. She accepted it.

"How is your bastard, I mean your husband, taking your joining Sorosis?"

Casey laughed. "In our house, Madame Demorest is the anti-Christ."

"Because she's a socialist?"

"No. Because she changed fashion, diluted it for the masses—the women of the rag and the bone."

"She's a pioneer, and a very rich one. She's one of the four hundred."

"Another reason why Waddy despises her. He can't brook a woman who makes millions."

"That's just the attitude we want to eradicate."

"But it's complicated, you know? On suffrage, he's more or less ambivalent. In his own words," she paused to consider using his vulgarity, "he doesn't give a flying crap one way or the other if women vote, as long as they're wearing a *Googan* voting costume. His hatred of Madame Demorest is more personal—his own insecurity, economic insecurity. And ... ," she paused as if surprised by the thought that had come to her mind, "he does ... he really has loving eyes."

Rosemary shook her head. "I don't know how you stand it."

Casey glanced off, as if seized by some memory. "He's not all that bad, actually, as husbands go."

"Women make better friends." Rosemary squeezed Casey's hand.

Casey smiled and nodded.

"What did you mean 'not that bad as husbands go'?"

Casey stared at Rosemary, who returned the stare with greater intensity. "We're intimates, right?"

"Sorosis sisters, and more."

"So ... I can tell you everything, woman to woman."

"Of course."

"For one thing," Casey smiled nostalgically and looked diagonally up as if into some ether, "you know how we made snow angels as kids? He does that, on cold nights, on the bed, while I'm in my toilette. I can hear the sheets shussing. And he's between them, naked, he always sleeps naked, even on the coldest nights. He's waving his arms and legs like he's making a snow angel, but what he's doing is warming my side of the bed so I won't feel frozen when I get between the sheets. It's so Waddy. He never mentions it, never looks for gratitude. He can be such a good man."

Rosemary looked like she'd lost her knitting. "Maybe he's just ... feathering his nest, his love nest."

Casey gave a short, low laugh. "Such a good man," she repeated, as if Rosemary had not spoken or as if she was ignoring her. Too good, actually, and that's what I can't stand." She looked directly at Rosemary. "He knows how to please a woman, beyond her imaginings, and he's arrogant about it. Not that he says anything, really, but you can tell. He kind of wears it, the arrogance, in place of clothing. He loves giving pleasure, and I suppose I should be grateful, but it's like an addiction, like he's giving me opium instead of love, and I can't stand the dependence, and what he wants most deeply is not to *love* a woman, or for a woman to love him, but to crave him, for *that*. And I don't want to be dependent on a man, like that, for anything. So I turn into a cold fish, and he resents it."

Rosemary had become an obelisk. Casey waved her hand in front of her face.

"You said we were intimate, right? I thought I could tell you."

"You can." Rosemary shook her head. "Women aren't like that."

Casey laughed. "I know."

Rosemary stared at Casey and squeezed her hand. "They're not like that."

Casey found it curious that Rosemary hadn't said 'We.' She resented feeling discluded from her own gender. "Now you know everything."

The line of an acknowledging smile broke across Rosemary's face like a new crack in the clay of a sun-baked arroyo.

The knock at the door was Mrs. Jack, in a daring décolleté with an entire parure of emeralds and leading a pack of sorosis members.

"Pray, who *un*dressed you?" Casey joked.

"Why, your husband. Didn't he do it well?"

There were titters. Casey led her Sorosis sisters on a tour of the house. Mrs. Jack looked at the mirrors draped with clematis, then at the dried pampas grass and thistles. "Wildness should not be contained by cloisonné jars." She fingered the palm boughs and spoke to them. "How surprised you must be to be in a Satsume jardinière."

It was looking dim for Casey. Among her collection of statues and bibelots was the whale member previously used by the Wharf Rats, a yachting club, as a gavel. It was discarded after it had been distorted and partially charred by the fire of 1872. Mrs. Jack finally smiled as she read the inscription describing it.

"It doesn't even look like a phallus," said Rosemary.

"No, but it closely resembles what some women think of phalluses." Mrs. Jack threw Rosemary a telling glance. "That will be *our* gavel, if Mrs. Googan has no objection."

"It would be an honor."

Mrs. Jack passed the whale phallus to Rosemary and inspected two twin statues. "What are these?"

"Lothans," said Rosemary, "the only objects in Casey's collection absent phalluses."

Mrs. Jack patted the belly of a Lothan. "Poor guys, no enlightenment and no phallus to make up for it. You don't suppose there's a connection?" Noticing the clock over the mantel, mounted in carved, almost brambly wood, she ejaculated, "Oh, dear, the Medusa is being tortured into telling time."

She frowned at the worn tines of some of the forks and at the darns in the tablecloth but smiled at the yellow Japanese silk that softened the glare of light globes, and she seemed to admire the tête-bêche armchair. "There's a *douceur de vivre* in a well-appointed house," she pronounced, leaving Casey to guess whether hers was or was not well-appointed. Then she smiled. "*Sic situ laetantur lares*," and she translated, "the household gods delight in being here." Though the translation was unnecessary, Casey smiled.

Mrs. Jack had approved.

# Chapter 9: Jack and Flora

*W*hile Casey awaited Mrs. Jack and the Sorosis crew, Waddy decided there was still enough daylight to check on his new fighter before celebrating at Mooney's. He drove his Phaeton across the Chelsea Street Bridge, Chelsea Creek and the Boston-Maine railroad tracks to The Sporting Club where Laz was coming out the door.

"Going home?"

"Yup."

"I'll take you."

He drove down Shawmut Street to Laz's house at the corner Marginal Street. A comely black girl dressed like an Irish ragamuffin was catching eels in the soggy marsh grass by the Chelsea River. The wind pressed her dress to the leeward thigh. Old and small, the dress in the back had two buttons missing, and where it flapped open her bare flesh pressed Waddy's eye.

"Who is *that*?"

"My step-sister. Triffeny."

*A long salty pull of dark taffy*, Waddy mused.

"Don't mind her. She's daft. Dropped on her head or

something. Ain't her fault."

"I don't mind at all," said Waddy, enthralled. She smiled at her step-brother as she approached. Her teeth were perfectly set. Her face, if you ignored the strange eyes, was handsome. Her body was as well-formed as that of any women he had fitted, and that cast included his wife. Triffeny's uncorseted waist was impossibly thin and its juncture with her buttocks reminded Waddy of a shaft joined to an arrowhead. Most dazzling of all was the bronze luster of her skin, light refracting in a captive shimmer.

"How old is she?"

"Fifteen."

Waddy smiled broadly. "She's going to be my showstopper."

Laz's brow wrinkled. "What do you mean?"

Waddy smiled. "Model. She has the body of a twenty-year old, a twenty-year-old Aphrodite."

Laz didn't get the allusion, but he understood *model*. His head jerked incredulously from Waddy to Triffeny to Waddy again. "She's a Negro."

Waddy smiled. "Madame Demorest began using Negro models twenty years ago."

"She's ..." Laz agitated his hands. "She's exalted in the head."

"*Exotic* is what the audience will see. Models never look anyone in the eye. All models take on an air—arrogance, insouciance, haughtiness, primness. They all have an unnatural look. It's all restrained or disguised sexuality, of course. But it doesn't matter. What the white audience will see is African-translated haughtiness, an enslaved princess. What they'll see is *exquise*," Waddy lapsed into French.

Laz kicked the dirt and shook his head. "Ex-what? I don't think so. Don't want anyone making fun of her."

"They won't. All she has to do is smile and walk. Can she do that?"

"Sure, but ..."

Waddy thumped Laz on the chest. "Smile and walk. That's two things. She doesn't even have to do them together. She can smile at the end of her strut."

"But her look—it's a little daft."

"Those Piss-in-the-*pail-ian* Brahmins think all Negroes are daft. They won't see any difference. What they'll see in Triffeny is exotic."

"What you fixin' to pay her?"

"One silver dollar."

Laz startled.

"With a bonus if we win an award."

Laz waited till he got Waddy's eye good. He was tempted to put a hand on Waddy's shoulder but restrained himself. "Boys are always trying to take advantage of her. She don't know nothin'. You know what I mean? You gotta take care of her like I do. Men around here know what'll happen to them." He raised a huge fist.

Waddy didn't hesitate to put a hand on Laz's shoulder. "You have my word. Waddy Googan will take care of her." He smiled reassuringly. Laz took it in.

"Can I come?"

"To the fashion opening?"

"Yeah."

"Are you kidding? You're a prize-fighter."

"That's my kid-sister."

"She's not really a kid anymore."

"She's still my sister."

"Are you as daft as she is? You don't even own a suit."

"You could make me one. I'd look good in a suit, specially a Googan one."

"I'm your manager, not your tailor."

At Mooney's an hour later Hugo Bartolini bought a round to celebrate Waddy's own fistic victory. Foxhall Codman and Jawing Kerry lifted their mugs. "Here's how."

"Same here."

"And one for the strongboy, John L. Sullivan. It's his birthday."

Mugs were tipped again, while the schnorrers occupied their usual niches, looking for marks. Bounding Dick and Marbles, so-called for his sempiternal dexterous rolling of marbles between his fingers, engaged in an arm-wrestling contest. Frank the Gyp, who spoke more Irish than English, hung his new tile on the rack and demanded a *uisgahbetha*.

"Neat?" said Skeets.

Frank clearly didn't understand, and Skeets poured him a whiskey straight up from a bottle labeled 'Firewater.'

Foxhall Codman's pal Deke Merriwell ordered a glass of house red. Skeets took an unlabeled bottle of Guinnea Red from the shelf and let it flub and splash into a schooner. Deke frowned.

"You're not putting out a fire," Codman corrected the barkeep. "Pour like you're baptizing a baby."

Skeets gave him a look but said nothing.

"Fucking fancy pants," scoffed Nemo from his cups.

Codman ignored the jibe and looked at Jawing Kerry. "You're not talking too much tonight."

Kerry swallowed. "Can't. Mouth's half full of blood. Gotta swallow it to talk. Don't know where it's coming from. Just keeps filling up."

"Let's have a look," said Waddy.

"I've already looked in a mirror. It's a slow leak somewhere. You can't see it happening. But I can taste it all the time. It's like I'm tasting death. I keep swallowing it, and I swear my piss is turning pink."

"You're just drunk," Codman reassured him.

"How long's this been going on?" Waddy asked.

"All day."

"You feel weak?"

"Yeah."

"Everything can't be rosy, now, can it?" said Codman

"No. Some things must be shit."

"Go home and sleep on it," Waddy advised.

"Tried it. If I lie down, my throat starts to fill up. I'm

afraid it'll fill up if I fall asleep. I won't be able to breathe."

"Sounds like you're dying, Kerry."

"I'm afraid so."

"How much blood's a person got?"

"I don't know," said Hugo. "Do you, Foxhall?"

"No."

"Hey, Waddy, how much blood's a person got?"

"How do I know. I just stick pins in 'em," said the fashion designer. "I don't clean and dress 'em."

"Ask Skeets, he'll know," said Jawing Kerry.

"I'm tired of asking everybody," said Hugo. "You ask him. Hell, you're the one who's dying."

"Just ask him, will you, for Chrissake. He might throw me out if he thinks I'm dying in his place."

"All right," said Hugo. "Hey, Skeets, how much blood's a person got?"

Skeets came closer. "I don't know. But it's a bitch to mop it all up." He laughed like a ratchet that slipped, notch after notch, like someone pulled the catch out. It came out in perfect intervals, like a cuckoo, the tone falling too with each laughing rasp, and the listener felt his chin dropping notches, following it. "What do you want to know for?"

"Jawing Kerry's bleeding in his mouth. He swallows it and pisses it. I guess he wants to know how much time he's got left."

"Oh, shit, what did you tell him for?" said Kerry.

"You ain't spitting it up, are you?"

Kerry swallowed. "No."

"He ain't spitting it up, is he?" Skeets asked Hugo.

"No. He just swallows it."

"If he spits it up, you don't want to get it on you. You might get what he's got."

"He's pretty clean, Skeets."

"That's good." Skeets wiped the bar and spread his hands as if measuring a fathom on the polished mahogany and walnut bar. "Judging by what I seen, appertaining to that, a man can't lose more than a quart before he falls into an unconscious state."

"What do you think, Jaw'n?"

"Yeah. Penny for your thoughts."

"My thoughts? Jeeesus ... My thoughts are crummy."

Waddy tried to humor Kerry, who sold patent medicines and was working on a contract to have them mass-produced. Waddy held an imaginary bottle in the air and imitated Kerry's spiel. "Nature needs some help in overcoming obstinate bleeding mouths, and fortunately nature has some valuable assistance in Dr. Kerry's Pleasant Pellets."

A bit of blood spurted through Kerry's lips as Foxhall laughed and slapped him on the back.

"Give him some good whiskey, Skeets, on Codman," said Waddy.

Just past ten p.m., Waddy watched Big-Mouth Babs waltz in with a sailor while Father Divine on his fiddle played Mozart's *Schlittenfahrt*—Sleigh Ride, while Waddy mentally opined that no sleigh he knew of could accommodate the barn-door ass of Big-Mouth Babs. She nonetheless impressed him with the inspired habit of carrying a purse with a strap separating and highlighting each breast with an egalitarian if not sumptuous spirit, and Waddy wished each of them beneath his breath the best of evenings.

The sailor wore a flat-topped brimmed cap with a black tally sporting yellow silk lettering and hanging in a bow over his left ear. The couple were almost immediately replaced by another demimondaine cum sailor, as if they had inherited the tavern space, as if Babs and her beau had merely been place-keepers of an emotional state—like a bottle of beer that excesses into the permanence of a cardboard coaster and then is replaced by another. The thirtyish Babs had drawn down off her shoulder her striped cotton top, revealing a birth mark the color of tobacco juice spat years before on a dugout floor as well as the ugliest tattoo Waddy had ever seen; it looked like a stocking fallen and misplaced on her biceps. It all depressed the couturier, who was distracted from Babs by Jans Mangin, dressed all in black and cradling a brown package. He put it on the bar next to Jawing Kerry, who just stared at himself in the bar mirror. Jans unwrapped a chocolate cake and asked Skeets for a knife.

"Cake for everyone who can belly up to the bar," he said.

"Who died?" said Waddy.

"My brother's wife. They wouldn't let me in the wake, so here I am."

"You feuding with your brother?"

"Dirk wouldn't mind. It's the wife's family. I'm a black sheep because I married a non-gypsy and settled down. They never forgive you. Even when my wife died. You think it's forgotten, then there's ways of reminding you."

Codman waved his hand, refusing a piece of cake.

"You have to nip the cake. It's bad luck if you don't," said Waddy.

Codman took a piece to be polite. "Not bad."

"Damn good," said Skeets. "Say, Jans, where the hell are the rats?"

"Swipes is bringing them. He'll be here any minute. Fifty of the best. Killers. 'Fraid of nothing. Dirk says if they taste human blood they become fearless. He pulled them off some stiff down on the tracks. In and out of death he was, fallen in the blackest water between you, me, and God."

"Jesus, this is good cake," said Hugo. "Your brother's wife ought to die more often."

"I heard your brother made you a special cage, for a pet rat, a real monster," said Hugo.

"Some cage. The rat disappeared, what I heard," said Father Divine.

"It was a phantom rat anyway. No real rat is that big. Big as a dog, I heard," said Waddy.

"Know what Jans did with the cage? Chopped a hole in

the back of his shanty and stuck it in, like a window."

"What the hell good is that?" said Codman.

"Ventilation. You ever been in his place?" Hugo pinched his nose with his fingers. "The pig he lives with has a livelier eye and cleaner toenails than he does."

"I heard someone caught that rat again," said Nemo.

Codman was relieved when no one seemed to know that Jans had acquired the phantom rat, which he gifted to Skeets, who nodded to remind him of their prearranged signal, then looked away. In cahoots with a gypsy and a barkeep, Foxhall Codman was *in extasis*; while his Brahmin cronies merely *hunted the elephant*, he had it slain.

~~~~~~~

Swipes came in lugging a burlap bag that kept shifting shape. Hugo snickered. "Jans, the kid brought your lunch."

"How much?" said Skeets, shaking the bag.

"Eleven cents a rat." Jans looked at Hugo and snarled. "Assholes like that drive the price up."

"You know my price. Ten cents a rat."

"These are killers."

"Yeah, we know," said Skeets. And I heard you bought 'em for a nickel apiece."

"Seven cents, for half of 'em. The other half I caught myself."

"Skeets, you ever met a gypsy that didn't have all twelve toes crossed when he talked to you?" said Hugo.

"I'm no more gypsy than you are," said Jans. "I've lived in the same house for twenty years."

"Yeah, and you still play that gypsy fiddle shit. I bet you still can't play *Yankee Doodle*."

"Maybe he don't like *Yankee Doodle*," said Father Divine.

"*I* like *Yankee Doodle*," said Waddy.

"I'm not surprised," said Hugo. "As Thoreau said, 'The culture of an Irishman is an enterprise to be undertaken with a kind of moral bog hoe.'"

"It was the bastard Cromwell said that," Waddy disputed.

"Thoreau."

"I've read Thoreau," said Waddy. "He went to live deliberately, he did. And a man that lives deliberately has no occasion to disparage the Irish."

Hugo looked at Skeets, the constant arbiter. "Well?"

"Well, it was Thoreau, unless Googan is buying, then it's Cromwell."

Everyone but Waddy laughed, because he'd just lost all the cash he had on a bum steer at Mystic Park. He couldn't stand anyone a drink, and he was angry at Skeets because Skeets should have known it. And the joke should have been on Hugo. Everyone was fed up with his rainy day mentality and cruelty. Everyone knew how he beat his horses and his dogs.

Waddy gripped his pint of ale and contemplated throwing it at Hugo, but Codman read his mind and put his heavy hand on Waddy's forearm. Codman had a grip like John L. Sullivan's, and Waddy's idea was put to rest. But Hugo noticed, and he slowly rested one hand on his lucky horseshoe, just in case. Hugo was the horseshoe pitching champion of Cambridge, and several plaques in his honor hung over the bar, just above the sign that read: *No Profanity Tolerated*, and below the sign that read: *Take a little wine for thy stomach's sake.*

Jans lifted the burlap bag and planked it on the bar. Skeets looked at the bag, then at Jans. "Ten and a half, and you put your hand in the bag."

"Eleven. Take it or leave it," said Jans.

"A ratter's got to prove his product. Goes with the turf."

"He don't have to worry. Ain't a rat yet that's bit Jans. Never bite their own kind," said Hugo.

Jans' hand was in the bag and out again in a flash. Hugo let out a sickening yelp, and Skeets's beagle lifted its head and ears as Hugo's hands flew to cover his face that had already gone fuzzy brown, four feet scratching for a foothold, and a piece of his nose was hanging by a shred. Now the rat was pinned against the bar by half a dozen human feet. It bounced around and escaped to the waiting maw of Skeets's beagle, who took it in a quick scuffle.

Blood was pouring from Hugo's nose. He got close enough to drip on the bag and he bled on Jawing Kerry, who bled more silently and didn't move a muscle; bled on Jans' right hand too, squeezing the ice pick skewered through the top of the double burlap bag. The rats smelled the drops of blood and were frenzied.

Father Divine and Nemo grabbed Hugo by the shoulders. He was gushing and screaming for a piece of Jans.

"Throw the meatball out," said Skeets.

Hugo was in the street calling for help, his left forearm pressed to his nose, with his head held back to diminish the bleeding, his elbow pointed straight ahead like the sight on a rifle. He heard a familiar thud, turned and scanned the ground for his lucky horseshoe. He picked it up with his free hand. Unable to see well with his head tilted back and his arm elevated, he bent every few steps from the waist to make out where he was going; moaning figurehead slicing through the Cantabridgian darkness. In front of the Gaiety was a poster that caught Hugo's eye only for a moment, announcing that MacBeth, whom Hugo knew not, was coming.

"Satisfied?" said Jans. "The price is still eleven. Gotta make up for the one I just lost."

"Yeah, yeah, eleven. Get them rats the fuck out of here."

"The pit ready?"

"It's ready."

"Who's on?" Waddy asked Skeets.

"Jack and Flora. Some real carnage tonight."

The noise level in the bar jumped as the men reacted to

the news of Jack and Flora. Fifteen minutes later the bar drained patrons to the back room where Jack and Flora would take on the rats. Father Divine took to his pulpit early.

"Blessed God..."

"Who blessed him?" chided Waddy. "Did he bless himself? That would be narcissistic, no?"

Father Divine stared at Waddy. "Alien illiterates rule our fair city. The saloon is their church and the toddy stick their scepter."

Father Divine ducked a billiard ball aimed at his head. "You mean the Irish, don't you, Father? Give the underdog a bath, a decent kennel, and some wholesome food and he won't need the mange of religion," said Waddy.

Codman raised his glass. "And pay them the way Googan does, especially the ones in skirts."

"We need rum, not Romanism," said Waddy.

"Look what rum's done to poor Jawing Kerry?" said the priest. "It's a short trip from the saloon to the morgue."

Skeets now took umbrage. "This ain't no saloon. It's the Temple of Bacchus."

Codman laughed and slapped Waddy on the back. "Jack and Flora—like Sullivan versus Flood. "Who do you want?"

"My choice?

"Hundred bucks. Pick 'em."

"I'll take Jack. Always liked his style. Calm as can be. Like tiptoeing up to the wife, put a little nip on her neck, then give her a toss and out again."

Everyone laughed but Kerry, who bled.

"Blessed God," Father Divine began again and knocked over his beer.

"Shaddup, ya fuckin' moron," inveighed Nemo.

"And don't be drowning us with holy water on a frosty night," Waddy added.

Jack and Flora were a top draw. Admission to the pit tonight was a dollar. Ladies free. A six-foot woman entered Skeets' *Sanctum Sanctorum* wearing high-waisted trousers held up with galluses, over which she wore a seal-skin saque; on her head a wig the color of Yellow-Jack molasses candy. She stopped to light up a cigar under the signs: *Smoking While Dancing Prohibited*, and *No Lovers Wanted*. Skeets nodded at Big-Mouth Babs and let *her* pass with no charge.

Roof rat, barn rat, field rat, house rat, sewer rat, water rat, wharf rat, alley rat, gray rat, brown rat, climbing rat, white-bellied rat—they're all here, subtlely differentiated, but all monikers for the same *Rattus norvegicus*, nervously sniffing the air from a cage and whetting their teeth on the iron bars. One stands out, freakishly large. He's a *rex*, which in pet parlance refers not to size but to curly hair and whiskers.

Before the fight Jack and Flora were washed and tasted—the handler of each dog licked his own dog's fur to prove that no poison, morphine, or other substance had been applied to slow down the rats that bit it.

Codman combed his right hand through his hair, the prearranged signal to Skeets to put his gargantuan brown rat in Jack's pit. The rat was nearly double the size of the others. The odds went three to two on Flora when Jack's corner lost the fixed coin toss and drew the pit with the huge rat. There were fifty rats per dog. It was to be a *simul*, Jack and Flora to be dropped by their handlers when Skeets blew the whistle. No stopwatches. Whoever finished his/her quota of rats first was the winner.

"Twenty-five monsters like him and old Jack will be walking on their backs," said Nemo.

Jack and Flora had met twice. The first time, in New York, Flora set a record for fifty rats in eleven minutes, thirty-one seconds. In the rematch, in Boston, Jack evened the score.

Both were bull terriers, both eighteen pounds, with

deep chests and muscular legs. Jack, a black and tan male. Flora, a white slut. Their tails were cut back to give the rats less to hang on to. The ears too had to be trimmed or they would be torn to shreds. And it slowed a dog down—rats clamped on and held the bite while a dog shook its head with another rat in its teeth and tossed it dead to the side. The best dogs, like Jack and Flora, would go through the whole pit, and when all the others were dead they would take on the hangers. Bull terriers were bred for this. They didn't panic. Still, it was best to trim the ears as much as possible.

"Who are you betting on?" Waddy asked Father Divine.

"Whoever Codman bets on. I've never seen a man so lucky. Did I tell you how he won two thousand dollars on a horse race in Hartford?"

"No."

"Amazing piece of luck. He was drunk as a boiled owl and bet a thousand on a horse named Jim at three to one. When he sobered up a bit he panicked. Found the nearest bookmaker and covered his thousand on Jim, putting a thousand on the field against Jim. Well, the strangest thing happened. This horse, Mona, was entered at the last minute and won. Jim finished second, but Codman still won because Mona wasn't in the field when the first bet was made. But she *was* when he bet a thousand on the field against Jim. So he won twice in the same race! That's some lucky sonofabitch, huh? They ought to put the sonofabitch in jail."

"What do you mean?" asked Waddy.

"I mean the fix was in. Why do you think he wins so much? He's a crook."

"Codman? He's the pillar of fucking society."

"Take the roll at any jail and you'll find the majority are Irish," Nemo said, knowing Waddy's nationality.

"So, lock me up. I'd be better off. Besides, Codman's not true Irish. He's Anglo-Irish."

Nemo almost sprayed a mouthful of beer, laughing. "As if that made it any better. I don't understand why you defend the bastard. Hugo was just saying he's got it in for you."

"For me? What for?"

Nemo didn't want to say. And he wasn't sure he believed Hugo himself. Time would tell sure enough.

Skeets poured whiskey from a pocket flask into Waddy's ale. "On the house. One for the Irish."

Waddy lifted his mug to Skeets. "Know what the fucking British are doing now? Taxing sunlight! If you've got two windows instead of one you're a rich man in Ireland, and the peasants are eating dogs with sapless bones."

Skeets laughed and lifted his schooner. "Here's how."

"Same here."

Nemo's hat fell into the pit and was immediately set upon by rats looking for an ark of salvation. "Hazardous hell!" Nemo imprecated, waving his hand, but the rats did not shoo. One stood on its hind legs on the hat's brim and spread its jaws, revealing small but very sharp yellowish teeth, with two almost-tigerishly long incisors that could produce six-thousand foot-pounds of pressure. Nemo took a chance, grabbed the brim, and the rat latched onto the webbed flesh between his forefinger and thumb. He recoiled, screaming, and the rat fell back into the fray with its last supper. Nemo cursed and shook his hand. Skeets approached and poured a tumbler of whiskey on the wound as antiseptic. The hat remained in the pit, which was clapboard, waist high, about 15' by 6', with an improvised wooden divider that formed two nearly square sections. The two-inch wood was deeply gouged by rats scratching and biting for way out. Skeets in fact had a kitchen table made from a discarded divider, its deep gouges lacquered but still clearly visible. All four corners of each pit sported triangular tin flashing that prevented the rats from scrambling up and out. Men lined three sides, three-deep, while on the fourth side a steep three-tiered set of bleachers afforded a good view. The dirt floor, soaked with beer, stunk. The pit itself stunk of live and putrefied rat. "Douse the glim!" shouted Skeets, and Swipes turned down the gas that lit an anomalous, magnificent crystal chandelier also rescued from the fire of 1885, from the same Episcopal church where Skeets got the pulpit, with the help of Father Divine, a drinking buddy of the rector. The brighter it was lit, the more the small room was heated, and the hotter it got, the more it stunk.

Swelly Bangs and Happy Huntz began snarling at each other, baring teeth, imitating dogs, each trying to outsnarl the other. Rats leapt like popping corn, searching for an exit. Jack seemed to enjoy catching rats in their flight, while Flora, *The Borgne* (one-eyed) Boston Bitch, excelled at catching two rats with one bite. Some crouched, trying to hide between the back legs of the bitch that had lost an eye to a rat at Kit Burns' pit in New York.

It comes down to this. Flora has three rats left, while Jack turns at one corner of his pit and sees the heaving sides of just one living rat—the leviathan. Jack takes a few sprightly steps and stumbles. He gets up and shakes his head and just stands there, and Flora is down to two rats.

The huge one is in a corner near Nemo, who bends over the wooden railing as far as he can without falling into the carnage. One of Jack's handlers is worried. He's screaming to pull him back, but it's hard to hear a thing in the din, and Nemo has no money on the contest; he just wants to get a good look at the rat that must sense that the executioner is stumbling.

Its eyes are small and set very high back on its head, slanted, red, and terrified. The pit is not level. A rivulet of blood flows down toward the rat, and if you had Nemo's eyes you would see the rat's head almost submerged and you would see the cheeks contracting and the mouth wide open—bloating itself on the blood, hardly even aware of Jack's jaws stretching to get a grip around the back of its thick neck, but suddenly almost no one but Nemo is watching the lethargic, glassy-eyed Jack take his last rat, because Flora is already well into her victory lap.

Jack's handlers argued that two of Flora's rats were still alive. Skeets jumped into the pit and kicked rats away from a small chalked circle in the center of the pit. He placed the two contested rats in the circle and brought his shillelagh down on their tails. The rats twitched but did not move out of the circle. By house rules, they were considered dead. Flora was toasted and washed with a pitcher of ale, and a red ribbon was placed around her neck.

No tomb, no monument, for the rats. No engraved words. For the patrons of Mooney's Temple of Bacchus there is an atavistic puzzlement. It's done. What now? Losers departed like unstuck dogs, cursing Flora. Winners bellied up and shouted drinks for their companions. The curious, the inveterate, and the *elephant hunters* ordered drinks and sat back to throw quarters at Jack-the-Rat and Snatchem Leese, who bit the heads off live rats for a quarter, or off mice for a dime. Snatchem entered the pit imploring, "I'd like to be an angel, so's I could bite off Gabriel's ear." Lower class establishments than Mooney's offered local rum-dumbs free beer to do the same, guys with delirium tremens, who were as likely as not to have a piece of their lips bitten off by the rats. Skeets was true to a sign he had hung outside advertising: *A Good Night's Sport and No Humbug.* Only pros like Jack-the-Rat and Snatchem Leese were permitted to do their geek act.

Father Divine followed Waddy out the door, stopping to let the bouncer drag a man out face down by the heels.

"Who's that?"

A man with pearl-studded galluses turned to the retired priest. "Some rum-dumb. Fucking mess. Bled all over he place. That's the way to go, though—on a bar stool. I hope I go that way."

"May your wish be granted," said Skeets, throwing a

shovelful of sawdust on Jawing Kerry's blood, then sweeping it with all of his motions *toward* the door to avoid bad luck.

Waddy loosened his cravat, inhaled the smokeless air, and drank in the indifference of the stars with the emasculating feeling of not being able to pay his debts again. He literally felt his testicles retreating as if someone had lifted him by the back of the trousers, turning his crotch into a snare. The raucousness of Mooney's hit him again as Foxhall Codman left the door open behind him. Codman crushed out his cigar and fussed with the top buttonhole of his suit jacket. "Damn thing never lines up right."

In the corner of his eye Waddy saw Codman take off the jacket and thrust it at him.

"Fix it."

"How many times do I need to tell you—I'm not a tailor. I'm a designer." Waddy tried unsuccessfully to pass the jacket back.

"Well, you employ those kind of people. Have it fixed. We'll call it even."

Waddy managed to stop himself from retorting that it was just a two-dollar job. He resented being the recipient of Codman's *noblesse oblige*, being let off the hundred-dollar hook for his lost bet on the fixed match. Waddy held the jacket at arms length, inspecting it as if it were a carcass. He extended a sleeve. "Needs two more buttons. Anything less than three is disgusting." Waddy looked at the label. "Brooks Brothers. John Brooks is a fucking fripperer. Christ, you look like *an épicier en dimanche*. Style counts."

Codman disagreed. His eyes drew a bead on Waddy's. "Style is the essence of concealment."

Waddy saw Codman's wry smile as smug. The good feeling of having brandished his French on his high-hat friend dissipated. Codman had him pegged but good—the concealed man, antipathies bursting at invisible seams— toward the class system that excluded him, toward John

Brooks and his ridiculous collars, toward his wife—the paragon of withholding, toward the women too stupid to wear his fashions and the women who wore them without spreading their legs for his creativity, his genius.

~~~~~~~

## (Waddy)

*I dozed a bit on the way home, in my Phaeton, which was no problem, since the horse knew the way. I dreamed about Patti the Cantatrice and awoke thinking about marriage itself, its scents, its bows, the powders, the fluff, the very religiosity of its rituals, a shaky business with its small dividendum, and for this—all that man must do is provide. I hung my hat, tiptoed to the bed, and made my presence known. My wife is at times as cuddly as a barrel cactus. From the day we were married she has undressed in the closet. And when she has replaced all the wrappings I have designed for her with a pink night dress with only a scarlet ribbon at the throat, she whispers something indiscernible but French. She lies facing the window on the far side of the bed, and I reach over her shoulder and pull on the bow till it is no longer. My hand dives around her tiny waist and the summit of her hip then down about the smooth thigh, as her head on the pillow/salver stretches toward the window as if for air or as if the spectacle were somewhere else. I feel almost like an incubus, invisible, and ageless as a ghost, Biblical in the intent to know the unknowable but plunging ahead in what is ultimately a game of tag with the nothing that stirs the thing that I am, until one and then the other player explode into* **it***, and we have each our private Babylon, waters commingled, her head falls limp to the pillow as I fall from her, with the faintest sound of a wave slapping its final* **not it***. Then I run my hand again from her breasts to her armpit to her knees, as I had done earlier. I drape the gown again over her exposed parts and twist the ribbon around itself. I retreat as I had arrived but with no tiptoeing. I love then the sound of my bare, flat feet against the parquet floor like a piece of raw flank steak slamming on a butcher's block.*

—Waddy?

—Who else?

—Were you with the rats?

—Yes.

—You washed your hands?

—Of course.

—May I see?

—My hands?

—Do you mind?

—No. There, what do you think?

—It's all in my head, but would you wash them again?

—I didn't touch the rats, but if it helps put your mind at ease ...

—And the dogs?

—I touched a couple of dogs.

—And the dogs were bitten by rats?

—Yes.

—Would you mind?

—Sure.

—You're such a good man.

~~~~~~~

Casey felt the same cold nose as the house dog's, the same earnest, eager humping. In *media res* Waddy had the strongest urge to disengage, run downstairs for a growler, toss it down, and scuttle back upstairs, back to business ... Whatever it was that made him tick had enough cuckoo in it that he himself shook his head in wonderment. By the time he lay back, all of his whistles whetted, she noted that the earth had turned enough that the brightest star in her field of vision out the window had dropped from view.

Naked, spent, he lay against her, his arm over her, their fingers clenched. He fell asleep immediately and dreamt, waking Casey with his laughter.

—What are you laughing at?

—Oh, I was dreaming. I was at the Copley, at the

Spring fashion opening, and the women were mobbing the racks to get at my collection. I was smoking a long thin cigar in front of it, and when the downtown high-hat ladies got too close I'd press the hot tip of the cigar to their flesh and they'd jump back. I don't know why that was funny, but it was.

Casey rolled over. Waddy remained awake, thinking of their honeymoon in Bar Harbor:

> The wind blew boats off moorings, signs off their chains. Rain flew twenty feet horizontally through the inch-opened window to both of our cheeks, and at 1:30 a.m. the ghost of the East Wind Inn opened our locked door, then closed it, squeezing by me on its way to the bed where it turned the lamp on and off. Half the night the rain repented against our windows, the rain a crowded rosary of the dead, clicking beads in that wildness, me wild for you.

> In the morning the single knock on the door startled me. I thought it would be you, back from your early walk, but it was the chambermaid who entered upon my bidding and was shocked at the sight of me, naked and at the ready, and I could think of nothing to say but to inquire about the ghost, upon which she fainted, having heard of the incubus that had had its way with a score of chambermaids, and I remember thinking—what the hey—it would only take a minute; what could a chambermaid say anyway, knickers down in a man's bed? Barely a minute. Why not? Is what I thought ...

> We left an hour later. On the rented buggy, owl scat and a half-eaten rodent, the owl hooting in the tall linden, moons in his eyes; hoot—an owlish wink, calling my hand, one male to another, his carcass splayed on the buggy table, the quick and the dead in tandem steaming in the shimmer of morning. I opened the buggy door. My wife got in.

# Chapter 10: Walk in the Park

$C$asey's victims included not only good scullers, but runners on the banks of the Charles, Harvard track men usually. She'd race them in her shell, hawklike, predatory. But there was something special about this one—the grace of his movement, the strength of his legs. Different, too, because this one would sprint, almost as if he *knew* he'd been entered into a secret race. For short stretches, he would gain a full length or more on her. She needed a full mile to best him, at her top speed, a little under six minutes. She was almost glad when he crossed the bridge for Boston, perpendicular to the river and directly over her.

She couldn't clearly see his face, but the scarf the man had tied around his left biceps could have been a Googan. It could have been hers. Her heart jumped as the odds jumped that the muscular black man was Waddy's new fighter, Lazarus Godfrey. A week later she ran into the man with the scarf around his arm again, at Shrafts in Back Bay. It was Sunday, and he'd already done five miles. He'd stopped—rather, he *was* stopped, by the display in the window. He was careful not to let his head actually touch it. The sweat would leave an occluding stain, and there'd be hell to pay from the white shopkeeper. It was like a shoe display, the way each rectangular tray faced the viewer in rows of two. Row after row of pastry cream; white, gray, and chocolate blended into a muddy standing wave of sweets. How much pastry could Back Bay eat? Turkish delights. Date shortbreads. Almond nougats. Chocolate pyramids. Caramel rounds. Apple tarts. Rum-baba—what was that? And what were these bright pink confections that looked, precisely, like breasts? How had that motif—ubiquitous—escaped him until now? The chocolate bells? The nippled merengue dyads? He pressed his lips together, tasting the texture—spongelike—they had to be ... *"Lazarus!"* ... jam-saturating the pink... *Lazarus!* ...

Turning, he noticed first her hat—stiff and broad-brimmed, reaching almost to her shoulder. With her head cocked to one side, the pink hat covered most of her face. Along with the high-collared blouse with two buttons free of their loops, the hat with a real rose on the brim suggested *louche*, a word that he didn't have, but the concept was as clear as the premonition of beauty in her chin and mouth, exposed by the tilt of the enormous pink hat—Waddy's color, desperate attempt at possession.

Uncomfortable, exactly, the penetration of her eyes, like Bob Fitzsimmon's renown solar plexus punch. He felt almost paralyzed ... *Lazarus!* ... The sound of his own name came as if from underwater.

"Lazarus." She stood and offered her hand. "Casey Googan, Waddy's wife. We met once, on the Common. I apologize for staring. I didn't recognize you at first. Bad eyes."

She looked away and let him breathe. Mute and feeling awkward, he watched a middle-aged woman at a neighboring table drop a spoonful of sugar into her coffee and sip as if it were cod liver oil, giving him a baleful look.

"Waddy is thrilled with you. He said you break punching bags with your fists."

Looking at his callused knuckles, Laz became even more shy. "Just once."

She realized that she couldn't ask an underdressed black man to sit with her. She picked up her purse and blue parasol with tassels and a tiger-eye handle. "Let's walk."

They strolled diagonally across the Common, turned down the path parallel to Arlington Street, down to Charles Street and back up the other diagonal, past beds of multicolored flowers. He pointed out the tree where her scarf had been caught. He felt uncomfortable with the looks he was getting, though, dressed as he was, he ironically drew less attention than if he'd been duded up. He looked like her gardener. A few white men looked at him—he thought— threateningly, but their attention was divided between him and the woman he was walking with. Worse was the look from the women, directed at her as much as at him.

"I've seen you before, you know."

"Where?" he said, surprised.

"Running on the Charles. You're very fast. You almost outran me. No one outruns me."

"You run?"

"I row."

"You're one of them scullers." He smiled.

"Yes."

They walked a while in silence.

"You know who's enjoying this day most?" She pointed to a gnarled creature, burl, a man of the rag and the bone, under five feet and lost in loose clothing and clutching a cane. His blue eyes looked stretched open. "This could be the last sunny day of his life. He's soaking it in the way I'd like to ... Do you ever have a death wish?"

It took him by surprise. "No."

"You should. Changes your perspective on things." She

smiled. "I could treat you to one."

He was still a bit shocked. "I thought wishes were, you know, you've gotta wish them yourself."

"I guess I mean near-death experiences. You don't have them, in the ring? I mean, the reason you box—it's not at bottom a death wish?"

"Living's hard enough. Don't think too much about dying."

"What about pain?" Almost a whisper. It sounded to Laz like an invitation.

He mockingly recoiled, as if ducking a punch. "Try to avoid it."

Casey deflated a laugh. Eyes downcast, she inhaled audibly, as if to erase her previous question.

"You laughed."

"No, I didn't."

"Yeah, you did. What *about* pain? When you're rowing."

Her eyes sidelong, pensive, she was wondering how much to let him into her personal world, how crazy it might seem. "Pain is ... just something I inhabit."

He now was almost used to being stunned. He smiled. "You're one of them guys that keep coming. You can hit 'em with a lead pipe and they still keep coming." *Bull terrier*—came to his mind. The thought too indecorous. He quickly let it go, let himself inhabit her softness, or try. It was there, he felt. Under wraps, maybe, but it was there— the way a hand could be all knuckles, then fingers could uncurl into an open palm.

They'd passed the carousel before. Well-dressed kids from Beacon Hill with governesses dipping into their purses for a nickel. An unkempt adolescent boy in third-generation hand-me-down trousers shook down a squatting shoeshine-boy for five pennies for a ride, leaving the kid in tears. Laz wondered if, by himself, he would have intervened.

It was an unusual carousel. Steam-operated, with an ungainly wide rubber belt drive. Elegant prancing horses, fantastic frogs, long-maned lions, zebras, and unicorns. She almost failed to notice the elderly woodworker turning to her the unmistakable profile—nose and chops—of Charlie Hot Dog, drill in hand.

Tools were scattered about him—ball-peen hammers, saws, drills, sandpaper in various grades. Casey couldn't stifle a chuckle at Charlie's bending and putting his lips to the new horse's ostensible anus, blowing the shavings and sawdust out before affixing the large, glue-globbed dowel that held a fabulous, wonderfully-detailed, carved and painted tail, as big as Casey's torso. She turned her head toward the pond and tried to concentrate on the ducks, gulls, and pigeons vying for tossed peanuts, while two bony urchins seemed to contemplate the indignity of entering the struggle for dominance in the pond's food chain.

"That's the hot dog guy," said Casey.

"You know Charlie?"

"Can't miss him—those Santa Claus chops."

Casey was lost in thought. What perplexed her more than seeing the hot dog man turned woodworker was the old tool box with its large, engraved capital letters: CODMAN BOATWORKS; how it seemed to be a fitting piece of the wrong puzzle, the hot dog man who set up by the river and watched all the scullers, stopwatch in hand.

"Hey, still here?" Laz queried the entranced woman.

She stopped. "Let's get on."

He pulled at his empty pockets. "Got no money."

She grabbed his arm. "Money's nothing." But he wasn't budging. She looked at his face and smiled. "You're scared."

He looked blankly, then shook his head, staring at the sky.

"Yes, you are. You're afraid of flying horses."

He looked at her seriously. "I don't like horses. I mean, they don't like me. They get spooked, jump, do crazy things. Like they got an allergy to me."

She waved a hand in front of his face. "Wooden. These are wooden."

He took an unwilling step towards the carousel, then stopped and pointed at the horse on the ground, the one Charlie was obviously replacing. It was not just dilapidated. One leg looked charred, like lightning had hit it. It looked like it had taken a detour through hell. "That one probably got a good look at me when we were walking."

She laughed. "You're safe with me. I love horses. I've got my own—Minden Lo. She's an Andalusian. Used to belong to a Hungarian prince." She smiled at him. "I'll ride a horse. And you get a frog." She laughed again.

"Frog? Me?"

Casey heaved a deep sigh, pressed her lips tightly and looked away. "You may turn into a prince. Doesn't take much," she said—he thought—slyly, stepping toward the carousel.

His eyes on the back of her head, Laz earnestly replied, "Not much chance of that."

The man operating the carousel also collected the nickels for the rides. He looked like a moonlighting clown. Red face. Hair in grey clumps. Bulbous nose, eyes the color of mid-winter sky, cheek puffed out with a wad of tobacco. Laz and Casey were not the only interracial couple on the carousel. A light-skinned black man, five or more years older than Laz, was with a very Irish-looking, red-headed young woman. The clown-like operator let go a spate in the path of the other interracial couple, through the gap in his front teeth. Laz had time to consider his reaction if the man were to spit in front of him. Maybe it was the sight of Laz's huge clenched fist that made the man think twice and just let them pass.

Laz gripped the frog's ears, watching the mechanism that drove the fantastic animals in their perpetual circle, a mechanism he could no more divine than construct. And when the ride ended, so soon, his grillwork grin turned sheepish, as Casey understood what he was embarrassed to articulate—*he wants a second ride on the wild menagerie.* She laughed, bought the tickets, and again they were spinning through arcade-space, rising and falling on these stars of junked galaxies; he no longer the terrified kid, fingers frozen to the wooden ears of a frog. This time it was on what he'd told Pearline as a kid what he wanted to be, a *lion.*

Casey was still perplexed by the nameplated toolbox. It was like a nut that wouldn't crack.

"What are you thinking about?"

"Charlie. He times everybody."

"You?"

"Yeah. Well, sometimes he doesn't know who I am."

She noticed, in her peripheral vision, Laz turning to look at her. "I kind of dress like a man. Use a different boat. Nobody really knows me."

The words Laz wanted to articulate got knotted up in his throat. A bed of tulips entered then passed from his field of vision, and a simple thought came to him. "How fast you go?"

She shrugged. "Don't know."

"You could ask Charlie."

"What for?"

Her question surprised him. He thought for a moment. "Know how far you are behind the best time."

"Behind?"

He looked at her. No laugh, no smile. *He* laughed, incredulously.

"I don't row for time. I just don't let anyone beat me," she deadpanned.

It was his turn to be perplexed. She didn't seem to be putting him on, nor did she seem demented. "Nobody?"

Arms folded, eyes to the ground, almost embarrassed at her self-revelation, Casey sighed. Laz didn't quite understand the attitude but he found it funny. She seemed almost sad, as if what she had said could cost a friendship. She expected that all men would share at least part of

Waddy's attitude toward her—freak, *Amazon*, as he sometimes called her.

"Nobody." She looked up with a false smile that was almost paternalistic. "Can we change the subject?"

He felt he had no choice. He also resolved to ask Charlie himself, for the truth.

From his chauffeured Benz, Foxhall Codman squinted, in spite of perfect vision, at what he saw. The beautiful Mrs. Googan and the boxer, strolling. Respectfully separated. But there was something coquettish, he thought, in the way she held or twirled her parasol. He couldn't articulate the feeling, but he could imagine how the incident would play in *Town Topics*.

They walked by the duck pond. "Do you think a person can row herself to death?"

Laz became more uncomfortable, on untrodden terrain. "Never heard of nobody doing that."

She sighed. "So far, it hasn't worked. I just row into another body."

He gave a questioning look.

"I don't know how to explain it. Sort of like if you punched yourself, or got punched, into John L. Sullivan."

"Tom Molineaux—maybe. Not Sullivan. He's white."

"Who's Tom Molineaux?"

"Greatest fighter ever lived. Would have been world champion, but the English crowd jumped into the ring."

"Negro champion?"

Laz nodded.

She recalled her conversation with Waddy, right here on the Common, urging him to make the young man just that.—*Premonition*, she said to herself, reflecting on its root—*monition*—warning.

He found her gestures playful, even boyish—twirling her parasol, then in the shade using it almost like a cane. Downtown ladies didn't. He was becoming more comfortable, in spite of having little to say. She seemed to fill in all the blanks. He started to feel good. This could go on, he thought. They continued walking in silence till it dawned on him to ask a simple question. "Why do you row?"

"Why do you live?" was the tossed off answer, her attention diverted by a beautiful circle of daffodils enclosing a cluster of red flowers she did not know the names of, musing that Waddy would. She laughed. "Waddy only talks about Sullivan—and you. He thinks he's related to Sullivan."

Laz laughed. "Every Irishman thinks he's related to John L. Sullivan or Yankee Sullivan."

She chuckled. "Funny thing is—I am."

Laz stopped, taken aback. "You are?"

"The Caseys and the Sullivans go back to Cork. I'm a third cousin or something." She stopped. "Don't tell Waddy. He'd die of jealousy."

"Does he know about your death wish?"

She looked at the ducks moving serenely across the pond, then at the cattails. 'Bulrushes' came to her mind— the fact that she didn't know what they were, but Waddy would. And from *ducks* her mind again wandered to the reality of snapping turtles. She shook her head. "I think I'm giving you the wrong impression. I'm not a dangerous person. Honest."

She started to reach for his arm, to squeeze it reassuringly. Not to be done, she realized, in public. And she wondered if her two hands could circumfuse his biceps.

"I like your hat."

"In the wind, no way to keep it on," she said, putting a hand on the wide brim.

"I like the color."

"Pink? It's Waddy's color. He's the only man I know who can get away with wearing pink, besides Haliburton."

Laz stopped and laughed heartily at the thought of Waddy in pink. Casey smiled at him. "What's your color?"

He shrugged. "I don't have one."

"Everyone has a color. I think yours is white," she said, looking at his shirt.

Seeing a kid playing with a toy wagon, Laz reminisced, then nodded in the kid's direction. "The only toy I ever had comin' up was like that. My aunt Lily gave it to me. Mom found out and got angry. Don't know why. Maybe cuz she couldn't afford it. Anyway, she took it away."

"That's terrible."

"I found it. Played with it in secret. Used to dig a hole in the floor and bury it, like a dog, to hide it."

"You had earthen floors?"

A short swarthy man in a high black felt hat walked by carrying a wooden sign, latched front and back with leather straps over his shoulders: *Dr. Kerry's Safe Elixir: The Invalid's Friend And Hope.* The man was so short Casey wondered how the sign managed not to impede his walking. He reminded her of a medieval penitent.

"Dirty Dozen, 's where I grew up." He noticed her look of incomprehension. "You never heard of the Dirty Dozen?"

"No."

"Twelve rat holes. So bad the Hunkies and the Irish all moved out. Negroes only ones'd live there."

"I'm sorry."

"We don't live there now. Got wooden floors, like most folks."

It struck her that he didn't say *like everybody*. "What happened to your toy?"

"One day it was gone. Thought maybe I'd misplaced it. Dug up the whole floor, looking for it." He stopped talking.

"And?"

"Nothing. It was gone. Mama must have dug it up."

"That's cruel."

He shrugged. "That's mom."

"Still live with her?"

"Not for long." He felt good, hearing himself say it.

134

The shadows of the Beacon Street townhouses covered the path they'd walked several times. He thought he could actually see the single shadow rising, edging over the grass. A whole block of townhouses. Twelve, maybe. He refused to count. A dozen, roughly. Shadow—just a shadow.

~~~~~~~

Dusk turned to dark. Waddy turned to a crystal decanter and mixed himself his Pick-Me-Up: a jigger of absinthe, two dashes lemon phosphate, and a half jigger of Italian vermouth. He shook it at two o'clock—semi-vigorously, without spilling a drop on his pink silk smoking jacket with gold embroidered dragons snorting red stylized threads. He took a sip before turning to his nightly chore, watering the plants in the greenhouse, where Casey never set foot, making it a safe place to tryst with the maid, Mary. The greenhouse had, by design, approximately the same number of plants and flowers as Mrs. Astor had invitees on the most exclusive guest list in NYC. He could tell you the names of each of the flora, but he wouldn't. He'd profess as much ignorance as the common man, though he could tell a Jupiter's Beard from an Anise Hyssop. He loved the names as much as the colors, though he'd joke that the petunias were Cabots and the geraniums Lowells, situated just behind the Prince of Orange. And here, while he could be monarch of all the aristocratic 400, he chose to abnegate, to relish instead his role as caretaker, common gardener. In a greenhouse no flower knew another's name, and you could simply be what you were. He was Waddy Googan—a man with a watering can.

The Latin names pleased him most. *Verbena* was his favorite, for sound as well as for bordering his floral assemblages. The only Latin term he disliked was *petunioideae*—petunias, a name he associated with a snot-nosed kid. He loved their reddish-crimson, a color that was beyond name, beyond the arrogation of Harvard's crimson, a color that shimmered into a brilliance that resonated when a critical mass was present. He loved the exuberance of the purple-veined petunias that bellowed "*varicose*" so loudly the word lost its ugliness. He also loved the way they overflowed their boxes and fell on the greenhouse floor. It was at once an act of humility and a kind of *noblesse oblige*—laying down one's cape for a lady to walk on, a kind of inner nobility, not the kind conferred. He loved their fierce violet radiance, for which he had his own jargon—"*farouche*," he intoned when he saw them, in effect renaming the petunias.

Along with *the 400* were the herbs and vegetables he cooked with—amaranth, lemon balm, cicely, calendula, hyssop, and fenugreek, along with the ingredients Nemo needed for the healing potion he used on the fighters and bull terriers he attended to—marijuana, yellow dock, gentian root, rhubarb, and wormwood, which he seeped in buttermilk.

Placing the watering can on the shelf, he retired to the study, a delightful place to read, sip an absinthe cocktail, or just to be. He picked up the *Town Topics*, settled into a plush, dark leather chair and read, relieved to find nothing about himself.

Casey arrived shortly and sat in a matching leather chair, with lamps on either side. She opened a large-print version of *La comédie humaine*. Waddy interrupted occasionally with snippets of news, most of which Casey ignored, which did not bother him. The current events of Boston or of the nation were a man's domain, about which he assumed she knew or cared little. In effect, he often talked to himself—himself projected onto another person, his wife. He enjoyed dialoging at times more than chatting with her. And she was content to let him perorate. When she did reply, there was seldom any eye contact. Each carried on as if the other were miles away.

"I had onion rings for dinner," he said.

"Not a felicitous choice," he rejoined himself after a burp and a second of silence. The ostensible reply—crinkle and snap of refolded newspaper. Casey picked at some crackers without taking her eyes from her book.

"Typhoon in Japan."

"Coming our way?" she deadpanned, not moving her eyes.

Waddy was astonished at these *touchés* from his wife. He didn't know how to respond. He disliked being riposted while admiring his wife's wit. At times he would laugh in spite of himself, and cut it off after a single *ha*, mouth agape in a sort of *rictus interruptus*.

The thought of the typhoon made him aware of the cool air deliciously blowing through the windows. After a brief reverie of Mary on a bed of petunias in the greenhouse, he returned to *Town Topics*. "In 1890, one hundred fifteen Negro lynchings."

"Any in Boston?"

"Doesn't say exactly. Eight in the North. Murder, mainly. Then rape, attempted rape, suspicion of rape."

Moments later she added, "Suppose I was black."

He raised his eyebrows and laughed. "That porcelain skin of yours?"

"All it takes is a drop." She closed her book and put it on an antique Chinese end table, Ming Dynasty. "Suppose my great-great-grandmother in Richmond was a slave, raped by the master, and the child was high-yellow. Passed for white, and married white for generations. Would you be able to tell?"

He cocked his head, crossed his legs, and sipped his absinthe cocktail. "I don't suppose I would ... Do you want to proclaim this Negro heritage, or just let it be our secret?"

Casey picked up her book, and Waddy sat, lost in thought for ten minutes, staring at his wife. Then he rose, looked out the window, whistling *By the Light of the Silvery Moon*, and ambled around the room, ruminating, looking at her sculpture collection, virtually everything with a phallus. He put down the newspaper and browsed the table supporting a fraction of her collection of glass flowers and animals. He rubbed his finger across the tusks of a woolly mammoth of untinted glass. He put it down and stroked the slightly chipped table. She brushed past him, to make some hotter tea in the kitchen.

"It's hard to tell, sometimes, where the lacquer ends and the furniture begins," he said. He surprised her with his arm around her midsection. "Can I tell you a secret?"

"Of course."

He squeezed her to where, she thought, passion ends and violence begins. He sensed her apprehension and released her slightly.

"The idea that ... the fantasy of you being a Negress, octoroon or whatever. I mean, I'm so ... so seeped in ... I've boxed with Laz. Did I tell you?"

"No."

Waddy laughed, brushing her neck with his lips, inhaling her scent. "Drew the claret on me, all right. Gave me the nobber. Bled all over the both of us." He squeezed her breasts, then unbuttoned her blouse. "His mother keeps poking around. Brings his sister sometimes."

"Laz has a sister?"

"Stepsister. Not all there. Comely, nonetheless, in a strange way. Buxom for a fifteen-year-old. Let's ... right here."

"On the rug, the Qom?"

Waddy laughed. "All these animals—in the rugs, the tapestries, the statues. We're in a veritable jungle, aren't we?"

His hands, his lips—he had a touch, she had to admit. He looked her suddenly in the face. "You don't have anything African."

She was shocked. "Yes. I can right that."

He turned off the lights and closed the curtain. He fumbled to find her and spoke through a slight laugh,

"You're practically ... the dark itself." He pressed her near-naked flesh to him and kissed her. She kissed him back.

"So are you."

This time she let herself go. It was like what Waddy said of being hooked to the head by Laz—seeing stars, her whole body a nebula.

She dreamt her standard dream. But this time the trireme sailed on calm, sparkling waters. And when she woke she couldn't dress fast enough, to get to the stable, to mount, to ride the roads where he ran, to tell Laz ... what? On the border of Chelsea she reined in Minden Lo, slowed to a trot. She heard the drum beat of the horse's hooves, the message sent by that in itself

—*I can't.*

She turned abruptly and gained on Boston, on Cambridge, the house on Putnam Street, the backyard maze—her sanctuary, her own life ruin enough.

# Chapter 11: Mrs. Jack

*Town Topics*

    *The land of the bean and the cod is now sporting gondola races, or so some would have the ingénue believe. Mrs. Jack (Isabella Stuart Gardner), Boston's first lady of fashion, arts & all things social, as well as champion of young gentlemen artists and writers, is back from Spain, where she attended a bull fight. The bull gored a horse. The people went, 'Ole!' Mrs. Jack went, 'Oy!' and left. In her hotel she had a painful attack of angina that the Spanish press said would have been fatal had not a parade with a giant crucifix been passing by. But given Mrs. Jack's vaunted escapades at home and abroad, we on this side of the ocean can't help but wonder if a spiteful crucifix may have been responsible for the angina in the first place. At home and fully recovered, Mrs. Jack has championed local couturier Waddy Googan, who made her costume ball gown. We can't say just how many fittings Mrs. Jack needed, but the four horses that dragged her Brougham to Googan's Emporium of Fashion are reputed to be in the knacker's lot from exhaustion. The ball was greeted as a great success, especially by Miss Constance Lodge, who left early to attend nocturnal gondola races on the Charles River, viewed from a flat-bottomed barge. We won't say who accompanied Miss Lodge, but she certainly was in fashion and so was her accompanist. Some Boston fathers are known to protect their daughters with a feminine 'Prince Albert.' Others simply warn against Mrs. Jack's parties. We recommend sealing wax for the thighs. If lavender is for condolence, we know what color to use on the seal of our correspondence with a certain Boston patriarch. Any father can make a little mistake. We can only bemoan such a 'fitting' fate.*

*—The Saunterer*

The saunterer was Colonel William d'Alton Mann, a scoundrel of the first water by any man's standards. His scandal sheet, *Town Topics*, in the late years of the nineteenth century, was read by everybody who was anybody or wanted to be. Mann had it in for high society. They snubbed him, he snubbed them, don't get mad get even. Mann was the nemesis of the 400. Most of their servants were on his payroll, for gossip, as well as their livery men and dozens of telegraphers. Revenge seekers, the scorned, the deceived—were even better sources, and they offered their tidbits for free.

Mann operated primarily in New York, but he had men on the beat in Boston and Philadelphia as well. Waddy Googan made more than a few bucks himself from Colonel Mann, with tidbits gleaned from making gowns to disguise pregnancies, some unwanted, some unexpected, some scandalous. Even Pearline Godfrey, Laz's mother, made a few bucks from *Town Topics* when a well-to-do lady sought out the services of the well-respected abortionist that the socialite thought could not be traced back to her milieu. Mann offered the rich a deal. Stories could be canned if the exposed party bought a subscription to *Fads and Fancies of Representative Americans* for a thousand dollars, or two thousand, or more. The vanity book was never published. The rich didn't seem to mind. There was something almost ineffably perverse in the accepted fact that you were nobody if you were not paying Mann's legal blackmail.

Mann was right about Mrs. Jack's devotion to Waddy. A Googan fitting was jazz before the jazz age, a sui generis performance. Waddy was both mesmerized and mesmerizing, a human dynamo—though he would have hated the metaphor. A pin-cushion wizard, he darted around his subject like a spider spinning a cocoon; pins between his lips and in his lapels were withdrawn and inserted with the panache of a gunslinger, the accuracy of Annie Oakley. He'd step back, pause, as if composing a symphonic piece—and in his mind he was. Tension and relaxation were perfectly balanced as he rearranged the angles of the lace here, depressed or elevated the V of the bosom there, readjusted the length of the hem, the position of a rose or a floret. No pause was too long. His hand tripping the air with a harpist's glissando felt, to the breathless fit-tee, like a caress across the breasts, which often enough it was.

"Whew!" ejaculated Mrs. Jack upon her first fitting, and immediately arranged for another the next day. She had Googan gowns and dresses she never wore. What Waddy was selling, unintentionally, was a quality of attention, unparalleled in the fashion world of Boston or New York, that made the subject feel special, a work of art. It left some breathless. Left some shirtless, bloomerless, but always satisfied.

Elizabeth Peabody compared Waddy to the Boston Symphony Orchestra conductor. "He's like Wilhelme Gericke, but with pins in place of a baton,"

When his mouth was not full of pins, he provided the score to his composition, muttering to himself, "More ripeness ... succulence ... the grace, yes, the grace."

"A woman has her own tempo," Waddy averred á propos to Foxhall Codman over an absinthe cocktail. "Vaguely put, the tempo is inversely proportional to the urgency of being clothed." Waddy philosophized as he fitted, and middle-aged women like Mrs. Jack were flattered by his deliberately up-tempo work.

Women's names were entered on a ledger, along with numbers representing bust, waist, and hip measurements and garnished with a musical key and a time signature.

As the fitting came to a close, he would slow, like a fantastic beast rising and falling on a nineteenth-century carousel, and punctuate his movements with bravos, fantastic's, and *formidable*'s—the last a French verbal tickler.

In the end it mattered little if the gown fit well or was well put together, though it almost invariably satisfied both criteria. What mattered was the buzz at the Mayflower Club or the Chilton Club. Through the fog of Turkish cigarette smoke, Mrs. Jack could be heard to say, "I just love Googan. *Semper accelerando*," her hand whirlwinding.

Constance Lodge, who bore Waddy a grudge, disagreed. "I prefer Haliburton. Pianissimo. A glorious economy of grace. Not a wasted movement or motion. I much prefer the giuoco piano of the master to the whirling dervish gambits of Googan."

"Enough with the Italian," Rosemary Frothingham needled Constance. "You'd think Googan was a gondolier instead of a couturier."

Constance blushed at the innuendo linking her to the lothario and to the piece in *Town Topics*. Lady Playfair arbitrated. "Googan is a pagan ritual, Haliburton an ethereal prayerfulness. Suit yourselves."

The day of the fashion opening at Mrs. Jack's house, Laz threw off his gloves before noon. "I've got to go to 152 Beacon Street."

Waddy was taken aback. "The fashion opening? It's women only, except the press and the designers."

Laz smiled. "Bunch of blue blood dames want to see a prize fighter flex his muscles. Gonna pay me five dollars."

Waddy scratched his chin. "Did my wife put you up to this?"

Laz kept his eyes on the floor.

"Did she?"

"Somebody knew somebody who knew Mrs. Googan

knew a fighter."

Waddy looked Laz up and down. "I'll be damned!"

Laz would be a distraction, and Waddy was anxious enough already. His remedy for anxiety as usual was a bottle of whiskey.

~~~~~~~

'Outraging the bourgeoisie' was a large part of what Mrs. Jack was about. It made her chuckle, especially at the scandalous cleavage in the portrait by Sargant. Startling her friends was harder, but for her own fashion event, she took her lion cub and a servant for a stroll on the Common. She was not disappointed to be accosted by a middle-aged man with immense mutton chops getting out of a Bachelor Brougham. She knew it was gossip-king William d'Alton Mann, who had made the trip to Boston just for the opening.

Mann adjusted his Bodier cravat. "Good day to you, Mrs. Gardner."

"Mr. Mann." She smiled though she found the Colonel as grating as the scissors grinders on Arlington Street.

"I love your hat. Such a ferocious violet."

"Apple sauce," she deprecated. Mann was in loud tweed knickerbockers that she resisted commenting on. Passengers on the Station Omnibus on Beacon Street gawked at the lady with the lion, where the three horses of a cocking cart started snuffling in agitation, smelling the cub.

Mann took out a small leather-bound notebook and withdrew a sharpened pencil, eyeing the lion with clear apprehension. "Does he have a name?"

"She. Not yet, but I'm considering 'Maude.'"

Mann scribbled the name. "Charming."

They paid no attention to the weepers—panhandlers—or to the blinkers with their hands out, pretending to be blind. Mrs. Jack watched Mrs. Horace Mann, no relation to the Colonel, arrive in a demi-d'Aument buggy, then a woman in her own Pony Park Drag, a buggy much in vogue with women in the Boston Four-In-Hand Club. Mann noted that her horse was in a pigskin harness with white doeskin reins that bore Googan's **WG** insignia.

"And that?" Mann asked as the woman stepped out of the buggy.

"That is Katherine Rogers."

"Her ancestors came over on the Mayflower, no?"

"Yes. They weren't very strict about immigration then, were they?"

"She's a corking good-looker."

"Yes, but why is she wearing the dome of a mosque on her head?"

Colonel Mann recorded the insults for *Town Topics*. He watched the gay young sparks in sulkies on the Common and a man in a Herdic keeping pace with a woman on a bicycle. Mrs. Jack stopped abruptly, surprised by the tall, well-dressed woman walking in the opposite direction, catching only a glimpse of her face in profile. She felt upstaged. "Who is that ungodly beautiful woman and where did she get that hat?"

"That's Mrs. Wadsworth Googan," said Mann, "so the hat must ..."

"Obviously." Mrs. Jack then recalled having just met the newest Sorosis member. Casey didn't have to take Beacon Street to get to Shrafts, but she did so just to peek at the women arriving at Mrs. Jack's. She didn't like attending Waddy's openings, and he never encouraged her, feeling freer to make passes at the available society ladies.

Mann showed unusual discretion, not mentioning the gossip he'd printed about Mrs. Jack's innumerous fittings at Googan's Emporium of Fashion. "Mrs. Googan's a fine whip, and a dab at sculling," the Colonel asserted.

"So I've heard." Mrs. Jack did not like to be one-upped with gossip in her hometown.

"What I mean is," said the New Yorker, "rumor has it

that Mrs. Googan would, if you'll pardon the expression, beat the pants off of half the men in Boston."

Mrs. Jack, with the uncanny ability to look down her nose at someone slightly taller, turned to the white-bearded New Yorker. "Does your magazine have a column on missing persons?"

"No. Why?"

"By your account, half the Bostonian male population has gone missing. I should like to know where they are."

Forsooth, the Colonel and Mrs. Jack were privy to the same rumors. How the stories of Casey's unusual abilities were passed on, however, depended on the filters of gender and rank. Mrs. Jack heard whispers from her Sorosis sisters. Mann heard third-hand from servants like the Googan's maid Mary.

Mann already had a photographer waiting at the famous house at 152 Beacon. Mrs. Jack drank in the calculated oohs and ahs, directed at her lion cub, at the entrance and kept the audience waiting a half hour as she changed her dress.

Hal Haliburton sidled up to Waddy. "Brooksie says you're using a Negro model."

"Why not? Madame Demorest used Negro girls going back to the end of the war years."

"But this is Boston. It's 1892, and there's a twenty-year lag between acceptability in New York and in Boston."

Waddy grinned. "Not with Mrs. Jack, and she's handing out the prizes."

For Waddy, there was a lot riding on the outcome—the Sporting Club, his house, limbs, and teeth. He desperately needed prizes to keep the fickle *tout*-Boston coming to his shop to pay his *semper accelerando* gambling debts.

Mrs. Jack descended the staircase in the same décolleté that Sargant had painted her in and proceeded to a back room. She had insisted on meeting Laz personally, though she did not shake his hand. She instructed him to strip to his boxing trunks behind a screen that was back-lit with holophane lamps, so that the ladies could see his shadow but not his person.

"The audience wants you to flex your muscles, then jump around the way you do when actually fighting."

"Yes, mam."

Mrs. Jack took a front row seat. Mrs. Monty Sears leaned toward her. "We've already seen muscles, Isabella. You had what's-his-name—Wando—the circus strongman flex behind the screen."

"You mean Sandow."

"Sandow. I think we can dispense with the screen."

"He's black."

"I didn't say dispense with his trunks. His color makes no difference."

Mrs. Jack summoned two servants, who removed the screen. Laz appeared much smaller in vivo, but more shocking. Constance Lodge stood up and stormed out. She looked back from the door. "My father warned me. He said, 'With Mrs. Jack you never know if it's going to be Mozart or muscles.' Not to mention half-naked Negroes."

"*Cocodette*," mumbled Mrs. Jack. The reference to a smug but loose and fashionable woman brought laughs from Mrs. Sears and a few others.

The boxing show lasted only fifteen minutes—ladies only, while the competing couturiers and their models waited in a salon. Some of the ladies were too shocked to clap. Mrs. Jack's favorite refreshments were served—doughnuts and champagne, while she went upstairs to change again, into her most outrageous costume gown, created earlier that year by Drew Lashton, who was known to be on the pipe, as his creation attested. A half-hour later she reentered with, as *Town Topics* reported, a halo-like arrangement on her head—gold wire tipped with diamonds that made her look like a cross between a Burne-Jones and an Aubrey Beardsley. Her gown was Egyptian. She was dressed as a nautch girl, tightly swathed in layers of golden embroidered gauze that covered much of her face except for her eyes, nose, and mouth. A string of enormous pearls hung around her neck. Three of the four competing designers, chatting in a circle, collectively gasped.

"Gad! She looks like Henry James!" said C. E. Quimby.

"It's brilliant—you can't see the wrinkles," quipped Waddy.

John Brooks approached the group, his eyes bulging. "Why is she wrapped up in sheets?"

Haliburton wrinkled his brow and pulled on his goatee as if puzzling for an answer. "Because the pillow case wasn't big enough?"

Waddy rested his hand on Brooks's shoulder. "Imagine going to a costume ball as a nightmare."

Thurlow Bleekman, owner of a department store and master of ceremonies, joined the only male coterie. "My god! She's a mummy!"

"But with diamonds. They say you can't take it with you, but Mrs. Jack did," said Haliburton.

Waddy kissed her hand. "Your gown could be better only if it were diaphanous." He knew how to pull her strings, how wit permitted a multitude of ostensibly outrageous comments. Middle-aged Mrs. Jack smiled.

Haliburton kissed her other hand. "Yes, in fact Waddy just remarked that if he had his way you would be garbed in nothing but pearls, with Rajah here and the Light of India here," Hal referred to her famous enormous diamonds, pointing to his own nipples.

"I've always thought that pearls should adorn one's finest features. Don't you agree, Hal?" She left Hal flustered for a moment. "That's why mine are on my head."

Brooks pushed through to kiss Mrs. Jack's hand. "I'm so glad you could make it. I heard you were ill."

"I was, but I hadn't consented to illness, so it had to go."

Master of ceremonies Bleekman introduced the first

model. "C.E. Quimby's model Daphne is wearing a costume of Nile green faille with court train of rose-pink faille trimmed with green ruchings."

"Why doesn't he simply say Nile scum. 'This is a Nile scum gown.'" Haliburton swished as if wearing the gown. "I know it's tawdry, but I do have a nice asp." The fortunate segment of the audience, with seats near the designer, laughed loudly.

"It is identical to the one Mr. Quimby made for Marchesa Chigi. The bosom is opulent, while not overtly revealing."

"Marchesa Chigi? Sounds like a bedbug," Lashton scoffed.

"Looks like something bedbugs would inhabit," Hal added.

"That's why she's carrying a carpet beater."

"Walking stick. Society women don't beat carpets."

"Yes, but in that thing, maybe they should. Maybe they'd beat themselves for being stupid enough to wear it."

In the end, in spite of the ribbing, Brooks took the Costume Ball Gown prize. Waddy and Hal looked over the shoulder of the *Town Topics* reporter. Haliburton read:

> *The usual gathering of fossils, wild flowers and fawning couturiers... Boston is on its hind legs with excitement at Mrs. Jack's fashion opening."*

Waddy whispered in his other ear. "As is Cambridge." The surprised reporter glanced at Waddy, then at Hal, who whispered, "Boston—the beast—I like that. I see Boston's forelegs hooked over Cambridge's shanks in a paroxysm of excitement. Write that."

Among the Brahmin dames were Lisa Rotch, the wealthy widow, equestrian and cyclist; Mrs. Apthorp, who had a nose ring, and Corinne Putnam, Mrs. Monty Sears, Louise Endicott, Corina Smith—who all had their nipples pierced, a fashionable thing to do in the 1890s. What Mrs.

Jack threatened to do outside her bodice—string pearls on a necklace over diamond nipple studs—a few of these ladies had already done beneath the bodice.

"And now," Bleekman announced, "the bonnet competition." Hal's model Clarissa advanced slowly and carefully across the floor. "Haliburton is famous for his wonderful headdresses, along with forgotten combinations in dress."

Lashton quipped, "They're better off forgotten."

"Headdresses are for Comanches, not Brahmins," Waddy scoffed.

Clarissa's bell-festooned scarlet boots jingled. On her head was a lyre lit up by gas jets. The audience ooh-ed.

"I get it. She thought this was the Costume Ball Gown Category and she's the Boston Fire of '72," Lashton jeered.

Waddy punched him on the arm. "No. With those buttocks, she's more like the Amoskeag pumper."

The lines drew some laughs, but the audience was clearly impressed. These outrageous poufs were nothing new. Marie Antoinette's coiffeur á l'independence featured a boat on her head and her coiffeur au jardinière sported a vegetable garden with carrots, radishes and a head of cabbage. Not to be outdone, the Duchesse de Choiseul wore a three-foot high pouf that replicated a garden with a windmill. Waddy had to produce something extraordinary to top his rival. Triffeny took the floor in a bonnet with fake ivy and real flowers that formed a nest for a real bird, enclosed by thin wire. There were smiles of astonishment all around. The bird chirped happily. It appeared that Waddy might have a winner till Haliburton histrionically covered his face with his hands and blurted, "Oh, my god, the bird is shitting on her head!"

The sparrow appeared to be scratching at something with its feet. Triffeny shuddered while trying to keep her composure.

"Don't spray it on us!" Hal objected, twenty feet from the model. Triffeny hurriedly exited. Momentarily, Mrs.

Jack announced, "The winner is the bonnet without bird feces, the confection of Hal Haliburton."

"Fucking mummy," Waddy mumbled while applauding Hal's triumph.

The last category, announced by Master of Ceremonies Bleekman, was 'Most Outrageous Gown.' Haliburton again clearly stole the show with a confection called 'The Rape of Europa or Terrier-torn Terciopelo.' Everybody knew that Mrs. Jack had paid a fortune for Titian's Rape of Europa. Bleekman read, "Haliburton's model sports a long Zouave jacket with velvet reinforcement at the shoulders, a hood for bright sunshine, and a pair of terciopelo knickerbockers. The jacket, in case of inclement weather, is cut fly front effecting a loose appearance."

"Corresponding to the habits of the wearer," Quimby added.

"She looks like a cross between Little Red Riding Hood and the Grim Reaper," Waddy added.

Anticipating the torn jeans of a century later, Haliburton approached his model with a tethered terrier that tore at the terciopelo. Much of the audience stood in fright and huzzaed. It was outrage to the third degree. Mrs. Jack applauded and handed Hal a check for his prize. His fellow couturiers applauded, de rigeur. As Waddy approached and shook Hal's hand, the terrier ripped off a sleeve of his jacket. He seethed. It was no accident. "Christ, he's swallowed one of my pearl-studded sleeve-links."

Hal soothed and petted the beast that was chewing on a swatch of Waddy's jacket. "Poor Fido. I hope it doesn't make him sick."

"I hope it does! That's a fifty-dollar item."

Indignant, Hal chastised, "The least you could do is give him the rest of your jacket. It's of no use to you now."

Waddy tore off the remnant of the suit jacket, dropped it over the terrier's head, grabbed his portmanteau from a servant at the door, and left without another word. After tipping the whole nine at Mooney's, he went home. A fine rain had just begun to fall on Waddy as he unlatched the finely-worked wrought iron gate of the Putnam Avenue house. Two iron cherubs just over his head swung back with muted trumpets as the gate creaked open. He closed it and stopped to catch his breath half-way up the irregularly high, six stone steps. A little drunk. A little penitent. A little needy. Without looking, he hung his hat on one of the two elephant tusks Casey had installed as a hat rack, the 'something African' Waddy had said was missing. He heard her step. He turned with his portmanteau partially unbuttoned and held his arms out wide to embrace her. She retreated from being enveloped in wet twill, elbows tucked into her navel, a tiny fist over each breast, as if to pummel the advancing beads of water.

"You're all wet."

He hung up his portmanteau, resenting how she always turned her hip in toward him as she hugged.

"How did it go? Did you take any firsts?"

"Haliburton and Brooks did better, even Quimby, to be honest. There was a disaster with the hat." What Waddy did not say was that without prizes in the important categories, women would be flocking to other shops, leaving the sporting man with even less income to pay his debts, but Casey understood the repercussions of losing.

Waddy sniffed. "What's that smell?"

"Desperation. Mary is at her wit's end with the mice. She's put rat poison everywhere. Let's go to the kitchen."

Waddy hesitated at the top of the stairs that lead down to the kitchen. He stretched his fingers across the wide oak handrail, almost paralyzed in thought. He stared at the kettle, his brain feeling mildly coddled. Finally, he descended the stairs and reached for the brandy decanter.

"Mary broke a snifter today. She's been getting careless," said Casey.

Pensive, Waddy held the decanter just short of horizontal several seconds before pouring and replying,

"You know, when I came through the door ten minutes ago, you pushed me off because my coat was wet, but it wasn't the water. You're such a facade. We're such a facade. I knew you would recoil from my wet coat, and I set you up for that. Do you see? I wanted to feel unfairly victimized, so I could silently reproach you. But what I was doing was making you a surrogate, a whipping boy for my rejection at the show today. Do you see? We—not just us but the entire human race—we're such a pathetic charade."

Casey wouldn't argue. "You're overwrought." She kissed his forehead and turned in. Waddy couldn't sleep, his new model Triffeny on his mind. An uncommon lass. What flower would he choose to represent her, with the verbena, at the fringe of The 400? Black-eyed Susan? A virgin, he reflected, turning the many-petaled flower in his mind and plucking. His thoughts alternated between Triffeny and Laz. Sheep were for those devoid of imagination ... She loves me ... Loves me not ...

Hours later, he was able to sleep. He awoke with Casey shaking him.

"Waddy! Wake up!"

"Hm?"

"You were talking to yourself, but you weren't you. It was terrifying."

"Who was I?"

"You were a black man, talking like one."

He could not tell her the dream in which she was standing in the center of the boxing ring while he lay on his back in the ring, naked, with a towel over his head so that his friends could not recognize him. Then how she removed the towel, exposing him, black and naked, then how he was mounted by an Amazon that transformed into some kind of monster out of Hieronymus Bosch, her vagina the beak of a bird/person descending on his loins, swallowing him up.

~~~~~~~

The cool, fragrant morning air came right in past where Casey had lain, and blew up into Waddy's nostrils an explosion of nectar that pulled him out of bed. His head felt like a balloon, and he walked with his toes curled in the carpet to keep the taut string of his body tied down. He put on his monogrammed dressing gown, made of pink terolama—fabric about which Balzac had commented, "felt like wearing the sun." He walked out to the balcony and looked down at the garden where new blue flowers had opened. The garden earth cracked, broke, and rose around the pitchfork planted the previous fall, straddled by a chorus of bluebells. Hysteria in the green.

Casey was still at her toilette. Waddy went down to breakfast. More than the exhilaration of spring, it was the sting of the fashion show fiasco that motivated him to vow that, this afternoon before Casey got back from rowing, he would finally crack her backyard maze. Mary heard Waddy's slow steps on the last flight of stairs to the kitchen. She wiped her floured hands on her apron and shook the apron, remembering the morning when she had spilled flour and Waddy took it out on her buttocks with Casey's riding crop as if she were a rug—how it stung through the several layers and raised welts and how she and Waddy raced around the kitchen trying to keep down the volume of their laughing and crying, and how Waddy waited for the first click of Casey's heavy clogs several flights above to lift her skirts, and the terror in her eyes and Waddy's heavy breathing and his fury to finish before Casey made the final turn in the kitchen basement. "Good morning, Mary."

She turned her broadly smiling face in silhouette to the light just coming in through the ivy encroaching on the small, high kitchen windows. "Some hotcakes, Mr. Googan?"

Waddy's smile turned into a leer. "Indeed. Hotcakes, indeed." He peeled away the layers of cotton over her bosom. He leaned her against the wall and pressed his head between her exposed breasts. He tore down the undergarments of the standing servant, knelt, and kissed the insides of her thighs, then rose and kissed her breasts, again burying his head between them.

"Mrs. Googan is still upstairs?"

"Yes."

"We must be quick."

True, but at the same time, part of Waddy wanted to be caught in delicto flagrante, getting from the servant what he infrequently got from his wife.

"The greenhouse, Mr. Googan, like last Friday."

"This is more exciting."

"I love the bamboo. It reminds me of you."

"It does? How?"

"You're tall, strong."

"What else?"

"I don't know."

"Think," he said, grinding at her.

"Hollow?"

"Hard, Mary. Is it hard?"

"Oh, yes. Very."

"Did you know that you can eat bamboo shoots?"

"I think I hear Mrs. Googan. Could you ... hm ... ah ... could you hurry, Mr. Googan ... please? Oh, yes! Please God!"

~~~~~~~

Looking sadder than a pan, he emerged from the maze around noon, wanting to chop or burn it all down. He blamed his luck, but his spatial orientation was hopeless. Maze 3; Waddy 0.

# Chapter 12: Encounters

*A* week went by and Casey had not seen Laz on any of her early morning workouts on the river. But she knew where he ran—across the lowlands of Chelsea Creek, where John L. Sullivan used to do twelve miles in two hours, running and walking. Laz never walked, and he was down to nearly half of Sullivan's time. His path intersected a trail shared by riders of the Revere Equestrian Society. And Casey, for reasons she did not entirely understand, took to riding there more frequently and rowing less.

Close to the beach was a pine-studded cinder path that passed through a narrow old gate which was never closed. Here, on the first Sunday in May, as he approached the gate, Laz heard a horse behind him and moved to the right side of the path, not looking at the rider till she was directly abreast. Turning, he did a double-take. "Mrs. Googan."

"Casey," she corrected him. "I've been following you for a mile. Checking to see that you don't stop and eat berries."

"Berries ain't out yet. It's too early."

157

Her horse jerked, and she stroked its head. "Now I know. You've got a brisk foot. What's your pace?"

"About ten miles an hour. Depends how far I run." He glanced at her attire. "That's some fancy gear you're wearing."

She sighed. "It's what they make women wear. If I had my way, I'd be wearing twill, like you."

"You race in that?"

She laughed. "I don't race. I do dressage."

"Don't know what that is, but I'd like to see you do it some time."

She turned her head diagonally downward with a meek smile that Laz correctly read as saying that the only way he could attend a Revere Equestrian Society event would be as a groom. Politely, she disparaged the proceedings. "You'd be bored. Just a bunch of girls on horses."

He smiled. "Sounds good to me. What's it like?"

She exhaled dismissively. "Oh, it starts with fancy teams, then a *jeu de barres...*"

"What's that?"

She shrugged. "A game, which," she seemed to apologize, "I win. Then there's the Lilliputian ride by sixteen feminine juveniles, a gallop quadrille, and a grand maneuver by twenty-four ladies. It's all very boring, actually." She was having trouble keeping her horse still.

"Like I told you on the carousel, horses don't like me," he said. "But it's even, 'cause I don't like them either."

"I wish Waddy didn't like them. This bookie is after him all the time. He even comes to the restaurant where I work." Laz smiled, recalling the incident with Moose.

Minden Lo acted up again. Casey whispered to her. Laz backed away slightly, as if that would help calm the mare. "What do you like more, riding or rowing?"

She bit her lip, thinking. "I just like competition. I mean, I like to win." She stared away, a jumble of contemplation, and addressed the blue sky as much as Laz before she became conscious of it. Self-conscious now, she blinked, blushed, and looked directly at him. "But it's ironic, I mean, funny ... Riding, I always get a ribbon or two but I'm never number one, overall. And sculling, I can't lose, but they won't let me race."

"Cuz you're a woman?"

She nodded, looking again at the sky.

"So, you must like riding more."

She contorted a smile into a frown, the gesture itself sufficient metaphor for her feelings. "Riding, when you win, it's not you that wins. It's more the horse." She patted her mare's snout. "Minden Lo keeps her head high. She's always had a high step and a good gait. That impresses the judges. You can put a novice on a great horse and take ribbons. You put a novice in a great boat and chances are she'll sink. Horse—you can't always make it do what you want, but a boat—if you're strong enough and skilled enough, unless it's a scow, you can make it a winner."

Laz's eyes remained focused on Casey's face, while hers wandered as she spoke, from him to Minden Lo to the white oak one might make a boat out of. "Sounds like the boat's more tame, like you like to tame things."

She smiled. "Yeah. My boat is housebroken. My horse is not."

As if to prove her right, Minden Lo jerked her head and took a few steps backward.

"You're right. Minden Lo doesn't seem to like you. This is embarrassing. I should have absolute control over her." Minden Lo pranced a bit, retreating from him.

"It's not your fault. Like I say, horses don't take to me. I got kicked by a horse once. For no reason at all. Almost broke my leg."

She strained to keep the horse still. "This is unbelievable. I've put her through obstacle courses with two live elephants for gates, and she didn't get this jumpy. Must be her heritage. She used to be a race horse. Got too jumpy at the gate, so they made her a dressage horse."

"You never told me exactly what that was."

"Kind of competition." Casey saw a way out of her dilemma. "Say, how about this—it's two miles from here around the stable and back. And it's two miles to the shoe factory and back, in the other direction. You go that way, I go the other, and the first one through the gate wins. I'll ride all the way at your pace, except the last hundred yards, then we sprint."

"How are you going to know my pace?"

"I know your pace, Laz. It's what dressage horses do. But I'll start out a hundred yards with you to make sure."

Laz was dubious, mainly because he hated to lose at anything.

"Come on. They say a fast man can beat a horse at fifty yards."

"You said the sprint is a hundred."

She laughed. "Laz, you're going to cheat, like all men. You'll start your sprint early."

"And women?"

"Cheating? Depends on the circumstances. You sprint from a hundred, and I sprint from fifty."

He smiled. "Well, I could give it a try." Then he looked at the gate—the finish line—and shook his head. "Suppose we come through at the same time?"

"We can fit. Besides, the chances of us coming in dead even after two miles are pretty slim, aren't they? But we don't have to race. I thought it might be fun, even though you don't stand much of a chance..."

"All right. You've got it. What's the stakes?"

"Anything you want."

Laz mulled that over. "Your scarf."

"To what?"

"I don't know. Don't think I've got anything you'd want."

"What's the smallest thing you've got?"

"... Button?"

"All right, a button. Go!"

Casey snapped the reins and Minden Lo broke into a

trot, catching up to Laz and adopting his pace. After a hundred yards, Casey turned her horse in a small circle, keeping almost perfectly the same pace. As Casey predicted, Laz cheated. But to cheat down from a six-minute mile was no small thing. Sprinting from two hundred yards or so felt like a fish-scaler drawn across his lungs each time he inhaled.

Casey, Waddy, Pearline—they blew through his mind but did not hold. What he felt as a dim memory was pure darkness out of which his hands were punching and his feet were kicking—a vague revisitation not of his birth but rather his refusal to die, bundled and discarded by Pearline Godfrey, abortionist and midwife. How he came to be raised by Pearline he never learned. All he knew—from Pearline's friend Lily—was that his birth mother was not Pearline. Now, coming around a bend, he could see the gate, less than a hundred yards ahead, and there was no sign of Casey or the equus. His mind said, 'Push it,' but he had already been sprinting, and there was nothing more to kick in. She saw him and slowed her pace to make the sprint fair—or did she want then to reach the gate at the same time? His feet hitting the cinder path reminded him of Pearline's tapping out the rhythm of her Santeria chants and spells with an oval, hand-sized stone. He recalled bits of a chant she used for someone to win a horse race. Then, as he saw Casey in full sprint with fifty yards to go, he found his own chant—*Beat the sumbitch horse!*

He chanted, feet pounding the trochaic rhythm— *Beat the sumbitch horse!* The pain in his legs pulled toward his lungs at the last small incline; his head already seemed to have lifted off like a balloon. Fifty feet from the gate he could see Casey hunkered down low over the horse's back. Her grin looked demonic, her blue eyes bulged; the only frightened eyes were those of the horse—he could see it—like a fighter who knew he was overmatched; the horse had its fear-filled eyes fixed on a white-shirted, white-trousered figure running at it head-on.

Her silhouette could have been time capsuled and pasted on a scotch bottle, icon for young woman in full riding regalia; maybe a straight-on shot would have been better, two eyes focusing between the sights of the horse's ears on the twin posts of the finish line that was about to be clogged with a two-legged boxer in white pants. Was it accidental that Minden Lo was aimed at Laz, Casey's chin tucked so that the black button on her hard black cap created a strange triangle with the two black horse nostrils at its base? His eyes moved to the perfect flanks of the woman bouncing off the horse's brown flanks. *Jodhpurs*— he didn't know their name, but they reminded him of the canvas bag, Big Paddy, that he pounded daily. The riding crop in her right hand reminded him of what he was beaten with by a sadistic ninth grade teacher until he laid the old man out with a roundhouse right and said goodbye to the schoolhouse forever. The crop came down on the horse's flanks as regularly as its tail would swish away flies in the stable.

"Right!" she yelled. "Right!"

He wasn't listening. His *right* arm *was* already cocked, moving in a short arc by his ribs up to his shoulder. Leaping now, ahead and to his left, out of the path of the horse showing its teeth as its head tilted to the left and almost out of range of the leaping, lunging right hand that landed off-center on the snout and slid up the right side of its head, making the horse rear back, to where there was nowhere for her to go but down off its backside. She hit the ground moments after Laz, who was flat on his face. She bounced on her rump and rolled.

When his head cleared of blur and the dust settled, he saw in his mind an almost photographic image of two sets of teeth, identical, top and bottom lips pulled all the way back—Casey's demonic determined-to-win grin and the terror of a mare choking on a bit and about to be struck by a hard-charging madman. He could see her lips moving now, but he didn't hear anything. The blood beating his temples seemed to echo the chant—*Beat the Sumbitch Horse*! Eventually, the words registered: "What did you punch my horse for?"

She seemed to be laughing in pain, which made him laugh too. "I don't know. I thought it was coming at me. I told you horses don't like me."

"You should have stayed to the right. What in the world possessed you to cross over? I had to rein her in."

"I don't know. I'm sorry. Are you okay?"

"I'm okay, but ..." She shook her head again. He got to his feet, wiped himself off, still breathing deeply. "One thing, though ..."

"What?"

"You didn't rein in that horse."

She stared out at the budding maples and the blooming forsythia. Then she nodded, and finally laughed and looked at him. "You're as crazy as I am."

"What do you mean?"

"You'd die before you lost."

"Guess that means I won."

She walked Minden Lo in a circle, calming her. Then she walked over to him and pulled off her scarf, which he took reluctantly.

"So, I did win."

"No. It was a draw. You owe me a button."

He looked down at the only buttons he had—on his duck trousers. She laughed. "One button. Next Sunday, delivered to my house, at three o'clock." Waddy, she knew, would be at the Franklin Trotting Park.

"I'm sorry," he repeated.

They both turned. Over her shoulder Casey said, "A big, shiny one." She stared at him.

Laz mustered up a small, humble grin to match hers. It would last him all afternoon. Forty minutes later he was back at the Sporting Club. He borrowed Waddy's bicycle and found himself riding through the dump. He rode in a figure-eight, around and around. To avoid a heap of rubble, he had to cut the bottom half of the *eight* longer. The figure looked to him like the thorax and hind quarters of a bee, and not unlike the figure of Mrs. Googan.

Thoughts buzzing.

~~~~~~~

At three on Sunday, Waddy at the races, Laz knocked at the Googans' door and was treated to tea in the backyard. He was curious about the maze, and she showed it to him. It was on the plateau at the top of the slope in the back yard, high enough that from the top floor windows of the house one could not look down to see the secret pattern of hedges. It had been started by Sam Casey, who ran out of money and couldn't finish it. Its expansion was a post-nuptial gift of a man eager to please, for a bride who had to recreate, for reasons she was not conscious of, something from her past, something of her mother, her mother's escape with her Russian exile. The maze that the Count had in Russia—so he claimed—was more elaborate than the one at Versailles. And used more imaginatively.

"The Count called it the—*labirint svidanie*—a trysting maze," Casey explained. "The czar of Russia, Nicholas II, chased Muscovite demimondaines through the maze in summer, collecting discarded garments as they were shed along the true path to the center." With a laugh, she dropped her scarf. Laz picked it up. She felt like skipping—'*gambol*'—she said to herself, noting the *double entendre*, and without another word disappeared into the maze. At the first decision point he found a shoe. Lost at a few other decision points, he retraced his steps, took another path and found a sock. It was as if the more lost he got, the more he found.

The words spoken inside the maze, neither Casey nor Laz recalled. Her only thought was *safe*. In her own back yard, *safe*. The irony of it. The grass at the center bore the imprint of feet. And elbows? Heads? The memory, much of it, was expunged by fear. Along with denial? Dream? What happened, or was imagined, blended into an event that all but vanished. Different versions of it came back at different times. In all versions there was little dialog. What need to talk when she could gaze, unrestrained by time or convention, at his smooth skin and muscular arms. Did she touch them? Slowly graze the forearm with the back of her nail? Circumfuse his biceps, or try?

He vaguely recalled talk of families—the run-away mother and the mistress of black arts, the absence of fathers, one dead, one never known and reputed to be an animal. Speaking was superfluous. Eyes decoded eyes' messages. *Do you remember the maze? What maze?*

He had imagined that the maze would be concentric, but denied himself even that assumption, wanting it to be a total surprise. Couldn't it, he wondered as he collected garments, be heart-shaped, that metaphorical center? It was a perfection of isolation, silence, that circular heart of the thing. So open to a clear blue sky, but closed to the rest of the world. Enchanted knoll. The freedom of childhood, recaptured in Waddy's back yard, independent of time. How long does it take to pop a button? Five seconds, five minutes? It didn't matter. Everything slipped off, or by, so slowly, deliberately, deliciously. Laz thought he remembered the smell of fallen apples. A sort of sweet putrefaction. Apples out of season.

How long did it last? The only reference point for time in the *labirint svidanie* was the blue sky that went a darker blue. He had no watch, just the moon-glazed clouds. It had to be time to leave.

~~~~~~~

The day had not quite dawned. Waddy slept. Laz fingered his new scarf. Fumbling in her pocket for the key to the boathouse, Casey smiled, fingering the button Laz had given her. She felt a need that she couldn't quite express to herself to show Laz her passion—rowing, whatever the risk of gossip, and to break him of his fear of water. Her will to thwart the illicit courtship dissipated like a circle left in the water by an emerging oar. She unlocked the backdoor to the boathouse and struck a match to help her find her way through the high-vaulted interior to the heavy doors opening onto the dock. She had little problem locating the boat. He lifted the stern off its rack and she lifted the bow. They carried it onto the dock. The sculls were kept in racks by the door. In the dark she picked out hers by feel, by the very small but peculiar dents and dings in the grain of the handles she had gripped for thousands of hours.

It was Saturday. Over the Charles, Venus hugged Jupiter, chaperoned by a thin crescent moon. An oddity— the three celestial objects at the dark cerulean horizon forming a triangle that Euclid, no seer of love, called scalene. As the sun wheeled up, they dimmed into nothing but portent. Laz and Casey slipped out onto the Charles in a pair-oared shell. He had never been in such a tippy boat. Feeling it so easily rock as he stepped into it, he was hesitant to move from the dock, and he stuttered out the source of his anxiety. "I can't swim."

"You won't have to. You're with me."

"What are you, my guardian angel?"

"For Pete's sake, Laz, even if we capsize, you just hang on to the shell. It can't sink. Believe me, I tipped more than one when I was learning."

"You're doing wonders for my confidence."

"There was a Negro sculler in Australia, one of the best. You get over your fear of water, and there's no limit to what you could do. Just like horses."

Laz shifted his weight very slightly, side to side, getting a feel for how much leaning leeway he had. "Horses are scared of *me*. Not the other way around."

He had the uncomfortable feeling that, if he tried to get out of the boat, it might tip right there. From the shore, these shells looked stable, the sculls almost like outriggers. The truth was that rowing or even sitting in a shell was like walking on a rail.

He leaned forward and pressed his mouth to her back, blowing hot moist breath through her woolen sweater onto her skin, tasting both her sweat and the undyed wool. Then she drew hard on her right oar, swinging the boat and him with it, on that teeter point of perfect equilibrium, so precarious that he did not even breathe.

Some part of her envied him, living like a Mayfly his whole life in the moment. His stroke now was all jabs and hooks. So ineffectual for swimming, but all he knew. She drew up her knees, rested her forearms over them, then her chin, and waited for him to live up to his name. Flailing, he grabbed onto an oar.

Relieved, she smiled. "You *can* swim. I knew it."

He held onto the stern as she rowed back to the dock. He hoisted himself up, then just stared at her, unsure whether he had fallen from the boat or had been jettisoned. Momentarily, without a word, he surprised her by getting back into the shell. She followed his lead and shoved off. They rowed. When he caught a crab, which he did several times right at the outset, there was the same frightening, sinking feeling of walking a rail and hearing a train whistle behind him. In a way, Casey was right. He had the same balance and coordination in a boat as he did in the ring. A fast learner. When he caught a crab, she would compensate so that the lurch was less. Occasionally, after ten or so good strokes without a hitch, he even enjoyed the calmness, the serenity, the beauty of moving on water in the early morning. Then he would catch a crab or think about being seen by one of Waddy's buddies and the mood would be broken.

When Casey felt that Laz had his rhythm, she pushed him to row a couple of hundred-meter sprints, which taxed muscles he was not used to using, and his respect for scullers soared. This was real endurance. The stress of the concentration needed drained more from him. He was glad to be in the bow, unseen, veins bulging in his forehead as he strained for all he was worth to keep up with the woman and failing at that. When his sculls synchronized and grabbed water at the same depth as hers, the boat seemed to leap forward with several more inches of freeboard.

Laz had no technique. He was a *hammer*. But on effort alone, he and Casey rowed a pretty fast double, a fact that did not go unnoticed by Charlie. On the Cambridge-side river bank the old man smiled, knowing that Casey *and anyone* was a pretty fast double. For a few moments Laz heard nothing. There was not enough blood in his head, or oxygen in his blood. His eyes squeezed shut as if pain were light that could seep in. Death would almost be a relief. Yet, were he offered that mercy, he could not have responded, could not have noticed even Skeets's cannon shot by his ear.

With the sun penetrating the trees at the horizon, leaving a red, burnt trail, she turned toward the boathouse, away from the blood-red eerie water. Laz gulped air, his stomach muscles in a knot. Casey could tell from his grunts when he had reached his limit. She turned slightly and he glanced at her, looking so serene that he did a double-take. She looked like she'd just finished a brisk walk.

"How do you ... ," he paused to catch his breath, "deal with the pain?"

She shrugged. "Like I told you that day on the Common—you inhabit it."

"Inhabit?" His oars dragged while she rowed.

"Like dancing. When you inhabit the music."

"So pain is like dancing?"

"If pain is all there is, it ceases to be pain. It just is."

*Freak. Amazon.* The words sped through his mind. But this was something else. *Spectral?* He didn't have the word. *Otherworldly*—yes. Something from the other side.

*Frisson*—he didn't have that one either. But he felt it. On the dock, he leaned on an oar, head bowed—a still-life backlit by water. The moment, hoarded. Minutes later, the boat was back on the rack. Casey scanned the still dark boathouse. No one was about. Laz could see her smile but not the glimmer in her eyes as she pushed him towards one of the *equipment* rooms and laughed at the man hopping, struggling with his trousers.

Caprice. Passion. Imagination.

Mrs. Googan.

The boxer was overwhelmed.

# Chapter 13: Gone Too Far

*T*erra firma—his element; the ring—his own personal chunk of it. After his near-drowning, Laz was never so glad to be back on his own turf. The Doherty fight and the subsequent Malone rematch were prerequisites for a showdown with the famous Joe Choynski. Outside the Chelsea Sporting Club, organ grinder John Williams set up next to the peanut vendors. His hand organ was mounted on a crutch. In 1892, the Civil War hero was still wearing his faded blue Civil War uniform with sergeant's chevrons. Waddy was one of the few who remembered John Williams, and he always dropped whatever change he had in his pocket into Williams's tin cup, even if it left him penniless. The organ grinder would give a nearly imperceptible nod of the head but always stared straight ahead, lost in the hurdy-gurdy that was to music what his wooden peg was to leg.

Williams was in the war from the start, with McClellan on the Potomac. He was shot at Williamsburg; and at Fredericksburg he lost an arm but refused to leave the army. At Chancellorsville, he was taken prisoner and force-marched to Libby prison. Exchanged for another prisoner, he rejoined Grant at Cold Harbor, where he met Waddy, lost his right leg, and called it quits. Back in Cambridge, the only work for a one-armed man was grinding an organ, which he did every day but the Sabbath for twenty-seven years.

Swipes had had his eye on Williams's tin cup for some time, and contemplated snatching his organ, too. It didn't take Waddy long to figure out what the kid was up to. He put a heavy hand on Swipes' shoulder. "That man only has one arm, but if you make one mistake and he gets ahold of you, he'll crush your spine and turn you into a pretzel."

Waddy let go of Swipes' shoulder. "That's John Williams. He gave his arm and his leg for this country." Waddy took a nickel from his pocket and handed it to Swipes. "Go drop this in his cup."

Swipes had the nickel in his hand and could have run. He could have taken the gamble and grabbed Williams' cup, too. Something didn't let him. He dropped his nickel on half a dozen others: fights were always good for John Williams.

In the locker room before the fight, Nemo rubbed Laz's shoulders. "This guy Doherty is a copy-cat, a counterpuncher. Never leads."

"So, how do I fight him?"

"Like you always do. Put his lights out. Then he can't copy nothing."

The first round was uneventful. When the bell rang, there were hoots and screams for blood, or at least action.

"They're loud tonight," said Laz. "What's happening out there?"

"Hard to tell," said Nemo, waving his hand at the ten-cent cigar smoke. "Big haze. You can't tell the high-hats from the hoi-polloi."

"What's *hoi-polloi*?"

"What everybody is in the shitter."

A good road-runner like Doherty could keep almost

anyone off for a number of rounds, waiting for his opponent to tire. But all it takes is one mistake, or in Knucksey Doherty's case, for the rabbit's foot to fall out of the glove.

Knucksey's trademark was a long left jab to the belly, a safe, defensive punch. And he was a clever fighter; he'd double the jab to the belly with one to the head. He was lighter than Laz, lighter than most heavyweights, but he was tough, sinewy, fast, and well-coordinated. He was 25-4, with the vast majority of his wins by decision, an accumulation of punches landed. He knew how to take advantage of an opponent's size and momentum. When Laz tried to get in close, instead of pushing him off, Knucksey hooked his arm under Laz's, then pulled him forward, off balance, while spinning to his right and throwing left uppercuts to Laz's stomach.

The referee was loathe to break up the only action in the fight, so he let the holding go, and by the time Laz tied up Knucksey's left arm, he had taken a pummeling. Knucksey also made good albeit illegal use of his elbows. He would throw a hook to the head that just grazed by, followed by an elbow, which cut Laz on the temple and did a job on his ear. Still, by the third round it was clear that Knucksey gave away too much in the power department and that he was canvas-bound. The dirty tactics smacked of desperation—until he caught Laz with a shot below the belt that the ref did not see. Knucksey was quick enough to take advantage of the momentary incapacitation. He dropped the hammer on Laz's face, wedging Laz's upper lip between the gap between his front teeth. The bell rang and he stumbled back to his corner.

Hugo, in his ringside seat behind Laz's corner laughed. "Look, he's got a wedgie in his mouth!"

Laz's face was so contorted that if he were on the street people would point and laugh.

"Cut it."

"What? You're already bleeding. You want a gusher?"

Nemo protested.

"Cut it, now. I'll knock him out."

Nemo could barely understand what Laz was saying, but the imperative was clear enough. He lifted Laz's lip with a thin cotton-swabbed stick used to stop nosebleeds and quickly slit the flesh stuck in his teeth with a razor blade. Blood gushed, Nemo wiped, and Laz kept his mouth shut, swallowing blood every five seconds or so. The bell rang and he knew he had to end it fast. Nemo had barely pulled the stool from the ring when he leaped across the ring and landed a shot to Knucksey's ribs.

"Hooray for Old Chocolate!" Hugo looked around. He was the only one standing. "What'samatter? Don't anybody get excited? Stick 'im now, Laz! Stick 'im!"

Hugo's commentary was cut short. Laz feinted a jab to the head, drawing the anticipated counter left to the belly. But Laz simultaneously moved in and to his left, throwing a hook to the head that landed simultaneously with Knucksey's body jab, blunting its power but taking nothing from his own, which derived from the twist of his torso. It was just the tempo Laz needed to get inside and nail him to the body till the slim edifice collapsed. Knucksey got up at the nine-count but held his hands low, his elbows tucked in to protect his body. Laz hooked him to the head and this time he went down for the full ten. And more. He wasn't moving.

"What a dumb-looking smile," said Hugo to Father Divine. "What's he smiling for? I got better dreams than him."

"How do you know?" said Father Divine. "Maybe he's dreaming he won."

Moments later, Knucksey turned his head to the side, away from the cotton soaked with ammonia. Then he rolled over and over, like a dog trying to crush some fleas. Waddy was ecstatic. Knucksey staggered to his feet under the resuscitating power of ammonia and seven hundred pairs of eyes, and stepped through the ropes.

Bill Fitzgerald, his manager, was at the foot of the steps, holding out his hands as if he was waiting for his child to take his first steps. Knucksey held his arms out straight like a sleepwalker. He took one step down and Fitz took the gloved hands in his and backpedaled. Knucksey took another tentative step, as if only the left half of him were coming down, then he shook his head as if Fitz had the wrong partner, still with the dumb smile of a wallflower dreaming she'd been asked to dance. He turned his head slowly, as if to say goodnight to the shiny walnut stool that looked like four legs and a head pounded flat.

"Come on, Knucksey. It's over."

Fitz put an arm around Knucksey's shoulders and waltzed him to the dressing room.

KO — Godfrey.

Just two weeks later Laz was back in the ring with Mountain Malone, for the second time. The first Malone fight had been a brawl. Laz went toe to toe with the big guy and came away with a knockout, but he took some big shots in the process. And Waddy came away with an extended grace period. He still lost as much at the track as he made off Laz.

In the first fight, Stu Steerman sat behind Mountain Malone's corner. Now he was sitting ringside in Godfrey's corner. Waddy was eating peanuts, waiting for the main event and checking out the arena for tarts or slumming suffragette types. In the corner of his eye, he saw two large Negro women. He recognized the one on the left as Laz's mother. Watching the referee check the resilience of the ropes, Waddy avoided eye contact with the women who approached him.

"You know who I am," said Pearline in an almost accusing tone, as if she knew that Waddy had been deliberately avoiding her. He turned, smiled the trademark Googan smile, rose, and doffed his white fedora.

"I think you must be Mrs. Godfrey."

"That man have a wicked smile," said Pearline's

companion Lily, herself smiling.

"Thank you," he said, not knowing quite what to reply.

"But he don't dress like no manager. More like the gentlemen downtown."

"Managing fighters is a sidelight. I'm a fashion designer."

"I thought you was," said Pearline, staring at the **WG** insignia on his tie. "I seen that before." Pearline then fixed Waddy with a stare that nearly made him rock on his heels and convinced him that everything he'd heard about Laz's mother was true.

"I like to think it's ... everywhere," he said, grinning. He felt uncomfortable, and found in Pearline's large, horn-like gold earrings something distracting to comment on. "Those are very interesting. Where did you get them?"

"Oh, I did something for a woman who didn't have no money."

"That skirt is interesting, too. Looks ... I don't know, African."

"You don't think it makes me look fat?"

"No."

Lily laughed, as did Pearline, and Waddy felt more uncomfortable.

"I kind of think it makes me look big in the hips."

"Believe you me, Mrs. Godfrey, the skirt is entirely innocent." Waddy again gave them his trademark grin. Lily and Pearline laughed, as if they caught the sarcasm and it rolled right off them. Waddy was relieved when they walked off without another word to their seats.

Hugo turned to Swelly Bangs. "Who are you picking?"

"Godfrey will take the sponge. The weight of Malone's fist is well-known."

Father Divine scoffed. "You mean *wait* like waitin' for a train? That's how slow he is. Godfrey will kill him."

Hugo bent Father Divine's ear all night, sitting next to him in the good seats. He wasn't back in everyone's good graces, but he'd apologized for his role in the fiasco before

Jack and Flora. And his nose was intact. He had a hell of a scar, but the nearly lost nose had been sewn back on. Now he studied the handbill. "I don't get it. It says Malone is twenty and one, with twenty-one knockouts. How can you win twenty fights and have twenty-one knockouts?"

"Can't be done," Father Divine noted, "but just in case, Laz better watch out for this guy."

Piggy Everett leaned forward. "Yeah, I'd like to know why Stu was taking three to one on Godfrey yesterday, and today it's even money."

All eyes were on Stu, who relit his cigar and checked his watch. "Well, since we got only a minute to fight time, I'll tell you. The first time they fought, Godfrey busted his eardrum with a hook. I didn't know that till this morning."

"I know a fighter who got his eardrum busted and he couldn't walk a straight line. Messes up your balance," said Hugo.

"It healed up. But I told Godfrey, just to see how he'd react."

"And?"

Stu sipped from his flask, reveling in the attention and suspense. "And the kid's a sap. I told him the truth, which is that if he clocks Malone on the ear again, he'll fuck him up permanently. The guy will never be able to walk again. He gave me this smirk, but you could see the compassion behind it." Stu smiled. "And on the other hand, Malone is out to even the score. He's never trained so hard. Lost fifteen pounds. So now, gentleman, we've got an interesting fight. Malone has lost only one fight, to Godfrey, who can't knock him out without a hook. And everybody knows Godfrey's a hooker."

"I knew there was something funny about this fight. Twenty-one knockouts in twenty wins ..."

"Yeah, they threw in an extra one for the eardrum."

"Ha! Ha!"

Malone was undefeated in Ireland, before coming to Boston in 1890. Few knew it, but the pugilist was first called 'Mountain' not because of his size but because it was his mother's maiden name. He was, in Stu's words, a dumb Mick, but tough. And in truth he looked like his mental energy would barely suffice to light up a twenty-watt bulb. The stupidity seemed to well up under his eyes and bury them. Perfect half moon scars on both sides of his face, just under the cheekbones—against which the flesh had split from the impact of hooks. You had a feeling that if a scarred cut were reopened, a solid shot on the back of the head would pop his eye out like dough from a cookie cutter.

His punches were deadly if they connected, but he had trouble with quick boxers. Malone's management was usually successful at getting him matched against slow boxers, but that pool had gone dry. Now there was Godfrey, the other up and coming slugger in the heavyweight division. He could brawl with the likes of Malone, but he could also box. Malone was one of the few white guys left between Godfrey and the *tip-toppers* of the heavyweight division.

## Round one

Laz fought defensively, countering with a jab. He landed little, and Malone landed next to nothing.

"Come on, you sissies, do something. Hit him with something. Hit him with your purse," said the sandy-haired goomba.

"Sissies! Bums!" said the bald goomba.

Nemo turned and said indignantly, "Why don't *you* get in there with *her?*"

"I would, but I left my purse at home."

"Ha! Ha!" The bald guy laughed at Nemo. "He's pissed 'cause that's *his* sister in there."

"Yeah, and his sister's a nigger. Ha! Ha!"

Waddy ignored the banter and the slow fight-action. Pearline attracted his attention with her capacious ass hanging half off the chair and listing to starboard. He couldn't understand why she did not keel over. So defiant of the laws of nature was Pearline's act of sitting that Waddy could hardly watch the fight. Her ass-overhang looked like stuffing coming out of a mattress. When the inevitable occurred, he felt a sense of relief that the laws of gravity and physics were intact.

"Hey, look! The old lady keeled over."

"Are you okay?" Waddy asked.

"She's fine," said Lily. "She just needs something to eat. Got low blood sugar. Ain't that right, Pearline?"

"Shut up and help me up. And somebody get me a hot dog."

"Give her another beer," said the man behind her.

Those compendious buttocks, if properly centered with equal portions of flesh overhanging both sides, would make her the ace of hydrant-sitters—thought Waddy, recalling the fire of 1872. Madame Pearline Gibraltar.

## Round two

"What are you waiting for?" said Nemo. "This guy is as slow as a hay wagon."

Still Laz was tentative. What Stu said about Malone's ear had got to him. He was reluctant to punch. In the seats right behind Waddy, the two goombas kept up their steady hectoring and heckling.

"Head! Head!"

"Ribs!" exhorted gray-haired Giacomo Barbagelata.

"Sic 'im! Ah, missed that time. Sic 'im again."

"Shaddap! What is he, a dog?" said Waddy.

"Stick 'im!"

Giacomo spat. "Hey, is it true that Godfrey broke a guy's ribs last week and couldn't get no one to spar with him except his mama, and she put a beating on him?"

Nemo turned and snarled. The first assertion was true, but he did not know how word had got out.

"Wouldn't want to cross her. I'd rather cross her kid. Fucking birds drop dead in front of the old witch, what I hear."

Sandy-haired Sergio Buttazzo was distracted by one of the prostitutes working the balcony. "Hey, dollar-fifty, baby, sit on my face!"

"Go fall in a hole!"

As round two wound down, Laz butchered Malone's scarred face with jabs. Malone's head popped back like it was on a spring. One eye was nearly swollen shut, but Laz hadn't thrown one hook.

## Round three

Malone came out flat-footed, both hands held way out in front. If he turned his head sideways you could put a bat in his hands. The style was effective at picking off a frontal attack, but it left him vulnerable to a hook to the head, a punch he knew Godfrey wouldn't throw.

Malone weaved and threw punches from his batting stance like he was shoveling snow. But Laz got careless and got stung with a right uppercut to the stomach that nearly lifted him off his feet. It took him thirty seconds to recuperate, but when he did, that sense of being coiled up and needing to spring out had come back. He let loose a barrage of straight lefts and rights to Malone's head, mixed with hooks to the body, so that the fat man would drop his hands. The butcher now. At work. A white carcass flecked with red. Punches picking gristle off the tendered ribs. A body that, every time it breathed, lifted the ribs and their black and blue trellis of hemorrhaged veins.

Malone never got off another of his homerun shots. He would dream it, stretched out in his own corner, looking like he had been stung to unconsciousness, red welts all over his arms, chest and head. They had to carry him out, which was not easy, with a three-hundred pound guy.

Nemo lit his stogie. "I'm gettin' a Rican tonight, after the last fight. Y'interested?"

"Where ya getting her, the Providence?"

"Whadaya mean? It's a new sandwich they got at White's."

"You mean a Reuben."

"Yeah. Wanna get one?"

Waddy shook his head.

"Want a peanut?"

Waddy held out his palm and Nemo dropped a few peanuts into it, till he signaled *stop*.

"I don't know what the world is coming to. I bought these from the guy out front, you know? And the kid in front of me said to the guy, 'They ain't poisoned, are they?' What kind of talk is that from a little kid? If you can't trust the peanut man, who is there?"

"You finished?" said Waddy. "I've got a thirst I wouldn't trade a fiver for."

"So, I give the guy a penny and he gives me this bag with only a fistful of peanuts, and every one of them is rotten. They've got this fuzz on 'em. So I try to get my money back and he says, 'Fuck you, pal.' I've been buying peanuts from this guy for years. How do you like that? The kid was right. You can't trust nobody these days. Nobody will give you an honest break."

Waddy slapped Nemo on the shoulder and smiled. He cracked open a goober and meticulously slid the paper shirt off. "As far as I'm concerned, nothing's changed. It's always been like that. You just never had your eyes open."

"I've just never been fucked by the peanut man."

Waddy had trouble getting the next peanut out of its shell, and he spoke gnomically, "My wife's like that."

"Like what?"

Waddy hesitated, then said, "Never been fucked by the peanut man."

In the locker room Nemo congratulated Laz. "You know who was out there tonight? ... The Boston

Strongboy himself. He said he could have taken you out in one round."

Laz laughed. "He ain't changed. Sonofabitch's been duckin' my cousin George for years, on account of his color."

A small tunnel of darkness before the locker room door. Casey, again in men's garb, took a deep breath, stiff-armed it open and breezed through it. She was surprised at the door's lack of creak and by the bent and apparently headless black man with his back to her. Now his scrunched-down head rose, the many beads of sweat sparkling. She knew this was crazy and akin to a death wish, but the thrill of the risk was irresistible, congratulating him in his element. Her eyes focused on the maze of muscles on Laz's back dripping with sweat. The two long stiff cords along his spinal column bulged as he raised his head and shoulders and tossed a shoe aside. He saw in the cracked mirror to his left Waddy's movement, and he turned, grinning, catching an unexpected eyeful of the androgynous figure with a brown woolen cap down almost over her eyes. Hearing Waddy's voice, she stiffened. She turned with a baleful stare at the door she propelled herself out of, avoiding eye contact with the interloping manager. Laz dropped the grin—meant for Waddy, then his shorts and protective gear, and walked naked to the non-functioning shower where Swipes was waiting with two pails of heated water, leaving Waddy alone, halfway between the fighter and the absent intruder.

"What the hell is going on?" he asked, torn between marveling at Laz's naked body and staring at the door. In the room lit by two gas lamps he was not sure who it was that bore a resemblance to his wife. A hallucination, maybe. A male look-alike, maybe. Laz with his back to him gave nothing away. For days, Waddy pushed the question around like a soggy biscuit after a slippery quahog in his mental stew. Too vast for him to get his mind around. For the moment, with Patti the Cantatrice waiting for him outside the door, there was no choice but to let it remain an enigma.

~~~~~~~

*Gone too far,* she said to herself—from *amour fou* to pure folly. She saw herself in Madame Bovary, in Anna Karenina, Hester Prynne. Yet, there was not even the solace of fiction: there was no woman who did not come to a bad end, who did not destroy herself or someone else in the pursuit of her passion.

—*I can't,* she said in the evening, imagining a perfectly desultory encounter with Laz that always ended up sounding like Tolstoy. She rode where he ran, and when she spotted him, she bore down on him, let the sound of the close hooves scare him into turning to see her.

"Hi. I've got something to say to you. Can you stop?"

He slowed to a walk, breathing heavily, hands on his hips, then wiping sweat from his forehead with his forearm. He tried with little success to calm Minden Lo. Before she could speak, he did. "That was you, in the locker room. You know what would happen ... Down South, a white man rapes a Negro girl, he gets a twenty-dollar fine. Black man and a white girl, they lynch him. This is Boston, but you're married, and the sonofabitch has friends. All kinds of friends. Some of 'em ain't good."

She groped for words, to delineate the boundaries of what had to be their relationship, but Laz didn't want to hear it or even think about it. She just stared at him, then, lips turning to frown, looked down, turned her horse and trotted away. Laz let his eyes sweep over her one last time, just another part of the marshland background.

# Chapter 14: A Race

*T*omorrow would be the first regatta of the season on the Charles, and Foxhall Codman was on the river at sunset, maneuvering his shell to where he could catch the sun going down over the river. He felt strong. Felt that no one was going to beat the King of the Charles. And he felt lucky, as usual. Ineluctably lucky.

Casey was standing at the counter of the Holly Tree, trying to think of a way to get free of her job, not just to watch the regatta but to row—her secret race. Her glasses felt suddenly heavier. She removed them to relieve the pressure on her nose. She rubbed the permanent indentations pocking both sides and put the glasses back on. Outside, the trees were as full as they would get, their color still that virginal new green. The last of the azaleas bloomed. The dogwoods were out, pink and white. Some rhododendron purpled the riverbank.

She had been on her feet since the restaurant opened at eight. It was now twelve, and her feet throbbed. She felt like standing on her hands, which she could do, to let the blood flow back. She fantasized it—her apron falling,

followed by the white uniform and slip, layer by quick
layer, till her white legs and cotton-panoplied, **WG**
insignia-ed undermost garment filled the hearts and minds
of the toast-crunchers, the tea-slurpers, as their mouths
dropped open. The dried, caked egg yolk at the corners of
their mouths would crack and fall as she turned one
hundred and eighty degrees and scissors-kicked, toes
pointing gracefully to the tin-plated ceiling, then hop—
show's over, pass those dirty cups with the black greased
fingerprints on the insides of the holes of the handles,
please.

But this was not Scollay Square and she was not Fanny
LaFlamme. She was Mrs. Waddy Googan. Her heart did a
quick one-two beat as she stepped out of the dream onto
the safety of sawdust and salt that diminished the danger
of slipping on the grease and whatnot on the floor.

Keep up the good work. Refill cups. Coffee; shit:
happiness; big tip. May the cycle remain unbroken.

At the counter these louts tended to become
gentlemen. They were suddenly *over easy*. They spoke softly,
almost as if they were in church. There were exceptions,
but most of the men behaved as if they feared having their
hands slapped if anyone complained about them gripping
their forks overhand with two inches of fork showing out
the back end of their fists, or if they belched too loudly.
She felt at times like laughing at them. The men of Casey's
fantasies, the men of the stage, were not men to be
snickered at. But there was not a smart-looking Jack
amongst these who might tear open her uniform and cup
her warm breasts in yet hotter hands. Instead, there were
men like Will, who wrote songs for Tin Pan Alley as well
as operas, who would sit on a corner stool with reams of
paper filled with octave bars, which he would fill with
circles and other do-dads. Will once asked Casey if he
could give one of his opera characters her name. She said
yes, and the budding Mozart shook his head in spasmodic
happy jerks, like a puppy trying to shake off water. Were

there any white Godfreys on a fast stallion who could whisk her away, to somewhere there was flat water?

*Did other women fantasize as much?* she asked herself. Was a cruller just a cruller? Did they ever see in the way coffee brewed and found its way hot up the glass level tube a slow steady tumescence? She slapped herself mentally into the reality of sugar-coated fingers, which she licked, while cups and saucers rattled in the sink and mouths opened and closed with the humility born of a hole. Munchings remained private affairs, eructations muffled, slurpings modulated by the lukewarmness of the coffee.

A sallow-faced woman from another century sat down, an aged Follies-Bergère diva with grey and white hair that curled up on top like a pig's tail, reminding Casey of the diva Patti, with whom everyone knew Waddy was running around. Her companion, a corpulent arriviste ordered them donuts and coffee with cream. He read his paper without a word to the diva, who reciprocated his silence. They dunked their separate donuts, softening them up for the old gums. After twenty minutes they were gone, without a word spoken save the ordering, their empty cups close but not touching, the spoons in them erect and touching.

Codman's asshole-buddy Deke Merriwell pushed through the screen door and was taken by Casey's gaze—pale, distraught, and transfixed by the empty table. He waved his hand in a long arc to get her attention. She brought him coffee and stared at his two chins, waiting for him to stuff his stogie into the crease above the wrong chin. This was at least more exciting than watching flies get stuck in the jelly on the counter. Casey disliked him. The lapsed aristocrat saw through the aspiring one. She watched the parvenu hawker into a hanky and laughed. The true aristocrat, like Foxhall Codman, would create the appearance of wearing a cape from a starched short-sleeve shirt. He would push coins to the waitress like a cat's paw on a votive mouse. He would have a nose that cut his face with a sense of eminent domain, and hewn stone features of incongruous cut and slant from Cretaceous inbreeding. His tippled discourse would be almost symphonic, full of cataclysmic *nays* and explosive disparagements. None of which was Deke Merriwell.

Hugo Bartolini stunk so bad of grease and oil that Casey said, "Hello, Hugo," without turning to see him enter. Hugo thought at first that this was a pretty quaint trick, but when the mental processes got greased and moving he resented it.

"Dark," said Hugo, "and a jelly donut."

Casey's eyes widened, watching him chow down on the donut.

"Jaysus, Hugo," she said, "you start with a white donut and by the time you're half done with it, it's chocolate. Why don't you wash your hands?"

Even Hugo's lips looked blackened. He wiped them with a napkin, genteelly turned it inside out and wiped again, wet his lips with his tongue and wiped them till they were a dull pinkish grey.

Waddy walked in and sat on the stool next to Father Divine. He seldom came by the Holly Tree when Casey was working, but he knew the pickle she was in today. He wanted to savor the irony of competing freedoms. Freedom to work. Freedom to row. He knew how much she wanted to *see* the regatta, but he did not know she planned to *row*.

"Hey, guess who's in the hospital?" said Hugo.

"Who?"

"Charlie Hot Dog."

"Charlie's seventy-two. What are you going to do?" said Waddy.

"Too many hot dogs," said Father Divine.

"How's he doing?" said Casey, returning with a donut for Hugo.

"He's got a tube down his throat and another up the ass. Hell, he might as well get out of the way—connect the tubes and leave himself rest in peace," said Father Divine.

"How does he eat?" asked Hugo.

"He don't have to. They shoot blood up his veins—like an automobile—human lube job. Poor guy will probably never eat again."

Hugo lamented, "It's a shame. He was a very talented man."

Waddy thought this was boorish sarcasm. From his silence Hugo sensed the misinterpretation. "He was a very talented man. I don't mean hot dogs. He worked with my old man."

The mention of Hugo's old man, the anarchist Americo Bartolini, drew some muffled laughter. Americo also had worked for Codman Boatworks, founded by Foxhall Codman senior, now deceased. Americo would sit on his front porch and rail at capitalism in general and the Boatworks in specific. "*Theerty, forteen* year I work in that forkin' place," he would say, rhyming *work* with *fork*. The line became famous in Cambridgeport.

"Charlie worked with my old man. He was one of the best," said Hugo. "Then he messed up his hand in a machine and got arthritis. He could hardly use a hammer, so they fired him. I swear to God. You can ask Americo."

"What kind of boats?" said Waddy.

"He specialized in rowing shells. Singles, pair-oared, eights, everything. You can still see some of his boats on the river. Most Codman Boatworks shells—ten, fifteen years old—chances are Charlie built 'em."

Casey felt a mild shiver, having seen Charlie with his tools.

"It makes sense. He's always out there with a stopwatch. And he never misses a regatta, except this one, poor sonofabitch." Hugo looked up to be sure that Casey was not standing there as he cursed.

Waddy left for the race and an assignation with Patti the Cantatrice. He felt a silver dollar roll across the quarter in his pocket, the only money he had. All the big bookmakers—Hacket & Delacy, Lovell, Johnson, Steerman—had elevated stands that looked like sentry posts. There was a station every fifty meters along the bank. Waddy stopped at Lovell's. "What are the odds?"

"Jumpier than a terrier in a rat pit, but you can have the underdog at two to one."

Lovell took Waddy's marker for a hundred bucks on the challenger, O'Sullivan. Those odds had been three to two the day before. But rumors that O'Sullivan's boat had been sabotaged the night before turned out to be true. He had a light, fast paper boat. Many racers favored paper because of their weight. They were constructed of shellacked paper in layers pressed around a mold, then varnished. Their problem was fragility. As O'Sullivan was bringing his boat into the boathouse the evening before the race, he was rammed by a skiff, completely crushing the shell. He suspected Codman, but later was convinced that the culprits were hired by a Boston bookie who was giving long odds against the kid. Reverting to a wooden boat after training with a paper boat would be tough, but O'Sullivan couldn't deal with the ignominy of dropping out. He wouldn't leave twenty thousand spectators, who'd come from all over New England, New York, and New Jersey, high and dry. He decided to race, to whip the old man.

After the other bookmakers found out about O'Sullivan's boat, odds went to three to one on the champion. The odds even went back to two to one after Stu Steerman propagated a rumor that Codman not only was suffering from ague but had badly blistered his ass, which had become infected with the dye in his worsted trousers.

Steerman was the race's promoter. He put up the five thousand dollar purse himself, winner take all. In return, he retained rights to all advertising at the race site. He had his own hot air balloon at Magazine Beach, emblazoned with *Dr. Kerry's Safe Elixir*. A spur of the Commonwealth

Avenue trolley shot out to Alston, close to the river bank, and it too was covered with *Dr. Kerry Elixir* ads. The start-and-finish line was plastered with more advertising. Steeerman exacted five per cent from excursion boat operators and sightseeing boats, from the grandstand builders, local hotels and boarding houses, and from all games, straight and skin, operated on or near the race. Even the thimble-riggers and the catch-penny operators paid their five per cent, enforced by Steerman's gang of henchmen.

Approaching the boathouse Cambridge-side, Waddy passed a bearded lady, some jugglers, a pony ride for kids, and a Brahmin woman with a cambric ruffle walking a Havanese with luxating patellas and bad eyes. *As inbred as its mistress*, Waddy said to himself, fighting the impulse to give them both a hop in their well-groomed asses.

Back at the Holly Tree, Swipes stole a donut and ran. A block away he eased up. No one was chasing him. He leaned against a fence and devoured the donut, licking the sugar from his fingers and from his dirty sleeves. Then he continued running toward the river, sneaking up through the thick lilac bushes in bloom against the east side of the Riverside boathouse and peeking through the window to the *famous* back room where Cambridge sporting men trysted with their paramours.

He hit a rich seam. Waddy Googan himself was sporting with Patti the Cantatrice, whose cheeks were bright red and whose head hung over the side of the bed as Waddy kissed her neck before reciting his part of the litany that he had taught her.

—Do it!

—Do it to me!

Waddy's light opera came to a crescendo and ended with a shriek as Patti, head hanging over the edge of the bed, noticed the upside-down grinning face of the boy who disappeared as she blinked and looked again. Waddy gave Patti a peck on the cheek and rose from the bed feeling emptier than before, wanting only to lie back in the sun on the river bank. He looked at himself in the mirror that was so dusty he could not see his features clearly. But his normally impeccably groomed reddish hair was clumped in spikes that found their own configuration, and he ran his fingers through it.

"Lose you comb?" said Patti, brushing her own hair.

"Yes," he intoned. Looking for his comb, he noticed behind the bed a condom he had used some time ago with Patti. He brushed some of the dust off the old condom and thought with melancholy of Patti's legs kicking in accompaniment to her insistence on immediacy as he fumbled about, trying in the darkness to ken the direction of unrolling the condom, then dropping it on the floor covered with dust, ashes, cigarette butts and whatnot. He'd retrieved it and plunged ahead, driving home the adhering ashes and dust; a half hour later, uncoupling and leaving— like an Anchorite—everything behind. It was hers to reckon with it. Until this moment he did not know the fate of the dispossessed condom. From the dust cache he retrieved the two-bits worth of insurance he had purchased from Mitch the iceman. The mystery was solved, not that he had lost any sleep over it. Still, it surprised him that she had just tossed it over her shoulder. *He* would have treated the object with more respect, would have wrapped it like a dropped communion wafer in tissue and deposited it in the trash.

"Tony, Tony, look around. Something's lost and must be found."

"What?"

"Your comb."

"Who's Tony?"

"St. Anthony."

"He's got it?"

They dressed. Waddy was impeccable in a white suit, black spats and white shoes. His hair, with the aid of the newly-found comb, was perfectly parted. The grayish-red hairs over the graze on his cheek, remnant of Gettysburg, ran with the current of his beard.

Patti took his arm. "What about that ermine coat you promised me months ago."

"I'll make it. Just a little pressed right now."

"If I were Mrs. Googan, I could wait."

"There already is a Mrs. Googan."

"I figure I've got ten years before my looks are gone."

"You'll still have your voice."

"You'll still have an impossible wife."

"It's not that I don't love you."

"With you it's not love that's the problem. You just don't *like* women."

Waddy erupted. "You're right. I don't like women; I love women. I'm devoted to women. I make their clothes, for god's sake. You know who doesn't like women? Charles Worth. For two decades he's been torturing women with bustles. He's made a caricature of them. Rumps sticking out, looking like a horse attacked by drapery. I've been in the vanguard of liberating women from their bustles, and we've damn near eradicated the thing. Sorosis should make me their patron saint."

"You're talking about women's bodies, not women. You work with their bodies. You love their bodies."

Waddy raised his hand in a stop sign. "I'm not listening to any more of this rubbish." He felt a pain in his stomach and stared at the mirror, as pensive as Patti. They each inhabited their own little planets. Waddy weighed the evidence against him. Indeed, he did not like the pastes and the rouges women applied to their skin. He did not like their menstruation. He did not like their chatter or their intolerance of sitting quietly and introspecting without intercourse. He did not like their bad piano playing and their forcing it on everyone, or the way they ate little in public but gorged themselves when no one was around. He did not like their aping men in athletic competitions, and he found odious the sight of a woman with a drink in one hand and a cigarette in the other. He didn't understand how they could have such little insight and self-awareness, couldn't see that they were making themselves in the image of men. They might as well have strapped a phallus on the front side to go with the bustle strapped on the rear. That was the extent of the evidence against him. The indictment just didn't add up. If he were to think of the things he disliked about males, the list would be much longer. And no one ever accused the gregarious Waddy Googan of misanthropy.

"We'd better go. The race will be starting," Patti said after the long pause, as if Waddy's words had traveled miles to get to her.

The strong scent of the lilacs, which Waddy could not stand, reminded him of Casey, who put them everywhere. They passed a huddle of Brahmins—Brink Thorne, Todd Farrel, Cosmo Croninshield, and Deke Merriwell, the inner circle of Codman's entourage, swilling champagne in anticipation of Foxy's victory. Waddy overheard Todd say, "Did you hear the Monday Evening Club is closing its doors? Declining membership."

"Foxy told me a month ago. Sort of an old hat club anyway. Besides, no one really wants to dine out on Monday all that much," Deke observed.

The linen suit seemed to wrinkle on Waddy's sagging shoulders. He wondered if the tidbit was *meant* for him, if word was out that he'd been put up for membership in a club that was demising. As galled as embarrassed, Waddy picked from a bag of grapes Patti offered. He found them bitter, which made him take another and another, with the optimistic faith that eventually a sweet one would pop into his mouth and erase the taste of the bitter ones. Patti was amazed at the rate of Waddy's devouring the barely ripe grapes. Waddy too was perplexed at his rabid ingestion of bitterness. He excused himself to use the boathouse bathroom. Back at the old sycamore, Patti's fingers found a groove, a scar in the ragged bark. She traced a heart's irregular edges and the shaft of the arrow to the initials: **WG & RC**. And she jumped as she was touched on the shoulder by the quondam sycamore scrivener himself, whose face looked as if the weather inside his head had taken a turn for the worse. The barometer was falling, and his cranium was caving in. The ballast in his tummy rolled uneasily. His eyes luffed in their sockets. Not a well man, and the grape bag he gripped as if with rigor mortis was nearly finished.

"Jaysus," he said, and sat on the ground.

Waddy looked like a man who had gone through three of the four stages of a fever in five minutes. His face and neck were sweating. His head fell back, watching the few strands of West-bound cirrus in the blue sky.

"Can I get you something?" said Patti.

"Get them to delay the race. Tell them ... tell them my horse ain't saddled," he joked.

In The Holly Tree, Casey's eyes followed her arm into an oblivion of cleansing circles on the counter in front of Hugo, who wanted another donut but could not afford it.

As she walked to the sink, Hugo said to Father Divine, "You know what I'd like to be? A fly. Get a free meal anywhere. When I'm rich I'm gonna get rid of the fucking kerosene stove. I can't even get it up when I smell the stuff. Even when you stop using it, it smells. I can't even get laid till June."

"Count your blessings, Hugo," said Father Divine loudly enough for Casey to hear. "You could have a wife like Googan's—frigid."

A train rumbled by. Flat cars. Tanker cars. Cars with logos of places as exotic as Florida and Baltimore. Hugo and Father Divine watched Casey, who listened to Will's piano playing upstairs and fantasized about Laz Godfrey while the refrigerator rattled and rumbled like a miniature freight car going nowhere. At night these trains played an encore in her ears as she lay on the flat car of her bed. But the reverie had to end. There were tables to be wiped, grease stains on the glass display window to be removed. She picked up a newspaper, letting the confectioner's sugar and crumbs slide into an ashtray. Her eyes focused on an article about a derailed train. She tore off her apron and ordered the three remaining patrons out. She switched off the fan and the lights. The gents left with no argument. The race was soon to begin.

~~~~~~~

The figure in brown wool—pants, sweater, and cap—that emerged from the Putnam Street house was completely androgynous. Tall for a woman but with a girlish gait. Shoulders of a thin young man, but with a bit of pale, smooth skin between the sloping cut of the sweater and the capacious woolen cap.

Ozone lingered in the high-pressured air. The few twists of cirrus seemed unlikely to band together. The breeze was redolent and constantly shifting from seaward to landward, bringing different smells at each turn. Seeing the crowd on the river bank, Casey felt her heart settle like a champagne cork several notches higher in her throat. Foxhall Codman emerged from the boathouse carrying his sculls like standards, their orange tips vertical to the ground and grazing the sky. The pageant had begun. Resentment for the Brahmin curdled in Waddy's stomach. Betrayal mixed with shame at his lack of pedigree. All his monograms, even his Harvard diploma, could not give *it* to him. *It* was something that Foxhall Codman oozed and that Casey flashed. They carried themselves with a kind of arrogance and self-assurance that Waddy could never understand. Even when Codman lost a bet—a rare occurrence—it was as if there were some fluke in the preordained cog of things—God was napping.

*It* was *just there*, like they were born with *it*. And *it* was one reason why Waddy was so attracted to Casey—his lapsed aristocrat, why he put up with her defiance. He felt privileged to have *it* under his microscope so he could study it. It bewildered him when, while they were courting, he would do something spontaneously nice, some gesture of generosity or kindness that was simple and natural to him, and Casey would respond, with an air of cosmic astonishment, "You're such a good man." She would say this not directly to him with any eye contact, but directed almost at the heavens, as if she were making some kind of pronouncement that should be recorded by someone. There was a lack of personal connection, a kind of objectivity through which she seemed to observe him—the common man, some sort of specimen. Which was why he had to have her. In bed she would get off that pedestal and enthrone him. He would see those sharp eyes go opaque as a dead fish's, cerebral cortex flooded with seminal input. It was why, too, he had to have her in every room in the large house, except the greenhouse. Even in the bathroom. *Hoi-polloi*—Nemo had said—what *everyone* is in the shitter. *Waddy in his defiant soul.* It wasn't that Casey and Codman and their ilk did not have faults, but these were invisible. Not that they did not make mistakes, but these were never setbacks to the march of things, regardless of how big they were. They just did not count. These Brahmins lived life like a kid's game where they just made up the rules as they went along.

It irritated Waddy to his bowels that Foxy was right about everything, even when he was wrong. He would misquote Dante or Horace, whose work Waddy knew thoroughly; then it was as if either Dante or Horace was obliged to change his utterance to fit Foxy's misquotation. But Waddy had his own brand of arrogance—the arrogance of common sense and logic. He just did not see it as such. Waddy was more intelligent, more charming, and better looking than Foxhall Codman. He had a better sense of humor, irony, better wit, better taste in clothes and women. To Waddy, it was only logical that men like Codman should acknowledge these facts.

Back on the river, Codman's camp looked over the opposition. O'Sullivan looked fidgety.

"He's got the needle," said Deke Merriwell.

"Everyone gets the needle," said Codman.

"He's just a kid, Foxy. You'll row through him," Deke assured him.

Codman laughed confidently. His biceps flexed as he carried his sculls to what was called, ironically a *needle boat*, just thirty feet long, twelve inches wide, and weighing only about thirty pounds. He looked good and he well knew it. At forty-one, he knew that his reign on the Charles was near its end, but he was confident that on smooth water like this his technique would carry the day. One day an upstart crow would take his laurels, but he felt that it was not his time—he would bet on it. He did. He did not perceive himself as old. He could lift more weight in barbells than when he won his first regatta on the Charles, ten years earlier. Of the fifteen pounds more he carried, most was muscle. The small layer of fat in his midsection could not even be called a spare tire. Three-quarters of the hemisphere's Chateau d'Yquem had to go somewhere. And the proof was that on the water he was only seconds behind his best times.

These times, of course, did not mean much, because so much depended on the wind and the water conditions, and even the tide. But though there was no objective standard to judge by, he felt fit, he felt good, he even felt glad for the challenge. And as ever, he felt lucky.

"Tell O'Sullivan there's a new kid on the block," he laughed, thumping a finger on his disproportionately thick chest.

O'Sullivan's seconds seemed dismayed by the champion's powerful physique. "He'll be tough, but you can do it, Declan."

"I was not born in a wood to be frightened by an owl," replied the confident challenger.

Winding through the crowd at the river bank, Casey

smelled the clam fritters and chowder. There was a fat man's race and a baseball game. Boys were chicking dice on a barrel top. A triad of Mud Foley's gang were catching eels, waiting for the race to start. There was a minstrel show and clog and reel dancers near the Western Avenue bridge, Cambridge side. And on Captain's Island (Magazine Beach), members of the Riverside Boat Club challenged both men and women to row their famous "Downie" without taking a spill. No one succeeded. Many suits and straw hats had burn marks, result of the ubiquitous firecrackers. Googan's Emporium of Fashion would be busy on Monday.

Casey felt the old tingle of excitement along with the push of confidence born of mastery. She got to her distant starting mark with barely a half minute's rest before the gun would sound the start of the race. There were many small boats on the river, far from the racers' course, including some other sculls. The Commodore of the Cambridge Yacht Club had noticed with some vexation the single shell with Riverside Boat Club colors cutting diagonally across the race course two hundred meters downstream, but did not delay the start.

Codman had several strategies to get upstart kids to hammer then go down in a blaze of fatigue. Sometimes he would go out very fast, then ease off, letting the less-experienced sculler pass him. The adrenaline would feed in, and it was hard to turn it off. And Codman would almost shake his head at the stupidity of the racer who had burned out at one mile. If the false start didn't work, he would throw in a few sprints to accomplish the same thing. He enjoyed the first mile of game playing, but the second mile was a torture he had to get through. If he was ahead or even two lengths behind at two miles, he knew the race was his. He enjoyed the pain of a hard sprint. His extraordinary endurance, married with impeccable technique, paid off. The boat moved at a constant and inexorable rate to the finish line. First.

Codman *shipped off* to the toasts of dozens of Boston Brahmins, the densest collection of Louisburg Square residents after the caroling procession of Christmas eve. They were entouréd by a bevy of Boston's foremost debutantes, dressed to the nines in the fashions of Googan, Haliburton, Brooks, Quimby and Lashton. No shortfall of well-wishing for Declan O'Sullivan either, the people's champion and sportswriter the *Boston Globe*. The two men shook hands and got into their shells.

The protocol-ish false start did not work as well as Codman had expected. At the half-mile mark, both men sprinted short pieces, playing games with each other, and the lead seesawed. O'Sullivan was proving to be a wily Mick. Codman was being called on to respond in unanticipated ways, and he worried about depleting more energy than he wanted to in that dead zone of the middle mile. The race, he realized, would go down to the wire. Meanwhile, Casey had carefully charted out a point, exactly three hundred yards past the starting line and had her own marker another three hundred yards past the half-way point, where the shells turned. She rowed on the Alston side of the river, where there were far fewer spectators. The androgynous figure was hardly even a diversion for most spectators, speeding past her finish line, except for Stu Steerman, whose binoculars shifted back and forth between the race and the secret race.

With a quarter mile to go, Codman had pulled to a half-boat lead. Then the unthinkable. Inch by inch O'Sullivan closed the lead. The inches became feet, and the boats were dead even with two hundred yards to go.

Codman upped his stroke to thirty-nine, and as soon as he pulled slightly away, his opponent capitulated, mentally, and Codman seemed to slingshot by, winning by a full length. But doubt had been born in a small corner of his mind. Doubt of his invulnerability on water. He turned toward O'Sullivan and looked through him, never making real eye contact. He threw a smile, *noblesse oblige*, the way he would blow his ex-mother-in-law a kiss.

As Codman crossed the finish line, Stu Steerman looked downriver, towards Boston, still clenching his chronometer in his hand. He watched the diminutive figure take one more stroke before letting the sculls glide. He slammed the button on the chronometer, and could actually be seen jumping up and down, flabbergasted. He had seen the distant sculler before, running the same secret race in the early hours of the morning. He and Charlie Hot Dog, in a sense, shared a secret, but it was only recently that Stu had discovered the shadowy racer's identity. What he didn't know was that she had caught a crab two hundred yards out and lost the rhythm of her stroke. And the crab was due to a stitch in her side that almost caused her to stop rowing.

Now Stu and Moose ambled past a group of Negroes that included Laz Godfrey. Stu had already learned through the grapevine that Googan had lost his wad on the race, spreading his bets with every bookie on the banks of the Charles. Waddy would probably lose either his house or some limbs as a result, which delighted him. But more important to him than the loss of blood and face was the possibility of making a financial killing. He waited until Laz took notice of his presence, then said to his companions, "It's a crying shame ... Someone ought to tell Googan that the only man with even a Chinaman's chance of beating Foxhall Codman ... is his wife!"

Laz was stunned. He could see now, at the water's edge a half mile downstream, the slim figure who had rowed past a few minutes ago, and he noticed her trying, and failing, to get out of her boat. He sprinted down to help her. Foxhall Codman was an amateur in the realm of pain where Casey now found herself, a hallucinated world that was constant enough to be very real to her, a world where a trireme doppelganger rowed for his life—and that of, some might say, a schizophrenic housewife.

As firmly as Casey believed in her duality, she did not

believe in reincarnation or previous lives or anything that would explain this phenomenon, how she could row out of herself, row so hard that she no longer possessed a body and that every perception was dimmed into a wall of dull light, and it all seemed like a rehearsal for someone crossing over and crossing back. It was as if this poor rehearsal was made possible by a man in another place and time, who rowed into the future with the same passion that Casey, directionless, simply rowed out of herself. She was a vehicle somehow of his salvation, but in these episodes he never quite escaped his pursuers, and she was terrified of what it might mean for him to be saved.

"Casey!"

She knew, without looking, who it was, and she felt lifted by the palliative voice even before he strode into the water and raised her like a rag doll from the shell. She wanted to hug him, to cling to him, for reasons he could not understand. But this was still a public place, however remote from the crowds, and then she felt grotty, drenched with perspiration. And for all that anyone knew, this would be two *men* embracing.

Laz rowed the boat back to the boathouse while Casey walked. He put her boat back on the rack while she changed clothes.

"You know, after that horse thing, I thought you might not talk to me again."

"Minden Lo's very understanding."

He laughed. "And you?"

She threw back her head, gazed quickly at the clear blue sky, filled her lungs with inspirational air, then moved her head side to side, letting the air out audibly.

"Me ... I'm just ... reckless." She started to lean her head against his shoulder, then pulled it back.

"You know what you really are? You're the mystery woman, the woman in the brown woolen cap Codman always talks about."

Casey laughed, without assenting to her unmasking.

"Those highhats all get together at Mooney's, and they sip their top-shelf whiskey and their vintage Port and smoke their Marguerite cigars, and they talk about the phantom sculler. Some of them actually think you're a ghost."

"And Codman?"

"He said as far as he is concerned anyone who can row through him has to be a ghost. But he remembers a laugh. He's haunted by it. Did you really laugh at him?"

Casey hesitated, turned and scanned the faces of the people sitting on the river bank. "I don't know. Maybe."

"How did you do it, I mean, beat Codman?" He squeezed her hand excitedly.

"Well, it was easy—he stopped ... I kept on rowing. You can't let a little thing like a bridge slow you down."

"Or pain?"

"Or pain."

"Or a three-hundred-dollar boat you don't want to smash up."

"It's just money, Laz."

For the first time in his life, he had disposable cash, but it still seemed strange to him that one could talk cavalierly about smashing a three-hundred-dollar boat.

"You know what else you *really* are?" Laz stared at her and wanted to put his arms on her shoulders, but someone would notice. He took a deep breath and spoke deliberately. "You're the only sculler with a Chinaman's chance of beating Foxhall Codman in a real race."

Casey avoided his eyes and shrugged self-deprecatingly. "We might be a dead heat."

"So, why do you do it—row so hard? You looked ready for the undertaker, getting out of the boat."

Her immediate response was almost like a confession. It stunned him. "For my father," she said with a rising, questioning intonation, "... I guess."

"You know, you really did me in, that day in the pair-oared."

She squeezed his hand surreptitiously and looked him in the eye. He had the feeling she was going to say something important, but a yacht siren went off, warning some boys on logs to move aside. She inhaled deeply, looking at other boys pulling model boats by strings on the river's edge.

"No one's going to beat me." She exhaled with almost a sadness, which flummoxed him. The line was spoken with such certainty, as if she had already seen the future, but almost, he thought, as an apology—to those she would beat. It was beyond him. She seemed so genuinely sad about the men, many of whom she admired, having to face the fact that they'd been bested by a woman.

Laz had heard of a guy who rowed himself to death. He was worried, for her. He had total confidence in his boxing ability, but he knew in his heart that a man like John L. Sullivan might beat him. What really struck him about Casey was the absence of any fear of losing. Zero. Nil What she felt, and what was impossible for her to put into words, was that in the final quarter mile of a race she metamorphosed: she truly rowed right out of herself and felt the presence—she could even smell his sweat—of someone taking over her body, that trireme doppelganger, rowing in some distant sphere for his life, a man with bronzed arms as strong as Laz's, and if she-and-he ever crossed over, she would not lose the race, but she truly doubted that she-in-her-body would ever come back. She occasionally wondered if the nutcases who believed in reincarnation were right, but she'd immediately dismiss the thought. So she looked at him with an earnestness, almost a desperation of someone who knew her days were numbered.

"Damn," he said after a long pause, "I hope you don't take up boxing."

She changed clothes and headed to the hot air balloon staging area to meet Waddy. He'd missed the race. He was starting to feel better in his stomach but morose over the results.

"Who won?" he asked Patti.

"Your friend, Foxhall."

Waddy managed to trudge through the dispersing crowd to the staging area in Cambridgeport park, half-hoist over Patti's shoulders, his stomach still queasy from grapes and champagne.

"Googan! Ahoy! I say, Googan!"

Waddy and Patti made their way to Codman's balloon—*The Garden of Unearthly Delights*—its name in bold black letters in three lines on the rubberized, German-made envelope. The Codman family had always trusted the Germans for workmanship. The Benz V*is-à-Vis* was imported from Germany. Codman Boatworks was staffed mainly by Germans. For all of his cars, Foxhall kept a stockpile of tires made in Germany. They lasted, he claimed, twice as long.

The balloon was tethered to a dozen stakes by thick ropes. Foxy took Waddy aside. "You'd best ditch the mistress. Your wife is on the horizon."

"Can you get one of your entourage to take her home?"

Codman summoned Cosmo Croninshield, who escorted Patti to the periphery of the park, but not before Casey saw her patting Waddy on the shoulder.

Foxy gestured toward a group of balloonists. "The one with the Imperial beard is Count de la Vaulx. To his right is Jacques Balsam, then Charles Stewart Rolls and the famous Brazilian balloonist Alberto Santos-Dumont." He turned and pointed in the direction of a middle-aged man with a Van Dyke. "That's A. I. Mountenoy Jephson. He was with Stanley."

"Oh, good," said Waddy. "If you encounter any Africans in the sky, he can interpret for you."

Casey sidled up and Waddy gave her a peck on the cheek. Codman nodded and bowed toward her, then pointed to a tall gentleman in a top hat. "That's James Gordon Bennett, OBE, publisher of the New York

Herald."

"OBE, PGP—if you believe *Town Topics*," piped Waddy.

"I understand Order of the British Empire, but what's PGP?" asked Casey.

"Pissed in Grand Piano. He was outcast from New York society for doing just that, so he slums with Bostonians now. Speaking of which, *look* at you, Foxy! Is that a hanky or a fichu?" Waddy stuffed the handkerchief farther into Codman's pocket, then straightened his tie. "This a vestimentary disaster. The cravat is to clothes what truffles are to dinner."

"You don't say."

"*I* don't. Balzac did." Waddy enjoyed identifying the author of a phrase the Brahmin had never heard. He then flicked the flower out of Foxy's button-hole with a chastising, "Perennials don't belong in button-holes. Everybody knows that." He knew that Codman and his cohorts had no inkling of which flowers belonged to the set of 'perennials' and those that didn't. So it didn't matter whether the button-hole flower was or was not.

Casey scanned the rucksacks, flasks, hampers, and megaphone. "What do you do in the balloons?"

"They fuck in the balloons," said Waddy.

Foxy ignored him. "We play *Hare and the Hounds*."

"In the sky? How charming."

"Ask him where they piss?"

Foxy tapped on his balloon's *nécessaire*, out of which the *golden rain* was gleefully thrown down on the peasants. "You feel yourself soar as you piss. It's magnificent. Ballast, too, if one needs it."

Deke Merriwell raised his horn to his lips, then used it to brush away a terrier at his feet. "What's that dog doing sniffing up my feet?"

"He had four other rats for breakfast."

Deke gave Waddy a dirty look and blew on his horn, then picked up his megaphone. "Tally-ho!"

Codman smiled. "Deke is the best tally-ho toodler in Boston."

Deke had one of those healthy, cheery faces, head swelled like a hop toad and anchored to his thorax with a starched dickey, that made Waddy wish it could be fastened to the end of a pike. Good-fellow-well- ... *capitating—end-of-pike.*

Codman put his arm around Waddy, helping to support him. "You and Casey are coming with me!"

"Thanks, Foxy, but I don't think so. Not today."

"This is my day. I won't stand for any dissent."

Casey's face lit up. "Come on! I've never had such an adventure."

"You'll love it. A half mile up, even the most dreary appendages of a city turn glamorous."

Waddy, who was not only sick but afraid of heights, looked at *The Garden of Unearthly Delights* and frowned. "It's just not me."

Deke whispered to Todd Farrel, "Get her some fizz. I hear she's awfully good game when she's tipsy." Todd handed Codman a magnum of just-opened champagne. He guzzled some and offered the bottle to Waddy, who pushed it away. "Don't you people use glasses?"

"Todd! Three flutes."

Todd brought the peacock-tailed crystal flutes and Codman filled them.

"Cheers!"

"To the victor."

Codman put his arm back around Waddy, and Casey let the champ support him. "Actually, Waddy, it *is* you! It's utterly *anachronistic.*"

"Just ask Daedalus," Waddy muttered, his stomach still grumbling.

Codman laughed. "These balloons have hardly changed since Pilâtre de Rozier made his first ascent with the Montgolfier brothers in 1783."

"All the more reason not to set foot in one."

"Come on, old sport. If you're afraid of flying, stay here. But don't deny your wife the opportunity of flying."

"A maiden ascent," Todd added.

Waddy wrinkled his brow.

Codman smiled. "As unique as it is enjoyable."

Casey spoke up, "He really doesn't have the power to deny me anything."

Waddy gritted his teeth and stared at her. Casey was ambivalent about him losing face. She pulled him by the sleeve. "Let's talk."

"Let her go, Googan. It's a celebration," said Deke, handing a corked magnum of cold champagne to Todd Farrel.

"Yeah," said Todd. "Let her go, or you'll be ballast on my balloon."

Behind them, Oswald Short's *Kismet* had already lifted off, followed by Lord Llangatuck's *Crystal Palace*, carrying the considerable ballast of Casey's friend Rosemary Frothingham. Todd pointed a finger at her. "She's got two hundred acres in her estate, and she needs all of them." He spread his arms to approximate her girth and laughed. Then he trotted to his balloon and jeered at besotted W. Worby Beaumont, who had to be grabbed by his legs, twenty feet off the ground, to keep from falling—drunk— out of *Kestrel*.

Codman's crew withdrew the long, twelve-inch pipe that had pumped fifty thousand cubic feet of gas into *The Garden of Unearthly Delights* during the last half hour. It was the last balloon to be filled. Casey took Waddy further aside. She was dead-set on going, and Waddy knew it, but she knew his feelings had to be soothed.

Waddy disliked being pulled by a woman, but he still needed her support to stand. He looked menacingly at the balloon. "It's very small in there."

"There's room for four."

"Room to lie down in."

"Oh, Waddy."

"They're decadent, those Brahmins. Who knows what they do up there? Even foursomes are not . . are not ..."

"You sound like an old lady."

"Well, what does a woman do if she needs to pee, for Christ's sake? You can't just step out."

"I'm sure they've thought of that."

"I'm sure they *have*. That's the point."

"Well, don't get apoplectic about it. It's just a balloon ride."

"And if you want to say *no*?"

"If I wanted to say *no*, I wouldn't go."

He gulped. Casey laughed and put a hand on his chest. "I'm teasing. If I wanted to two-time you, would I do it right in the open, in a balloon?"

"A mile up, *open* is hardly open. Just ask Mrs. Jack, or the Winkler woman, the one with Farrel."

"I've always believed in one man at a time, and you're still living." Casey gave his cravat a flip with her finger. Waddy felt to some degree reassured. There was no time left to argue. The balloon was on the point of leaving of its own accord, piloted by Foxhall Codman, who was tossing out sand bags. He looked up. "Last chance. No pleasure like hazardous pleasure. What do you say?"

"Bal*loonacy*," croaked Waddy.

"I'm going." Casey slid from under Waddy's shoulder.

"Wonderful." Codman lifted her into the wicker basket. Waddy envied his strength. She looked, he thought, beautiful, but ill-dressed for a balloon flight—large brimmed, flat-crowned hat trimmed with hydrangeas and green tulle, dainty white muslin blouse, cream serge skirt, and white feather. Waddy made mental notes of the balloon colors and its structure, already fashioning a proper female ballooning costume. These thoughts helped him manage a small grin of empathy for the adventure as he blew Casey a kiss good-bye. She surveyed the well-provisioned basket—tins of beluga caviar, boxes of Bath Oliver biscuits, cold chicken legs, a jeroboam of vintage

Taitinger champagne, blankets, fire extinguisher, telescope, *nécessaire*.

"Promise me you won't ..."

She laughed, waving Waddy a pshaw. "If I were going to cheat on you, it would be on water, not in air." She glanced at terra firma. "Maybe on land," she joked, "but definitely not in air."

A crew of twenty men held the balloon with ropes against the strengthening East wind. Waddy watched the balloon lift off to the accompaniment of a score of champagne corks. It occurred to him that he knew neither their destination nor when they planned to return. He stammered, "Where are you going?"

"Wherever the wind takes us. West, most likely. Cheerio, old sport."

"How will you get back?"

Codman scratched his head and raised his eyebrows. "Gosh, I haven't thought about that. Maybe we'll have to stay." He laughed and gripped Casey by the shoulders, dislodging her white feather boa. In fact, the chauffeur Sawyer was already in Codman's Benz V*is-à-Vis*, preparing to give chase. Cheers rose. Holy Cross men shouted *hoya*. Hats were waved.

Waddy jumped as he cursed at the rising balloon, deriding its pilot to the spectators. "He's got raglan shoulders in his pajamas! And lapels on his underwear! He's got Bible verses embroidered on his table linen, like Princess Beatrice!" No one paid Waddy any notice. He looked back up at the ascending balloon. "The curse of the seven orphans on you!"

The more Waddy fumed, the wider Codman grinned. Looking down, he cupped his hands like a megaphone and recited, with an Italian accent, "Roméo! Roméo! Wherefore art thou, Roméo?" with stress on the accented *e*.

Graduate of Boston Latin Academy, Waddy clenched his fists and reddened in the face. "It's Rómeo, you dolt!

Why would Juliet run off with an ass who accented the antepenult when the penult was long?"

Codman made an inquisitive face and looked upwards, as if thinking of a reply, then cast his eyes down and a pulled on a non-existent beard. "Because, perhaps, *he* has a balloon, and the other man can't afford one?" He laughed. "It's no disgrace to be poor, Googan, but it *is* inconvenient."

Waddy cupped his hands around his mouth and shouted, "May the seven terriers of hell bark at your soul!"

Codman tilted his head with his hand around his ear. Waddy didn't waste his breath repeating the curse. Casey became smaller. The balloons became specks. Between spasms of vomit, Waddy stared at the sky. Casey's words came back to him: *one man at a time*. Why had he been so naive? As long as there wasn't one cock in her cunt and another simultaneously in her arse, it was *one man at a time*. He thought of what he would be doing with Patti now a mile up in that balloon. A whirling dervish of fuck. Cunt, ass, cunt. Little Black Sambo, dissolving into his own pancake batter. Or was it whipped butter? He couldn't remember. His head spun. The earth, then Casey, took turns above and below him. Circumscribed by fuck. Circumscribed again by vomit. He fell to his knees, put his head to the earth. He tasted the grass. Like a sick dog. No one even watching.

~~~~~~~

Six hours later, near sunset by a wide river in Western Massachusetts, *The Garden of Unearthly Delights* was near touch-down in a corn field. Sawyer was still a few hours away but hot on their trail in the Benz, stopping every ten miles to inquire if anyone had seen balloons passing overhead. He was lucky. The wind was due west.

Two rustics in overalls ran after the anchor trail-ropes that cut a swath through their cornfield. Casey tidied her skirt, pulled her bodice more firmly into place, then pulled her hair back and fastened it with a device Codman couldn't fathom.

"Where are we?" Codman asked the men.

"You're up in a balloon."

Back at Putnam Street late that midsummer's night, Waddy was re-possessed by a desire to crack the maze, finally, in the light of the full moon. Casey had not told Laz that the trysting maze was a gift also of Tattler, a long-shot two-year-old who smelled the roses at the finish at Mystic Park and would not be denied. He recalled her appreciation at his hiring the landscapers to finish the job and the heartfelt kisses on his forehead and neck.

—*Perennial or deciduous?*

—*Perennial.*

—*You want yews, arborvitae, barberry, burning bush?*

—*Burning bush? ... Yes, perennial burning bush!*

The already tall *arborvitae and burning bush* that Waddy bought to finish the maze grew quickly, to where only the top of a top hat of a man as tall as Waddy (5' 11") could be seen. Waddy never asked about or peeked at the layout plans. He was much too egotistical, sure that no maze in his own back yard, designed by his wife and her father would stymie a Harvard man. But his egregious sense of direction and poor spatial memory had caused him to fail thrice. Or was it four times? Five? He'd stopped counting. He remembered only the intense chagrin of getting lost in the maze. He had had to shout, at intervals, till Casey returned from work and led him out.

Waddy began to lay mental siege to the thing that loomed like Charlie's Peugeot, just days after his last failure. He wandered through it now, *musing*—shouldn't every *cul de sac* have a name, like the rooms of a mansion or an inn? The names of the women he had lain with, those dead-end ladies? Here was the Sally Amesbury room. Here the Charlotte Leda Valery room. And the swank Constance Lodge quarters—dead end with a view. He wondered why at this moment he felt an ever greater urgency to tackle the maze. Was being lost a metaphor for his life? Was the maze an extension of his wife? Of all women? Of their psyche? Taking a cue from the Brothers Grimm, he had loaded up his pockets with buttons from his shop, having already calculated the circumference of the maze and that of presumptive inner circles, figuring the approximate length of dead ends and taking enough buttons to drop one every ten feet, not following the same dead end twice. Along the way he finished off a pint flask of whiskey.

Miscalculation. He ran out of buttons before finding the center. But not clothes, he thought, in mild panic. Taking inspiration from the Muscovite demimondaines, he tore off his own buttons, then dropped pieces of his own clothing, finally resorting to tearing his shirt into strips.

For all of this he succeeded. He lay back at the center, flush with the joy of success. He napped a while, then began his retreat, which came to resemble Napoleon's. A nauseating feeling made its way slowly from his mind's gut. He tried not to let it register, but eventually he had to accept that *having buttons on virtually all of the paths was the same as having no buttons at all.* He could not find his way out. Reversing the original process might have done it— picking up each button as he left. But he had literally skipped with joy back through the first few turns where his clothes lay, and had gotten to a place where his poor sense of direction did not allow him to find the correct path out. His head spinning from the whiskey, again he panicked, running down wrong paths, stumbling and cursing. Worst of all, feeling like a complete jackass. He calmed himself with a line from an Andrew Marvel poem he'd had to memorize at Harvard:

*a green thought in a green shade ...*

It worked, at first. It calmed him. But did nothing for his searching skills. Green thoughts got darker. Being thoroughly besotted didn't help. His frustration grew intolerable, and Marvel's full couplet sang in his head:

*Annihilating all that's made*
*To a green thought in a green shade.*

The lines that had for years both intrigued and baffled him became clear as he found himself forcing his body, right foot first, through the perennial burning bush and arborvitae.

*Annihilating all that's made!*

Grotesque, the shirtless hedgehog that emerged through the last thicket row—arms, hands, legs deeply lacerated. His face looked as if it had been stuck in a burlap bag with Jans Mangin's monster rat. When Casey saw him the next morning she gasped. Her first thought— *my God, he's shed his skin.* She said nothing. The pattern of welts, scratches, and cuts made it all obvious. No need for a man to lose face when part of it had been left in the hedges. At Mooney's, it was assumed he'd been in a cat house fight. That was acceptable. That was Waddy's last foray into the maze. Picking up the buttons, Casey was treated to a foray into a private place, the mind of Waddy Googan—strange, tenacious, and perhaps already a trifle mad.

# Chapter 15: Dive

*D*une shadows retreated. The mist dissipated, blue dawn imposing on Laz's eyes, his feet stretched indelicately over the scattered corpse of a sandman. On the beach he escaped both the heat and Pearline. He closed his eyes again and imagined waking in the grass and the bluebells of Casey's maze. He shook off the reverie and began his morning run up Spruce Street.

Waddy found Laz on the last leg up Powder Horn Hill. Huffing, hunched over the handlebars of his bicycle, fifty yards behind and losing ground. Just a few puff-ball clouds with bellies the color of soft-shell crabs, the color of Waddy's face now. And how he had become determined these days to catch the lad.

"Laz, slow down! We have to talk."

Waddy caught up, stopped, and straddled his bicycle. When he caught his breath he asked, "What's the one thing you want more than anything in the world?"

"Jesus, what happened to you?"

Waddy waved a hand. "Cat house thing. Forget it. What is the thing you want more than anything in the world?"

Why Laz hesitated, with a strange smile on his lips, Waddy couldn't fathom.

"To be the champ, world champion."

Waddy nodded. "The trouble is, nobody wants to fight you. Sullivan doesn't want any part of you. You're too strong, too fast, too like Corbett."

"So what are you trying to say?"

"You've got to look vincible."

"What's that mean?"

"You've got to lose one."

Laz gave Waddy one of his mother's patented mean looks. "I'm not throwing no fight."

"There's nothing to it, Laz. You lose the first, then win the rematch."

Laz picked up the pace and made Waddy struggle. "No, sir. I know how that game works. You lose one, then they ask you to lose another, and it don't never stop."

"Trust me. Just this once. That's all I'm asking. I've got some very serious debts to pay."

Laz scowled. "I don't take dives. But if you need money, why don't you bet on your wife?"

"What's that supposed to mean?" Waddy tried to concentrate on Laz's mien but had to pay close attention to the rutted path.

"I mean Mrs. Googan can row a boat right out of the water. Let her race. You can get a hundred to one odds."

Waddy was piqued. "What makes you think that?"

"I keep my ears open."

"Well, you'd better keep your nose closed."

Laz kept his mouth shut. He shoved his hands into his pockets and kicked at the ground.

"There's big money for you, too."

"Can't do it, Mr. Googan. Put your money on me. I already did—a thousand, so there's no way I'm gonna lose."

"I'll make up the thousand. You're even money against

Choynski. That's not a money-making proposition. If you don't play ball, you leave me only one option. I've got to sell your contract."

"To who?"

"John McKane. Maybe Foxhall Codman. I don't want to, Laz. I want to manage a world champion as much as you want to be one. But these guys will cut my nuts off. And if McKane runs you, you'll be throwing more than one fight. These New York guys don't care about developing a fighter. They don't give a shit about anything but money."

"I ain't gonna do it. I don't need you, or McKane, or nobody. You understand me?"

Waddy glowered, then turned away with a deadpan, reflective look. "Sure, kid."

He gave the bike a push and started down the hill. The bike picked up momentum and he thought of braking but didn't. He was out of control and he liked the feeling. He saw himself gashed and bleeding all over his white suit, but the mental images had no currency in the new territory he had entered. He lowered his head, his hat blew off, he squinted into the wind on the long downhill, and as he conceived an idea, a great, world-eating grin spread across his face. The idea was mad, but so, perhaps, was he. The next day, he passed by the Sporting Club where Laz was punching bags.

"There's a card game tomorrow night, at my house. If you want to make a few bucks bartending and making sandwiches, come on by, and rush a few of Skeets' growlers on the way."

~~~~~~~

On cold nights Nemo sat inside with a hot brick for his feet and a mug of stock ale warmed on the hub of his stove. On warm nights he sat outside on a barrel and talked to the stars or to himself, to anyone that would or would not listen. When Laz arrived, he was half in the bag, talking to the court of celestial appeals.

"Pull up a log. What fetches you out this starry night?"

Laz shrugged and sat on a stump. Nemo proffered his bottle of ale. "Here's to the future champion."

Laz waved it off. "Future champion?"

"Hell, yes. You're as fast as your cousin George Godfrey, and you hit even harder." He pointed to a jug. "Guinnea red, if you prefer."

"Why are you always comparing me to colored fighters? What about Sullivan and Corbett?"

"Cuz they don't want any part of you."

"I'm going to challenge both of 'em. After what I did to Malone and Dooney McCool, they've got to fight me."

"John L. says he won't fight a colored. There used to be one reason for that. Now there's two—George Godfrey and you." Nemo rolled his eyes and took a long swig of ale from a bottle in one hand; in the other he held a coal shovel with two pounds of calves' liver over the coals of a fire. Laz emptied Nemo's jug of wine onto his tongue, strained it through his teeth and spat out the sediment with a sound like jabs on the light bag. He dipped a ladle into a rain barrel to rinse out the remaining sediment. "Why is there oatmeal in the rain barrel?"

"To settle the mud out," Nemo said, as if it were the most obvious thing in the world.

Laz dropped the wine jug to the dirt floor of Nemo's shack and headed for the door.

"Pissing or leaving?" said Nemo, whose eyes were closing.

"Leaving."

"Just don't piss inside." Nemo cut a large chunk of liver and stuffed it into his mouth.

Laz stopped and turned. "Nemo, can I trust Waddy Googan?"

The trainer laughed, then surprised him by saying, "In certain matters, yeah. So long as you stay away from his women."

"He's married," Laz said sheepishly.

"Yeah, and she's bad news. Just keep your mind on fighting. You got Joe Choynski coming up, and if you beat him you'll challenge Corbett when he beats Sullivan. You're two steps from the title. You read *Town Topics*?"

"What's that?"

Nemo did not mention how an unnamed Negro boxer had been indirectly linked to the wife of a prominent sporting man, going to his fights in men's clothes. "I'm sure Waddy does. Keep your guard up. Lead with your left, not with your pecker."

Nemo offered Laz some of the liver. He declined. He shooed gnats and swatted mosquitoes with the *Chelsea Ledger*. He was moved by the aesthetic of splats on the paper, but stopped short of showing Nemo in the dim lantern light the mottled red patterns of his blood.

Nemo gazed at the stars, then spoke without looking at his guest. "Your mama's no good, all that witch shit. Googan neither ... just to open his mouth there's mud coming through your door."

Laz laughed. "Mama—you don't know the half of it."

Laz stared into the black Chelsea sky that glittered more than usual, wondering if the stars really did tell the future the way that their absence told his past, the way his mother told both. He'd never bared his soul to anyone, and in truth he believed that his body was barren of soul. But there was something in Nemo that he trusted, mainly because the miracles he worked with fighters' hands and cuts was so diametrically opposed to what his mother did. And what his mother did was something he had to spill.

"You remember when I first cut up Big Paddy and you asked me what it was that I didn't like about the bag?"

Nemo slugged some wine and nodded.

"It was the laces. I guess I better backtrack and say that my mama ain't really my mama. That was just an accident. Mama's an abortionist and a midwife to women, sometimes society women, who don't want the kid. She disposes of them the same way—puts the fetus or the kid in a burlap sack with laces at the top, then has someone throw it in the dump at night. Rats take care of it."

"Shit." Nemo's head shook back and forth.

"One of those kids was me. Rats ate through the bag, but before they could get to me a couple of gypsies heard something and brought me back to Pearline. They knew about her and they made sure the cops would know if I got dumped back. 'Course the legend is that I fought off the rats, some kind of supernatural baby." Laz chuckled. "Then my job, until I was big enough to say no, was to take the burlap bags to the dump at midnight and toss 'em. So, now, think about a goodnight kiss from a mother like that ... or don't. I was just making that up. Never had no goodnight kiss from mama, from anyone."

"Praise Jesus. Your mama's a fucking vampire."

Nemo slumped to sleep on the ground by the fire. Soon, Laz did too. Moonlight sheeting his body, he fell asleep and dreamt of holding a flute with his boxing gloves on, playing an awkward tune, one note after another till the opponent went down. Pied Punching Piper of Boston.

A week later, Casey rode to the flats where she knew he would be taking his early evening run.

"I want to see it."

"What?"

"Your box."

"What are you talking about?"

"You said you fit all your clothes in one box."

He took her to his room, building #3 of the dirty dozen. At sunset, the walls were a washed-out burnt umber, reminding her of pictures of Pompeii. Drafts came through the cracks in the corners in spite of the multifarious things stuffed in them. The open window did not afford much view but had a ladder on the ledge outside by which he could reach the roof, his favorite spot. He took her up to where they could see the river. It started to drizzle. They retreated to his room. The dull walls lit up in a flash of lightning and faded to the same color as the clouds. With the first roll of thunder, she squeezed his wrist and turned on her side. He watched the storm clouds descend over her haunches.

"Waddy's losing it. Ever since that card game, he seldom leaves the house. He's afraid of running into the bookies he owes. The last time he was out he came home with a black eye and a swollen jaw. He spends half of his time in his study with a bottle, and half in the greenhouse with the shotgun." Casey started to cry. "He won't let anybody in. Except yesterday—a man from the bank. I think he's re-mortgaged the house."

It took Laz only a few seconds to hatch a plan. "I'll take care of it."

"You'll take care of it?"

"I'll talk to Waddy in the morning."

He found Waddy slumped in an old leather chair with wooden, lion's paw handles, too hungover to reach for the shotgun at his feet. Waddy grinned through four-day stubble and waved, then he took a slug from the half empty bottle of bourbon on the table.

Laz considered slapping him to momentary sobriety, but his idea would be sobering enough. "You've got one chance to keep breathing. You listening?"

Waddy nodded and waved. Then he mustered enough energy to throw a well-worn copy of *Town Topics* at him.

"Don't pay no attention to rumors. Listen, your wife is going to race Foxhall Codman, three miles, with a two-length spot, and you're going to arrange it."

Waddy pawed the air to dismiss the idea. "She's a woman."

Laz's stare didn't waver. "With two lengths and a new boat she'll croak him."

"She's already got a boat."

"It's all dinged up. She hit a dock in the fog. The boat's paper."

"Paper?" Waddy laughed.

"Paper and shellac. It's light, but when you ding it good, it's pretty much a goner."

Waddy felt the weight of brain cells washing up against the side of his head as he shook it.

"Even if she could win, Foxy won't race a woman. It's humiliating."

"Less humiliating than when every suffragette in town says he ducked a woman? When's the last time Codman turned down a bet, on anything? The man believes in his luck and his skill."

"What have I got to wager? I don't have a pot to pee in."

"You've got the house."

Waddy grinned, knowing that the bank effectively owned most of it now.

"When Steerman and Forse get through with you, what good's a house gonna be? Bet your house against his. In dollars, that's fifty to one."

Waddy chuckled and asked, breathlessly, "You think she can beat him? Casey?"

"In that old scow of hers, she's probably a length off Codman's best time. A new boat—she'll blow him out of the water."

Waddy's resentment of Foxhall Codman came up like heartburn. "What kind of new boat are you talking about?"

"A Neblung."

"A Neblung ... Charlie?"

Laz nodded. "Master boatsman for Codman senior. His hands got messed up with arthritis, and the old man let him go. You and him got something in common. He hates the Codmans as much as you do. He'll make the boat."

Waddy's head began to spin again. "Charlie's in the fucking hospital."

"He ain't dead yet. This will give him something to live for."

Waddy tried to sit up. On the third try he succeeded.

"Tell me you're not pulling my leg. Tell me my wife has a remote chance of pulling this off."

"Nothing remote about it. She can cook it. She already beat him once."

Waddy squinched his eyebrows together, not comprehending.

"The phantom—the one in the brown woolen cap Codman always talks about—that ain't no phantom. That's your wife."

It took a moment to sink in. Then Waddy cachinnated and shook his head incredulously, muttering, "My wife ... "

Staggering down Mount Auburn Street to the hospital at 8:00 p.m., Waddy watched an orange hangnail of a moon going down, leaving its partner Venus gawking brightly and alone in the western sky. He was thinking of Charlie's heart, of Casey's father, of Jawing Kerry staring at the tumor jackaling his throat. *What to do? Buy Charlie some white carnations with pretty red vessels and watch their water go murky?*

The creaking of nuns who stalked the hospital corridors freaked Waddy out as much as the colors—white that had yellowed, or yellow that had blanched. Charlie's room was an unheartening beige, the color of a light-skinned earthworm. The hospital miasma had converted the walls to its ends and was presently recruiting the patients' pale-drawn faces.

—*Charlie's a goner here*, thought Waddy. He saw a nun and a priest praying and the prayers getting soaked up in off-yellow walls like flies hitting flypaper. He crossed himself unconsciously, held his breath, and entered Charlie's room. Charlie was awake, staring at the paper flowers on the wall. Several closed notebooks were at his side. Waddy started to smile, then pressed his lips tightly together and nodded when Charlie caught sight of him.

"Waddy Googan?"

"Hey, neighbor. What'd they get you for?"

"Ticker. I had terrible pains, so I came in and had a heart attack in the waiting room. Pretty good timing, *jah*?"

Waddy smiled. "You look pretty good for a guy with a bad ticker."

"I'd feel better if I could get some real food, and beer."

Charlie smiled, and Waddy coughed nervously. "Kids have been breaking into your basement."

"Mud Foley?"

"Swipes, probably. He's got his own gang now."

Charlie raised his hands dismissively. "Nothing lasts forever." He looked down the length of his body. Waddy searched for something to sit on, but there were no chairs. Charlie moved the tray of half-eaten soup and crackers to the other side of the bed and told him to sit down.

Waddy squirmed into the soft mattress. "I've got a confession to make. I didn't come just to see how you were doing ... I came to ask you a favor ... They tell me you used to make boats—for Foxhall Codman Senior."

Charlie gave him a scornful look, but did not speak.

"Well?"

The old boat-builder frowned. "A long time ago."

"And he fired you because you got arthritis and couldn't use a hammer?"

Charlie nodded. "I couldn't get the fine tolerances with the tools I had. So, yes, that bastard fired me."

"Well, we got something in common—I've got as much use for his sonofabitch son as much as you had for the old man. And I have a way to get back at both of them."

"You want a boat," Charlie preempted with a snicker.

Waddy's brow knitted.

"How do I know?" Charlie preempted Waddy's question rhetorically and looked at three of the four walls. He turned up his palms, then cocked his head and shoulders several times. "I know."

Waddy scratched the back of his head.

"Not the particulars. But anyone who watches the river

could see it coming."

Waddy stood and turned his head back and forth, working out a crick. He paced towards the window and turned back to Charlie. "What am I ... the only putz who doesn't know my wife is a world-class sculler?"

"Take it easy. You can be a reformed putz."

Waddy raked his hair with his fingers, weeding out the weak.

"In a race, Codman averages thirty-three strokes per minute over a mile, and your wife does about thirty-two, more or less. It's hard to tell. Sprinting, they're dead even."

"A stroke a minute over three miles, how much is that?"

Charlie shrugged. "With Casey's scow, two, three lengths. Depends on the boat you're pulling and on how you sprint. All things considered, hard to tell. There's variables."

Waddy's face fell, his fingers interlocked above the thinning hair.

"Of course, with a new boat ..." Charlie stared out the window into the night for a few, to Waddy, interminable seconds. "... with the boat I could build ... she would kick his Brahmin ass right out of the water."

Lurching, Waddy hugged the old man.

"You smell like a brewery," said Charlie, pushing him away. "I have the worst .. . nostalgia for this stench."

Waddy walked to the closet and opened it. He tossed some clothes at Charlie. "Come on. We're getting out of here."

Charlie pointed at the closet floor. "There's a suitcase too. Put these notebooks in it."

Waddy opened a tattered notebook. There were hundreds of sketches, finely drawn shells of different proportions. There were notes in German and English, close up sketches of sculls, oarlocks, toe plates, etc. There were sketches of a hull, drawn almost perfectly without instruments, with three views around a baseline. On the outside Charlie was a recluse who walked across town every morning so regularly that Codman called him Emmanuel Kant. Inside, he steamed. And designed.

Waddy turned to the last page of the newest notebook. Charlie looked at it. "This shell is six inches longer than the one Casey is using now, but it's got less draft, and it's twenty percent lighter than Foxhall's old scow. You might say this boat is the equalizer, and more. A boat like this—there is nothing like it on the river. Their eyes will pop."

Waddy grinned, thinking that if the river weren't already the *Charles*, they'd have to rename it. Later that night, after a half-quart of brandy, the difference for Waddy between a hot dog and a racing shell diminished to nothing more than fate turning a few screws at odd angles. There would be a day of judgment for Codman, too, he thought. Accountability by water. The shell would be hammered through the blue blood heart by the Amazon that *was* his wife.

The night that Waddy made the deal with Codman at Mooney's there was a stillness in the tavern air, even bizarre moments of silence. Mugs clinked in a lower key. Stumbling out at 4:50 a.m., followed by Codman, Waddy was distracted by the bleating of a goat. "What's that goat doing with the dray?"

"I thought it was an Irish thing—so *you*'d know."

"Know what?"

"You're not really a horse-man, are you?"

Waddy glared at him.

"Horses, like men, need companionship at night. There's a good many racing horses that have goats as companions. If you owned one, you'd know. Stonewall Jackson's still for sale. For you, I'll let her go for $500."

"Don't have it."

Codman surveyed the quiet, with the benign softness of drizzle on his shoulder. "You could win it."

Codman smiled and Waddy knew he had another wager in mind. Waddy groused, "I don't go around putting eggs in the hay. You haven't lost a bet since horses started trotting."

Codman shook his head in pity. "A horseless man."

"I've got horses."

"Spineless drays. I mean real horses."

"All right. What's your wager?" Waddy intoned like a condemned man.

"You put the goat in one sulky. I put the dray in another, and we race around the block."

Waddy looked at the horse, which had a wrapped bum leg and obviously could not run. He looked at the goat which, albeit slowly, could. On Sundays the poor of Cambridge had goat races on Mass. Ave. for fun.

"Foxy, the horse and goat—they ain't ours." Waddy's grammar mistakes were always deliberate.

Codman knocked loudly on the door of the caretaker's abutting shack and handed the occupant a dollar. Waddy still wasn't convinced. "What's the catch?"

Codman shook his head disdainfully. "A horseless man." He looked at the reddish, hemorrhaging sky over downtown Boston. A mosquito alighted on Waddy's forehead. He could feel it, but he did not shoo or slap at it. He always waited till a mosquito had begun the process of slipping in its proboscis and either could not get it out quickly or was so drunk with the taste of blood that it kept drinking despite the approaching hand. Then Waddy would slowly crush it, with an off-speed slap while muttering to himself, *"in sangriento delicto."*

The mosquito had as much chance as he did betting against Codman, but he had to ask, "Stonewall Jackson to what?"

"You tell me."

"The cookie jar's got about twenty bills."

Codman gave a scornful laugh. "That would keep me in snuff money, and I never use snuff. Look, since you're chronically short on cash, let's make it Stonewall Jackson to your hat."

Waddy took off the derby and pressed his fingers into the wet brim. "Made it myself."

"Admirable work. I like it."

"A hat to a horse? There's a catch."

"The only *catch* is what you and the goat will try to do to me and the hobbled, knacker-bound dray."

The wager was too attractive to turn down. Waddy smiled. "Lay on."

"Hold on," said Codman. "I need to rush the growler."

Waddy inspected the sulkies. "Wait. This one's busted."

Codman looked at the broken spoke with his hands on his hips. He scanned the area and pointed. "I'll hitch up that donkey cart."

Waddy laughed. The Brahmin would look ridiculous in the kid's cart. "You sure about that?"

Codman slapped him on the back. "I'm sure. The night needs more sporting."

While Waddy hitched the goat to the racing sulky and checked to see that everything was secured, Codman went back into Mooney's, then momentarily disappeared into the shadows of the stable with a bucketful of ale, which Waddy didn't see. Steeds secured, feet up in stirrups, the men gripped their whips in one hand and the reins in the other.

"One more thing. Loser rides to Mooney's tomorrow in this rig." He pointed to the donkey cart.

Waddy nodded. "Ready? Go!"

The goat and the three-and-a-half-legged dray raced off into a nearly black street. The goat took the lead and Waddy heard the strange canter of a hobbled horse behind him. Mud flew off hooves into their faces, Codman getting the worst of it at first. Then Waddy took a wet clod in the eye from the horse pulling abreast. He cried out, reached for his eye and dropped his whip. He wiped his eye on his sleeve and forced it to open. Probably even with the whip the goat would have slowed. As they pulled around the final corner of Greene Street, he heard Codman pulling ahead. He blinked his mud-stung eye clear. More than seeing, he was hearing and feeling himself behind Codman's dray-drawn cart. Only a bolt of lightening could save him from losing. That risk, it seemed to him, was as great as his chance of beating his rival at anything. The greater ignominy was the clods of mud thrown up in his face by the dray as his goat slowed to a walk, and he had no whip, only curses at the goat's patrimony, about which goats cared little, to urge him on.

"A horse's hooves—is there a more cheerful sound, Googan?"

Waddy handed him the hat. "Too dirty for my taste anyway."

"Anything can be cleaned, Googan. Even a pure blood Irishman." Anglo-Irish Codman laughed at his pun, having *cleaned* out his friend.

"How did you get that knacker-fodder to run?"

"Well, I wouldn't exactly call it running, but His Nibs—that's his name—was the fastest quarter-horse in the East, till he pulled up lame a few years ago. Henry Lodge loved him so much he couldn't put him down. Let him get fat on oats, hops, and barley. You put a bucket of ale in front of his nose and he'll run on three legs to get it. He'd pull out of a mare if he smelled a quart of fresh-pulled."

"That's why you rushed the growler."

Codman laughed. "I'll bet you wouldn't pull out for a bucket, with that wife of yours." He patted him on the shoulder and laughed. Waddy's goat was got but good. He'd been had again. He sneered. "May your cows take the crippen and your calves the white scour."

Codman laughed louder, summoning Sawyer with the Benz. "You croppy!"

Waddy's ears reddened. "May you go so blind you don't know your wife from a haystack."

"Divorced. Remember?" He waved. "So long, old sport. By the way, there's a balloon race next month. Your wife has agreed to crew for me."

"You don't need a crew in a balloon."

"Someone has to empty the *nécessaire*."

Sawyer pulled up in the sputtering Benz *Vis-à-Vis*, which had just flattened a squirrel—what the upper crust was up to with their infernal machines of internal combustion, Waddy reflected.

"We all have to suffer the caprices of the petrol motor. It's a new century coming, Googan. Might as well get used to it."

The moon was still visible in the East when Waddy started up Mass. Ave. From the North, great blotches of dirty white thunder clouds were moving fast toward the moon, which seemed to move through the tops of the elm trees as he walked. He deliberately crossed to the other side of the street so that the moon floated just above the trees, uncaged. He sniffed at a honeysuckle saddle over an old fence, the humid, cool air full of nectar. By the time he found his Stanhope Phaeton, the moon was blacked out by clouds. It began to drizzle, making ghostly the headlamps on the occasional automobiles and the hansoms. Shortly, he was sitting in the rain on the hill adjacent to Mooney's, in a bosquet with an ash tree that leaned over the footpath at a sharp angle. It was one of the oldest trees in Cambridge, and from the top of the hill on a clear day you could see much of the city. But now visibility was near zero. Waddy listened to the mizzling rain being fended off by the canopy of leaves and boughs. This close to the dense ash and under a coachman's umbrella, he was untouched, untouchable, concealed. He concentrated on the rain's cadence in the amazing dryness. He lit a pipe in the warmth that seemed collected under this tree, himself huddled in it, his back dry against the seat, his eyes suddenly wet. On such a night no one could tell that Waddy Googan was crying, and it's no book that wants his tears.

The following evening Father Divine spied something out of a window at Mooney's that made him rub his eyes and look again. "Look, lads, it's Googan spanking along in a donkey cart!"

The regulars flocked to the windows and the door. Natty as a speckled wren, Waddy was all smiles, in highly polished black shoes; the setting sun itself seemed to beam from his toes.

"Jaysus, he's in a donkey cart driven by a goat and he looks like he's at the reins of a four-in-hand Brougham. And look—there's primrose tied to the goat's tail."

"What's that for?"

"To prevent fairies from stealing milk."

Hugo looked blankly at Skeets, who slapped him and turned his palms up parallel to his shoulders. "It's a joke."

Hugo wasn't sure if it was Skeets' joke or Waddy's. He felt confused by the Irish, and at times it seemed that the whole crowd at Mooney's was nothing but Irish.

Inside the tavern Waddy called for drinks for the house, on Codman, who could not say no. He excused himself and made for the men's room while Waddy studied Skeets' selection of whiskeys.

Hugo shook his head with a wry grin. "It's humiliating nonetheless. Pretty clear Foxy has it in for Googan."

"Seem like asshole-buddies to me," quipped Father Divine.

"You know why Foxy got divorced."

"Sure. His wife was cheating on him."

"With who?"

"Oh, come on. With his employees and friends, Googan is as loyal as they come. Not even the Saunterer suggested such a thing, and if there was even a whiff of it, it would be in *Town Topics*."

"Yeah? How come I got a whiff?"

"Cuz you're Hugo Bartolini, son of an anarchist and a bitch," gibed Fanny Bronski, delivering a platter of ten oysters she'd just shucked. Father Divine handed her a quarter. Fanny had overheard the entire conversation.

"And I'll tell you one more thing," Fanny pointed the

short shucking knife at Hugo, "the man has kind eyes."

Normally, that would be the end of it. Fanny Bronsky almost always had the last word. Hugo didn't recognize the irony in his tacking on, "And he gives you four bits for a two-bit platter of oysters," followed with a slurp and swallow.

"Don't mind if I do," said Waddy, whiskey in one hand and squeezing a lemon quarter with the other.

# Chapter 16: Gunboat Smith

$C$asey was elated to hear Laz's plan for a new boat, financed by his fight with Joe Choynski. Laz was taking Choynski apart in the guise of Big Paddy when Waddy staggered in with a baleful look. "Bad news, kid. Choynski pulled out."

"What?" Laz's face fell. He slapped at a heavy bag.

"Hurt his hand. Doctor says he can't box for a couple months. I'm working on a replacement."

"Who?"

"Gunboat Smith."

"You mean 'Piano Mover'?"

"They changed his moniker. Hey, he's 20 and 0, all knockouts. The guy is huge. Hits like a sledgehammer."

"Yeah, but he's a fucking piano mover."

"What can I say? It's his profession."

"He's supposed to be a boxer."

"He is. Piano moving is just his former and future profession. You can't box forever."

"Some guys can't box five rounds," said Nemo.

"He doesn't have to. Knocks most guys out in the first.

This guy is huge, Laz. Lifts pianos by himself."

"Goes three hundred and change, I heard," said Nemo.

"And he's dirty. You gotta protect yourself. He'll whack you in the balls every chance he gets."

"He won't even see me. He'll go down like a dropped piano. One hook to the temple." Laz demonstrated the knockout punch on Big Paddy.

"Yeah, well, watch out, or you'll be singing that song in a higher key."

Nemo realized that his cigar had been out for a while. He spat and relighted it. "He ain't that good anyway. Got booed in Brooklyn."

"In Brooklyn they boo Santa Claus."

Waddy laughed. "If he's that bad, you'll take him out in the first, right?"

"I'd knock him out sooner but they don't allow it."

"That's big talk, kid." Waddy slapped him on the back. "You just let your fists do the talking. And when they do, I want them to quote John L. Sullivan. You went to school, right?"

"Couple years."

"You can count to ten, can't you?"

"Sure. Why?"

"You don't want to stay down more than that."


Training at the Casino Athletic Club on Tremont Street, Gunboat Smith was out of sorts. "I don't know if I should take this fight, Mr. Googan. My chest hurts."

"Breathe in ... Take a deep breath. Hold it ... Okay, now let it go ... How's that feel?"

"Okay, but ..."

"But what? Nothing's busted. If it was, you'd feel it when you took a deep breath."

"You sure?"

"Have I been in this business twenty years, or what?" Waddy exaggerated.

"Yeah, but, when I cough sometimes, or when I

sneeze, it hurts. Hurts a lot."

"When you sneeze?"

"It's the sunlight. When I walk into the sunlight something happens and I sneeze. And now I get a sharp pain up here."

Smith slapped himself lightly with a closed, sideways fist, like doing a *mea culpa*, just below the clavicle.

"Who hits hard enough to bruise ribs on a big fuck like you?"

"Wasn't nobody, Mr. Googan. We were hoisting this piano and it kind of slipped. The leg hit me here."

"Jesus Christ!" Waddy tore at his hair. "Piano fell on you and you're still alive?"

Smith acted like it was nothing abnormal, like everybody had pianos fall on them from time to time.

"Listen, son, you gotta stay out of the sunlight. That's the main thing. Stay in the dark. And if you go out in the day, wear horse blinders. I'll get you some that let you still see your feet, see where you're going. You can't afford to sneeze. I had two more guys pull out of this fight."

"Who pulled out?"

"Stonewall Bob Allen. Got shot point blank in the head over a craps game in Cambridge. Then Frank Craig, the Harlem Coffee Cooler. He kept hearing how strong Godfrey was and he chickened out. That's why I wanted someone bigger and stronger, like you."

"I appreciate your confidence, Mr. Googan, but what if I stay inside and I sneeze anyway?"

"If you gotta sneeze, hold your chest in with your hands. Push down and out with your stomach, and the sneeze can't build up any pressure. I saw a lot of broken ribs at Gettysburg. Believe me, it works."

"You were in the war?"

"I was a kid, sixteen. And stupid. Don't ever go to war."

"Problem is, I like sneezing."

"Gunboat, you ever pull out?"

"Pull out what?"

"Your dick, you moron."

"Yeah, couple of times. Sure."

"Well, it's the same thing. You like something, but you gotta do something else."

Waddy slapped him reassuringly on the back. Gunboat nodded with an uncertain smile, thinking he understood the allusion but not entirely sure.

"Hey, it's just three days. But don't forget the blinders. Best policy is not to sneeze at all. And just try to stay in the dark for three days. Stay in the gym, why don't you?"

"You think it'll be okay if I get hit?"

"Didn't anybody tell you?—the idea is *not* to get hit."

"Yeah, but this Godfrey ..."

"Cover up, like this." Waddy demonstrated. "Don't give him a shot at your chest. And hit him in the balls. Niggers can't take a good shot in the balls." Waddy still held out hope that Laz would take a dive. In any case, if a fight proved no contest, the fancy was known to smash chairs and even set fires. Malone had to look like he had a chance. And Waddy had other reasons for wanting Laz to take a shot to the balls.

From his jacket pocket he took a tube of *Dr. Kerry's Salve And Unguent* and handed it to Gunboat. "This'll take care of you. Rub it on your chest, where it hurts."

"That good for bruised ribs?"

"*Dr. Kerry's Salve And Unguent?* Good for anything. Stomach, arms, chest ... except the balls," Waddy deadpanned, Gunboat stifling a laugh he knew would cause him pain.

The morning of the fight, The Society for the Prevention of Vice was still trying to get an injunction to stop it. The drinking and gambling at the Chelsea Sporting Club were excessive, and the back rows were practically turning into a brothel. The Society had paid a visit to Mooney's, and Skeets overheard them saying that The Sporting Club was next on their list. They assailed Skeets for the goings on at his saloon.

"Temple of Bacchus," he corrected them, and he defended the various spectacles, the *Miscellaneous Entertainment of High Character*, that took place in the *Sanctum Sanctorum*. "They're just rats. Who gives a rat's ass?"

As for *les belles impures*, Skeets noted that, unlike other Cambridge temples, his was off limits before 10:00 p.m. Queried on Big-Mouth Babs and her affections for sailors, he pleaded ignorance.

Waddy was where Skeets thought he would be, at his desk in the top floor office. Nemo let him in. It was almost noon and Waddy had just roused himself. He had a three-day beard and was at the end of a three-day binge. He forewent coffee and poured himself a half glass of scotch. The ink on the ledger on his desk was blurred from spilled booze. Balancing the books was out of the question and not just from the spilled ink. Foreclosure was imminent and Waddy felt powerless to do anything about it.

"Skeets."

"Googan, I've come to warn you. The vice squad has Archbishop Williams in their corner, not to mention Henry Cabot Lodge, and they may show up at any minute. Lodge has it in for you, if you didn't already know."

On the one hand, rumors tended to be just that. On the other, where Waddy Googan was concerned they were more than likely to prove true. And little more than a fortnight had passed since Constance Lodge peered out at him from a four-in-hand Brougham on Brattle street and seemed to cover a snicker with a white-gloved hand. *Barge-bottom-Connie, snickering at him*? Distilled spirits were the constancy Waddy took refuge in from the welter of rumor. Cognac, bourbon, rum—it didn't much matter as long as it resulted in oblivion that obviated reflection.

"If the Archbishop sees you like this," Skeets continued, "I'm afraid you're done."

"Then we'd best not be here. "Champagne breakfast at

Dunfey's—on you. What say?"

"Waddy, the roof's caving in, and you've got to get it ready for tonight. We'll tip the teapot after the fight. By the way, what's this talk about Godfrey taking a dive?"

Waddy chortled, "Truth is—Smith won't come to scratch for the second round. Not that I haven't tried to get Laz to throw it. But the kid is solid. A veritable coal mine."

Skeets felt, in the floor's creaking beneath Googan's well-shined shoes on his way out, a hardwood tattling; he felt that Laz might throw the fight, but he misunderstood Waddy's affect. Waddy opened the door, which also creaked, and he turned back but did not look directly at the barkeep as he spoke. "Who's going to cry when I'm gone, Skeets? ... Who's going to cry?"

Skeets stared at him in the doorway. "I don't understand."

"Yes, you do ... Yes, you do." Waddy laughed, a bit demonically in the barkeep's view. "I've got a sure thing for once, with Laz, and there's not a bookie in town who'll take my marker. "

Leaving *Sodom By the Sea*, Waddy was thinking about Foxhall Codman's boast—that he owned three-quarters of the Chateau d'Yquem '*in this hemisphere*.' But the Chateau *itself* was not only in this—the northern—hemisphere but in the part of France that was in this—the western—hemisphere, so his boast was impossible. Mistakes didn't seem to matter for aristocrats. A hemisphere was what Codman said it was, geography be damned. If there were a Chateau d'Y*Quim*, Waddy would own it. If they counted the coup that mattered, he too would have a plaque over the bar at Mooney's.

Skeets had just gotten into his Cabriolet when he noticed Waddy raising his foot toward the Phaeton's floorboard then lowering it and histrionically pounding his fist. He had no desire to kill the long-legged spider that kept advancing even in face of the benevolently warning fist that shook the plank it walked. He noticed with some chagrin two women looking askance at him as he scraped off the moist mass and watched it fall on his shoe, then noticed a long auburn hair flailing from his raised heel in the morning breeze and shining in the bright sunlight. Casey's? He thought of the fine web the spider could have spun with it to trap its dinner, to decorate a love nest, while from across the street Skeets watched, bewildered. As the auburn hair snapped back up and the light burned down its length, the barkeep could see Waddy kicking one shoe against the other, then slapping at it, his lips moving, and were the barkeep closer he would hear his desperate whisper, "*Let go, hair!*"

He wiped the shoe against the sidewalk and crashed into some geraniums. He kicked as if fighting off a mad dog, scrambled to his feet and walked quickly to the Phaeton. And Skeets Mooney said to himself, "There's something wrong with Googan."

~~~~~~~

—He used to come in now and then. He's a very gentle man.

—Are we talking about the same Gunboat? Laz asked at the counter of the Holly Tree.

—Yeah, said Casey.—Gunboat Smith. Big strapping guy, but he's afraid of bridges. He can't even cross one with his eyes open.

—So, said Laz,—when we get in close, I'll just whisper *bridge* in his ear, and he'll shake in his shoes.

—Why not?

~~~~~~~

There was still some light in the sky when Waddy stumbled out of his Phaeton at Laz's house. He knocked, but there was no answer. He walked around the back, where Laz was pulling a towel off the line.

"Let's go. It's time."

The tone sounded to Laz like an executioner's. He stuffed the towel into his bag, and suddenly the wind picked up. The clothesline became chorus line; shirts and skirts, towels and trunks, all dancing. He saw in the chorus line ghosts of dead fighters materialized, putting on clothes, getting giddy, then luffing back into non-being. He nodded to Waddy and followed him to his Phaeton.

There was a line at the ticket window of the Chelsea Sporting Club, and vendors of various comestibles were scattered near the entrance or on the steps. Laz recognized the one-armed, one-legged, hand-organ player, John Williams. Next to Williams, a man in a ratty topcoat kept saying, "Hit me twice for *yes*, once for *no*." The voice sounded familiar to Waddy. The large man was selling peanuts from a gunny sack he had attached to one wrist with a rope. He was noticeable also for the old ear trumpet he would put to one ear when he needed to converse with someone.

As Waddy and Laz got closer, it was apparent that the man was blind along with hard of hearing, and that the fist he asked people to hit him on was enormous, which completed for Waddy the process of recognition.

"Beast?"

"Peanuts. Penny a bag. Hit me twice for *yes*, once for *no*." He held out his giant fist. Waddy hit it twice, then twice hit the ear trumpet, which the man put to his ear.

"Beast?"

"You know me?" The man, who was bigger than Godfrey, smiled. Waddy recalled that after his bare-knuckle fight with John L. Sullivan, Bobby 'The Beast' Casper went completely blind, at least fifty percent deaf, and suffered memory loss. "Hit me twice for *yes*, once for *no*."

Waddy hit him twice on the fist. "Waddy Googan," he shouted into the trumpet.

"Did I fight you?"

Waddy hit him once.

"Want some peanuts? Penny a bag."

Waddy pressed two pennies into the open hand that reverted to a fist after placing the coins in his pocket.

"Did I fight you? Hit me twice for *yes*, once for *no*, to remind me."

Waddy hit him once. He had an impulse to invite Beast to see the fight, but realized that not only could he not actually see it, he could barely hear the excitement and would forget even who was fighting, not to mention the difficulty and aggravation the ear trumpet would cause, all of which saddened him.

The Beast had a second gunny sack, one with the entirety of his material possessions. Waddy could make out two skins—boxing gloves. Their undersides had a large hole where the fingers could emerge, and a hole where the thumb could poke through. They were now, evidently, winter gloves, for working.

"Would you turn the lights on, please?"

*Hit him twice? Once?* Waddy was too stunned to think. The Beast could not even remember that he was blind. Waddy dipped into his pocket for two more pennies and put them in the Beast's fist, hoping the Beast would forget his request for the lights while getting more peanuts from the sack he kept attached to his wrist so that the Chelsea gamin would not steal it.

Waddy pocketed the bag, then walked quickly toward the entrance. "He was a great fighter."

"Yeah, I heard of him," Laz acknowledged.

"Biggest hands I've ever seen. That's how I recognized him. He could hit harder than Choynski. Nobody hit harder than the Beast, not even John O. But he just waded right in. No defense whatsoever. Took a licking in a lot of fights. Then Sullivan ended it. Poor son of a bitch can't even remember what happened to him." Waddy turned to look at Laz. "Let that be a lesson to you. You can't just wade in. You gotta dip for the oyster, dive for the clam. But then, you already know that." Waddy grinned wanly at the allusion, doing a foreshortened bob and weave. And Laz thought—*dive for the clams* ... then turned down to the locker room while Waddy sat ringside, next to reporter Declan O'Sullivan.

Nemo looked out at Pearline, who was gesticulating with her hands as her lips moved. "What's that mumbo jumbo coming from your mother's lips?"

"Let's just say she's praying," said Laz.

"For what? Rain?"

Laz laughed. "Yeah, rain. Rain's in the sky and mama's in the front row. Lace me up now, Nemo. I don't want to know who I am no more. And don't be looking at her. She can draw the claret from a man's eyes."

"What do you think, Skeets? Is Godfrey going to beat Gunboat?" Codman asked.

"Gunboat's gonna get his whiskers clipped. Sure as thunder sours milk. Look what Godfrey did to Malone, then Billy Hill the Pick and Scaldy Bill Quinn. And Elbows McCracken? He had one ear swolled up like Fanny Bronsky's summer squash and the other hanging by a shoestring."

Deke Merriwell winced. "Back in the days when John Jackson was fighting, it was a gentlemanly affair. Politicians would come. Judges. Great authors. You'd have the likes of Benjamin Harrison at a championship fight."

"They didn't allow Coloreds in the ring then," said Codman. "Then it was pugilism."

"What's that?" said Skeets.

"That's boxing raised to an art, or a science."

"Make up your mind," said Skeets. "Which is it?"

"Then it was a white man's affair."

Nemo was tying the laces of Laz's gloves and reminding him that his jab was the key. Father Divine trundled up to Waddy and nudged him. "Last instructions or voodoo shit?"

"Last ... Forget about it. Go over to Malone's corner and give him last rites."

Waddy staggered up to Laz and slapped him on the back. "How ya feelin', champ?"

Waddy felt almost a burn from Laz's eyes.

"Scared, Mr. Googan."

Waddy's eyes widened, exposing globes with red lines of latitude and longitude gone haywire. "Scared? Scared of what? The guy is slower than a hay wagon."

"Scared I'm gonna kill 'im."

In the center of the ring Smith and Godfrey stared each other down. As they touched gloves, Smith muttered something that Laz could not quite make out. The only word he heard clearly was, "balls."

The first two rounds were void of action, each man feeling the other out. In the third, Smith looked awkward, arms across his chest in a bobbing style that he was not used to. Laz was leery, and stayed his distance, just popping jabs at Smith's head, since Gunboat's arms were shielding his chest. But the short ribs were open, and Laz went to work with an arpeggio of left hooks, sometimes coming in low with a left to the ribs followed by a right to the other side, then tying up the piano mover before he could retaliate.

Gunboat Smith's sides and belly were covered with so many welts it looked like one mass of red, like somebody had sandpapered the man. By the end of the round, his nose was bleeding. While he backed into a corner, the ropes cut into the flab at his sides. He looked like a stuffed and sewed up turkey, basted in sweat and blood. And Godfrey was either biting his ear or whispering into it.

At the end of the tenth round, Gunboat could not find his corner. The canvas between him and his corner seemed like a bridge. The referee gave him a push in the right direction. He sat, and his trainer, Joe Welsch, put an icebag on the back of his neck. Gunboat's mouth hung open and he was shaking his head to get the cobwebs out.

"I think my hand's busted. The nigger's got a hard head."

"Which one?" asked Joe's brother, Jemmy.

Gunboat turned quizzically to Joe Welsch. "He's only got one."

"No, dummy. Which hand? Which hand's busted?"

"Left."

"Then hit him with the right, for Chrissake," groused Jemmy. "Jesus, you got more pains than a broad on the rag."

"Give him the haymaker." Joe threw a right uppercut to underscore his point.

"Yeah," Jemmy paused. "Make hay while the sun shines, cuz, if you don't, it's gonna be nighttime for you, pal."

Gunboat touched his glove to his chin. "I'm gonna wallop him."

"That's it, champ."

Gunboat folded his arms over his gut. "It's cold in here, Joe," he groused.

"Sure," said Joe, removing the ice bag from Gunboat's neck.

"It was burning up when we came in. Musta been a hundred. It's freezing now."

"Everything is gonna feel different. When it's hot, it's gonna feel cold. When it hurts, you're gonna feel good. Okay?"

When the bell sounded for round eleven, Gunboat felt almost exhilarated, thrusting forward effortlessly. He felt like a three-hundred pound robin red breast pushed from the nest. His cornermen lifted him by the armpits and pushed him forward, not knowing themselves what it felt like to have ingrown ribs or to have *your lunch* eating *you*.

Clinching in the fifteenth round, Gunboat again spoke to Laz, and it became clear to Laz what he was saying— "*Don't hit me in the chest and I won't hit you in the balls, okay?*"

As they circled, Smith would nod his head and say,

"Okay?" waiting for Laz to nod assent to his offer. Laz had sparred with Mysterious Billy Smith, who whispered in his ear and then bit him on the top of the head, so he wasn't going to be distracted by Gunboat's whispering. But he couldn't help wondering why Gunboat was holding his arms in tight. Laz fired a left and right combination to the short ribs and then clinched. As the referee shouted, "Break," Smith jumped forward and nailed Laz a shot in the balls. The referee gave Gunboat a warning while fans yelled, "Kill the coon!"

Laz took a minute to recuperate, then danced to his left then shot a hook off the jab that wobbled the piano mover as the bell rang. As he turned toward his corner, Gunboat repeated, "Okay?"

"You're doing great," said Nemo. "How do you feel?"

"Hurts to talk. I've never been hit in the nuts like that."

"I told you," said Waddy, "protect yourself."

"He said if I don't hit him in the chest he won't hit me in the nuts."

"What is he, crazy?"

"He must be hiding a busted rib," said Nemo. "You hit him there, you might puncture his lung. Might kill him."

"What are you talking about?" said Waddy. "This isn't a picnic, it's pugilism! You've got to knock this guy out, this round. I've got money on this."

Laz spat into the bucket. "I thought you couldn't get a bookie to take your marker?"

"You don't want to know where I got it, but I got it. What do you think he'd do to you if you that had a busted rib? The fat fuck would kill you," said Waddy.

Laz seemed to have taken Waddy's advice. By the nineteenth round, there was little Gunboat could do but plod relentlessly on and pray for rain, or a lightening bolt. He seemed to paw with his jab. He practically fell on his stool when the round ended.

In the twenty-first, Laz ducked under a Smith jab that seemed immeasurably slow and Laz hit him with a huge right to the ribs, a shot that he threw with a slightly downward motion in order to separate the ribs from the cartilage. It worked. It hurt Gunboat now to throw a jab, and even more to pull it back, so he left his arm out, pawing at the stalking cat. Now Smith threw a right that seemed to float, and Laz had all the time in the world to weave and throw a hook that rattled the ribs on Smith's right side.

Gunboat dropped his elbows to protect his body and Laz followed with another hook, this one to the head, and Smith's knees genuflected involuntarily. Hands at his sides, he looked both sleepy and like he was praying. Then the lights went out. He keeled forward onto his chin, which ironically seemed to bring the big man to his senses. Referee Terence Reilly started the count slowly, moving around to look Gunboat in the face as he counted. At *six* he looked at round timer Happy Huntz, who picked up the hammer. As referee Reilly counted *nine* and Gunboat was on one knee, Hap hit the bell signaling the end of the round. Nemo fumed, but such collusions were common. He knew that a knockout had to be definitive.

The bell rang late for the twenty-second round. Smith had almost no offense at all. He just countered when Laz got close, and most of those blows were smothered. He was taking a pasting, but showed no signs of checking out.

"What's he hitting him in the head for?" complained Waddy when the round ended. "The guy's got a rock for a head. You'd need a sledgehammer to knock him out."

"Nah, nah, the hook will do it. Give him time," said Nemo.

Shortly into the twenty-third, Smith spun out of a corner and landed another uppercut south of the border. Laz collapsed to his knees.

"Get up!" shouted Nemo. "Hop on one foot!"

The referee cautioned Smith that another blow like that and he'd be disqualified. In a minute, Laz was up but still incapacitated. The rest of the round was hardly contested by either fighter.

"What did I tell you?" scolded Waddy.

"Tell Mr. Googan to shut up," Laz told Nemo.

"Shut up, Mr. Googan."

"Shut up? I managed to find a sucker to take my wager for a hundred!"

"Well, go bet five hundred on this round. He's gone."

"I haven't got five hundred."

"You didn't have one hundred either."

"Yeah, well, right now, I don't have a pot to pee in."

Deadpan, Nemo handed him the ring bucket, then gave Laz a serious look. "He's not going anywhere unless you hit him in the chest. Waddy's right. He's got a gravel bag for a jaw."

"He's gone. Bet your house on it."

"That's about all I've got left," said Waddy.

"And your monogrammed undershorts," said Nemo.

"Laz, you'd better be right, or you'll be on he next boat to Liberia."

Laz sneered and perched himself on the stool. "He's gone, goddamn it! Make that bet before he hits the canvas."

Waddy leapt off the ring lip and headed for the action. He got lucky and found some gents from out of town who did not know his reputation, and giving odds was able to wager another hundred on a Godfrey knockout in the next round.

In his corner, Smith grimaced. "He smit me a soaker to the ribs. Hurts like hell."

"Hit him in the balls if he gets you again. It'll give you time to recover," said Jemmy.

Gunboat shook his head. "Time ain't gonna help."

No sooner had the bell been struck than Laz flashed across the ring. He hit Smith with a right barely after his stool had been removed. Hit him hard on the arms that protected his chest. Laz's right hand was a pile driver, and Smith grimaced when a blow slipped off his arms onto his chest, as if his top two ribs were a tuning fork set by force to a lower key.

Laz then stunned him with a hook that created an opening for a straight right to the chest, and he threw it. Smith saw it coming but could do nothing. He grimaced, but the pain was not there. Laz had pulled the punch. The piano mover's moment of truth had come. The eyes of the rat before the pit bull bores in.

Laz let the big man clinch and whispered, "Go down. Go down or I'll fucking kill you. Your ribs will be sticking through your heart like a fork."

Suddenly Gunboat Smith was not a boxer but a piano mover. He pushed Laz away and nodded. Laz weaved and leapt forward with a pulled hook. Gunboat fell like a tipped cow. Waddy was ecstatic, with relief. He had recouped enough to keep Stu Steerman happy, or so he thought. He was relishing the ability to show his face and talk trash with the well-breeched at Mooney's till closing time when, at the count of eight, Smith suddenly got up. Covering his ribs, he clinched with Laz and said, "Gotta make it look good. Throw the same punch at the end of the round."

Laz backed off and nodded. They clinched again, Laz simply waltzing Matilda, then Smith turned Laz, imposing his broad back to referee Reilly, and unleashed an uppercut to Laz's balls. Laz went down, writhing and rolling. Nemo stared at the referee and threw up his hands. Reilly suspected a low blow, but he hadn't seen it. He had no choice but to count. To ten. Laz was still on the canvas, with the first loss of his career. Waddy stood, motionless as a wooden Indian, mouth open like a hole in his pocket.

Laz had bet a thousand dollars on himself, the entirety of the loser's purse. He came away from the Smith fight with nothing.

# (Town Topics, July 15, 1893)

*Waddy Googan has had his rapacious maw in many a good thing, but nothing quite so pleasing as the Chelsea Fighting Club by the sea, which he acquired from quondam King of Coney Island John McKane. It has turned out to be a veritable gold mine, and many Boston pols are shaking hands with themselves for coming in on the ground floor, but not for Googan. Unquestionably, politics has its remunerations, but successful fighting clubs are bonanzas, and Foxhall Codman's Charles Street Bank hasn't hesitated to foreclose on Googan.*

*The spacious building on the shores of the Atlantic was taxed to its utmost last night for the appearance of one of Boston's favorites, Grappling Godfrey, Kid Chocolate to some. Over one thousand followers of pugilism ventured out into the rain, journeyed to Googan's Sodom by the Sea, and tramped through the muddy waters regardless of exposure to pneumonia and other ailments to witness the fight, packing the Chelsea Club from pit to dome, as if Patti the Cantatrice were singing the Star Spangled Banner clad only in bloomers.*

*Even standing room was at a premium, and long before the entertainment began, reserved seats for the affray were selling at $10 and $15. It was an immense gathering and a good show. At first sight, the $5000 purse, $4000 to the winner, $1000 to the loser, looked big money, but the investment, by judicious booming, was an excellent one. The most conservative estimates placed the receipts at $20,000.*

*Gunboat Smith is largely unknown to fame in Boston. He gained fistic laurels in the antipodes, whither he went in quest of fortune. While there, he coped favorably with other shining lights of the short-haired fraternity.*

*At the outset, 'One was afraid to lead, and the other daren't', as the poet said. After a series of requests from all parts of the house, the men decided to make matters lively in the middle rounds, the result of which was a sharp exchange of blows, some of them low, but neither man was damaged to any alarming extent.*

*By then it was obvious that Godfrey, who has beaten McCracken, Malone, and Quinn, was the more scientific man. He delivered blow after blow on the face of his foe without receiving a blow in return. Several times, however, Smith grew vicious and appeared to lose his temper and unleash the fury that has sent the likes of Joe Choynski to the canvas. Then Godfrey forced his opponent against the ropes and once delivered a telling swing on the Californian's left eye. He had the man in serious trouble but could not, or would not, follow through, which raised some questions in the minds of the spectators who, at the end of the 21st, had finished all the beer, soda-water and sarsaparilla in the house and had demolished several carloads of sandwiches. After having satisfied the inner man, they sat back in their seats and mournfully whistled, 'Home Sweet Home', 'That is Love,' and 'We Won't Go Home Till Morning.'*

*In the 24th, Godfrey managed to get in a swinging right hand blow to the ribs that floored the big man. When he got up, the Californian sent out an uppercut with telling force and Godfrey lay insensible on the floor till the count of nine, when suddenly he tried to right himself, but like a man intoxicated he fell back over again. He lay there a helpless man. As soon as he was counted out, Smith picked him up in his arms and deposited him on a stool.*

~~~~~~~

"Godfrey is washed up," said Hugo.

"It was in the bag," said Skeets. "Godfrey was waltzing Matilda in the 20th. Coulda put him away easy. He had to lose to a white man some time or other. Otherwise, he'd never get a title shot."

"Who ever heard of a twenty-four round fix?" said Hugo.

"I've heard of stranger things," said Skeets. "Remember how Malone was 20 and 0 with 21 knockouts? Anyway, everyone is looking for the fix, right? You've got to make it look convincing."

"In dark town," said Hugo, "they're saying his old lady put a hex on him, to get back at him for something."

Hugo laughed.

"What's so funny?" said Skeets.

"Isn't it Mothers' Day or something?"

"Mother's Day is in May, you dumb bastard," said Skeets. "Today ain't nuthin', 'cept maybe Googan's funeral." He chuckled and opened his *Town Topics*. "Have you guys heard the Saunterer's latest? I'll read it to you:

*Is dear old puritan Boston undergoing a transformation? From the land of the bean and the cod we have avant guard fashion openings, and now we hear of a maze with dark goings-on that rival those of Manhattan. And how we would have enjoyed a seat at a most extraordinary card game, where the vindictive host, crazed by rumors of his wife having an affair, excuses himself to rush a quick growler after raising her to the tupping point, then sends a black male servant into his bedroom, in complete darkness, to serve her, as retribution. As the servant exits, he enters, or reenters if you will, leaving the unfortunate woman to either marvel at his recuperative powers or imagine the worst fate that could befall a woman of her status. But ten minutes later she is all smiles downstairs, serving the men cookies. It leaves one's head spinning. It is all so implausible we wouldn't believe a word of it if we didn't have it from a firsthand source, a maid in the house who is dallying with the master, which caused the wife to have her affair, we are told, in the first place. A crazy hub—Boston, head chasing tail, spinning yarns that make even Gotham's hair stand up.*

*—The Saunterer"*

"Frankly, I don't believe a word of it," said Hugo. "Sounds like servant gossip to me."

Father Divine folded back his upper lip. "I've never heard such rubbish."

Hugo nodded. "Typical *Town Topics* baloney."

Skeets nodded and folded his paper. "It's probably mutton done up as lamb, but Googan is an afflicted man, if not entirely crazy. He identifies with Godfrey. You should see him prancing around the ring, sparring with him. What if it turns out to be true, and the guy his wife is having an affair with is actually a nigger."

Hugo shook his head. "Jaysus, I'm confused."

Skeets laughed. "It's just like Foxy, but the reverse. Remember that time Foxy won twice on the same horse? He can't lose, and Googan can't win. And if Godfrey has been tupping her, Foxy too, Googan just lost twice on the same mare."

Hugo shook his head. "I feel sorry for the guy. He loses his fighter, he's got bookies after him, and the high-hats are laughing at him cuz he's tried so hard to get into their social clubs."

"They're not *all* laughing," said Skeets. "The reason he's blacklisted is because he's fucking half of their wives. Why wouldn't they keep him out?"

# Chapter 17: 152 Beacon St.

*B*etting on himself, Laz had parted with the loser's purse, which Casey had been counting on to finance her new boat. She was left with a moral dilemma that resolved itself in her appropriation of Waddy's 'book,' as he called the oversized, leather-bound sketchbook with all of his new fashion ideas. She dropped it into a cloth satchel, walked to Massachusetts Avenue, and caught a hansom to Haliburton's shop on Newbury Street. She rationalized that she was saving Waddy's life, indirectly, via the new boat the 'book' could pay for. And he had retreated again to the greenhouse with several quarts of whiskey and a shotgun.

She stepped onto the white, crushed-shell, semicircular drive at Haliburton Fashions to gasps behind curtains and lorgnettes. She was dressed to the nines, in a violet organdy ensemble with a thick embroidered hem in a Celtic pattern, torn from the shoulders of a mannequin in Waddy's workroom. An elongated boater was kept at a perilous slant by one huge pin ending in a chignon. The hat elicited more gasps from browsing women. She flopped the heavy folio onto the counter and didn't lift her eyes. Haliburton knew what it was. He had several guesses why, and his heart thumped.

"What's this?"

"It's like Dickens, when the ghost of the future walks in. If my husband were dead, this would be mine, to sell."

"You want to ..."

"He is as good as dead, unless I get my hands on two thousand dollars."

"Two ..." Haliburton's breath ran out again. Offhand it seemed like a huge sum. Without asking, he opened the sketchbook and was stunned by the two pages he glimpsed before Casey slammed it shut. Even with her poor vision Casey could see his eyes widen, his Adam's apple rise and fall, and she knew that he could recall everything he saw in the book.

"I could give you ... maybe five-hundred."

Casey read his face the way Waddy did at his weekly poker games, but more successfully. "What do you think John Brooks would offer?"

"Brooks never liked Waddy's work."

"That doesn't mean he wouldn't steal it."

"All right. Waddy is a competitor, but he's also a friend. I'll give you $1,000."

"You're right about 'friend.' That's why I came here first. But there's always Quimby and Lashton, maybe Worth."

Haliburton shook his head with a flat smile. "It'd be a pig in a poke. No one will bid on what he can't see. And if you show it, it's worthless."

Casey looked around the shop. Two women who'd been staring at her turned to a hat rack and whispered. Casey leaned forward and dropped her hat on the counter. "When I walk out of here, those two women will break a leg getting to this counter, begging for this hat. It'll keep three milliners busy ten hours a day. And this dress, which you've memorized—they'll be asking if you've got it in beige or mauve. Tell me I'm wrong."

Haliburton just stared.

"Look, Hal, we both know what this is worth. And we know that Brooks and Quimby and the rest of Boston's imaginatively threadbare collection of couturiers would pay $2,000 for it. I came to you because you're closer in spirit to Waddy than they are."

Haliburton looked at the women eyeing Casey, then at the hat. He turned it and tilted his head to see it from a different angle. "$1,500. You'll want it in green, I imagine."

Haliburton pulled out a money clip and gave her $500. "Come back in a week for the rest, and bring that dress."

Casey smiled, reached for her hat and pushed it to Hal. "Get ready for the stampede."

Casey looked back through the window and laughed. She was right. Two women were fighting for the hat.

The book turned out to be a version of Seward's folly. Two weeks later Haliburton took all the prizes at the New York Emporium fashion opening. But Casey needed $500 more, and she knew of only one person who might loan it to her. She rang the bell at 152 Beacon and was escorted upstairs.

"We're Sorosis sisters, right?" said Casey.

"Yes, but how are you so sure you can beat Codman?"

Casey breathed deeply and exhaled, extending her hand. "Shake."

After a moment's hesitation, a befuddled Mrs. Jack clasped her hand lightly around the much larger hand of Casey Googan, feeling the crush of her heavily calloused palm. Momentarily, she let out a shriek. A concerned servant rushed upstairs, only to be dismissed immediately by his mistress.

"I'm sorry," said Casey.

Mrs. Jack inhaled deeply. "Dear, you did what you had to. I would write you a check, except that my hand is broken." She forced a laugh and momentarily flexed her fingers and found the wherewithal to write.

# Town Topics

*Opening his shop one recent Christian morning John Brooks was met with a veritable cemetery of whalebone skeletons. Fifty or more corsets littered the stairs and walkway of his shop. Pushing them aside with his gold-handled cane, the famous designer was the laughing stock of Newbury Street. It was a trick worthy of the seldom seen Wadsworth Googan, the day before Gotham's Fifth Avenue fashion opening, the trick a gibe at Brooks' heeling to the antiquated. Indeed, Haliburton, undoubtedly the perpetrator, stole the show with his "Boxer" collection, featuring paddled shoulders and loosely cummerbund-belted waists.*

*Haliburton has already put several lengths between himself and his Bostonian competitors. Even Gotham's own Charles Frederick Worth is shamelessly copying Haliburton's sporting line, so in vogue with the evolving woman of the new century, and who but Mrs. Jack would be Haliburton's first and foremost model, paying dearly for the honor?*

*Is there any end to Haliburton's novelty? There's a masculine edge to all the feminine finery. Which makes us wonder about the true origins of Haliburton's genius. The evidence: a high-collared sweater, such as scullers wear. Jodhpurs cut to a woman's figure. Rounded shirt-collars with a man's necktie or a large, feminine, loosely tied bowtie. So who is the model, the inspiration? ... Who rows boats? Takes ribbons in dressage? And is reputed to attend boxing matches in men's attire? Who but the woman known all over Boston as Casey, the wife of Wadsworth Googan. Ye women of Boston, let not the legendary woolen cap be pulled over your eyes as the cognoscenti say it was over Foxhall Codman's. You're not wearing Haliburtons. You're wearing Googans.*

*—The Saunterer*

# Chapter 18: Off

*A*t the Union Boat Club, Deke Merriwell swirled his glass, watching a single small cube make a half-revolution in his cognac. He sipped the *Very Superior Old Pale*, and swirled again.

"Something's funny, Foxy. Something's going on. The niggers in the West End are taking the odds, betting on the broad."

Codman let go of the wooden handles, attached to ropes and weights, that he had been pulling down from a sitting position. "Fifteen to one—I'd bet against me, too."

"They say Godfrey's mother put a hex on you. They take that stuff seriously."

"So?"

"So, I've done some investigating."

"And?"

"Word is Charlie Hot Dog is building her a boat that will fly past anything on the water. Even your chauffeur is taking the odds against you."

Codman's poured himself a glass of Verdelho Madeira, demijohned in 1850. "Charlie Hot Dog?"

Deke refilled his glass, dipped two fingers into the cognac, removed the partially melted cube, and replaced it with a new one.

"Charlie Hot Dog Neblung. The guy seems to have some kind of grudge against you."

Codman stared out the window, two thoughts vying for dominance; one—the spat that followed his father's dismissing a man named Neblung; the other—that the maids had done a shitty job on the windows.

"There are more rumors. They say the Googan woman dresses up as a man. Goes to fights, races under assumed names. They say she raced you and rowed through you."

Codman laughed. "Bullshit! No one has ever rowed through Foxhall Codman."

"This morning ... I couldn't find a bookie giving even five to one ... You know what they say—money talks."

Bullshit ... *don't row.*

~~~~~~~

"Find out everything you can about her. Strengths, weaknesses. What she's like. Her history, particularly rowing."

Deke starts at Mooney's Temple of Bacchus, where leads take him to Bryn Mawr, U. Penn, and the Schuylkill, a hotbed for rowing. Several days later he's back with a story. He meets Codman in the lawyer's study. Empty bottles of vintage champagne fill an entire shelf, souvenirs of victories past. On another shelf a dozen filled bottles. They spray no one; on Beacon Street imagination's in dry dock. Codman lights his pipe with lucifers that never fail, sucks in the cooled smoke through a dark briar tunnel, lets it tease his throat and lungs before exhaling what leaves a familiar taste. History, he knows, can be controlled like that. Much of the history of Boston has been written in rooms like this, rooms that smell like the inside of a cigar box. The cobbles on the street outside are inlaid in a pattern conceived right here.

And the history he doesn't know blows in with Deke Merriwell, blows in off the Schuylkill, clear sky, late afternoon or early evening, the distinction washing out on the sterns of four shells, three long and one short:

*a few straggling cloud-wisps practice entropy, shape-shifting arriviste angels, spectators of dories, scows, and sleek, narrow shells with eight men pulling oars in synchrony, but. One of them looks like a furled leaf. He's done his best to vomit mostly outside the shell and his gut is a wringer on fire. He won't row again for three days. And so now seat 2 of Boat 2 takes his place in Boat 1. B3's number 2 jumps to B2, and on B3 the table is set, the porridge is poured, and no beast to take the seat.*

*But Billy Spires didn't earn his seat in the stern with muscle. The U. Penn senior cox has been distracted for the last half hour of their warm up on the Schuylkill, and it's a big day for the U. Penn crew. The Child's Cup race is a week away. Seat-swapping still looms and the three boats are ready to race. Had been. Three down now to two, and eight men in Boat 3 are cursing, shipped off to the Lethe now without a seat 2.*

*No one but Spires has noticed the impeccable form of the lone sculler who has yet to churn up a single splash from the boat's oars.*

Codman smokes as Deke narrates, "Spires realizes there'll be ice on the Schuylkill before that happens. And the other talent Spires has is a magnificent whistle, the kind where forefingers pull down the corners of the mouth and the tongue folds back to let out a shrill blast. He's got to put down the megaphone to do it but it's still loud enough to hurt the ears of anyone within a hundred feet and turn the head of anyone on a river where sound carries a whistle like that for more than the fifty yards between him and the sculler who turns her head—yeah, now you know—and turns the shell toward the beckoning arms of the cox."

*"It's a fucking girl," says Toad—affectionate corruption of 'Todd.'*

*Spires kicks Toad hard on the shin and Inky Ingram, the English major behind Toad, whispers, "Redundant redneck."*

"She draws her boat gracefully sideways to the docking B1, and Spires asks her if she can row an Eight, and she tells him she's stroke for the Bryn Mawr girls' crew. Spires calls coach Ward over and tells him they've got a replacement for the puker and that the three-way race can go on.

*Ward nods almost imperceptibly, maintains his sempiternal distant gaze. He's as impervious to weather as the figurehead on a ship. He stands just as still, his face as motionless. He watches the clouds. If they be angels, whom were they here to herald? Torn apart now, as if in dissent to their calling. Once every year Ellis Ward smiles, but only to let the world—his crew—know there are teeth behind it.*

"Some of the guys in B3 are laughing, but most of them are glad for the chance to race, and when the freak gets through glaring at them like some kind of fucking Joan of Arc holding an oar like a staff and they realize she's as big as their stroke, there's no more laughing, and the laughers feel like assholes, and they are.

"So now they do a 500 meter piece, and B3 whops the shit out of B2, and B2 can't believe it. They do it again—same result. Coach scratches his head and sees Spires nodding his head toward the girl in B3. He shouts at 7 in B2, a kid named Schieber, to swap with the girl. Schieber mumbles and curses and coach Ward won't tolerate that shit and lets Schieber know he'll be banished from the crew if he says another word.

"Next piece, B3 is left in the dust and Spires in B1can see the bow of B2 poke into the periphery of his vision, which B2 has never done before. So the guys in B2 are cheering and slapping the new 'guy' on the back. And she says, 'What are you, a bunch of happy fucking losers?' That's exactly what she says—*a bunch of fucking losers*! The only broad they've heard talk like that is the one who makes her living on her back servicing Delta Sigma Phi or some horseshit Greek thing. Salty bitch turns out to be as talented with her tongue as with an oar. One wily broad. Knows how to get their goat but good. It's one thing to be called a loser, but being called a *fucking* loser by a girl kicks up the testosterone in all of them. One wily broad."

*The girl knows them all by their names because they're painted in black on a white swatch of broadcloth sewn on to the backs of their shirts.*

*"Barnacle, you wash out at the release. Your hands have to be like a bicycle chain, go around without stopping.*

*"Vespoli, you've got to be more connected through the last phase of the drive. Keep the pressure on your footboard all the way through.*

*"Dupont, ..."*

*"Dumont! At least Swarthmore girls can read."*

*Her shoulders shake and Dumont knows she's laughing. "Dumont, you're skipping your blade too much. Splash is getting in my eyes. Get higher out of the water.*

*"Harrison, you're slouching over your oar. Keep your head back. You're losing half of your efficiency."*

*"Half?"*

*"Bryn Mawr math," says Vespoli.*

*"You know what I'm saying. It all adds up—you, McCarthy, Dumont, Harrison, you may be a beast yourself, but you've got to be one beast, a beast with eight arms, all connected to Hart, who's your brain."*

*"Hart, the brain? Shit, we ain't got a chance."*

*The crew laugh, including Hart, the cox.*

*"McCarthy, you pull like a Clydesdale, but you also stop at the finish. Efficiency slips out of your stroke like poop after lunch at Romero's. You might as well be a girl."*

*More chuckles from Boat 2.*

*"Barber, you lift too soon after the release. Your blade is half way to Philadelphia before your stroke is finished. You know what that means over 2,000 meters? Look at Wolff's release. His oar leaves a big puddle that implodes. That's what you want to see at the end of your oar."*

*"Miss," says Barnacle, "how do you see all that? I mean, McCarthy's back is as broad as a barn door. Not to mention that his sweat would knock out a bloodhound."*

*McCarthy splashes Barnacle.*

*"Save that for your shower."*

*"I get bored sculling. I watch you guys and I feel sorry for you, but you're not all that bad. You might beat my girls' boat."*

*"Trouble is—we just don't have the power first boat has. I mean, McCarthy does, but the rest of us are on second boat for a reason."*

*"It's not about possessing the power. It's about getting whatever power you possess behind the oar. Everybody does that, and the boat swings. You can beat anybody, or almost anybody. And it's got to hurt beyond anything you think you can endure, cuz it's about the pain that possesses you—taught to respect the body."*

"So she's chewing them out and everybody can see it, everyone in B1 and B3, and the coach, and everybody's wondering what she's saying cuz it looks intense. Looks like Madame Blavatsky giving a séance. Then Ward docks them and points one hand at the girl, and the other at Barnacle, the B2 stroke, then crosses his arms like a well-witcher. Doesn't say anything. Stands there like a cigar store Indian. Now the girl is stroke and Ward cups his hands like a priest signaling the congregation to all rise, and they get back on the water. This time it's 2,000 meters and for all the marbles. B1 and B2 both go out strong and you can tell that B1 has the needle. They settle into thirty and B2 follows suit, and the girl shouts at the cox, 'Up it!' From the launch Ward reads the lips of the dumbfounded cox questioning, 'Up?'

*"Up it! Now! And hold it till you clear their bow."*

"So B2 blows past B1 for the first time ever and Spires knows it's crazy to go out that fast, but even he gets the needle. He's got Madame fucking Blavatsky stroking a boat that has never looked half so clean. He picks up the pace and the B1 boys aren't used to seeing only B3 behind them and they get a little sloppy, which is just what the girl is counting on, and B2 picks up a half length more.

*Can you bend, actually bend the blade in the water? And if you can pain, can't you do it again, and again? One pain to the next—isn't it the same delirium, like the in and the out simply dissolving into one—breathing?*

"Meanwhile, Barnacle's arms are going like a bicycle chain and he's right behind the girl who's still perfection incarnate and Barnacle is learning from the new stroke. The boat's got a harmony it's never had. Vespoli and Harrison follow suit, and now McCarthy looks like a kid with a new toy and the toy is an oar and the oar feels like a toothpick and it's like a toy too because he can feel the boat lift on the drive and he knows power is finally coming from him. Now the boat is in swing and they've got almost a full length on B1, so Spires picks it up but not full out because the sprint is 200 meters away, but the girl knows that he's just managing to hold back panic. They pull their bow up to B2's stern and stay there for five strokes and B1 finds its old rhythm. It picks up a seat. And now Hart gets the needle. He wants to respond and he raises the megaphone to his mouth and the girl says, 'Wait!' Hart's stunned because B1 has a full seat lead and Spires is grinning. B1 is in full sprint and even the crew are wondering why Hart hasn't pulled the trigger, then the girl says, 'Now, pick one.' Fifty meters to go and Hart spits out his own command, 'Pick Spires!' And the boat responds to the personal. It goes fucking airborne, blows past Spires and one more seat when they hit the finish line.

"Ward turns to Fritz, the assistant coach, says that's the cleanest, smartest blade work he's ever seen. The three boats dock and Ward gives that icy stare and Kittredge, the B1 stroke, knows what's coming. The girl is now stroke for B1 with Princeton coming to town for the Child's Cup. The girl isn't a U. Penn student, but everyone has ringers and everyone knows it. B1 gets their new stroke and the boat swings, puts up its best times ever. Come race day, the girl has her hair cut and tucked into a woolen cap. She's got a loose shirt on over a couple of yards of tightly pulled cotton bandage. But somebody snitches. I suspect it was Kittredge, but I suppose there's more than one misogynist in that boathouse. The girl's out. U. Penn goes down big time, loses to Princeton by two lengths.

"Cleanest, smartest blade work he's ever seen—what Ward said. And a girl stroking Penn's first boat! Who ever would have thought that Princeton would care about a female ringer in a men's boat? But a ringer is always a ringer. There's got to be a reason for replacing the varsity stroke at the end of the season. And the Princeton coach knew a guy who knew the girl's father, and turns out the girl has quite a reputation. So that was it. Princeton protests. And we all know who the girl was. I don't know what to say, Foxy. A girl is a girl, but a ringer's a ringer. I just don't know."

"I do," says the reigning champ of the Charles River, leaving Deke completely flummoxed."

~~~~~~~

Casey's new boat was constructed in the Googan's side yard by Charlie, Casey, Laz, and Waddy, under the surreptitious supervision of Billy Swipes Unger. The race was little more than a week away, but Charlie acted as if there was no rush. For two days he did nothing but sharpen tools, eight hours a day. It drove Casey nuts and Waddy to drink. He had a half-dozen stones, all of which looked the same to Casey but were slightly different to Charlie. With immense patience he sharpened his many wood-chisels and plane blades. The differences in blade angles were apparent only to Charlie. And when he finished a chisel, it was laid on velvet cloth with the deference afforded an antique Samurai sword. The thick steel chisels were razor sharp. To prove it, Charlie would mow down a few whiskers on his cheeks. Charlie treated his chisels, augurs, planes, and other tools with reverence. They were almost like family.

At the end of the second day, while Laz was whittling a miniature oar, Charlie set all his sharpening stones on newspaper to dry, threw out the ten-gallon pail of red-brown water, set the last chisel on velvet, gave Laz an icy glare and pronounced as if from the far end of a tunnel, "Ready."

The next day Charlie worked like a man forty years younger. The lost time was made up by twelve-hour days. The shell was right on schedule, but there was trouble in Casey's camp. Practicing in her old boat, she aggravated the muscle she originally tore during Codman's race with Sullivan. She dismissed it as a stitch, but everyone could see that it was something more.

Waddy kept himself pickled enough that the delicate balance of jealousy/rage and self-preservation could not be tipped by ratiocination. The first few days after the Smith fight, Laz was too beat to do much. He did, however, have the best eyes and feel for the fine detail work, which Charlie tutored him to do.

Charlie had gotten lucky—all the woods he needed were available. White oak from Michigan for the gunwales and ribs, Douglas fir for the hull. He had his own wood screws made—zinc-plated. Casey was worried about the hull that had a minimal keel, worried that the shell would have problems tracking. Charlie reassured her that her technique would make up for any potential loss in tracking, and the lesser draft gave her an edge in speed.

Waddy bitched loudly about the wood dust getting in his throat, which made him knock off for beer at 2:00 p.m., after which he was useless. Not that it made much difference—all he could do was sand.

Casey loved the aroma of yellow cedar, and the rooster tail of sawdust from Charlie's crosscut saw raining on her. Shortly after lunch, Charlie stood up straight and threw down his sandpaper. "I've got a bad feeling."

"We're almost done," said Laz. "We'll paint her tomorrow."

Charlie shook his head. "No. They've got something up their sleeve. I've seen too many of these races. Boats get sabotaged the night before. Driftwood fills somebody's lane and the race is over. We need a signaling device, to let Casey know if there's trouble."

"Like what? Megaphone? Bell?" Casey asked.

Charlie shook his head. "Can't trust you'll be able to hear much. There'll be a lot of fireworks."

"So, what do you suggest?"

"Heliotrope. You can see it a mile away."

"Where are you going to get a heliotrope?"

As if on cue, Swipes came bounding over the wall holding cabbage leaves over his loins and his ass. "I'll get you any damn thing you want. Just get me some clothes."

"What happened to you?" Casey asked.

"Was skinny-dipping at Magazine beach. Mud Foley's gang stole my clothes. So I lifted a cabbage off a *shtupvegel*."

Casey handed him a large towel to wrap himself in. "I'll run into the Square and pick you up some things."

"Thanks," said Swipes. "And I'll get you that helio-thing you want."

Waddy laughed. "How are you gonna get a heliotrope?"

"I'm gonna steal it. What did you think—I'm gonna buy it?"

"We don't approve of stealing," Casey chided.

"Yeah? What about losing?"

Waddy's voice was a low, unintentional tremolo, "We don't even think about losing."

"You even know what a heliotrope is?" asked Laz.

"Whatever it is, I can get it. Long as you got connections with the gangs and the cops, you can get anything on the Charles. The Quayside Rats owe me one."

"For what?"

"You don't want to know."

Before Casey could disagree, a man with a disheveled beard and long mustache showed up with a burlap bag,

"Americo Bartolini! What the hell are you doing here?" said Charlie. It was the first time in years the old anarchist had ventured from the front porch of his house on Magazine Street.

Hugo's father, Americo, hugged Charlie. "What are you doing out of the hospital?"

"Building a boat."

"I know you're making a boat. Everyone knows you're making a boat, even that bastard ...," Americo shook his fist in place of Codman's name. "I saw his car last night about midnight, and I said to myself, what's *a dat* high-hat *figlio di puttana* doing in our neighborhood? *Da boat*! He's a gonna *sabote a da boat-a*. Like hell, he is, I'm *a* said to myself. *Theerty, forteen* year you been *a* waiting to make-*a* dis boat. And I'm *a* gonna help you."

"What do you know about boats?" Waddy slurred, lighting a cigarette.

"When I come America first time, I come Pennsawanya by boat."

Waddy laughed. "How you come Pennsawanya by boat? Pennsawanya ain't *a* gotta no coast."

Americo shook his fist at Waddy. "I come by boat, then by wagon."

"Put him to work, Charlie," said Laz, sitting on a saw horse. "We can use all the help we can get. I'm still sore, and ..." Laz just pointed at the useless Waddy, who was constantly worried about getting something on his clothes.

"Hey, I'm *a* no builda da boat. I'm *a* guarda da boat. That sonofabitch—next time I'm a shoot 'im."

Americo opened the burlap bag and took out a twelve gauge shotgun and some shells.

"Okay," said Charlie. "Just be sure you know who you're shooting at."

Americo retired to the high ground—the wall between Charlie's property and Waddy's. He put the shotgun on the ground, rolled a cigarette, and offered one to Waddy, who declined, waved good-bye to everyone, and staggered around the corner of the house, toward where his buggy was parked.

No one had noticed bookie Seamus Forse arriving, till he was almost in the midst of things, except Waddy, who stood around the corner of the house, overhearing the conversation before he slipped off. Americo's shotgun went off and Forse ducked.

"What the hell?" said Charlie, grabbing his heart.

Forse raised, then lowered, his hands. "Don't shoot. Just looking for Googan. The race is off. His time is up."

"What are you talking about?" said Casey.

"Off. As in *o-f-f.* Codman pulled out. Where's Googan?"

Americo clicked his reloaded shotgun closed.

"He can't pull out. Everyone will say he's chicken."

Forse shrugged. "He said it's ridiculous to race a woman. She hasn't got a chance. I buy that." He threw a smug glance at Casey and tipped his hat. "Tell Googan I'm looking for him." He strutted back to his Panel Boot Victoria, drawn by a pair of anxious horses. When he got in, Laz threw down his sandpaper and took off across Charlie's lawn.

"Where are you going?"

"Find Waddy before he does. Did you see that Smith and Wesson in his belt? He's not coming to collect.

Waddy's been a deadbeat too long."

Casey trembled before searching for him too, checking first the greenhouse, discovering pots smashed on the floor along with a scythe, *The 400* decimated, decapitated and hacked.

~~~~~~~

The four-hundred pound double mahogany doors of Foxhall Codman's house on Beacon Street took a beating from the summer afternoon sun and from the elements in Boston's winter. Now they had to deal with Waddy's boot, which had already left a scuff mark just below the smoked glass. Loud enough to alert the Codman butler, who let him in. Waddy knew the way to Codman's study. One flight up, end of the hall to the left. Through the ornate Florentine doors, down the red carpet to the large Isfahan carpet with its gold and silver threads, past the wall-to-wall bookcases filled with first editions of Balzac, Flaubert, Dickens, Thackeray. He recognized immediately the red leather and quatrefoil of his beloved Dante, serving as a doorstop, unhocked from a Tremont Street pawn shop by Foxhall to spite him.

"We had a bet."

Codman shrugged and tilted his head. He reached into his humidor.

"You can't pull out on me!"

He lit a cigar. "What do you know about contracts?"

"Don't give me that lawyer bullshit. This is a gentleman's affair."

Codman swiveled and walked slowly toward a bookcase. "I'm talking transparency, indispensable in a valid contract, which is what a wager it. You never told me that your wife is an Amazon who rows forty strokes a minute."

"You calling my wife an Amazon?"

Codman shrugged. "*Amazon*'s not so bad. Better than ...

*cuckold*." He laughed, and Waddy lurched at him, managing to cockeye his cravat before being tossed to the floor. His tippled head was spinning and his mouth was filling with blood. He wiggled with his tongue the same tooth that was always coming loose and scaring him in his dreams. He spat the blood-specked incisor onto the back of the cockatoo in the rug. Back on his feet, he felt lighter. He began to laugh. "You're afraid of losing! ... To my fucking wife!"

"Fucking—yes. Losing—no. I just never let myself be suckered." He lit another Havana. "Give me back the two-length spot and the race is on."

Waddy turned and looked at him, but the champ's eyes were fixed on the sky through the narrow windows that ran nearly from the floor to the ceiling. Waddy walked to the door and opened it before giving his answer.

Codman grinned. "It's not pleasant being over a barrel, but at least it's been warmed."

Waddy gave him a quizzical look.

"Your wife ... and the negro."

Waddy opened the door wider, without looking back, feeling suddenly more sober than he had in weeks. "Maybe we're all keeping it warm." He took a few steps, then turned. "I'm not gentry, and I know it. And you're not really Irish. You're fecking Anglo. Your ancestors evicted mine." Waddy shook his index finger at his nemesis. "Only the dispossessed know their land in the dark. I know mine, and I'm coming to take it back."

# Chapter 19: Amazon

$D$etails change—Skeets' red shirt may be short-sleeved or rolled-up long sleeves. He may be handing a beer to Father Divine and chatting with Nemo, or vice versa—in a panoramic photograph not *snapped* in 1893 but *recorded* across a battered band of gray matter by Laz Godfrey: one sweet, sad, nostalgic moment in that year's biggest racing event.

In any version, Skeets has a shiner under his left eye, a remnant not of a bar fight but of an encounter with The Society for the Prevention of Vice at Cambridge City Hall's licensing bureau. The most prominent missing person in the photo is Casey, who would be behind them somewhere on the Charles, warming up for the race in her old patched paper shell.

Years later, the would-be photographer/boxer could be found on his back—of his own accord and not in the ring, up river on the grass, ostensibly taking in some sun but actually taking account of his life, relishing these moments, feeling that time was running out for him to tally it all up definitively—the plusses and minuses, the *joy* and *sorrow*, struggling with the pieces of the photo, as if they comprised a jigsaw puzzle, the final assemblage of which would magically spell out the *three* or *six* letter word in that tally sheet in his head.

He felt that if he could understand the whirlpool of emotions in him at that moment—the day of the race, he would understand the slower currents that spun out of that whirlpool, which subsided across time the way the release of a hard-pulled oar would leave a small and temporary whirlpool in the boat's wake.

*Who was in the background of Laz's 1893 photo?* Pearline and Triffeny, Waddy in his white suit, grass-stained from a drunken fall, black-banded white hat, spats, and pearl stickpin. He was wobbly but still flashing his broadest smile while Patti the Cantatrice sat placidly some distance upstream, on the outskirts of the Louisburg Square crowd, with her legs tucked under her, intrepid Swipes trying to catch a mole's eye glimpse of her monogrammed, **WG**, nainsook drawers trimmed with white Hamburg, recalling her performance with Waddy in the boathouse. There was Charlie, testing out Swipes' booty. Simple but effective, the heliotrope was basically a sun-mirroring device on a tripod. The Achilles-heel of the plan, Charlie realized when a cloud covered the sun, was that the heliotrope worked only when skies were clear. Finally, there was Foxhall Codman, wearing Patti's unmonogrammed scarf, blowing the Cantatrice a kiss goodbye.

In his new shirt and trousers, Swipes could almost pass for a Brahmin kid on a Sunday outing. In the years to come, Casey would informally adopt him, sending him off in Waddy's footsteps to Boston Latin. For the afternoon of the race, she made him a tongue sandwich. He sat on the grass near the Brahmins, where Mud Foley's gang wouldn't scuffle with him for the sandwich. A middle-aged woman in a Directoire style dress and a high-crowned hat with ostrich feathers smiled at the appetite of the boy ravishing his sandwich.

"Want to share your sandwich, sonny?" she joked.

"If you was really hungry, I would. But you look like you already ate the cow."

When he noticed Casey on the dock, he stuffed the remnant of the sandwich into his mouth, ran over, and said hello. He noticed a bronze statue of a man hurling a discus. "Why's that man throwin' a pancake?"

"It was a sport in ancient *Greece*," Casey answered, and had to wonder, in light of the boy's puzzled expression, if he wasn't processing a second question, about the substance the pancakes might be cooked in.

Shortly after Laz had stood at the edge of the water taking the mental photograph, he felt alone in the late summer sun and the white world of sculling. It all mattered because he felt it was only a matter of time till the white lady got tired of her black bibelot. He reflected on what she had done to her famous husband, whom he studied just days ago, from a corner at Mooney's where no one would be watching him. He tried to intuit the sporting man's feelings as he sat alone smoking at the bar on a slow, early evening. And he knew that if Waddy suddenly turned, if he looked into his eyes, he would know that Laz saw through the facade of the Googan grin. But at the same time Laz *wanted* Waddy to turn, to look at him, so he could get into the man's gut, into the fear and the sorrow, into the tempting, piss-warm emptiness.

It struck Laz that he was in a bubble by himself on the river bank, so unnoticed that even the curs all found someone else to sniff up. And though some rational part of the semi-catatonic man in the bubble thought his motionlessness should attract some attention, kids and even flies paid him no heed. Then the twenty-year-old ex-contender stepped out of the bittersweet bubble the way he would come out of his corner when the gloves were laced on; he filed the photo plate for a lifetime of dissection and contemplation, and with a *coup de* heartfelt grace said a silent hello to the woman on the water.

~~~~~~~

Downriver, Stu Steerman picked at the hair below his Adam's apple, while a horsefly landed on Moose's size eighteen neck. He slapped at the pain and heard the angry buzz of a fly that fell, still fanning its wings on a flat rock.

—*Die painful*, he said, noticing Waddy pacing the dock, as frantic as the fallen fly and feeling like he was complying with Moose's wish. When Moose looked again at the rock, with his hand raised to swat, the fly was gone, as was Waddy.

—*Sonofabitch*, he philosophized,—*everyone gets lucky sometime.*

Deke Merriwell helped Codman carry his shell to the dock. "Foxy, I know you're going to win, but if anything comes up, don't forget—she rows with the Harvard guys, up-river. She doesn't know the Boston part of the Charles like you do."

"What are you getting at?"

"If you win the toss, take the Boston-Alston side. You'll be in the current and away from the driftwood that builds up Cambridge-side. Swing out wide as you pass the point. Let her go straight into it."

"What you're saying is that there *will* be driftwood and you'll give it a shove before the race starts."

Deke smiled. "About a mile down. Keep your eyes peeled and swing out."

A blackfly landed on Waddy's head. He shoved its proboscis back into its skull. He was about to sit on a rock, but noticed that it was crawling with ants. They owned it, the way the Brahmins owned the river. Finally, he found a tree against which he could sit and relax, but the *blackflies* would not leave him alone. After a five-minute snooze he awoke, shouting and grabbing his crotch, thinking that a creature that would crawl all the way up his pants leg to feed on his pecker deserved a name less banal.

Upriver, a fat lady broke out a beer from a burlap-lined tin tub filled with ice. Stout for the stout. She smiled at Waddy with a thin beer fuzz over her lip. She offered him one. He smiled and waved it off. He staggered downriver, nervously. He spotted Steerman on the outskirts of the Mooney's gang and hesitated before joining them. Steerman too was in his cups, smiling. He had much to be happy about. The race was bigger than he had expected. He not only got five per cent from the rooming houses on both sides of the river, he was also renting out dry-goods crates to the shiftless and the pickpockets, for fifty cents a night. For seventy-five cents they could get a piano box. A dime more—hay and straw for bedding. For nothing the rats of Cambridgeport got drunk on the dregs of beer in split, broken kegs. For nothing they filled their bellies on crumbs and crud too small to tempt urchins like Swipes.

Steerman walked upriver, followed by Moose. Seeing Waddy, Skeets exhorted him to rush the growler. After a staggering jog to Skeets' table, he poured himself a beer in one of the steins Skeets had brought for the occasion. On cue, Skeets and Waddy and Nemo and Father Divine formed a half-circle with one arm around the shoulder of the next man, putting their steins to their ears, like a barbershop quartet that had practiced the routine many times. These Four Horsemen stood silent, bent, mouths open, mugging for Laz's invisible camera till Skeets nodded and uttered, "Yea-a-a-h-h," and they laughed. The beer had passed the test their fathers had put it through when they were tots—it had *growled*, and now could be downed; each man connected by some string to his father, eyes closed in transport; that string calling out to be plucked and fretted for its version of growl.

"Here's how."

"Same here."

~~~~~~~

At the boathouse, the victory celebration had already begun. Mrs. Jack arrived—in a Cleopatra barge, refusing the many hands offering to help her onto the dock. She accepted a glass of Taitinger champagne poured from a jeroboam by Deke Merriwell, who took the bottle toss from Todd Farrell.

The boathouse society was delineated into three camps: the Gales Ferry crowd, the Red Hat crowd (including J.P. Morgan Jr.), and others. The men wore blue blazers or striped jackets, white pants, ties, straw boaters or modified beanies. The women were in long dresses, floral hats, and carried parasols. The crowd, over ten thousand strong, not only lined the banks and boathouses, they spilled out onto the river, in shells, rowboats, sailboats, skiffs, fishing smacks, scud boats, punts, dories, scows, and schooners—men were literally hanging from the rigging. Near the finish line, the boats were so thick that men stepped from one boat to another to get to shore. Farther out on the river, a dozen yachts flew flags from every boom and bowsprit.

Foxhall Codman performed his standard strength feat for the admiring crowd, lifting his oars by the handles, parallel to the dock, then holding them straight out, as if they were extensions of his arms. The crowd *ooh*ed and clapped. Then the man with arms indistinguishable in color and bulk hardness from the oar shafts slammed the orange-tipped sculls into their lock plates. Todd Farrel and Deke Merriwell shoved him off on a warm-up run. His blades dipped in the water, catching and pulling with grace, speeding the shell against the drag of the water. The puzzled sculling champion watched his opponent dock and exit her slow scow, and was stunned as a sleek, light, beautiful shell was lifted off the top of Hugo Bartolini's hansom by Laz, Nemo, Waddy and Hugo, their efforts orchestrated by Charlie Hot Dog, who half the crowd thought was dead.

The new shell seemed to be slumming beneath Casey's

old sculls, folded back onto the stern, looking like the wrong wings grafted onto a butterfly. A lesser athlete than Foxhall Codman might have been more than fazed. A more dignified boat designer might have just shaken or kissed Casey's hand. But not Charlie Neblung, champion of nothing if not the sweet lumpen proletariat. He laughed as Codman approached to inspect the shell, three loud notes in a descending scale.

Momentarily, the two scullers shared the stillness, gliding to the starting line. Codman won the fixed toss and chose the Alston side. He tried not to look at his opponent, but was distracted by her letting go her sculls and reaching under her sweater. She was putting on a brown woolen cap, looking through him, laughing low and fulsome, and reminiscent. Treading memory, he let up on his sculls and felt a frisson of fear run up his arms. The laugh grew dimmer with the distance of the two-length spot she rowed to. He put two fingers to the corners of his mouth and whistled loudly at the woman staring at his broad back. He turned, smiled, and waved her back. Waddy hadn't told her, or anyone, that the two-length spot had been rescinded. Referee William Blaikie, the ex-Harvard stroke, blew twice on his whistle, in the stakes boat.

"It's going to be a fair start, Miss."

Laz and Hugo glared at Waddy, who sheepishly studied his spats. Casey backed her boat even with Codman's, on the Cambridge side. He returned her laugh, stared at her, and Casey's eyes burned back. She backed her boat another six feet, spotting Codman two yards, and smiled at him.

"The fucking arrogance!" grumbled Deke to his cronies in the boathouse, leaning over the railing, which was lined four deep. Blaikie blew his whistle again and ordered her to pull up even.

"Piker in the world of pain," she whispered.

"What?" But he had heard the taunt. Almost biblical.

*Piker in the world of pain*—was all she said, but enough to unsettle him.

*One daffy fucking broad ...*

But then the look, delayed, look of true compassion—for a loser, a kid in a *man*'s game. Her head moved slowly, side to side. He couldn't help noting the uncanny grace of it, the total lack of fear, the calm. She turned and looked at her reflection on the smooth water as serenely as if she were putting on makeup in a mirror. And what he felt break gently down his arms and legs was a jot and tittle of doubt that he hadn't felt on this river in fifteen years.

She looked at him again. "You know what a trireme is?"

He nodded with an air of belligerence.

"Never rowed one though, have you?" The question rhetorical. Some queer kind of smile, he thought. An almost contorted laugh as she turned to look at him again. "You don't have a Chinaman's chance."

The fucking finality of it, a bitch in flannel britches. He thought on the one hand that she was insane, and on the other—*that she was insane.*

Blaikie raised a small flag and brought it down sharply as he blew his whistle long and loudly. Ten strokes into the race, Codman's plan of a tactic-less race was scrapped. Her boat was clearly faster than his. The shell flew. He had no idea how much of a lead she would open up. So he did what he had never before done—he played catch-up at the start, went out hard just to keep her stern in sight, till he could feel her out, measure her pace.

Wary of being false-started, Casey slowed. Codman pulled even and she adjusted to his pace. A quarter mile out, Charlie was counting strokes and looking at his stopwatch. He fidgeted, and looked apoplectic. He seemed to be trying to jump in place, but his knees were of a different mind. He shouted, "Twenty-nine ... He's slogging it! He's slogging it!" They finished the first half mile in 3:05. The pace then picked up slightly, but not enough, in

Charlie's mind, to stave off the famous Codman sprint. And Charlie worried about Casey's ability to close against someone with the strength and poise of Foxhall Codman. Experience was his ace in the hole. If she panicked and hammered, she was lost.

Suddenly, Codman began to drift off course. Casey slowed to be sure that *she* wasn't drifting. On the river bank, Charlie had put down his binoculars and shook his head in frustration. A cloud was over the sun, and three logs were several strokes from Casey's path. The sun teased through, and Charlie seized the heliotrope that reverted to useless as the cloud redeployed. He glared at the cloud and at the useless winch on the dock and at the more useless gaggle of lawyers. His first thought was of his boat being lost, not the race, for which he felt immediately ashamed. Penitence was rewarded—the cloud was hoist. The heliotrope worked at the speed of light plus the speed of Charlie's arthritic hands. Casey's eyes caught the flash. She put two and two instantly together—Codman had swung out for a reason, and she followed. On her second stroke, her oar struck a log and she lost a tempo, but she avoided the pine flotilla. She had not swung out so wide as Codman, and as they made the turn at the half-way point, a mile and a half downriver, the lost tempo was negated. They were dead even, nine minutes and five seconds out. Casey then seemed to read Charlie's mind. She picked the stroke up to thirty-four.

*Piker!*

Did she speak or was he *hearing things*? He knew pain, and now he felt it more acutely as he watched her boat inch ahead.

"Now you're cooking!" shouted Charlie, whose face had gone white as smoke. Codman was forced to pick up the pace.

"She's pulling in the dead zone! The bitch is pulling!" Deke Merriwells's face reddened. He knew the only place Codman was vulnerable was the first mile after the turn.

Stu Steerman knew that Deke, Todd, and Cosmo would be looking to him for confirmation. He withheld eye contact, but his grin broadened. His own money was riding on the Neblung.

"She'll slack off. She's got to," Todd reassured himself, then felt relieved, if not prescient, when Casey did ease off. Feeling more confident himself, Codman decided to sprint by her just to see how she would react. She could see the tremendous speed of his sculls through the water, how they actually flexed and bent under his power, and she wondered if she could match the speed of that sprint. But she would not be panicked into matching him now. She knew it was still early. She kept her pace, and as Codman slacked off, they drew even and stayed even for the next quarter mile.

"He's got her now!" said Deke.

Codman was feeling the cost of the two early sprints. He didn't trust himself to have the full quarter-mile sprint in him. He thought that if he was to win, the Amazon with the faster boat would have to be broken early, panicked into hammering, so he began his final sprint early. And in part it worked. Casey was determined not to let him row through her, not to have to play catch up at the end with the hole that was starting to burn again through her abdomen. She would not let him take an inch. There were no more games. It was just get ahead and stay there at any cost.

"She's pulling thirty-eight. She can't have a higher gear," said Todd.

Stu dropped his binoculars, smiled, and stared at the lads as he spoke. "No one's ever seen how far she can take it. But she'll take it all right. That Amazon will row that Neblung right out of the water if she has to. Seeing is believing, gentlemen. See how Codman's boat leaps forward at the catch like an angry pitbull after a rat? Tremendous power, then the boat slows. Now watch Casey. She makes Codman look like Ed Hanlan. Her boat drives forward almost as fast, but then it just ghosts forward in the recovery with almost no perceptible loss of speed. It's the boat, gents. Codman, in a word, is fucked." He pressed his binoculars again to his eyes.

There were huzzas in the grandstand. Some of the rowing cognoscenti loved the early sprint. They saw records being broken. Others doubted that the two could keep it up. They pulled even. Codman turned to Casey with the smirk of superiority that wilted his competitors in the stretch, when he was going into his sprint. The look that was returned, he felt, was nothing less than demonic. *Pain? You're a fucking amateur*—it was saying, screaming. He averted his gaze. The image of the woman pulling the brown woolen cap was almost comforting, in comparison. He'd never felt such an urge to pull away from a competitor. At the next catch, his boat seemed to leap forward. It felt good—reminding him who he was. *She* had a cap ...

*He* had a crown.

"He's up to thirty-nine!" said Deke

"I think he's starting to buck," said Stu.

Todd Farrel laughed nervously. "Foxhall? ... Never."

Codman could see that the woman was not going to fold as easily as he had hoped. He knew that he had about twenty strong strokes left before his adrenaline was shot, and in those twenty strokes he had to row through Casey, to break her.

Her gut felt like a match was being held six inches below a piece of paper which browned in a widening circle till it became black, then a hole with flame at its edges. With twenty strokes more, Codman had pulled a foot past her. The pain intensified, to where her only recourse was to lift herself from it. Before it got so intense as to *make* her scream, she found herself screaming, but it seemed to be beyond volition, seemed to come not from herself, and she recalled the one time in her life she had allowed herself to scream—after her father's body had been brought to the house.

The otherworldly scream that startled Codman in spite of his concentration had a simple explanation: adrenaline shot into Casey's blood so that with the next few strokes her sculls flexed and the boat flew up even with Codman then glided past him, the adrenaline blocking the pain. But the sound startled Casey as well because it was not her voice. And she began to feel that the arms on the sculls were not hers either: the sleek new boat had taken on a different aspect, a *Trastevere* glow of ancient varnished wood. The *figlio di puttana* had come through for her.

The spectators—shouting—could hear nothing from Casey. Nor did they hear the chickenhawk-like screech of Charlie Hot Dog, who had isolated himself, standing in a drenching sweat, clutching at his heart, his feet dug prematurely into a hillock.

Casey matched Codman's last twenty hard strokes.

"He's washing out! Foxy's washing out!"

"He's as dead as mutton!"

Codman had lost his rhythm. And Casey still had ten hard strokes left. With the last piece of her stern out of Codman's view, both scullers let up, and her boat suddenly felt lighter, as if its trireme ghost had abandoned ship and dived for the bottom. There was still sixty yards to go, and it could still have been Codman's race. Casey's stomach muscles had ripped and she did little more than glide to the finish, but he had conceded, couldn't have understood, even if he had been looking, what his supporters were shouting from the clubhouse. He told himself that the woman just had a faster boat. The truth was the Brahmin had no scream in him. Nothing to transport him. Those final hundred yards Casey was not on the river at all. She was no more in her body than her old man was in the body whose cold forehead she had kissed for the last time two years earlier.

Casey's last race ended with torn abdominal muscles that never completely healed. Laz had to lift her from the boat. He didn't have to hug her, but he did. A crowd surrounded them. People Casey had never seen. Women who hadn't run in years were running to congratulate her. The euphoria of the moment deadened or overwhelmed the repugnance or surprise of a black man hugging a white woman. Men in ties and boaters, men in working clothes, women in long, elegant, uncomfortable dresses, all slapped her on the back.

For some, the shock was deep, visceral. Laz heard one man say, "What's that nigger doing?" But most of the epithets were drowned out by cheers, and much of the gathering throng did not see Laz lift her from the boat and hug her. He was just an oddity, boat-carrier. They were drenched in champagne, and Casey managed an occasional smile. She also managed to hold on to Laz, even as she was hoisted onto the shoulders of six fans and carried to the victor's stand.

Waddy saw it all. He stopped in his congratulatory tracks, with no heart to rub it in or even to collect on the biggest bet of his life. The champagne meant for Foxhall Codman was spilled over the victor and trickled onto the black man beside her.

And Waddy?

High, dry, and kindling.

# Chapter 20: Trial by Fire

*There* was a tomorrow. Casey woke up in it still Mrs. Googan, rose like a jackknife as if out of a dream, thinking *amour fou.* Waddy, on the couch downstairs, normally wouldn't awaken till noon. It was Sunday, Mary's day off. The kettle began to whistle, moving up the scale to a high pitch that wavered but established a certain pattern, a sound he hated. This morning he was too exhausted from his dreams to complain to her to turn it off. He turned over, pushed a cushion to his ear and nearly fell asleep. A half minute later the kettle was still whistling. He threw off the cushion and screamed, "Shut that damn thing off!"

"I'm in the bathroom. Shut it off yourself."

Furious, he got up and stumbled zombie-ish to the stove. He gave the gas knob a powerful twist, redefining *Off* by a quarter inch.

"You know that drives me buggy!" he shouted at the door.

"While you're up, would you mind pouring some water into the cup with the tea in it, the Madame Demorest tea?"

He gritted his teeth. "I'll pour it over your ass and

watch you shit a hard-boiled egg!"

She latched the bathroom door and made chicken noises, infuriating Waddy. He kicked the door, then hit the sack again and fell back to sleep. Twenty minutes later, in a semi-conscious state, he was vaguely aware of the repetitive pounding noise of her clogs on the stairs. Then he heard her changing shoes. He climbed the stairs, painfully stubbing a toe on the last one.

"Every day, that kettle steams my fucking brains open. And every day you go deliberately pounding up and down the stairs fifty times with those clogs while I'm trying to sleep."

She threw on a dress and ignored him.

"You think people don't know?"

She looked him directly in the eye with no emotion, and he just got hotter. She picked up a *Bison Jack* playbill from the desk with Patti's picture on it, and tossed it gently at him.

"I'm late for work."

"And my book!" he screamed. "You sold my fucking book!"

"If I hadn't sold it, you wouldn't be here. You'd be dead."

She walked out, leaving him screaming at her to come back and never come back.

~~~~~~~

A few hours later, Waddy got off the trolley at the corner of Massachusetts Avenue and Columbus Avenue, then walked toward the Cathedral in the South End, in the shadows of the tall warehouses where his career had begun in fire, fantasizing plans for his revenge. He found himself drawn to the Cathedral, where Henry Cabot Lodge and Archbishop Williams were meeting to discuss charity and the archbishop's condemnation of Sodom by the Sea— The Chelsea Sporting Club. *Quid pro quo.* Waddy took refuge in the Cathedral not to see yet another cross with a bearded man on it, but to attempt to disinter something within himself. He had come also to visit, not as an apostle, a devout, or even a believer, but as if to pay his respects to a dying and distant relative. He had come to see himself. He dropped a quarter in the box for the cult and veneration of Saint Anthony. He had also come, he realized, for a spiritual handout. He had come to be found. He looked up at the tired man on the cross and confessed nothing, but monologued as with a dull, aged aunt. He walked out thinking that Saint Anthony's box was no different than Fast Fanny LaFlamme's palm, and that His Divine Charitableness felt something analogous for his spiritual dowry. *Quid pro quo.*

He continued downtown, running on empty. In the past three days he had slept about six hours, had eaten almost nothing, and imbibed a liver-rotting quantity of alcohol. The back of his neck kept popping like a knuckle cracking. Looking up, he saw splotches of black, like small-gauge shot in the cobalt blue sky. The features of the gargoyle overhead on Washington Street were clear. And its acorn-like eyes reminded him of Laz's kid sister's eyes, and he had a vision of the woman he had seen jumping off the Franklin Street building in the fire years ago—thighs of chocolate, melting.

The diminished din of buggies and automobiles and the darkening sky made him realize that he had not moved from this spot in a long time. The last moment of afternoon sky shrank like a magic slate lifted at four corners at once. The violets and crimsons and mucous yellows blended into one bruise-colored bandage across the horizon. Above, where the aquamarine blue blended into black, a single star shone. Venus. He would follow it. A woman approached, walking a dog that picked up the scent up of the well-dressed, eerily-smiling man who behaved so bizarrely. She quickly crossed to the other side of the street. Now it was with a stinking grin that he set out at last with a realistic plan. *Quid pro quo*. He was going to fuck the hare-brained sister.

Maybe it was the smell of tripe that did it to him. Maybe it was harder with one hand over his nose. He told her he was measuring her for the clothes he would make for her and had to remove the old ones. He love-bit her almost in a frenzy, as if she were an ear of corn. Then to the welts on her body he applied the mustard plaster of his lips. He was over her some time when he realized that she was not crying, not pleading with him to stop, and he realized at almost the same time that there was no use any more flogging her with his flaccidness, his face as perplexed as hers.

He drove his old reliable Stanhope Phaeton back to Putnam Street. When Casey answered the frantic rapping at the door, it was not the same Waddy Googan that had left hours earlier. He pushed her back into the foyer, threw her against the wall, then over the umbrella rack whose wicket edges pierced her pelvis.

"You're hurting me!"

He was not listening. He had his hands full holding her down with one hand and lifting then tearing the layers of the clothes he had made, not so much to essay his one trick as to take from her everything that was his. She escaped and locked herself in her room. Alice the cat appeared and hissed. Waddy hissed back and shot out his leg like the punter for the Fighting Irish and went down hard and painfully for his effort. Casey heard him fumbling in the carriage house and rolling out a barrel of kerosene. She ran out of the house and took refuge in the maze. He saw her and set about the more daunting task of dousing the maze with kerosene. At the same time, it felt more satisfying than burning down the house.

~~~~~~~~

# (Billy 'Swipes' Unger)

*I was there for Waddy Googan's flaming end. I witnessed it from behind the wheel of Charlie's Peugeot. It was only ten minutes earlier when I sat there under the weeping willow, watching it undulate, different sections of it going different ways, like it was working against itself, but somehow the vying pieces all seemed to fit; they were all droopy brooms sweeping the sky as if the world had turned upside down. And it was all a metaphor for Mr. Googan himself, as the ironwood trees behind it were stand-ins for Laz Godfrey. Under a peaceful, balmy evening sky with puff-ball clouds, I sat in the driver's seat of Charlie's clunker, imagining rolling down Massachusetts Avenue at full speed, which—incredibly—I would be doing five or so minutes later. They call me Swipes; they call me* Billy Under; *they call me worse than that, but they all call me idle, and that's the biggest lie of all. You don't get to be Swipes if you're idle, but they never knew that because they never knew their ass from a hole in the ground anyway.*

*I say the willow reminded me of Mr. Googan, and that's true for all the reasons I mentioned, but sadly the one who was weeping was Casey. And when the weeping turned to shouting and howling and when Mr. Googan's eyes got as big as the knots in the willow and even from this distance as red as the chokecherries rotting on the ground, I knew it was time to hightail it. I couldn't save Casey myself, but I knew who could, and I knew where I'd find him— 'please, God'—I said to myself.*

*It was a quarter mile as the crow flies from the Googan's backyard across Banke Street, then Crane and up to the corner of Mt. Auburn where, God willing, I'd find Laz at Mooney's. The problem was getting across Americo Bartolini's backyard without getting shot. Like Mud Foley and his gang, I'd swiped my share of watermelons from Americo's garden, and truth be told the old bastard had a green thumb—as well as an itchy trigger finger. And he'd sit out on his back porch just waiting for us to raid his garden. After he nearly killed Mud with buckshot, the police told him to use rock salt, but at fifty yards the rock salt had little penetrating power, so Americo dumped only half of the buckshot, which could be lethal.*

*When I got over the fence of Americo's backyard I was running as fast as I ever had it my life. I was already at the fence on the other side when I heard the shot go off and felt a tremendous sting on my left arm. But I was over the fence before he could fire the second barrel. And when I got to Mooney's, Laz saw me before I saw him, and he knew from the look in my eyes more than from the blood on my arm that there was trouble and he knew where the trouble was. I was too out of breath to even speak, to warn him that Americo would be more on the alert than ever. Laz was gone, and if ever a man could run it was Laz Godfrey. I wouldn't have been surprised if he cleared Americo's fence and Sarah Palfrey's white picket fence in one leap. Nor did I have time to tell Laz that I had a better idea, one that would get us back to Googan's twice as fast.*

*It was rare not to see a buggy or a Model T parked outside Mooney's while the driver was rushing the growler. And this time I was in luck. Hugo Bartolini's Steamer was outside with the top down, the motor running, and a passenger in the back. The old man had no idea what he was in for, and I had no time to get him out. The first time I stole a Steamer I had a devil of a time figuring out what all the gauges were for, especially the winkler, but after wrecking that one I knew that for my mission all those gauges didn't mean a damn thing. I made sure the kerosene valve was open, and released the hook-up pedal for maximum engine power. I squeezed the brake handle and eased it forward. The Steamer shot forward and the passenger started shouting. Hugo ran out with the growler and I heard it clang off the Steamer's rear end. I took the corner on Putnam Ave. on two wheels, going close to forty, and slammed on the brakes at Googan's driveway.*

*I heard two shots and I knew Americo would assume the runner was a watermelon-stealing nigger and he'd have no mercy. Instinctively, I ran to Charlie's Peugeot and waited. And waited. And what I saw was Laz hobbled, falling and standing again, his left leg nearly out of commission. As he approached, I heard him gasping for air as badly as I had at Mooney's, and I knew he was in no better shape to stop Mr. Googan than I was. I'd heard Waddy ranting in the foyer and seen Casey run for the maze—Waddy whooping like an Indian, splashing kerosene all over it. That's when*

*I kicked the chocks from the back tires, jumped into the driver's seat and said push.*

*There was a small incline, only about three feet long, and Laz had to get us over it. I heard him grunt and the Peugeot moved an inch or two but that was it. I jumped out and we both pushed. Next thing I knew the Peugeot was over the hump. As it began to roll, I swung around the gaping door and into the driver's seat in time to turn the wheel, the Peugeot quickly gaining speed as it approached the yews, arborvitae, and burning bush of the maze, while Mr. Googan turned over a piece of slate and struck a match, holding his jacket drenched with kerosene. I shouted his name, "Mr. Googan!" But he was too crazed to pay me any mind.*

*He had to have heard the racket, the ominous clunking, recognized the clop and squeak of the rusted springs of the Peugeot approaching like an unchained beast, for he turned and stared, bug-eyed and defiant, at the steel nemesis that bore him no malice but was the only instrument of a kid with no better idea of how to rescue a woman from a fire. That look in his eyes is still with me—nightmarish, as if he were hallucinating an enormous locust coming through the grass. Was he frozen in his own private thoughts of doom? Had he fallen again in love, this time with the cataclysmic rapture of destruction, and gone catatonic? He never truly saw me. He just stood there like a magnet, hunted and persecuted even by inanimate steel that was referred to as 'she.'*

*The Peugeot struck the shocked fire-starter at the knees and propelled him head-first into an old granite hitching post at the entrance to the maze. The flames leapt nearly to the windshield of the car. I covered my eyes with my arm, then opened the door, but the inferno was too great to approach the flaming man who lay unconscious of his fate. It was Monday. In a few hours, the revived Monday Evening Club would be, for the first time in nearly a year, opening its doors.*

~~~~~~~

He looked, to Casey, like the iconic Christian martyr, on fire and staring at the heavens. His tortured mouth looked like it was saying, "Who's there?"—Casey reminded of the opening lines of *Hamlet*. Miscommunication, to the end, between herself and the just as mad and flaming protagonist.

What was he thinking, that fiery moment before all was ash? It looked like the Holly Tree but was clearly the interior of the Monday Evening Club where he waited at the table of honor while his love opened the Marcus Ward linen letter sealed with chocolate wax that somehow resisted melting, inviting her to his last banquet as tears fell—some ironic relief—like those petals that every girl, indeed even the red-blooded boy, counted, calculated—she-loves-me, she-loves-me-not, she-loves-me—until the blot of oblivion. Yet, she loves me.

# Acknowledgements

I want to thank Sharol Olds for a looted image and Elizabeth Bowen for a line: Irish lit scholars are challenged to find the latter (email me, senorkbking1@yahoo.com, if you do.)

Thanks to Roseanne Balsamo for a coffee shop (Holly Tree here) anecdote and to Lou Iaquinto, of Melbourne, Australia for another.

Thanks to Jaye Winkler for all the dressage tidbits.

Thanks to the *Boston Globe* for a wee bit of 1892 fight commentary.

Thanks to Aidan Wolff-King for the line about "possessing the power."